About the Author

Mark Hayden is the nom de guerre of Adrian Attwood. He lives in Westmorland with his wife, Anne.

He has had a varied career working for a brewery, teaching English and being the Town Clerk in Carnforth, Lancs. He is now a part-time writer and part-time assistant in Anne's craft projects.

He is also proud to be the Mad Unky to his Great Nieces & Great Nephew.

TENFOLD

The Fourth Book of the King's Watch

MARK HAYDEN

PAW
PRESS

www.pawpress.co.uk

First Published Worldwide in 2019 by Paw Press
Paperback Edition Published 2019
Reprinted April 07 2021 with minor corrections

Cover Design – Rachel Lawston
Design Copyright © 2019 Lawston Design
www.lawstondesign.com
Cover images © Shutterstock

Paw Press – Independent publishing in Westmorland, UK.
www.pawpress.co.uk

ISBN: 1-9998212-4-6
ISBN-13: 978-1-9998212-4-1

To Clare & Bee Christmas

Who live in the house where it's Christmas every day...

TENFOLD

A Note from Conrad...

Hi,

Some of you have said that it might help if there was a guide to magickal terms and a Who's Who of the people in my stories.

Well, I thought it might help, too, and my publisher has been kind enough to put one on their website. You can find them under 'Magickal Terms (Glossary)' and 'Dramatis Personae (Who's Who)' on the Paw Press website:

www.pawpress.co.uk

I hope you enjoy the book,
Thanks,
Conrad.

1 — New Friends

How do you know that I'm not dead?

'Simple,' I hear you say. 'Turn to the end and see if Conrad is still telling the story.'

The trouble is that I know a Witch in Lancashire who practises Memorialism: absorbing your essence into a tree or other object, and she's not the only one.

For all you know, this narrative could be posthumous. You'll have to wait and see, though I should point out that I am very much against dying, and I'll do my best to stay alive until the last full stop.

For now, I'll get back to where we were: driving down to London from the Lake District after a harrowing encounter with a very dysfunctional Lakeland family. We'd only prevented mass murder at the eleventh hour, and I was glad to see the back of the fells. The same was true of my partner, Vicky.

Captain Victoria Robson – soon to get the Military Cross – is my partner in magickal crime-fighting and we both serve in the King's Watch. You'll find out more about the Watch in due course; for now, I'll go back to telling the story.

'Are these guys we're going to see a part of your murky past?' asked Vicky.

'You could say that. I rented their cottage for a bit, and then their farmhouse got burnt down in an arson attack. I don't like to dwell on the past.'

'Trouble is, Conrad, you've got a lot of past to dwell on. I'll find out one day, you know.'

'I know. I can wait. Ribblegate Farm is at the end of this lane.'

She looked up the lane towards the cluster of patched and improvised agricultural buildings. 'Don't tell me they're real farmers. Howay man, I'm sick of the countryside. Nothing but evil and cowshit. And Dragons.'

Vicky is a Geordie lass through and through, born and raised by the Tyne and thoroughly contemptuous of anything involving grass and livestock. Except football. She quite likes football. I kept quiet because I've worked with her long enough to know when she needs to vent and when she needs to be wound up.

I drove into the yard, past the builders' vans clustered round the farmhouse, and pulled up as close as I could get to the cowshed because I broke Vicky's foot in the Lakes and she still needs a crutch. I got out, passed her wellies from the back of the car and held her door open while she struggled into them. I heard one of the small animals that inhabit farms skitter away from underneath the car. Vicky has a few phobias that I know of (tunnels and spiders), and I wasn't keen to find out if she was afraid of rats, so I spoke up to cover the noise.

'There's five Kirkhams,' I said. 'Dad Joseph and son David are the farmers, only David is called Joe.'

'Why? Is that another piece of country lore?'

'No. He's the spit of his Dad, that's all. He's married to Kelly. I can't remember whether she worked, but she's nursing a new baby boy and a broken wrist. Kelly has a daughter called Natasha.'

She carefully inserted her damaged foot into the Wellington boot. The splintered metatarsal had been magickally knitted but would need a week with only light pressure on it to heal fully.

'Why are you telling me this?' she asked.

'Just so you know. Briefing is crucial, even when visiting friendly premises.'

'Shut up, pass me crutch and give me a hand. In that order.'

I led Vicky into the cowshed, where the Kirkham boys were expecting us. On the threshold, she pointed to the forty or so pedigree Frisian/Holstein cows munching away in the pens.

'Why are they all in here? Why aren't they outside?'

'It's only the first week of April. Grass needs to be at least six inches high before they get turned out. There's the boys.'

I made the human introductions, and Vicky stared open-mouthed at the beasts. 'They're huge. I thought cows were cute.'

The farmers smiled indulgently, like proud parents. 'Size don't stop 'em being cute,' said Joe. 'You remember that cow we had in calf, Conrad?'

'I do.'

'What?' said Vicky.

'*In calf* means pregnant.'

Joseph and Joe took us over to a corner, being most solicitous of Vicky's foot. I'm glad to say that the floor was pretty clean. The Kirkhams are good farmers.

In a separate pen, a young bull calf was suckling its mother contentedly. 'We're keeping him,' said Joseph.

'Why wouldn't you keep him?' said Vicky.

'Boys go for beef,' said Joe. 'This one we're keeping to breed from. We'll make money from AI that way. I said we'd call the bull *Conrad*...'

Vicky laughed. 'You're having me on.'

'... but we couldn't face it, in the end,' continued Joe, slightly offended.

I was very offended.

Joseph picked up the story. 'So Kelly says, why not that writer bloke's first name? Then we found out he were called Joseph Conrad.'

'And there's enough Josephs already round here,' said Joe. 'We wondered if you had any ideas.'

'Nostromo,' I said. 'It means *our man*, and it was my mother's favourite book. That's why she called me *Conrad.*'

'Nostromo it is,' said Joe. 'You said you had a job for us?' I nodded. 'Good. We wanted to offer you something, too, and Kelly wants a word. We moved back in to the kitchen last week. You can tell us about it over a cuppa, but come and have a look over here.' He turned to Vicky. 'It's not far.'

Joe led us to a shed against the yard wall, a rough lean-to structure that looked nothing on the outside, but had been insulated and even had some old carpet on the floor. On a pile of old curtains in the corner was another mother, this time a border collie with her litter. She looked up, happy to see the Kirkhams, less so to see Vicky and me.

'Now that really is cute,' said Vicky. 'They're gorgeous.'

'They are that,' said Joe. 'Conrad will know this, but you won't. These are working dogs. Both parents have won prizes, and they're worth well over a hundred pounds each.'

'I can believe that,' I agreed.

'We wondered if you wanted one,' said Joseph to me.

The second he spoke the words, the back of my neck prickled and something shifted in the shed. These puppies were only a week old, eyes closed, barely moving. Except one. From the middle of the litter, one chap squirmed forward, out of the tumble of bodies and on to the straw that surrounded their bed. The mother looked up, concerned, ready to reach her jaws down and pluck him back to safety. Then he opened his eyes, way way ahead of schedule. One eye was blue, the other a vibrant green, and the eyes were staring straight at me in defiance of all the laws of evolutionary biology.

The tiny puppy blinked, and I knew that he was a he and that his name was *Scout*. He collapsed back on his puppy legs and his mother swiftly grabbed him back to the fold.

'Bugger me,' said Joe. 'What happened there?'

'I think Conrad's just been adopted,' said Vicky.

'Eh?' said Joseph and Joe together. I knew what she meant, in principle. I'm sure she'll tell me the details later.

'I'll take that one,' I said. 'Give me a shout when they're ready to leave mum.'

'Aye,' said Joe. 'Shall we get some tea?'

The farmhouse, on the other side of the yard, had been almost gutted in the arson attack. When Joe said that they were *back in the kitchen*, it was definitely the opinion of someone who didn't have to cook there.

What they had done was nail planks to the unit holding the sink, rig up scaffold batons for a table and put more batons on top of the kitchen units that hadn't been completely destroyed by fire or water. The only thing that stood resolutely undamaged (if a little singed) was the Aga. Cockroaches and Agas, both indestructible in times of nuclear war.

In fairness, the plastering had been done, so I'm sure the kitchen fitters won't be far behind. Kelly, Joe's wife, was poring over drawings on the 'table'.

'Hiya, Conrad. Is that…?'

'Mina? No. This is Vicky Robson, my work partner. Vicky, this is Kelly.'

'Pleased to meet you,' said Vicky stretching over the planks to shake hands.

'How's Natasha and the baby?' I added.

'Tasha's fine. Got a playdate at a friend's house. One with a proper kitchen. I am going to owe so many favours by the time we're finished renovating. The baby's doing well, and so's that weird plant you sent over.'

She pointed to a far corner, near a window.

'Oh,' I said.

'Blimey,' said Vicky.

That Witch I mentioned, the one who does things with trees, had cast a spell over a tiny cutting. The cutting was from another Witch's plant, a Viburnum opulus bush. I'd left the cutting with the Kirkhams – specifically the female ones – to look after, a few weeks ago. It was now half the size of the original bush.

'I'd better get that home, before it evicts you. Thanks for taking such good care of it.'

'Natasha watered it every day,' said Kelly. 'I had to help her pot it on twice. What does it do, apart from grow very quickly?'

'It's supposed to help with cramps,' I said.

'Specifically menstrual cramps,' added Vicky, 'but he's too much of a bloke to say that.'

Kelly cast a particularly sceptical eye on the plant and stood up to put the kettle on the hot plate. 'Tea?'

Vicky looked alarmed, and whispered to me. 'Where do they get the milk from? Is it safe?'

'They get their milk from ASDA, same as everyone else. Unpasteurised milk at body temperature is something you only drink if you have to. I once had tea with warm goat's milk upcountry in Afghanistan. It's an acquired taste.'

'Eurgh.'

The door banged open and the boys came in. We settled on the singed chairs around the planks, and while Kelly made the tea, Joe explained to Vicky that AI had nothing to do with artificial intelligence.

Kelly sat down and fixed me with a mother's gaze. 'What's this favour you're after, Conrad?'

The subtext was clear to me: *is it dangerous?* Kelly blamed me for the bother they'd got into because I was a much more convenient target than her husband or father in law.

'It's simple,' I said, placing my hands on the table in a non-threatening gesture. 'Pick Mina up tomorrow morning and take her to Preston station.'

The Kirkhams shuffled on their seats and looked at Vicky.

'Don't worry,' I said. 'Vic knows all about Mina. She's even met her in prison.'

'HMP Cairndale, in't it?' said Joe.

'Yes. She gets turfed out at eleven and the train's at twenty past twelve.'

'No problem,' said Kelly, 'I'll go up with Joe and bring her here for a cup of tea. It'll save waiting at the station.'

Vicky looked confused. 'Do you know her?' she asked.

'Oh no,' said Kelly, 'but we've heard all about her. I even helped Conrad with his wardrobe when he was trying to chat her up. Standards have slipped since then.'

Vicky snorted into her tea. 'You're jokin' me.'

'We'd better go,' I said, before things got really embarrassing. I took out a white box covered with Apple logos. 'This is Mina's phone. I've charged it.' There were a couple of twenty pound notes underneath the box that Kelly took charge of, stuffing them into her jeans.

I stood up and brought Vicky's Wellingtons to the table after checking the soles. 'I'll be back in a few weeks if not before. To pick up Scout.'

'Scout?'

'The puppy.'

While Vicky put on her boots, I passed a badge to Joe. He stared at the design of a mediaeval tower and twisted it to read the words. '*Merlyn's Tower Irregulars.* Who are they?'

'You're one, for starters. I thought the name *Team Conrad* was a bit vain given that Vicky and I are partners.'

Vicky gave an exaggerated sigh. 'I've tried to stop him, but he's like a big kid sometimes. Ignore the badge, or give it to Natasha. There's a number on the back. If anything happens to us, and you're worried, give that number a call.'

Kelly grabbed the badge in alarm and stared at the phone number. 'Is anything likely to happen? Should we be worried?'

'No,' said Vicky. 'My role in life is to keep him out of trouble.'

Kelly turned the badge over and pushed it away. 'Right. Safe journey, Conrad. Nice to meet you, Vicky.'

As we left the kitchen, I heard Joseph saying, 'I'm tellin' you. Its one eye were *green*. Never seen a dog with a green eye before.'

13

The satnav said that it was nearly a five hour drive to London. Vicky had that look on her face: she was going to use every minute to generate maximum humiliation. I decided to get in first.

'What happened in that dog kennel?'

'You've been adopted by a familiar.'

'Really? I didn't know they were a thing.'

'Hell, aye.'

'Is it dangerous?'

'Oh, no. It's a mark of status. Very few Mages get them, and even fewer Watch Captains.'

'Is there a central agency for these things?'

'Don't be daft. You should know enough about Spirits by now to work it out.'

'That dog looked nothing like Helen of Troy, or Madeleine. Tell me about familiars.'

'There are a lot of Spirits about. They can't always access a good source of Lux, they get attacked, get trapped. A Spirit, no matter where it's come from, can easily find itself starting to dissipate. At that point, a lot of them will bind themselves to a lesser vessel, lesser in that sense meaning *not human*. Animals are favourite, but machines work in a sense. Cheng is convinced that they're starting to appear in the Internet.'

'Whoah! A ghost in the machine. This is a windup, Vicky.'

'I wish. That's for another day, though. In your case, some Spirit has tagged along after you, draining a tiny bit of your Lux, not enough to notice. Word has got around, you know, about the Dragon. One lucky Spirit was in the right place when Joe Kirkham offered you a puppy.'

'I think it's been following us. Following me. I've heard random animal sounds near the car a few times.'

'Sounds about right. When it saw its chance, it dived into the dog and merged itself.'

'Merged?'

'Don't forget, humans are hugely, wildly more magickal than dogs. That Spirit...'

'Scout. His name is Scout.'

'Right. *Scout* has become something less than human but much, much more than a dog. We won't know exactly what he's going to become until you get him home and he's grown up a bit.'

'That's something to look forward to, as is our conversation with the Boss.' Vic and I answer directly to the commanding officer of the King's Watch, who is known as the Peculier Constable.

Vicky groaned. She's convinced that I make Hannah's life a misery on purpose. Hannah Rothman was in the Metropolitan Police until something happened to enhance her magickal powers and she joined the Watch as a Captain, like me. Shortly after, she suffered appalling injuries and lost her husband. She's now the Peculier Constable and a very good boss.

The problem is that she thinks – or pretends to think – that the universe owes her a quiet life, and that I've been sent to test her patience. I'm sure she loves me really.

'What now?' said Vicky. 'I thought we were supposed to be good boys and girls.'

'We are. In fact, I'm going to make her an offer.'

'Please don't. What?'

'How do you feel about Myfanwy?'

'Eh?'

Vicky turned to look out of the window while she mulled over the question. A few weeks ago, Vicky's heart was stopped. Deliberately stopped by a Druid. I was able to restart it, but only with help from another Druid, Myfanwy Lewis. Myfanwy is currently in the magickal prison, Blackfriars Undercroft. Before becoming a magickal paramedic, she'd been part of the gang that attacked us.

'Grateful,' said Vicky. 'Profoundly grateful. And sorry for her. And then I remember why she's locked up and I get angry. Then I feel guilty and I'm grateful again. It keeps going round in circles.'

'Look, Vic, I talked it over with Mina this morning, and she's not wild about the idea, but she can see where I'm coming from. How would you feel if I offered Elvenham House as a place for Myfanwy to serve out her time?'

'Oof. That's a curveball. Has no one else stepped up to the plate?'

I paused. 'I didn't know you were a baseball fan.'

'Eh?'

'*Curveball … stepped up to the plate.* They're both baseball metaphors.'

'Shut up and answer the question. And don't you dare say that you can't do both.'

'No. The Northumberland Shield Wall are still the only group to have offered sanctuary. You said you wouldn't wish them on her. If you can see a better alternative…?'

She sighed. 'No. I can't. We'll just have to hope that Hannah is in a good mood when we get there. She won't be after you tell her that.'

'I'll win her round.'

'Careful, Conrad. I know you like to flirt with her, but have you ever thought it might be mutual?'

'What? I don't flirt…'

'…Yes you do. Have you thought that the reason she's so against Mina is that she wants you for herself?'

That was a stumper. I opened my mouth several times to say something. I *suppose* it was possible. I thought Hannah's attitude towards my girlfriend was down to Hannah being an ex-copper of high moral standards, and Mina being a convicted criminal. I ran the possibilities round in my head.

'Nah,' I said. 'I'm too much of a goy for a nice Jewish girl like Hannah.'

'Maybe. Can you pull in to Knutsford Services? I need the loo, and you need a fag.'

'I do, but that's unusually thoughtful of you.'

She grinned. 'You need to fortify yourself. When we set off again, I'm going to torture you until you tell me all about how Kelly Kirkham gave you a makeover.'

I sighed and indicated left. It was going to be a long drive.

2 — *Old Friends*

'How's your foot?' asked Hannah as Vicky clumped across the office at the top of Merlyn's Tower. The Occulted (magickally hidden) headquarters of the King's Watch is in an off-limits part of the Tower of London. 'Are you sure you're all right?'

'The journey didn't help,' said Vicky. 'I think it's swollen. Conrad's leg is none too good either,' she added in a heroic gesture of partnership.

My leg *did* hurt, though. Vicky's fracture would heal fully in a week; my shattered tibia and its supporting titanium rod were only going to get worse as the years passed.

Hannah sniffed. 'He's a big boy.'

Tennille Haynes, Hannah's PA, had been listening and brought in the tea tray. 'Don't stop him hurting though, does it?' she said, staring at Hannah.

Our boss rolled her eyes and kicked one of the comfy chairs further into the room so that I could stretch my legs and enjoy the view of lights coming on along the Thames. London always looks better at night.

Tennille placed the tray, and said, 'Is that all?'

'Thanks, yes,' said Hannah. 'I'll go straight to Newton's House in the morning and catch you later.'

Tennille wished us all goodnight and pulled the doors closed behind her.

Hannah's grumpiness lasted as long as it took to pour the tea. She flopped down into the third chair and reached a finger under her black headscarf to scratch round the plate in her skull. As I said, she was very badly injured.

She grinned at me. 'Welcome, Special Constable Clarke. Did you know that you've arrested more murderers in two days in the police than I managed in ten years as a copper?'

I'm a squadron leader in the RAF, really, though I do have a Lancashire & Westmorland Constabulary warrant card, and I am a Special (unpaid) Constable. Long story.

Hannah leaned over to offer Vicky the plate of biscuits. When Vic had commandeered the last of the chocolate Hobnobs, Hannah put down the plate and said to me, 'And on that note, Special Constable Clarke, I have more good news. You're booked on to the Met firearms course at Gravesend a week on Monday, twentieth of April.'

'Thank you, ma'am,' I said, grabbing a custard cream.

I have a gun: a Dwarven copy of the 9mm SIG P226. It has my Badge of Office embedded in the grip, and it fires magickal rounds capable of penetrating an Ancile, the magickal shield that most Mages use to protect themselves. Well, it *would* fire magickal rounds if they weren't all locked in Hannah's safe until I complete the firearms course.

'How long is it?' I asked.

'Two weeks. Firearms in week one. When to deploy in week two. You're excused the two weeks after that because they're all about armed pursuit in vehicles, and you don't need that to get your ammo back.'

'Thank you.'

She crossed her legs and folded her hands. Hannah's wardrobe, as far as I know, consists entirely of heavy white cotton blouses, denim skirts and brown or black boots. I don't know what she'll do when the weather warms up. The blouse was still crisp, but now rather creased. She picked at a false nail on her left hand, the one with more scarring. 'Nice as it is to see you both – and well done in Lakeland, of course – why am I still here instead of at home checking the TV guide while the microwave cooks my dinner?'

Vicky coughed. Perhaps the Boss really does eat TV dinners. I doubt it.

'It's what's not in the report, ma'am,' said Vicky. We'd agreed that she'd take the lead.

Hannah massaged her forehead. 'I knew it, and now that Tennille's gone, I can't get to the painkillers. What have you done now?'

'One of the principals in the Lakeland business is a Diviner, ma'am.'

Hannah's eyes snapped open. 'What? Hashem preserve us. What did she say?'

Vicky is a Sorcerer – she can sense the patterns of magickal energy, of Lux, that they call the Sympathetic Echo. I say *they* because I can't feel a thing. A Diviner is a very special Sorcerer who can see both deeper into the past and also how that past might affect the future.

'It's about the First Rusticant, ma'am,' said Vicky.

Hannah's eyes bulged and she turned to me. 'Your ancestor?'

'The same.'

The principal magickal university is known as the Invisible College. It's based at Salomon's House, and at its heart is the Queen's Esoteric Library. That library is older than the Watch, and much older than the College itself. The *Queen* in the title is Elizabeth I, just as the *King* in King's Watch is James I. Sometimes the world of magick has difficulty moving on.

The second Keeper of the Queen's Esoteric Library was my eleven times Great Grandfather, Thomas Clarke. He was suspended – rusticated – when he became betrothed to a Witch, a big no-no in the 1610s. Apparently, he "borrowed" some magickal books when he moved to my home village of Clerkswell, and because he'd falsified the records, no one knows what he took. The Keepers have been looking for them ever since.

What they didn't know was that for all those years of searching, Thomas Clarke's Spectre had been happily haunting Elvenham House, and he's still there. As Vicky's already said, Spirits of all kinds need Lux, and sadly, Spectre Thomas's supply has dwindled to the point where he's barely coherent as an entity, and he can't access his memories. To preserve his essence and the details of what happened, he's asleep in the well at the bottom of my garden. The well where he drowned in 1622.

'Go on,' said Hannah.

I kept quiet, and Vicky said, 'The Diviner hinted that Thomas may be … associated with something bad. Conrad and I both think it's linked to Project Talpa.'

Hannah delicately massaged her temples. 'Why?'

Vicky pressed on, not catching the tone in Hannah's question. 'The sudden increase in the magickal death rates – particularly in Watch Captains – points to a source.'

'I know that,' said Hannah. 'I meant *why me*? Conrad? What do you reckon? Project Talpa was your idea.'

'Possibly. Very possibly, though you can understand me wanting to give Thomas the benefit of the doubt, what with him being an ancestor. Vicky is off field work for at least a week, and I'm going to Gravesend. We could summon my grandfather, charge his batteries and find out once and for all. Either way, we can then spend a week on Project Talpa, and I have a couple of suggestions.'

'You're going to pull a fast one, aren't you?' Before I could deny it, she raised her palms in an eloquent and very Jewish shrug. I'm something of a connoisseur of shrugs, and this was a vintage one. 'What do I care?' she added. 'Go on. Tell me.'

'Have you had a quote from the Dwarves to create the new Badge of Office for Wales?'

'Eh? Yes. This morning. I had to ring up and check. It was three times what I expected.'

'The Gnomes have said the same. The magickal economy has a problem, and I'd like to bring in outside help, both on the summoning of Spectre Thomas and widening the scope of Project Talpa. We need it.'

'You've changed your tune. A few weeks ago, you wouldn't have countenance a joint venture with the Invisible College.'

I was planning more than a joint venture with the College, but I didn't mention that. I'd said *outside help* and if Hannah chose to interpret it that way… I pointed to Vicky. 'My partner's influence. I'll approach the College tomorrow at the ceremony, if that's okay.'

'Fine. And I know who can do the summoning. It should be well within Li Cheng's capabilities.'

Vicky choked on her Hobnob. I stared at the opposite corner, from where the elephant in the room trumpeted loudly. Vicky and Cheng have, shall we say, a history. A history that I let slip to Hannah one day.

'Anything else, team?' said Hannah demurely. 'You both do look tired, and it's a big day tomorrow.'

That was my cue. I cleared my throat. 'Myfanwy Lewis. She should go to Clerkswell.'

Hannah stared at the unloved and unwanted plain digestives. She looked up at me. 'You're right. She should. Sending her to the Shield Wall would be worse than close confinement. I'll put the wheels in motion.'

I coughed. 'Forgive me, ma'am, I took the liberty of asking Annelise van Kampen to meet me at the Undercroft. Tonight.'

All three of us jumped as Vicky's phone revved up. Literally, with the sound of an unsilenced motorbike.

'Sorry. It's me brother. He's just arrived at the staff car park.'

'Go,' said Hannah. 'I'll see you tomorrow. Conrad? Quick word.'

'Ma'am.'

While I opened the doors for Vicky and watched her down the stairs, Hannah disappeared to her inner-inner sanctum. When she came back, she had a suit cover draped over her arm and was carrying her uniform cap. Whatever she had to say wouldn't take long.

'I'm sending Cheng down to your place because this summoning could be dangerous, for all that Thomas Clarke is your ancestor.' The lines around her eyes creased, and she pursed her lips. 'I wish we could wait until after you get back from Gravesend, but you're right. This needs doing quickly. I got this from the Dwarves. A private commission.'

She held out her cap, upside down. Rolling around the silk lining was a single round of ammunition. 'If you use it, you'll still be in trouble, but I'd rather you were in trouble than dead. The same goes for Vicky, Cheng and whoever else you rope in.'

I took the round and quickly stowed it away.

'Thank you, Hannah. I'll see you tomorrow.'

'Goodnight, Conrad.'

I was half way to the door when she added, 'I'm not going home to the microwave, you know. I'm babysitting for Ruth. I don't know which is sadder.'

'I think you do,' I said. 'Give your sister my regards.'

I didn't close the door behind me.

Annelise van Kampen, Mage and solicitor, was cooling her Dutch heels outside Blackfriars Station when I arrived. We don't get on at the best of times.

'This had better be good,' she said, before I could get out an apology, 'because I'm freezing. And it had better be quick because I have to be somewhere at eight o'clock.'

She was doing me a favour, so I resisted the temptation to say that she should have worn a longer, heavier coat. And that gloves would have been good, too. 'Sorry,' seemed the safest word.

'Hunh. Come on.'

She had to wait out in the cold because you have to be escorted into the Undercroft by a key holder. I have neither a key nor the magickal strength to open the enchanted lock. She took great delight in reminding me of this all the way down in the lift to Blackfriars Undercroft, the magickal prison.

One of the deputy bailiffs stuck her head out of the Wardroom and said Hello. Annelise wrote our names in the visitor log before marching off down the corridor as fast as her heels and her skirt would let her. I smiled at the bailiff and asked for coffee, if she wouldn't mind, then lengthened my stride to catch up with Annelise.

The whiteboard outside the only occupied cell had the name, Myfanwy Lewis, and the number of days since her imprisonment. Annelise didn't even check the one-way mirror to see if Myfanwy were decent; she just yanked open the outer door and sashayed inside. I did pause, and saw the prisoner jump up in surprise, knock crumbs off her shapeless tracksuit and reach for the remote to turn off Coronation Street.

The antechamber to the cells is big. Big enough to accommodate a hospital trolley for sedated prisoners. It's separated from the living area by a heavily enchanted steel grill, sort of like a portcullis. You get a good view of the space beyond, and it's better appointed than most hotels, barring one thing. The enchantment is on the grill to keep all magick out of the cell. They call them Limbo Chambers, and that's what the real punishment is. The impact on the soul/spirit/psyche/mind of the Mage inside is huge. Many are driven mad or take the *short route* of suicide.

Myfanwy blinked at us as the heavy lights of the antechamber came on.

'Watch Captain Clarke would like to speak to you,' said Annelise. 'Are you content?'

Myfanwy ignored her. 'Hello, Conrad. Been in the wars again?'

I leaned against the metal door frame. 'You know me. Another day, another scar.'

Myfanwy turned to Annelise. 'Just checking it wasn't bad news. He wouldn't look so cheerful if was bad news. Yes, I'm content to speak to him.'

Annelise turned to me, said, 'I'm leaving in fifteen minutes,' and clicked off in the direction of the Wardroom.

While we waited for coffee, Myfanwy and I looked each other up and down. By Thor's Hammer, she'd aged. Her bedraggled blonde hair was pulled back in a messy ponytail, which did nothing to disguise the puffiness in her face. The day she'd brought Vicky back to life, Myfanwy had passion in her cornflower blue eyes; today they were grey. Losing Lux is terrible thing to a Mage (or Druid in her case).

She hadn't lost the Welsh lilt though. 'I must look a proper sight, Conrad. I'd say I've been to the gym, but the fluffy slippers are a bit of a giveaway. None of my other trousers fit, for some reason.' She tried a smile.

Unsuccessfully. 'It is a bit better, you know. After I pleaded guilty, they let me go outside for an hour a day. One hour to drink in the Lux. It's like being stuck in the Sahara Desert for twenty three hours and being airlifted to a water park in Majorca for sixty minutes. And I can't stop rambling. Sorry. How's Vicky?'

'Still alive, thanks to you. Sends her thanks, obviously. I'm going to sit down now.'

There are comfy chairs either side of the grille, and matching side tables. They even have a brass funnel for pouring coffee through the mesh. The deputy bailiff appeared and did the honours – she's had a lot of practice.

When the bailiff had closed the door behind her, I looked Myfanwy in the eye and said, 'I felt a bit sorry for you before, out of empathy. It's different now. I was locked in a Limbo Chamber last week, so I know exactly what the effect is. I also know that it's worse for some. Vicky didn't cope at all well, and I broke her foot when we escaped.'

'Escaped? How? No. Don't tell me now. That can wait. Why are you here, Conrad? Not that I'm not glad to see you, and all that, but you're a busy guy.'

'I need a housekeeper.'

For a moment, she couldn't process what I'd said. She blinked. She put her cup down and frowned. 'Say that again.'

'Elvenham House, in the parish of Clerkswell in the county of Gloucestershire needs a housekeeper. I think you should apply.'

'Housekeeper? Really? You're having a giraffe.'

I put her out of her misery, saying, 'You wouldn't have to clean or do the laundry, but you would have to organise it. Cooking we can share. That's all.'

She sat back. 'Oh.'

I leaned forward. 'I know you're a Herbalist. You can have free rein organising the landscaping of the gardens, subject to my approval, and have your own patch to do what you want.'

She sat up. 'There's room for both of us in this house, is there?'

'We won't be under each other's feet.'

'And there's Lux?'

'Oh yes. Not a vast amount, but yes.'

'And Vicky's happy?'

'Vicky's happy. Even the Peculier Constable is happy.'

'Deal.'

She stood up and pressed a blue button on the wall, next to a large red button. Annelise's voice came over the intercom. 'Yes?'

'Ready when you are.'

Myfanwy raised her coffee cup and clinked it against the grille. 'To the future, Conrad.'

I did the same. 'To the future.'

3 — *Newton's Cradle*

There aren't many places where the magickal and mundane worlds come together. One of them is Newton's House in Whitehall, London.

Mages usually arrive there from the Old Network of tunnels underneath the streets; mundane visitors check in via a modern door round the side of a suitably obscure government building. Ministry of Paperclips, or something like that.

I'd been allocated two tickets to invite mundane guests to the ceremony, and I'd have loved to invite Mina. I didn't think the Prison Service would play ball with that idea, so Mum and Dad had caught the early flight from Valencia and were dawdling down the road towards me, gawping like tourists. I'd seen them coming because Mother is very, very tall, and this being a royal occasion, she was wearing a hat. I, of course, was in RAF dress uniform.

'Hello dear,' she said after a perfunctory hug. 'I had no idea that this place existed.'

'That's the point. It's a secret facility.'

'I thought I knew all of them. Mind you, it's been a while.'

'Hello, son,' said Dad, giving me a vigorous handshake. 'Looking smart.'

'So are you, Dad. Let's get in before it rains.'

The modern doorway is unguarded and unlocked, because it quickly leads round the back of the Ministry to the ornate oak doors of Newton's House. The original Queen Anne building is now completely surrounded by later additions, and much of Newton's House is underground.

Today, the oak doors were open, and Maxine Lambert, Clerk to the Watch, was on meet & greet duty. I introduced my parents, and we were pointed to the corner where coffee and tea were being served to Vicky and her family by two women wearing the uniform of a catering contractor. I'd seen that uniform on many occasions – along with the women's red photo-ID badges. Their employer has a contract to supply refreshments for high security events. Reassuring.

Mum and Dad wandered off, and I said to Maxine, 'Are you security as well as hostess?'

'Hostess! Only you would call me that. It's a good job I know you, Conrad.' She paused. 'Why would we need security?'

'They follow royalty like flies.'

She looked bemused. 'No one knows the Duke of Albion is here except the guests, and this building is invisible unless you've got the Sight or the doors are open. I had to get here at nine to let the caterers in and put the flags out.'

'Fair enough. I'll catch you later.'

Mark Hayden

She gave me the conspiratorial grin of the fellow nicotine addict. 'Smoker's Corner is there, through the kitchen. I'll see you outside.'

I made my way towards the hospitality table, which was next to the double doors where Maxine had pointed, not that you could see much table. When Maxine had said *putting out the flags*, she didn't mean hoisting them up a flagpole, she meant drowning the table with them.

Newton's House belongs to the Invisible College, and most of it is heavily magickal; the Occult Council meets in the lower levels, for one thing. Above ground is the Banqueting Hall and this space, the Duke of Albion's Room. Vicky says that the Banqueting Hall is a riot of rococo frescoes, which some of the newer students would like to cover up. No such nudity in the Duke's Room, but there is lot of Invisible College branding. The College crest is a golden sunburst on a blue background, and it features throughout the carpet. To say that our flags clashed would be an understatement.

The Peculier Constable has her own coat of arms, featuring a sword. It's quite something. The Watch as a unit has a slightly bonkers coat of arms – a red shield with a white diamond in the middle, lying on its side, and that's it. No crosses, lions or dragons, just a scary diamond. I'll have to ask about it one day. Several large red and white flags had been draped over the hospitality table just to show that this was a King's Watch event.

We had been corralled into one corner of the Duke's Room because the space is huge. Even the museum rope barriers were done in blue and gold, as were the velvet chairs laid out for VIPs and guests.

For reasons of history and HR, all Watch Officers are technically in the Army. Except me. I got to keep my commission in the RAF, and I get a lot of petty pleasure from the fact that Vicky – and Hannah – have to wear the uniform of the Royal Military Police on formal occasions, and that the whole of their officer training consisted of a visit to the military tailor, who also taught them how to salute. Badly.

Vicky was juggling her crutch and a cup of coffee when she saw me coming. 'Do I have to salute?'

'Yes,' I said with a grin. I outrank her, and we're in uniform, so yes, she did have to salute.

'Dad, take this.' She handed off her hot drink and sketched a salute. 'Happy?'

I returned the salute and shook hands with Erica and Jack Robson, Vicky's parents. Jack has been a coal miner, an alcoholic and a long-distance lorry driver, in that order. Erica, his second wife, was – and still is – a domestic violence counsellor. The last time we'd met was in a hospital after Vicky's involuntary cardiac arrest.

'That's a canny collection,' said Jack, pointing to my row of medals. 'I've got mine, see?' On the lapel of his new suit was a black and white badge with gold lettering round the rim. 'Season ticket holder at St James's Park for forty year. I've probably suffered more to get that than you did for yours.'

'John!' said Erica. 'Don't be so disrespectful.'

'He's probably right,' I said. 'Let me introduce you all.'

Dad (my Dad) was coming over with two cups of coffee, and Mum, who towered over everyone except me, took off her coat and revealed her own gong, the bright blue enamel of a CBE.

'It clearly runs in the family,' said Jack, pointing to the medal, 'and not just height.'

Mother frowned and drew her head back, then gave a rare, shy smile as she held up the gong. 'This? I got it for sitting in a dark room staring at Russian codes and ciphers. Seems a lifetime ago now, and I only get to wear it at closed ceremonies like this one. I'm Mary, and this is Alfred.'

The four parents shook hands, and Jack said, 'Is it Lord Alfred or something? Vicky tells us your house – Conrad's House – is a mansion.'

Mum hooted. 'Don't encourage him, please. I married Alfred because of his smile, not his ancestral money pit.'

Vicky was brought into the fold, shook hands and then whispered to me, 'Can I sit down? Me foot's killing. I wanted to wear trainers but me Mam wouldn't let us.'

I grabbed a chair from the side and settled her down.

'Your parents are lovely,' said Vicky. 'You won't believe how nervous Dad was about coming.'

Jack Robson's voice is quite loud. We heard him saying, 'You've got your own pool? No wonder you moved to Spain.'

'Nice to see the older generation bonding,' I said to Vicky.

She groaned and muttered at the group of parents. 'Put a sock in it, Dad.'

'Are you sure your brother doesn't mind taking you to Clerkswell?' I asked.

'Why, nah. He and his lass are making a long weekend of it.'

Vicky was coming tomorrow, Good Friday, after having family time today. My parents were heading straight back to Spain so as not to miss the Fiesta. Me? I'd got a text from Annelise saying that I had to collect Myfanwy and deliver her to Clerkswell before the sun rose tomorrow at 06:24. That was a magickal deadline: more crucial for my personal wellbeing was meeting Mina's train in Cheltenham.

There was movement in the far corner and two gowned figures came slowly across the ocean of blue carpet. In an instant, I was relegated to second tallest person in the room as the Earth Master of Salomon's House approached, escorting the Keeper of the Queen's Esoteric Library.

The Earth Master, Chris Kelly, has done me several favours, and is my only real friend in the Invisible College. He gave me a grin and moved the ropes aside to let through the Keeper, Dr Francesca Somerton.

Mark Hayden

I went to say hello, and got a warm greeting from Chris. Before I could stop her, Francesca had made a beeline for my father. I shuffled over just as Dad was sorting through his mental filing cabinet. They've met before.

'Mr Clarke,' said Francesca.

'Have you still got that occasional table?' he replied with a grin.

'No. I gave it to my goddaughter. She gave it to someone else.'

'It's been passed round a lot, that table.'

'Probably because it's very ugly,' said Francesca with a smile.

'You haven't changed a bit,' said Dad. 'It must be twenty years now.'

The other three parents were looking very curious. I saw Erica take her husband's arm to stop him putting his foot in it. Francesca introduced herself by name, and gave her job title as, 'One of Victoria's former tutors.' Chris did the same.

I managed to peel Francesca away from the group before she said anything else. She, of course, is the current holder of Spectre Thomas's former office, and she is the latest in a long line of Keepers to have gone to Elvenham House looking for the missing books. It was time for a confession.

Before I could say anything, she gave me a frosty glare. 'You haven't been honest with me, have you?'

My face must have said *who snitched*, because she softened her glare and held up a hand. 'Constable Rothman told me this morning because she said we might not get the chance to talk at the ceremony, and because she trusts me. I think. The Royal Occulter is going to give me a lift down on Tuesday. He's good fun.'

The thought of Francesca and Li Cheng hanging out together was rather alarming, but at least we were now set for the summoning. Vicky, Cheng and Francesca should have more than enough oomph between them to bring my ancestor out of the well.

More guests drifted in. Desirée Haynes, daughter of Tennille and Vicky's BFF from the Invisible College, was accompanied by two of the young Watch Captains whom I'd only met once and were definitely there under orders. They were followed by two members of, if not actual royalty, then the magickal equivalent – the Warden of Salomon's House, Sir Roland Quinn, and the Dean of the Invisible College, Cora Hardisty.

Sir Roland is effectively the senior Mage in England. Even those linked to the Circles of magick rather than the College respect him and acknowledge his authority. Cora Hardisty is in charge of education and research at the College, a formidable operator and (when you get to know her), a nice person. Still not sure I completely trust her, though.

Sir Roland is both a powerful Mage and a successful academic politician. He's also getting on in years, and it's widely discussed that he will be retiring in the near future. The manner of his 'retirement' is quite complicated, but he's definitely a senior citizen, and today he was using an elegantly carved

26

mahogany walking stick to get him across the room. The head was shaped like a lion, and there appeared to be gold inlay running down the body. He and Cora had no doubt arrived in Whitehall by chauffeur driven limousine rather than schlepping along the tunnels from Salomon's House. Cora wouldn't have got very far along the passages of the Old Network in those heels, believe me.

She made a beeline for Vicky, once her student in Sorcery, and I intercepted Sir Roland, asking if he wanted me to get him a coffee.

'In a minute, lad. Just wanted to offer you my personal congratulations on defeating that Dragon. You've seen something I never will. Not in this life, and I hope not in the next.'

This is what I meant about his retirement. He's going to perform something called the Final Projection – leave his earthly body behind and become a Spirit. Apparently, he's only hanging on to make sure that his successor is up to the job.

'I'm certainly not in a hurry to meet one again, sir.'

'I believe that Cora wants you to lead a seminar on it.'

'She does. I met an old friend of yours recently.'

'Oh yes?'

'Theresa, up in Lancashire.'

Sister Theresa is the Witch who does things with trees. It was her who told me about the Final Projection, too.

Sir Roland was taken aback. 'Theresa? Really? She mentioned me?'

'Yes, sir.'

'I must get up there.'

That was alarming. 'She's in a closed order of Circle Sisters, sir. She only mentioned you in passing.'

Sir Roland frowned. 'I know where she is and what they do. She wouldn't have mentioned my name if she didn't want me to hear about it. Something's up. Thank you, Conrad, I'm much obliged.'

I glanced around the room. Hannah would soon be escorting the Duke of Albion into the room, and it was time to consider who *wasn't* there.

The Inner Council of the Invisible College has eighteen members and five were here (six if you count the Duke). This meant that twelve had chosen not to attend. Granted, the College was closed for Easter, it was short notice, and tomorrow was a bank holiday, but twelve members could now say that they had boycotted a King's Watch official ceremony. Don't forget, we were getting these medals for saving the country from a rampant Dragon.

'Let's get a coffee,' said Sir Roland, 'and I can get rid of this stick for a bit. An old man is allowed a little vanity.'

We sauntered over to the table and I said, 'Do you want me to put it in the kitchen, sir?'

'Just shove it under the table. If you could bend down for me…'

'Certainly.'

Mark Hayden

I was distracted for a second when Maxine heaved the doors closed with a thump as the last two guests arrived.

One of them was Rick James, Senior Watch Captain. He's a good bloke and had come from the West Country because it was the right thing to do. The fact that he is another of Vicky's former lovers (or *ex-shags* as she would say) might have played a part, too. The room went quiet and the floor sloped a little as the centre of gravity shifted towards Rick and his companion.

I'm speaking metaphorically, but everyone, male and female, young and old, leaned towards the stunning vision of lithe blondeness on Rick's arm. Everyone except Sir Roland, that is, who said, 'Put your tongue away, son. It's only a Fairy. How in Nimue's name did he get invited?'

'He???'

'Ask Victoria later, and don't talk to him before then. Stick, Conrad?'

'Sorry, sir.'

My leg was a lot better this morning, and I didn't have too much trouble kneeling to pull up the yards of spare flag pooled on the floor. I lifted the edge, hooked it back and glanced underneath.

Oh shit.

I spent a long time in Afghanistan, and not just on military bases. I've attended a lot of Threat Briefings. I've even seen them in the flesh. I know exactly what an Improvised Explosive Device looks like, and I was looking at one under the table. A big bottle of clear liquid had a detonator dangling inside it from the tape round the neck, and the detonator led to a black box.

'Clarke, is that what I think it is?' whispered Sir Roland, trying to keep his voice down.

On the other side of the table, one of the catering staff, trying to be helpful, bent down and lifted her side of the flag. As soon as she saw the IED, she screamed. Very loudly.

I dropped the fabric, and…

4 — As Good as a Rest

Captain Victoria Robson FGW MC KW RMP

I've made this recording because when you wake up, you'll need to know the basics, Conrad. I imagine your Mam and Dad will be there, so you'll know they're all right, and I know you'll be worried about everyone else, too. Basically, they're fine. I think you know who isn't. In fact, your biggest problem is going to be how to fit everyone in at Elvenham House. I'll get to that later.

I wasn't watching you, Conrad, before the explosion happened. I was talking to Dean Hardisty and I had my back to the hospitality section. We heard the scream, and I looked over. The last thing I saw before the flash was the Warden lifting his walking stick and spreading Works around the room.

Thanks to you, you big oaf, I've been locked up, shot at and attacked by lions. Now I can add this to the list.

The flash blinded me, the sound made me drop to the ground and curl up in a little ball. I must have screamed, too, because afterwards I had a sore throat. Mind you, everyone screamed, I think. Except you and the Warden.

I dropped to the floor because it was instinct. If it hadn't been for the Warden putting up that shield, I wouldn't have been dropping anywhere, would I? I'd have been flying across the room in bits.

After the roar of the explosion, all I could hear was screams, and all I could see was white blobs floating in front of my eyes. It was the smell that got me moving. That and the bits of burning stuff falling all around me. It's a good job that Salomon's House carpets have a fire suppressant Work built into the weave.

I used my crutch to lever myself up and took a couple of steps towards you, and then my eyesight cleared and I stopped still.

There was a hole in the floor, punched out like a die stamp. You and the Warden were just in front of it, all in a heap, but that wasn't what made me stop. It was the wall behind the hole.

A load of the panelling had been blown away back to the brick. Bits of it were scattered across the room, smouldering, along with bits of table. Next to that gap in the panelling was a red and black smear. It was the waitress. The Polish one. The other one was off to the side. Broken. I put my hand to my mouth and heaved. Just once. I swallowed it back down and looked around.

Our Dads were out cold. My Mam was feeling round the floor, blind. The only other one moving was your Mam. She was trying to stand up and get to you.

I limped over and grabbed her arm to help her up. We leaned on each other, and as we got closer I drew some Lux and extended my Sight to check for your Imprint.

'He's alive, Mary,' I said.

Another two steps and we got to you. You were underneath the Warden, and he was gone. We pulled his left hand off your shoulder and rolled him off you. That's when I saw his right arm. It had been burnt, barbecued from the inside out. His right hand was just … not there.

I touched my hands to your neck and checked your Imprint. I know your Imprint very well, Conrad, and you'll be pleased to know it's 102% in good shape. Actually, that's not a good thing. The extra 2% shouldn't be there. An Imprint is like a 3D spider's web made of different coloured silks, or that's how I see them. Down in the bottom left corner, there was an extra few strands with a different texture and colour, as if another spider had snuck along and added a bit. Just a tiny bit, not enough to make me want to know more just yet. As you would no doubt say, 'Priorities, Vicky,' and the priority was the lattice of binding Lux, like a skein over your Imprint. I've seen that before. Healers do it as a magickal anaesthetic. The Warden must have done it as part of raising the shield.

I rocked back on my heels to think about it, and a very loud voice shouted, 'Help! Over here!' It was Dean Hardisty.

'Go,' said Mary. 'I'll put Conrad in the recovery position and keep an eye on him.'

I looked around in more detail. All the men were unconscious. You, Our Dads, your mate Baldy Kelly and the Watch Captains, Eddie and Oscar. That's completely typical of men in general, but Eddie? He's got the magickal constitution of a horse. And whatever you do, don't tell the Earth Master we call him Baldy Kelly.

All the women were stirring, more or less. Mam blinked, saw me standing up and went towards Dad. Dr Somerton was sitting up, clutching her ears. Maxine was on her feet and we both ran towards the Dean as fast as my foot and her lack of vision would let us.

Behind Maxine, the doors were open again, and there was no sign of Desi, Rick or the Fae Countess. I did wonder why Rick wasn't unconscious, but only for the two seconds it took to realise why the Dean was shouting for help.

She'd been hit by a great chunk of wood panelling dropping from above, and full of flames if the black holes and raw flesh showing through her dress were anything to go by. That wasn't the problem, though. It was the piece of metal sticking out of her abdomen that made me put on a spurt.

'Stop staring and call a fucking ambulance,' said the Dean. 'I'm holding my insides together with magick, and that's not a long term solution.' She twitched.

I glanced over to you, Conrad, because you're always in charge of emergencies. You've often been the cause of them, mind, but today everyone was in my hands. I think the gods realised that this was not a good thing, and I heard the thump of Army shoes coming across the carpet. Hannah to the rescue.

She clumped up, scanning around and taking it all in. 'Bomb?' she said to Maxine and me, ignoring the Dean.

'Yes, ma'am,' I said. 'The catering staff were caught on the wrong side of a shield the Warden put up. He's gone. Sorry. Everyone else is alive, but the Dean needs an ambulance.'

'Everyone who's still here,' said Maxine with a frown.

'Who?' said Hannah.

'I heard the main doors open while I was blinded by the flash,' said Maxine, 'and footsteps running away. Then I blinked and saw Tennille's daughter. She ran after the others. The first two must have been Rick and the Fairy.'

That made no sense to me, Conrad. None at all. Hannah opened her mouth, but the Dean got in first.

'They can wait, Hannah. I can't. Please?'

Hannah did that half-squat she does in her uniform and touched the Dean's shoulder. She turned to Maxine and said, 'Call it in. Say there's one victim of an industrial accident. Meet the paramedics on the street.' She turned back to the Dean. 'I'll wake the sleeping beauties. They can get you out, Cora.'

'Where's Tennille?' I asked. As you've noticed, I was having trouble getting my priorities straight.

'Escorting the Duke of Albion through the Old Network. I had to check the tunnels before I came through here. Have you checked everyone else properly?'

'Only Conrad. I think the Warden used some sort of anaesthetic lattice.'

'Right. I'll get to work. You need to help the Dean.'

Hannah moved quickly to check on the men and tell our mothers that everything would be fine. The Dean beckoned for me to sit down.

When I'd parked my backside, she grabbed my hand and grabbed a stream of Lux. I got a taste of her pain on the back channel. It was even worse than when I felt how bad your leg can get.

'Let me know if you're going to faint,' said the Dean. 'I won't stop drawing Lux, but I will make sure you don't bang your head.'

I turned away to avoid staring at the metal spike in her stomach. I think it was a piece of table. Hannah placed her hand under Eddie's shirt and frowned. 'Damn,' she said and looked at me. 'It's not a lattice, it's a net. I thought you studied Fraternity magick at Salomon's House.'

31

The Dean snorted. She, of course, is intimately familiar with my less than stellar academic record.

'I had to re-take my Geomancy exams,' I said to Hannah, 'so I missed it out, and not having a Y chromosome, I didn't think I'd need it.'

Hannah shook her head and got on with it. Right now, the important thing is that the Warden used it to help with the shield that saved all those lives, including yours, and then it hit me really hard.

The Warden only taught one undergraduate class, and that was Fraternity magick, and someone else will have to take over now. He's gone. I barely knew him as a person or as a Mage, Conrad, but he was like a living breathing foundation stone in Salomon's House. Sometimes it seemed like the whole place had been built with the sweat off his back, and the person who would miss him most was sitting next to him, holding his hand.

You twigged that the Warden and the Keeper were close. You don't know the half of it. Dr Somerton was sitting, sobbing, and your mother was trying to comfort her. I'm guessing that comforting doesn't come naturally to your Mam, Conrad, but she did her best. With your mother otherwise engaged, mine kept shuffling between our Dads, checking and looking at Hannah impatiently. She was taking her time getting Eddie back in the game.

Next to me, the Dean let out a huge sigh. 'Thank you,' she said, with a bit less psycho in her voice. 'I should be okay now.' She didn't let go of my hand, but the drain of Lux slowed down to a sustainable trickle.

'Did you see anything?' she asked.

'A flash. A big bang.'

'Victoria! You've been spending too long with the half-Mage.'

That would be you, Conrad. The half-Mage. It's not a nice thing to say, nor is calling me *Victoria*. I hate it when older people use my full name to make a point about their power. I don't like it when you do it to take the piss, but you're allowed, as you're almost family. The Dean might be having a near-death experience, but it hasn't made her a better person. I've had an actual-death experience, and it bloody well changed me. I'll let you decide if it made me better or not.

I took a deep breath. 'Do you mean the Dragonslayer, Dean?'

'Please don't tell me you call him that. The man's ego is big enough to start with; he doesn't need acolytes.'

'He's my partner, so I get to call him what I like. He prefers Watch Captain Clarke. Or Conrad.'

'Of course. Sorry.'

I hope you're taking notes, Conrad, because that sounded like an actual apology.

'That doesn't excuse you neglecting your Art. Use your Sight and tell me what you see.'

That would be a No, then. Strike it off your list: not an actual apology. One day, maybe.

Do all teachers forever think of you as a student? Would you get the same from your old RAF instructors?

She had a point, though. Since the explosion, I've been behaving like you, Conrad, and not like a Fellow of the Great Work of Alchemy.

You've never asked me what it's like to be a Sorcerer, probably because you don't think it can be put into words. I'd have agreed before, but being locked in that Limbo Chamber and losing my magick helped me see what you see, or rather, what you don't see.

When we went to the Sacred Grove at Lunar Hall, you saw a wood. When it comes to magick, that's all you see – a wood. My Sight lets me see the trees, the branches and how they connect. A really gifted Sorcerer, like the Dean, can see the veins in the leaves and the petals in the blossom.

I opened my Sight to the room. I saw the blurred Imprints of the six other Mages, all of whom wear Personae. You'll note I said *six*, not *five and a half*. I saw our parents more clearly. You can't see any secrets or nothing when you do this, you just see more vivid colours – my Mam's smile is sweeter, for example. Your Mam looks even taller, and that's quite a scary thing. I also saw a fading red pulse against the wall as the proto-ghost of the waitress dissipated. By the doors, I saw a line of glitter. Fairy dust. I concentrated on the hole in the floor. Wow. That was weird.

'I'll go to the foot of our stairs,' I said. Out loud. I cringed, waiting for it.

'Don't tell me he encourages you,' said the Dean. 'You're not at the football now.'

'Conrad promotes all forms of diversity, Dean, including Geordies. He may draw the line at Mackems, but we've not met one yet.'

Her breath caught and she squeezed my hand almost as hard as you squeezed my foot when you broke it. Little spots of light flashed in my eyes and I started to keel over. The Dean stopped breaking my fingers and pushed me upright.

'Sorry,' she said. 'I lost concentration. Tell me, what do you see over there?'

'It's what I don't see. There's no magick. None. That really was a bomb. A mundane bomb.'

'Good. Who was the target?'

'My money's on the Duke of Albion.'

'Think it through. Do you really think a mundane terrorist planted the bomb?'

I thought about Newton's House. 'A Mage could have told them about the presentation ceremony. We both know that some Mages have dangerous associations.'

'They do, and any Mage who knew about this event would know that the Duke wears an Ancile. She would have been protected. So why no magick in the bomb?'

'Because one of us would have sensed it. In that case, the target must have been someone without an active Ancile: Conrad, Dr Somerton, Professor Kelly, Mrs Haynes, Desirée, the waitresses and our parents.' I looked at the piece of metal sticking out of her. 'And you, Dean? What happened to your Ancile?'

'Vanity, Vicky. I didn't want to spoil the line of my new dress. But I only made that decision this morning. If it wasn't me, who does that really leave?'

'Conrad or Dr Somerton.'

The trace of a smile twitched on the Dean's coral lips. 'Or Hannah,' she said.

'Eh?'

'This is a King's Watch event. There are going to be a lot of people with their knickers in a twist over this. Hannah is going to be up to her neck in some serious shit and the world of magick is going to be in turmoil now there's no Warden at Salomon's House.'

There was a pause then, because there was nothing that I could say to the Dean. She, of course, is the hot tip to become the new Warden. For just a moment, all I could hear was the sound of Dr Somerton crying.

Hannah gave a grunt and said, 'Come on you great lump. Wake up.' Eddie gave one massive snore, like a volcano, then woke up and cried out in fear.

And then Desi ran in, minus the new shoes and holding her dress round her thighs. Things got proper mental after that, especially when Annelise appeared from the Old Network with Myfanwy at the end of a silver chain like a prize sheep.

I've got to go, Conrad. You can find out all the other stuff when Hannah sees you. If she hasn't been banged up in the Undercroft.

I've saved the most important bit until last. I called Mina. She knows there's been an incident, and that you were not seriously hurt. She's decided to carry on to Clerkswell, and I had to find out from your Mam where the spare key and the alarm code were so that she could get in.

I'll be seeing you soon, partner. Take care.

5 — A Rude Awakening

And the floor reached up to smack me. I span round like the rotors on a chopper, and up was down. I spasmed, but I couldn't move, and the room flew backwards in a carousel of nausea.

'Get him out of here. Quick.'

There was a wet sock in my mouth, and I couldn't breathe. A woman cried out. The spinning got faster until I hit a brick wall, and …

… And the sock was yanked out, and I vomited generously into a handily placed bowl, decorating the man holding it.

'Easy, Conrad,' said a familiar voice. A male voice. I focused on the now ruined white shirt of the man holding the bowl. It zoomed in and out for a second until it crystallised, and I could anchor my vision on the little white buttons. I breathed.

My head was raised and to the side, and I came to know that I was propped half up on a bed. I tried to reach for a handkerchief and I couldn't move my hand. It wasn't paralysed, it was restrained. Handcuffs.

That made me convulse. Everything was restrained: arms, legs, ankles, chest. The convulsion made me throw up again.

'Easy, Conrad. Try to relax for a minute. We'll undo the buckles as soon as the convulsions have stopped.'

The voice. I knew the voice. It was the Earth Master, Chris Kelly.

I flopped back and stared at the ceiling LEDs. Too bright. I closed my eyes and tried to swallow. Ugh.

'Water?' I croaked.

'Rinse first,' said Chris.

I opened my eyes to see a water bottle and took a long draught, rinsed and spat as delicately as I could into an empty bowl. Another draught. Swallow. Breathe. Time to speak.

'Either I'm alive, or Valhalla is not as I imagined it. No offence, Chris, but I was hoping for a Valkyrie.'

'Will I do?' said another familiar voice.

'Myfanwy? What?'

'Give us a hand,' said Chris.

Shadows crossed the lights, and I felt the restraints being released.

'Don't sit up,' said a third, less familiar voice. A voice that spoke of the sea. Aah… It was Septimus Morgan, Bailiff and Sergeant at Arms to the Cloister Court. That must mean…

'Why am I in the Undercroft? What happened?'

I was able to move freely and brought my hand up to my face to give it a rub before I looked around. Yes. I was in the antechamber to one of the cells in Blackfriars Undercroft. There was a hammering on the door to the corridor.

'I'll get it,' said Myfanwy.

She pushed the door slowly out, and my mother ran in, stopping short of the trolley when Septimus put a gentle hand on her arm. 'Give him a sec.'

'Oh, Conrad,' said Mother. 'Thank God you're awake. Goodness me, I've never been so worried.'

Chris was still holding the water bottle. I took it off him and drank. It was coming back to me now…

The King's Watch flags draped over the tables. The glass bottle. The detonator. The black flash of dark sunlight, and one flame standing against the darkness, until it guttered and died. The Warden.

How…?

I looked Mother in the eye. 'The others?'

'All alive, bar three. The poor catering staff didn't stand a chance, and Sir Roland died saving the rest of us, apparently. That Cora woman is in surgery, but expected to recover.'

There was an awful lot not being said, and Mother's face was a collage of suppressed anger, fear, suspicion, concern and curiosity. I looked around at the others.

'You've scrubbed up nicely,' I said to Myfanwy. The stained tracksuit had been replaced by a royal blue tunic, leggings and new boots (one unzipped for some bizarre reason).

Myfanwy flicked a glance at Mother. 'Well, I thought I was going to start a new job today, didn't I, and not as a nurse, that's for sure.'

Septimus coughed. 'Lie down, Conrad, and we'll push you to the Wardroom.'

I stopped to button up my shirt, then lay back on the trolley and tried to relax as they wheeled me down the corridor to the more homely surroundings of the Bailiff's Wardroom. With help from Chris and Septimus, I made it into an armchair.

'This way, Chris,' said Septimus. 'I'll lend you a clean shirt and give you a plastic bag for that one.'

'I'll make tea,' said Myfanwy, retreating to the galley and leaving Mother to perch next to me.

She fiddled with the bottom of her jacket. 'They used to say that my grandmother was a witch. Mother's mother, from the fens.' She looked up. 'I had no idea. None. Vicky's mother did. Erica suspected that there was a world of magick, and that Vicky was a witch.'

I made an effort and reached out. Reluctantly, she took my hand. 'Vicky's a Mage,' I said. 'Capital "M", not a Witch, capital "W".'

'Don't tell me,' she said. 'I'm just glad that you ended up on the side of the Angels.'

36

I coughed, and was about to clarify the Angels business when she held up her hand. 'Don't,' she said. 'My life won't be enriched by knowing the details.'

Fair enough. 'Where's Dad?'

'In Denial. That's a magickal term, according your CO. Hannah said that it was common for us ordinary people to reject a close encounter with magick. The same thing happened to Jack Robson.' She smiled. 'Currently, your father is trying to convince Jack that a complete news blackout is in the public interest. He's quite a man, is Jack. He doesn't want the deaths of those poor women to be brushed under the carpet by an establishment cover-up. How are you feeling now, Conrad?'

I paused. 'Better.' Myfanwy came over with two steaming mugs of tea. 'Better for this,' I added.

'Not for me, dear,' said Mother, standing up. 'Mr Kelly is going to help me collect Alfred and we're going to catch our flight. Alfred needs to be kept away from you for twenty-four hours at least, to help him adjust. Vicky is being driven to Clerkswell by her friend Desirée for the same reason: to keep her away from Jack.'

I stood up, a little more steadily, and went to give her a hug. Perhaps it was because of the audience, because for once she hugged me back. For a second. Then she disengaged and reached into her bag. She pulled out and handed over an MP3 player with headphones. It said *Property of Blackfriars Undercroft* in printed tape on the side.

'Vicky has left you a recorded message,' said Mum. 'She made it a few hours ago.'

I suddenly realised that I had no idea of the time. I glanced at my watch, and it wasn't there.

'Five o'clock in the afternoon,' said Myfanwy. 'I'll get your stuff in a minute. We had to take it off before the procedure.'

Mother picked up her coat and gripped my hand before giving me a kiss. Her parting words were not addressed to me, but to Myfanwy. 'Take good care of the house, dear. It's a burden, yes, but I was happy there.'

Chris Kelly, re-shirted, shook my hand, patted me on the shoulder and took my mother away.

'You should listen to that,' said Myfanwy. 'If you ask Septimus nicely, he'll let you take it to Cell 1 and switch on the extractors. It's the only smoker's cell, and don't worry, the Limbo Chamber has been deactivated.'

'If you must,' sighed the Bailiff. 'I'll get the keys.'

I took my tea, some biscuits and the MP3 player into the empty room and sat listening to Vicky's account of the bombing.

I took a few minutes to digest what I'd heard. I was worried for Cora, yes, and angry at the pointless waste of three lives, but more than anything, I was boiling with rage on behalf of the Watch.

During all the years I spent in Afghanistan and Iraq, I never forgot that we were aliens. Well-meaning aliens, mostly, but that was not our land.

This is my land. These are my people, and only someone with a truly evil heart could do this.

I returned to the Wardroom full of questions. The first answer I got was not the one I'd been expecting. Myfanwy was standing with one boot off, rinsing a sock.

'My god, you didn't…'

'Sorry, Conrad, but I had no choice.'

'Words fail me.'

She put the sock on a radiator and pointed to the table. 'Let's eat. You'll be starving.'

She took the clingfilm off several plates of sandwiches and cakes, and she was right. I was starving. She poured more tea and joined me at the table, grabbing a plate.

'You know Hannah got the others awake, yeah?' she said. I nodded. 'She couldn't wake you. Needed a male Mage and a special place.'

'Something to do with Fraternity magick, according to Vicky.'

'Yeah. It's called something different in Welsh.' She tipped her head to one side. 'Doesn't translate well. Suppose I'll have to get used to all these Alchemy terms if I'm going to be living with you and hanging round with Vicky.'

I chewed a rough-cut doorstop of cheese and tomato to avoid saying that this wasn't my interpretation of her sentence from the court.

She carried on, oblivious. 'Not my area of expertise, obvs, but it has to do with creating a displaced link. The Warden drew Lux from all the men, and he used a sort of net. Like fishing. Because he died with the bond active, the nets stayed in place. With you, he did something I couldn't begin to understand. To loosen the net, we had to put you in the Enhanced Limbo Chamber at the end. The one that doesn't just block Lux, it drains it, too.'

'No wonder I felt like shit when I woke up. I've never been so disorientated in my life. Worse than being drunk on a chopper ride through a thunderstorm.'

'Really?'

'Really. My only real talents in magick are orientation and a bit of Geomancy.'

'Orientation? What's that?'

'Never mind. Carry on.'

'It had to be a team effort. Septimus performed the procedure. When the net loosened, he peeled it away, but to do that he needed Lux, so Chris created a temporary Leybridge from the antechamber, and I anchored.' She looked down. 'It's what you did when we revived Vicky. You did that on instinct; I had to be shown.'

'Thank you, Myfanwy. Another debt I owe you. Doesn't explain the sock, though.'

'Septimus shouted that you were going to convulse. He couldn't move, and the cell was empty. Nothing there. I took my sock off so they could shove it in your mouth to stop you gagging or biting your tongue. Don't worry, it was new on this morning. Brand new.'

Suddenly, the cheese sandwich was very dry. I took a big slurp of tea.

I stared at Myfanwy for a second, until she met my eye. 'What have they told you?' I asked. She looked down.

'Nothing that I didn't see with my own eyes. As soon as I got there, Annelise tied me up like a horse outside the saloon and stuck a Silence on me while all the shit happened. Those two lads took the Dean out to the ambulance and Maxine took Vicky's mam and your dads away. All that, I could see from the other side of the room. Didn't need to hear anything. Then there was arguing.' She shrugged. 'Finally, the Constable came over and told me to go with you and Chris. The only thing that's been discussed in my presence was what related directly to the Charm on your Imprint.' She smiled. 'And I talked to your mam. Seems you hadn't got round to telling her about me.'

'Ah.'

'Don't worry. I told her I was under house arrest for three years. I didn't tell her why, and she didn't ask. She was too worried about you to care, really.'

It was time for cake. I've no idea what it was, but it was nutty and very tasty. 'Has anyone else been in touch?'

She gave me a sly grin. 'You mean your girlfriend? You never mentioned her.'

'I was thinking about Vicky. Mina can handle herself.'

She shook her head. 'If they have, no one's told me. We've been working on you for most of the day.'

Septimus reappeared and helped himself to a slice of the cake. 'Mmm. Gorgeous,' he said, and looked at me. 'Have you met Steph? My daughter? She's one of my Deputies, and a mad baker.'

'No,' said Myfanwy. 'She hasn't been on duty when you've been here. And don't worry, I've got the recipe.'

'Right,' said Septimus. 'I've been on the phone to let Merlyn's Tower know that you're awake. There was a message for you.'

This didn't sound good. In a situation like this, I should be having a conversation with Hannah myself. 'Yes?'

He looked at a Post-it note. 'Mrs Haynes told me to say this: you need rest and protection, and Myfanwy needs to get to Clerkswell in your company. Rick James is on his way to town to collect you and take you back. He'll give you more details.' He looked up at me. 'And before you ask, I do know that it

39

wasn't Rick in the Duke of Albion's Room. It was a Glamour, and it had something to do with the Fae Countess. They are currently prime suspects.'

'Duw God,' said Myfanwy. 'Really?'

'It must have been a hell of a Glamour to fool Vicky,' I added. 'And Cora, not to mention Sir Roland.'

Septimus pulled his beard and shrugged with one shoulder. A very economical shrug, that. He probably learnt it in the Navy. 'Just so you know,' he said. 'Rick is picking up your stuff, and your car, Conrad, and he'll be here in half an hour. I'll do the binding and you can wait upstairs.'

There was a certain amount of packing, getting dressed and some complaints about wet socks, then we were ready.

Septimus checked a few details, then took a small spool of fine silver cord. Real silver. He carefully knotted lengths around both of Myfanwy's wrists, and I saw why she had a long-sleeved tunic. He took another length and made an elegant loop which he passed over Myfanwy's head and dropped round her neck. He fastened a final bracelet of cord round my left wrist. It tightened all of its own, not enough to hurt, but enough for me to feel a slight drain on My Lux.

He explained it like this. 'You have to keep each other in sight for the whole journey, comfort breaks included. Myfanwy can't project magick beyond her body, but that's not the biggy. At dawn tomorrow, all three of her cords will tighten and shrink to nothing.'

'In other words, it will decapitate me,' added Myfanwy. 'So no taking the scenic route, all right?'

That was rather alarming. Even more alarming was what Septimus said next.

'The only way to prevent that is to cut her cords. If you do that outside the parish of Clerkswell, or tamper with the one round your wrist, you'll lose your left hand.'

'No pressure, then,' said Myfanwy.

As we rode up in the lift, I started to get a bit twitchy. Even if I wasn't the target of the bomb, I take it very personally when people set up explosive devices near me. I couldn't avoid the thought that someone wanted me dead very badly. *Why* they wanted me dead was a distraction. For now, I had to focus on staying alive.

Septimus was unlocking the final magickal door to the service corridor. 'Who knows I'm here?' I asked.

Myfanwy spoke first. 'Me, Chris Kelly and the Constable were the only ones left when they made the final decision. I know that much. Vicky came a bit later, just to make that recording.'

Septimus shook his head. 'I haven't told anyone, but I'm not really in the loop. Do you want me to wait with you?'

'Have you got an Ancile?'

'Not on me, no.'

'Then I'll take my chances.'

'Oy,' said Myfanwy. 'You mean *we'll* take our chances. I'm a sitting duck next to you.'

'Good luck,' said Septimus.

Myfanwy muttered something, and I shook his hand. 'Thank you.'

Before he shut the door behind him, Myfanwy reached up and gave him a hug. 'You're a good man,' she said. He blushed and disappeared.

The service corridor opens just down from the taxi rank. It has an overhang and a small doorway. No one could see us, except for the taxis pulling away with fares on board. I stood downwind of Myfanwy and lit a cigarette.

'This isn't normal, I suppose,' she said.

'There's nothing normal about my life, these days.'

'No, I meant that I got talking to your mam. I know a lot about you, and you know nothing about me. Not really. You know I'm not married, don't you? Of course you do.'

'I know you had a thing for Rhein ap Iorwen, and I know it wasn't reciprocated. I'm sorry about that.'

She tilted her head. 'Are you sorry that he didn't care for me, or sorry that you killed him?'

I knew we'd have to have this conversation, but I hadn't expected to have it in a station doorway. Myfanwy had hatched the Dragon and been in love with Rhein; both the Dragon and the Hunter had died at my hand, so I wasn't surprised that it had come up so soon. Before I could get out my carefully planned question, she started up again.

'I had a lot of time to think in the Undercroft. Not a lot else to do, really. My barrister showed me some of the papers, and he asked around, but no one who knows what really happened was saying very much, and not to me or Gwyddno. Listen, Conrad, I don't blame you, but just to clear the air, could you tell me what happened after I took Vicky to the hospital?'

The Brotherhood of the Dragon had turned on Myfanwy when she objected to their plans for Welshfire, the Dragon. They'd taken her magick and tied her up in her car as bait for a trap that Vicky and I fell into.

'If you promise to shut up for a bit and let me get a word in, Myvvy, I will,' I said.

'Myvvy! You sound like my dad.'

'You're not the first person to say I sound like their father. How old are you anyway? And yes, it is my business.'

'I don't see how.'

'You're going to have to give me your date of birth for the insurance policy.'

'Oh. I'm twenty-six. How old are you?'

'Thirty-seven, though I don't feel like it at the moment.'

'Smoking is very bad for you. I hope you don't smoke in the house. Is it really such a barn of a place?'

'Do you want my whole history, or just the bit with the Dragon?'

'Oh, the Dragon, please.'

'Good. Just tell me, from the moment I rescued you, what would have been your preferred outcome?'

'You didn't rescue me. I didn't need rescuing.'

'Myfanwy, you were tied up and they were about to release a man-eating Dragon. I'd call that a rescue.'

She'd been rummaging in her handbag while the conversation pinged back and forth. She found what she'd been looking for and held it up. 'Will there be an iPhone charger in the car?'

'No. We can stop at Beaconsfield Services for you to get one. They have disabled toilets we can share, and there's a phone bits shop there. Answer my question: what would you have liked to happen?'

She slowly put the dead phone back in her bag, and didn't look at me when she spoke. 'It was too late. They'd already done the *Blasu Diwethaf* by then, and Welshfire had a taste for magickal human flesh. I suppose the best I could have hoped for was a quick end for Welshfire and a reduced sentence for Rhein.'

'Did you really do any thinking in the Undercroft, or did you just talk to yourself?'

'Don't be nasty.'

'I wasn't. Just put yourself in my shoes. I had to stand back and watch Rhein release Welshfire. After that, he wanted some sport, didn't he? Instead of giving the Dragon a head start and hunting her down, he was going to unleash her on the sheep – and farmers – of the Brecon Beacons. I couldn't let that happen.'

'I suppose not.'

I really snapped at her. 'There's no supposing about it, Myfanwy. If I hadn't stepped in, how would you have explained to some poor parents that their little boy had been a tasty snack for your Dragon?'

'It wasn't supposed to be like that! I don't think I can cope with this. I feel trapped already.'

'Perhaps this wasn't the best topic of conversation.'

'Just finish the story.'

'What happened was this. I used a trick to lure Welshfire back down the hill and into a trap. Rhein appeared and they fought. When the trap went off, they were busy knocking seven shades of shit out of each other. I nearly got fried. She spoke to me, you know.'

'Who did? Welshfire?'

'Yes. She said – in Welsh – "Where's Guinevere?"'

'What? No. Why?'

'I'm afraid so. They'd promised her Surwen and Gwyddno's daughter to eat for the *Blasu Diwethaf*, and Welshfire was disappointed.'

She looked suitably appalled. One day, I hope, she'll come to realise that she was a useful idiot to the Brotherhood. In fact, that day needs to come sooner rather than later.

'Listen, Myfanwy, I wouldn't have offered my home as a prison if I didn't trust you, but I absolutely do not trust Adaryn ap Owain.'

'It was mostly Surwen,' she replied. 'Adaryn was the banker and she was going to be the public face.'

'Oh no. They were a team, and Adaryn was the senior partner. She's anathema now. Not only has every Circle of Mages been warned about her, even MI5 have her on a watch list. Don't forget, it was her who stopped Vicky's heart.'

'I don't want anything to do with her, all right?'

'There's more to it than that. She might want something to do with you. She might get in touch. She might want to use you. She might be behind the bombing.'

'I …' She stopped, and for moment she really thought about what I'd said. 'I give you my word, Conrad, that if she gets in touch, I'll tell you.'

'Good.'

6 — Homecoming

It was time to check my phone. It had pinged frantically when we emerged from the Undercroft, but I'd wanted to have that conversation with Myfanwy first.

In short, Mina was worried, but safely installed in Elvenham House. She'd finished her message by saying, *Your house is huge, cold and intimidating. A bit like you in a bad mood.* Vicky had also arrived. I sent them both a message saying *Awake. Am fine. Waiting for a lift. More soon.* I added a bit to Mina's message, as you'd expect for the woman I love. By the time I'd pressed Send, a non-taxi was heading down the ramp.

The car was either my actual Volvo XC70 or a very close facsimile of it, and I caught a glimpse of a black face in the driving seat before I retreated into the shadows. Myfanwy is entirely too suggestible for her own good, which right now was good news for me. And her.

'Myfanwy, go up to the car and talk through the window.'

'Why?'

'You're not the target. If it's the enemy, they won't strike at you.'

'Okay…'

'Just ask Rick what Vicky's like in bed.'

'What!'

'If it's really Rick, you'll know from his response. Quick!'

She ran to the car and pressed her thighs against the door to stop the driver opening it. The window slid down. I couldn't hear what was said, but I saw Myfanwy's reaction. After a second, she put her hand through the window and patted the driver, now confirmed as Rick, on the shoulder and stepped back. I stepped forwards.

I thought about getting in the front, but for a second, I couldn't see Myfanwy and there was a tug on my wrist from the silver cord, so I installed her in the back and spoke to Rick.

'Way to go, bro,' he said. 'How to spot the Glamour without using magick. Not sure Vicky will thank you for spilling that, but better safe than sorry, eh?'

'It would have come out sooner or later. Myfanwy has no filter, and Vicky's a terrible liar.'

'Hey, I heard that,' came a voice from the back.

'Push that button, will you, Rick? I need the Hammer from the boot.'

'I'm ahead of you, bro.'

He pointed to the Dwarven crafted case on the front seat, and with some relief I got out the Hammer. The single round Hannah gave me is elsewhere in a safe place, but I needed the Hammer because it has my Ancile stamped on the grip. I felt a lot better with that. I got into the back and told Rick how to program the Satnav for Elvenham House. He set off, and as soon as the ETA appeared, I sent messages.

Rick waited until I'd finished and until we were in stationary traffic along the Victoria Embankment before he turned to face us. 'Are you okay, Conrad? Sounded bad.'

'I'm fine. What can you tell me?'

He looked at Myfanwy. 'I can't put a Silence on her with that binding, and I don't know much myself. I know that it's gone to CobroM, which is where Hannah is now.'

Myfanwy raised her eyebrows, but was too polite to say anything. I turned to her. 'Cabinet Office Briefing Room (Magick),' I said, 'and that's all I know about it.'

'Me too,' added Rick. He took a moment to drive twenty metres along the road. 'Have you heard about the Glamour of me and of the Countess?'

'Yes.'

'Then you know as much as I do. Hannah decided the operational priority was to get all potential targets to a place of safety, and that for all sorts of reasons, your house is the safest. When we get there, I have to wait until she can video call us all. Well, you, me and Vicky.'

'Then let's sit back and enjoy the drive,' I said. 'Wake me if I snore.'

'Seriously?' said Myfanwy. 'You're going to sleep?'

'Best thing. I'm shattered.'

Whatever the Warden had done, it had left me feeling wrung out and gritty eyed. In the safety of the Volvo, I had no trouble sleeping. Myfanwy shook me at the service station, and we had a fun time in the disabled toilet. Not.

After that, I made her stand under the outside canopy while I walked backwards until I felt the bond tug. I was far enough away for some privacy, and I called Mina.

'Has Vicky shown you where the thermostat is?'

'Conrad! Are you OK? Vicky kept trying to reassure me, but she was so upset I couldn't help worrying.' She dropped her voice. 'That friend of hers is scary. She doesn't like you.'

In the background, I could hear muzak. 'Where are you?'

'Tesco's in Bishop's Cleeve. Stocking up for Easter. It was ever so funny.'

'What was?'

'Desirée wanted to ask me if I eat British food, but she was too polite. She and Vicky have left me to shop and they've gone to the garden centre for some totally weird Mage reason.'

You will have noticed that I hadn't actually answered her question about whether I was OK. That's one of the reasons I love her.

'We'll be there at nine.'

'Good. I can't wait, though I hadn't expected my first visit to Clerkswell to be quite such a public event. Vicky actually used magick to find the airing cupboard so we could get bedding for everyone. Oh, one more thing. What should I tell people about me? Vicky says you're such a big figure in the village that everyone will talk. Are you really a local celebrity?'

Rick appeared from the shop and waved at me to get a move on.

'Got to go, love. Tell them what you like. It'll be fun.'

'It will. Take care. Love you.'

Back in the car, Myfanwy plugged her phone into the new charger and settled in for a mass catch-up session as soon as it had rebooted.

While she waited, I said, 'Tell me about yourself. Are your parents Druids? Brothers and sisters? What have you told them about all this?'

'Mam and Dad are Druids. They're not Gifted, but they know magick. They know I'm in trouble, and they'll have heard about the Dragon. I'm going to have a lot of explaining to do. You know they can't visit, don't you?'

'Yes.'

'Neither can my brother. His wife has a small Gift, and they have two kids.' Her phone pinged alive and her eyes were dragged down, like my eyelids. I was asleep before she'd unlocked the pass screen.

Rick woke me when we were ten minutes from home. Five minutes later, I told him where to pull in, just before the sign saying *Clerkswell welcomes Careful Drivers*. As we'd headed west, the clouds had piled in and it was raining. Being a true gent, Rick held the umbrella while Myfanwy and I prepared for the ceremony. Before we could get going, a BMW pulled up. It was Giraldo, one half of the husband and husband team who run the Inkwell pub. He's not really called Giraldo.

Look at it from his point of view. He's coming home from a shift at GCHQ, and in his headlights he sees a black man in combats holding an umbrella, me in my RAF uniform and a strange woman holding her arms out like a sacrificial victim. Of course he pulled over to see if everything was okay.

'Evening, Conrad, has your car broken down? Need a lift?'

'No thanks, Mike. This is my new housekeeper. She's Welsh,' I said, as if that explained everything.

This is the English countryside. Of course it explained everything. 'Nice boots,' he said to Myfanwy. 'Watch you don't get them dirty.'

'Who was that and was he really checking out Rick?'

'Later, Myvvy, and you need a proper cover story. Are you ready?'

'Go for it.'

'Myfanwy Lewis, you are bound to this place and parish for a period of three years and may not depart from this place or practise magick without leave from the Court. Do you accept this binding?'

'I do.'

I snipped the cords with my nifty enhanced wirecutters. I did have a moment's hesitation, but there was no magickal mishap; all four cords parted safely. Myfanwy rubbed her wrists and took a deep breath.

'*Cartref yw cartref, er Tloted y bo.*' She smiled at me. 'Home is home, however poor it may be. This is your home, Conrad, I'll try to make it mine.'

I stuck out my hand. 'Welcome to Clerkswell.'

The other two were in a hurry to get out of the rain. I wasn't, and not just because I was the only one with a proper outdoor coat. My paranoia was telling me, loud and clear, that this would be a good time to make absolutely sure.

'Open the boot, Rick, and both of you switch off your phones. In fact, switch them off and go and stand over there.'

Rick did as he was told; Myfanwy watched for half a second before joining him. I lifted the tailgate and heaved the luggage aside. The battery was under a panel, and I disconnected it.

'What's he doing?' I heard her say.

'Wait and see,' said Rick.

I've said before that Mages are not keen on the twenty-first century. In general. Why would you bother with a GPS tracker when you can use a crystal ball? But that bomb was a game-changer. It was mundane, but I'm willing to bet that magick played a part in its manufacture. And it had a radio trigger.

I took out my multi-spectrum RF detector and switched it on. Any vehicle tracker has to phone home, and that's its Achilles heel. The five lights on the little box flashed on, then went out. A few seconds later, one of them flashed on again. I walked round the car a few times and got confirmation. There it was. Every ten seconds, it was transmitting. I called them over.

'So now they know where you live,' said Myfanwy.

'If you do a Google search, you'll find a picture of me getting my DFC. The caption says, "Squadron Leader Clarke, of Elvenham House, Clerkswell." If they've half a brain, they already know where I live. I think there's going to be a reception committee.'

'What we gonna do?' said Rick.

'Vicky can't walk without a crutch. Desirée doesn't have an Ancile. It's down to you and me.'

'And me,' said Myfanwy. 'And don't say it doesn't affect me. It does. The court order allows me to perform magick in self-defence. And don't either of you *dare* say anything about me being a woman.'

'Three hours ago, you said you were a sitting duck. Your gender doesn't change that.'

I thought about the half mile to home. The best place for an ambush would be after we turn off what passes for the main road and go down Elven Lane to Elvenham House. On the corner is the church and churchyard.

'Myfanwy, can you make a Glamour of me sitting in the front seat?'

'Not my strong point, but yes.'

'Rick, are you happy to draw their fire while I try to intercept?'

'I can run faster than you, and you're not armed.'

'True, but I grew up here. I know every inch of this village, and you've only been once.'

He chewed it over. 'What's the plan?'

'Let's get moving. We've been sitting here too long.'

As we got back in, I had to get some items from the boot, and Myfanwy peered over my shoulder. She ignored the Kalashnikov and focused on the Cramp bark bush. 'Wow! Who enchanted that?'

'Priorities, Myvvy. Later.'

I told Rick to drive to the pub and called Vicky. 'Can you and Desi get to the end of the drive. No lights, just check for anyone lying in wait.'

'Seriously?'

'I'm probably just going to get wet and look foolish, but there *is* a tracker on the car, and someone did try to blow us up this morning.'

'On it.'

Rick pulled up at the Inkwell, and I got out. 'Drive slowly, but not too slowly, and watch out. Give me two and a half minutes to get in position.' I didn't wait for a reply.

I jogged across the village green, past the Elven Lane turning and along the north wall of the churchyard.

The main entrance to the churchyard is actually on Elven Lane, about three hundred metres before Elvenham House. No one would go to the churchyard on a dark, wet Thursday in normal circumstances, but tomorrow is Good Friday. To my relief, the church was dark.

I climbed over the side gate and used the black form of St Michael's Church to screen my approach to the south west corner of the churchyard. The main lights on the spire had been turned off for Lent, but there was still a spotlight on the clock, and a streetlight on the corner. Past the church, there were lots of graves to hide behind, if I could be bothered to crawl. I touched the Hammer and raised my Ancile.

Because of the rain, I couldn't hear anything, but I saw headlights coming up from the pub. I dodged up to the war memorial, and as Rick slowed down before the turning, I lowered my head and ran zig-zag through the graves.

It was pure luck that I had my head down when a blinding flash of light came from near the wall, followed by a boom and bass *crack*. What the hell?

Rick was on the Lane, and just in front of him, an oak tree was collapsing in slow motion onto the road. Rick slammed on the brakes, and I sprinted towards the gate.

A shadow flitted in front of me. The tree hit the road, and I couldn't tell whether Rick had missed it or been crushed. Either way, he and Myfanwy were very vulnerable. The shadow became a man, standing by the open gate and raising his hands. I had no choice but use the gravel path to close the last five metres, and he heard me.

A jet of flame arced round in front of the Mage, enough to grill me before I could duck, but he panicked and missed, and I was past his guard. I slammed into him and drove him into the gatepost. He wasn't a fighter. He didn't try any martial arts manoeuvres, but he did have a free hand to try magick. We both burst into flames.

Everything flammable I was wearing started to combust. That is not a nice feeling. He didn't much like it either, and he stopped whatever magick he was using straight away, but we were both on fire.

'Conrad! Mine!' shouted Rick.

I staggered back and dived into the gutter, where rainwater was gathering. The Mage tried the same trick on Rick as my comrade closed with him, but Rick has a proper weapon, not my empty gun. Rick was smoking when he dived forward and drove his Badge of office into the Mage's ribcage. I focused on rolling in the water.

'Conrad! Are you hurt?' said Myfanwy. She looked round and unfocused her eyes. 'I can't sense anyone else. Are you okay?'

'I think so,' I said, sitting up. 'Good job leather doesn't burn well, or my hands would be en croute. Can you pull my gloves off? They're still hot.'

I held up my hands and she carefully peeled away the leather before giving me a hand up. I stared at my fingers, flexing and checking. With no accelerant to sustain the flames, they'd gone out quickly. Everything was singed rather than burnt. I turned to look at Rick, and he was just standing there.

At his feet was the body of the Mage, Rick's long dagger sticking out of his chest. I went up and took his arm, turning him away. 'Well done. That was good work.'

'But I've killed him.'

'And I for one am very grateful for that. It's shit, isn't it?'

I held on to his arm while he processed what had happened. 'Yeah, it is,' he said with a shudder.

I looked over my shoulder. 'Myvvy, call Vicky.'

'I don't need to.' She pointed over the fallen tree. Two women were running towards us, with a third hopping behind them.

Desi and Mina dodged round the fallen tree. Desi paused to see what was going on, while Mina flung herself at me. Thankfully, she stopped herself in time.

'My god, Conrad. You ... you've been scorched. What happened? We heard the bang and came running.'

'We need to move,' I said. 'Myfanwy, keep watch up at the crossroads. Rick, help me shift the human torch into the car. There's enough room to get round on the other side of the tree, so you drive off quick. Desirée, you and

Mina check inside the churchyard, along the right hand wall. Look for a rucksack or something.'

'You can't order me around,' said Desirée.

'Suit yourself. I'll send Vicky in to give Mina a hand.'

'You can't…'

Mina marched up and grabbed her arm. She marched her past the body and said, 'I'm on licence. If I get arrested, there'll be no parole.'

Vicky arrived as Rick and I were trying to decide how to move the body. She was well out of breath, but didn't waste time. She opened the back door of the car and went to get a towel from the boot.

'Shall I take out my Badge out of his chest?' asked Rick.

'Not yet. He'll only bleed more if you do, and I only had that car valeted a few days ago.'

He shook his head and bent down to take the dead Mage's arms.

Rick drove carefully round the fallen tree and off towards Elvenham House, using a strip of grass in front of the Church Well, and until the Council came to clear the tree, the grass was likely to suffer significant damage, especially when the milk tanker turned up. Nothing stops a milk tanker.

'That was some homecoming,' said Vicky.

'I've had better.'

'Mind if I sit down. Me foot's killing me. A gallop up the lane to deal with an ambush was not what the Healer had in mind when she said "light use".'

She hobbled over and parked herself on the fallen tree. I joined her and checked to see if my cigarettes had been damaged when I rolled in the gutter. They hadn't. Good.

'Are you burnt?' she asked.

'A bit. Nothing too serious. My uniform's ruined. Hannah's going to love a £400 bill for a new one.'

She put her hand on mine, just for a second, just to let me know she'd have been there for me if she could. That meant a lot.

'How did he make fire like that?' I asked. 'It was nothing like a Dragon.'

'Pyromancy,' said Vicky. 'I can do a bit – you've seen me light the fire at your house. That was at a nice safe distance, with nicely combustible wood. Very few Mages have a talent for the serious stuff, and most don't develop it as such. They usually become Artificers. This guy clearly had a serious talent, but not much experience. That's why he's dead and you're alive.'

'Comforting thought. I hope I don't meet his master any time soon. Did you recognise him? He can't be that much older than you. You might have seen him at Salomon's House.'

'No. I even checked what was left of his Imprint after Rick disrupted it. Never seen him before.'

'Talking of Imprints, what's this about me having an extra bit attached? I trust you, Vic, of course, but it's a bit a facer when someone tells you your soul is no longer 100% your own.'

She made a gesture of uncertainty with her hand, a sort of shoulderless shrug. 'I had to tell you, but there's not much I can say. It happens naturally, over time. I bet if I looked at your Mam and Dad's Imprints, I'd find points of symmetry. This was sudden, and it has to be down to the Warden. I was exaggerating when I said 102%, more like 0.2%. It'll probably fade, but do let me know if you develop an interest in fly fishing.'

'Fly fishing.'

'Aye. It was one of his hobbies.'

There was a moment of silence, apart from the rain hitting the road.

'Thanks for the taped message,' I said. 'Very useful. Saved a lot of explanations.'

'You're welcome. Seemed like a good idea.'

I smiled. 'If there's a next time, try not to think you're telling it to me. Just give the story as if you're on the radio or something and it's not me specifically listening.'

'Why would there be a next time?'

I shrugged. 'Things are getting complicated. We might need to split up.'

'Aye, well. We'll see.'

I stood up. 'Can you walk?'

'I'd rather not.'

'I'll head to the house and give Rick a hand. He can come and get you while I try to drag Hannah out of the CobroM meeting. She needs to know this straight away.'

'Fine. I'll take charge out here. If Mina and Myfanwy let me, and if Desi doesn't have a diva strop.'

I said nothing and limped down Elven Lane.

7 — *Secret Santa*

The guy on Hannah's left didn't introduce himself, but he didn't need to. They were sitting rather closer to each other than they would have chosen, because the angle on the video camera wasn't good. Or maybe they were quite happy to share their personal space. For a bureaucrat, he's not bad looking, I suppose. I didn't check with Vicky to get a female perspective. We were rather more spaced out at our end, gathered around my partners' desk in the Elvenham House library. I never did find out where Hannah and her friend were sitting.

'This gentleman is from the security services,' said Hannah.

'Hi, John,' I said.

'Clarke,' he responded in a clipped voice.

'You two...?' said Hannah.

'Doesn't matter,' said Lake.

John Lake is a security liaison officer. He acts as a multi-purpose hinge when different agencies need to co-operate. I'd come across him during my debriefing after the Operation Jigsaw affair.

Hannah was still in her uniform, as was I. Hers was now rather creased, but at least it didn't have burnt bits. Her first instinct is for her team, and her first priority when Maxine had dragged her out of the CobroM meeting had been to make sure that we were all okay. She didn't need any further updates on our health, so I got straight down to business.

'Since we spoke, ma'am,' I said, 'the bomber's vehicle has turned up. I took the liberty of moving it to Elvenham House.'

Hannah cringed. She's still more a copper than anything, and I'd just ordered all sorts of forensic evidence to be compromised. Doesn't matter — there won't be a trial under mundane law.

Lake leaned forwards, edging Hannah off centre. 'Are you 100% sure that this man is the bomber?'

'Yes. He had a radio trigger in his pocket, and we improvised a test for nitroglycerin compounds. They were all over the vehicle.'

Hannah subtly elbowed Lake back to his place. 'Have you IDed him?'

'As I've said before, ma'am, we don't have always-on access to the PNC. I was hoping that this time we'd have support from other agencies. We can't do this on our own.'

Hannah went slightly red. She has very pale skin, and you'd have to say that she wears her heart function on her sleeve. 'Not yet. Maybe as a result of this incident, but not yet. Not without Council approval.'

She meant the Occult Council. This video conference was rather strained because John Lake was mundane, and because Hannah had been ordered to keep magick right off the agenda. The poor bloke must have thought we were all bananas.

Lake glanced at her. 'While we're still here, perhaps you could email a short report with any information. We can access the PNC and other resources,' he said.

'Yes,' said Hannah. 'And I'm afraid we have no leads on the other suspect.'

'I would have thought he would have been a lot easier to track down.'

'Not the bomber. The Countess.'

We were clearly suffering from a breakdown in communication. 'Yes. That's who I meant.'

'You said, "he".'

Now everyone thought *I* was bananas. Not unusual. I coughed. 'The Warden clearly referred to the other suspect as a male. Perhaps he was being snide, ma'am.'

Hannah's red face went white. 'We'll deal with that later.'

John Lake thought we'd all lost the plot, big time. He picked up a piece of paper to give himself a moment.

The soundproofing in Elvenham House is excellent, mostly because of the thick walls. Even so, I knew that there was a commotion going on outside the library door. I heard a voice, then a knock, then Mina slipped in. Something must be very wrong. She tiptoed forward and glanced first at me, then at the screen.

'Oh,' she said.

'Good evening Mrs Finch,' said Lake.

'It's Miss Desai now,' said Mina.

'*Oy vey ist mir*,' said Hannah, throwing up her arms and knocking Lake off balance. 'This I cannot cope with.' She pointed a finger at the camera. I think she was pointing at her image of Mina. 'What are you doing here?'

Mina drew herself up to her full height of 5'2" and shook her hair back. 'What is it?' I said quickly.

Mina sniffed and looked away from the screen. 'The police are here. Apparently someone heard the "lightning strike" and turned their telescope on the churchyard. They saw some suspicious activity, but not the actual removal of the body.'

'And you know about that, I suppose,' said Hannah.

Mina shot a withering look at the screen. 'Who do you think searched his pockets and found the car keys? Who found the car and drove it here?'

'Bloody peeping Toms,' I said, to change the subject. 'Who has a telescope out when it's raining?'

Lake stepped in. 'What are the police doing?'

'Drinking tea,' said Mina. 'One of them said they knew you, Conrad, so they were happy to wait, but if I don't come back in a few seconds, Myfanwy will put fentanyl in their tea and knock them out.'

It was Lake's turn to go pale. 'Tell them to radio the control room and ask for operation Delta November clearance, and try not to poison them.'

Mina nodded quickly and looked at Hannah. 'Nice to meet you, Constable. I've heard such a lot about you.' She was gone before Hannah could explode. And talking of explosives…

I'd guessed that there were others eavesdropping, and that guess was confirmed when and off-screen voice murmured to Lake.

'Clarke,' he said. 'Why did you test for nitroglycerin? That can't have been the bomb.'

'It was. I saw it. A full bottle, and yes I know how unstable it is. Also, I know how it was placed.'

'How?' said Hannah, grasping at something she could hang on to.

I held up the empty, red ID badge to the camera. We'd found it on the Pyromancer's body. 'Ask Maxine how many people set up the catering. I'll bet there were three. Our bomber would have been the lorry driver. He unloads the tables, waits until Maxine has covered them with flags, then slips the bomb underneath. I'll let the Constable explain why it didn't go off, and why we didn't detect it. He came back later, in disguise, to trigger it. He must have panicked when I found it and set it off to cover his escape.'

'That would work,' said Hannah. 'Anything else?'

'Not yet, ma'am. We'll prepare the report.'

Hannah looked at her fingers, then at Lake, who shook his head. 'Well done, Conrad, Rick. And Vicky. Now that the bomber has been removed, CobroM have decided to let the King's Watch lead on the investigation. I've also been to see the Dean.'

'How is she?'

'Cora is Cora. She's not going to let a hole in her abdomen slow her down. We've discussed it and we've agreed that this has to do with Project Talpa, and that pursuing the First Rusticant is a top priority.'

'About the First Rusticant, ma'am…'

'Going ahead as planned.'

'But Francesca…'

'She wants to be there when you question the Rusticant, and her brother's funeral won't be for a while.'

Oh. That's what Vicky meant: the Warden was her brother.

'I'd be there myself,' continued Hannah, 'but that new information about the Countess needs to be pursued. Stay safe, be careful, and … just be careful. All of you, OK?'

Lake looked away and cupped his ear to hear someone else. He turned back. 'That's Gloucester control room on the line.' He smiled. 'Are we done?'

'Yes.'

I stood up and saluted. We were both in uniform. Of sorts. Out of solidarity, Vicky joined in. Hannah returned the salute and reached forwards to disconnect.

Rick looked at us as if we were mad. 'What's with all the saluting and "ma'ams"?' he said. 'Since when has that been a thing?'

'Since eighteen years, for me. Since I joined the RAF. Bro.'

Vicky snorted. 'And for me, since I met him. He really believes in all that stuff. It's sort of infectious.'

Rick shook his head. 'I'm still trying to process what's happened today. Is it always this mad around you?'

'You don't know the half of it, man,' said Vicky with a wistful air, as if telling him about an especially fine restaurant that was now closed.

'I'd better go see the boys or girls in blue,' I said.

'I'll get cracking with that report,' said Vicky.

'And then I definitely need a shower. Are you staying tonight, Rick?'

'Nah. For once, my ex has come through. She's on her way to collect me, but that could be because it's my turn with the kids this weekend.'

Right on cue, his phone rang, and he answered it. A few seconds later he said to his ex, 'Oh man, I forgot about the tree blocking the road. Did you pass the pub? … Go back and wait there. I won't be five minutes. Promise.'

We left the library, and I gave him my profound thanks.

'No worries, Conrad. It's all good. Well, it's not, is it? You keep safe, yeah? And I'll tell you this: if you start calling me *Major James*, it'll be pistols at dawn. Okay?'

'I wouldn't,' said Vicky. 'Look over there.' She pointed to an old framed certificate in a gloomy corner of the corridor.

Rick peered at it. 'South West Junior Modern Pentathlon. Pistol shooting: First Place. Fencing: Second Place. Bro, you can call me what you like.'

I left Vicky to show him out and say their own goodbyes. There was quite a drama going on in the kitchen – a totally unspoken, intense and desperate drama, but a drama nonetheless.

Elvenham House has a big, warm, family kitchen with a four oven Aga. The Aga was Grandpa Enderby's wedding present to my parents, and Mother would have taken it with her to Spain if she could. The other striking feature is the ten-seater, battle-scarred farmhouse kitchen table. Dad likes to pretend it was from the original farm that pre-dated Elvenham House. Rubbish. He bought it in a clearance sale in the eighties. A female police sergeant and a male constable were seated on either side of the table, nursing large mugs of tea, but that wasn't where the drama was happening.

Mina and Myfanwy bookended the Aga like they were models at an ideal home exhibition, both trying to project ownership of a house that neither of them had stepped in before today. I felt myself go cold at the thought of a power struggle.

I spoke to the sergeant. 'Have you had word?'

She finished her tea. 'We have. I get it that we've been warned off, that's fine. We'll go, and nothing will be written down, but should I be worried?'

'No. Not in the least. I promise you that.'

She stood up. 'You also promised to call me.'

Mina's mouth dropped open, and Myfanwy's eyes widened. Even the constable looked interested.

'I did call you, and if you hadn't given me a false name and number, I'd have grovelled and asked you out on a date. The Chinese takeaway were not impressed when I asked if Gloria worked there.'

'No way,' said Myfanwy.

'Oh yes,' said Mina. 'That is entirely within his character.' She turned to the sergeant. 'What did you arrest him for?'

'I didn't arrest him. I was a young plod on my first beat, and here's this cricket team out celebrating and causing a riot in Tewkesbury.'

'We had just won promotion.'

'Hmph. The laughing lamppost here said that he was an officer and a gentleman.'

'Technically true,' said Mina. 'Go on.'

The sergeant motioned for her colleague to get a move on. 'Mr Clarke gave me his details and said that he'd get the others out of the fountain and back on the minibus if I gave him my name and number.'

'No. Seriously?' said Myfanwy.

'"Gloria" gave me an enigmatic smile and moved towards the door.

'Would you mind showing them out,' said Mina. 'I need a word with Conrad.'

And there it was. With a stroke, Mina had set the boundaries very firmly. Myfanwy jumped to it quite happily.

When we were alone, we kissed. Very carefully, but we kissed. I love the taste of her lips, and I was hungry for more. She pushed me gently away.

'That was so hard.'

'Dealing with the police or the encounter with Hannah?'

'Neither. Those were easy, but kissing a man who stinks like you do was above and beyond the call of duty. I deserve a medal and you need a shower.'

'Fair comment. Where's Desi?'

'As far away as she can get in this house, which probably means she's in Delhi. She is very, very *very* angry. With you, with Vicky, with Myvvy, with your boss and with God. Especially God. She wasn't angry with me until I said that Ganesha took a more relaxed view of things. Now there is only Rick. Give him time and he'll upset her, too.'

'He's gone. I'll let Vicky deal with Desirée. Coming for a shower?'

'I've bathed once today, and I've seen that shower. I bet the water's freezing. I will come with you though. I want us to sneak out when you're clean.'

'Where to?'

We heard voices and the thump of Vicky's crutch in the hall. 'Damn,' said Mina.

'Quick. This way.'

I led her to a narrow door in the passage. Beyond it, the servants' staircase let us get away.

As I peeled off my ruined uniform, I heard her on the phone. I think it was to Kelly Kirkham, and I think she said something about *he has two staircases. Two!* I might be wrong, though.

We had a much longer kiss when I got out of the shower, after Mina had checked a couple of sore places for serious damage. My back might blister, but there was nothing needing medical attention.

When I shivered, Mina pulled away from the kiss and said, 'You need to get dressed before you catch your death of cold. Put something warm on. We're going for a walk.'

Mina's case was open but unpacked next to the small settee. I started grabbing clothes and pointed to the empty cupboard space I'd prepared for her.

She looked round the room. It's not the biggest in Elvenham, but it is the only one with a proper en-suite bathroom. 'I like this room. It has a good feeling. Terrible decoration, shoddy furniture and draughty windows, but it has a good feeling. I can see why you chose it over the master bedroom when your parents moved out. I've put Vicky in there. I wondered about that blue room for Myvvy.' It was Mina who started me off with the pet name for our new housekeeper. Welsh is not easy to pronounce when your first language was Gujarati.

'Rachael's room. Her old room, anyway. Her stuff is in the attic – I rented the house out for a year, mostly so she couldn't drop in uninvited.'

'Oh?' Mina gave me that sharp look.

I hadn't told her all the details about Rachael's issues with my buyout of our childhood home. 'I'll tell you later. The blue room is fine for Myfanwy. Where are we going on this walk?'

'Where else? The well.'

Once upon a time (or so I'm told), Elvenham House was known as Elvenham Grange and was a working farm with nothing more than a generous farmhouse. One of my ancestors sold off the agricultural land, pulled down the farmhouse and built the Gothic pile that's there today. He kept enough land for extensive gardens and a paddock (which I rent out). He also made sure the Clerk's Well stayed in the family. There is now a pipe running from the well to the village pub, who brew their own range of excellent beers, and that's only the beginning of its many features.

To the south east of Clerkswell village, the land rises steeply up to the Cotswolds. At the bottom of that slope is a very old well, the original Clerk's Well (and not to be confused with the Church Well in the village itself). It was at the Clerk's Well that Odin, the Allfather, appeared to me and gave me the gift of magick. It is in the well that Spectre Thomas rests and from where we'll be summoning him. According to Vicky, the well was once a door to the realm of Fae (or Faery, depending on who you talk to). All of these things were very important, but none of them were the reason that Mina wanted to go there.

Last month, a snake woman, a Nāgin, appeared one night at the house. Her name is Pramiti.

We were able to sneak out of the house without being interrupted, and I held Mina's hand across the lawn until we were out of sight of the kitchen and I could switch on the torch. 'Will I be able to talk to her?' said Mina.

'I don't know, love. My magick isn't strong enough to detect things like that. She may not even know we're there, or if she does, she might not have enough Lux to materialise.'

'Hmmph,' said Mina.

Pramiti is a centuries old magickal creature from India. She can take the form of a beautiful woman or a giant snake, and probably others, too. She derived her power from a ruby – a mānik – that should sit in the middle of her forehead, where Hindus place the red dot, the bindi. Her mānik was stolen by an English Mage during the British Empire in India, and without it, Pramiti is very, very vulnerable. A small Jack Russell terrier bit her badly and she had to take refuge in the well, which has a small source of Lux in it. Again, this wasn't directly Mina's concern.

To get out of a difficult situation in Cairndale Prison, Mina had prayed to her favourite god, Ganesh, not expecting any direct involvement. The elephant headed deity is also the protector of Pramiti, and Ganesh had granted Mina's prayers – at a price. Although Mina and I can be together, we can't marry unless Pramiti's mānik is returned to her.

It was dark, and although no longer raining, the clouds were thick enough to make it pitch black out here. Mina shivered. 'I feel like we're in a wilderness, not the English countryside,' she said. 'Is it much further?'

I lifted the beam of the torch. The trees, and the well, were only twenty metres away. 'There.'

There is a stone rim round the well, four feet high, and a plastic cover keeps out leaves, birds and rodents. I heaved off the cover and shone the light down. With it being spring, the level was high, and all we could see was our reflections on the surface of the water.

Mina took off her glove and held my hand. 'Can you feel anything?'

I closed my eyes and tried to extend my magickal senses. In that recording, Vicky told me a bit about how Sorcerers see Lux. I don't. I feel it, like heat. I've got a bit better since the Allfather first enhanced me here, at the well, but not much.

To me, the well was like a small camp fire in the woods, and that's it. 'Sorry,' I said. 'I can't feel anything important. They could both be gone for all I know.'

'Let's sit for a moment.'

We perched on the lip of the well, and Mina put her rucksack on the floor. The first thing she drew out was a small box, gift-wrapped and with a bow. She handed it to me and said, 'It's not an Easter present. More of a Thank You.'

I unwrapped the gift and opened the plain brown box inside. Nestling in the box was a stainless steel hip flask. Being a man of simple tastes, I've been given over a dozen of these since my eighteenth birthday. I still have some of them. I didn't tell Mina that, but I did make a mental note to clear out one of the cupboards.

Something had been engraved on the side, and I lifted it out to look with the torch. When I did so, I realised that it wasn't empty. I read the engraving: *To Conrad. A Taste of Freedom. Love Mina. X.* I leaned down and we kissed.

'I think I should find out what's in it,' I said, unscrewing the top. I sniffed, and the smoky peat of Islay rose up to tickle my nose. 'Good choice, love.' I lifted the flask and said, 'To us.' It tasted as good as it smelt.

'I thought it might help you give up smoking,' said Mina.

'How come?'

'I gave you an engraved lighter. You can leave the lighter behind and still have something from me.'

That was a clever idea. I offered her the flask, and she took a small drink. 'I don't know how you can drink that,' she said. 'I'll stick to gin.'

I took another swig and stowed the flask in my coat. My tatty old field coat. I had now run out of decent ones.

'Join me,' said Mina, getting up and moving round the well to a sheltered spot.

I followed her and gingerly squatted next to her. This position was not good for my leg. I watched, intrigued, as she took more things from her pack. First was a small framed image of Ganesh, which she propped against the rim of the well. Next was a packet of tea lights, a banana and a packet of Tunnocks Snowballs. She took two out and unwrapped them. I could see where this was going.

She smiled up at me, her shy smile that I've never seen her give to anyone else. When Mina was twenty-two, when she had all her life ahead of her, she watched as her brother was murdered and her father beaten half to death.

When that was done, the killer used the butt of a pistol to smash her face in. Ganesh has a broken tusk, and that was what drew Mina to him, long before she discovered the world of magick.

'You don't need to say anything,' she said. 'Just being here is enough.'

Finally, she drew a sheer red silk scarf from her bag and put it over her head. 'Oh,' she added. 'Lighter.'

That first gift to me was a fake Zippo lighter with Ganesh on the side. I handed it over and she began her puja. At the end, she anointed both the picture and herself with red powder. She didn't place it on her forehead, but on her forearms. 'Don't want to upset Desirée unnecessarily,' said Mina. 'Thank you, Conrad. Do you need a hand up.'

'Thank you, love, and yes, I do.'

She left the picture, the tea light and the offerings next to the well and packed everything else away before standing up and holding out her hand. 'Try not to pull me over.'

8 — Entr'acte

We got back to the kitchen to find Myfanwy and Desi leaning over Vicky's shoulder as they all stared at a tablet computer. The tablet – Vicky's magickally enhanced device, which I call her sPad – stood in front of a stack of Tesco Finest Pizzas, still in their boxes.

'What's up?' I said.

Desi and Vicky looked slightly guilty. I'm not sure Myfanwy does guilt or regrets very much, and she piped up, 'Oh, we were Googling how to use an Aga. None of us have ever had one.'

Mina had hung up our coats and leaned against the kitchen door with an amused expression. 'Go on, Conrad, I'm dying to know the mysteries of country living.'

I folded my arms. 'There will be no dissing of the Elvenham Aga. It is older than all of us and will be respected. If any of you diss the Aga, it won't cook for you. Clear?'

Vicky snorted, Mina rolled her eyes and walked out, and Desi looked down, lips pursed. Myfanwy, however, gave me a big grin and shuffled over to the iron monster. I say *shuffled* because she'd swapped her smart boots for the fluffy slippers. She stroked the badge on the cooker and said, 'Hello, you. I'm Myfanwy. I'm sure we'll be great friends.'

I pointed to the four ovens. 'Roasting, baking, simmering and warming. Put the pizzas in either of the right hand two and take them out when they're ready.'

'On it,' said Myfanwy, turning back to the table.

Desirée straightened up and wiped her hand over her face. Like all of us, she looked tired, but seemed reluctant to sit down. Even so, she still has a natural grace and poise that rarely deserts her. Her mother, Tennille, was born in Trinidad, and I know nothing of her father other than that he is not around and must have been white or mixed race. Of the four women in the house, Desirée is the only one to have short hair. Normally, it's dyed and often in cornrows, but today it was black and messy. I tried to smile at her and get her to echo me by sitting down. She did sit down, but moved to the other side of Vicky so that she wouldn't have to face me. In doing so, she'd also moved further away from the Aga and closer to the door.

Mina returned with two bottles of red wine and started asking Myfanwy about glasses. Vicky was still staring at something on her sPad, so I said to Desirée, 'You're staying tonight, of course. Do you want to stay here for the Easter weekend?'

Oooh, had I said the wrong thing. Badly.

She lifted her head and looked at me down her nose. 'No, because it's not just a holiday for me. I will be at home, celebrating the resurrection of our

Saviour. Don't drink too much, because you're driving me to Oxford Services in the morning and our Pastor will pick me up from there. We're leaving at six, unless you want Mina to drive me.'

Vicky looked up. 'Howay, Desi man. Give him a break. He's been nearly fried. Again.'

I held up my hands. 'Sorry. I'll be ready at six.'

'Good,' said Desirée. 'And no wine for me,' she added when Mina put a glass in front of her. 'It's Lent. Excuse me.'

She got up and headed for the back cloakroom. Mina poured wine into the other glasses while Myfanwy rummaged in a cupboard and found a can of Diet Pepsi.

Myfanwy put the can down and said, 'Can we have some house rules, to save arguments later?'

I could guess what was coming next, but Myfanwy had to be happy here, so I nodded a reluctant agreement.

She sat down in the chair nearest the Aga, entirely without thinking. It had always been Mother's chair. For the record, Vicky was sitting in Rachael's chair, opposite me. Mina came round and sat next to me.

'Rule one,' said Myfanwy. 'No smoking in the kitchen.'

'Or the lounge,' said Mina. Traitor.

'Or the library,' added Vicky.

'Rule two,' said Mina. 'No beef served while I'm here.'

'Really?' said Myfanwy. 'Like really really?'

'Really,' said Mina solemnly.

'I've been here before,' said Vicky. 'That hot water tank isn't very big, so rule three: baths only by appointment.'

Desi reappeared and sat down. She held up the can of Diet Pepsi. 'Thanks for this.'

I leaned across the table and grabbed Vicky's sPad. 'Rule four. No screens at the table. I'd check that pizza if I were you.'

'Hey!' said Vicky.

'I think he's right.' That was Desi.

Good heavens, did she just agree with me? It seems she did.

Myfanwy took out the first pizza and started slicing it. When it was on the table, I decided that more diplomacy was in order.

'I think we've got five different faiths at this table,' I said. 'Shall we stand for a moment and give our own private thanks for the food?'

Desirée shot out of her seat immediately, followed by the others.

When Mina stood up, she said, 'And mourn those who died in Newton's House today, and give thanks for the safe …'

'…delivery,' said Desirée.

'Thank you. For the safe delivery of all those who survived.'

We took a moment of silence. I gave my thanks to Odin, gave a few more moments for everyone else to finish, then said out loud, 'Amen.'

Myfanwy and Desi joined in. Over the scraping of chairs, Desi said, 'Rule five. No magick talk at the table.'

A very good idea.

No one was keen to stay up late, and we were soon unpacking and finalising bedrooms. Myfanwy was muttering constantly about having to order new this and that. 'Thank God for online shopping,' was her conclusion. Her room was a long way from mine. Ours, I should say. It was next to the small bathroom, which is where she disappeared when I finally closed the door behind me. Mina was taking her makeup off and muttering about lack of a proper dressing table. I went over to kiss the top of her head, and I heard a scream from down the landing.

I ran back out and heard a curse in Welsh from the small bathroom.

'Are you OK, Myvvy?' I said. 'Have we got mice again?'

From behind the firmly closed bathroom door, she replied, 'I'm not bothered by mice. Duw God, it's these scales, Conrad. They're saying I've put on two stone. Two stone! They can't be right.'

'Actually, they usually read under. I'd add a few pounds if I were you. Night night.'

Before I left early the next morning with Desi, I fished out the parish magazine from the junk mail and propped it open on the kitchen table. I put a helpful ring round the time and place of the Slimming World club meeting and left Myfanwy a note suggesting that it might be a way to meet new people.

And before you accuse me of fat-shaming, she sent me a text at seven o'clock saying *Thank you.*

When Myfanwy had screamed from the bathroom last night, I'd been the only one to go and see what was going on. Given that there'd been a bomb and ambush that day, you'd have thought that Vicky and Desi would have appeared, too, but they didn't. I found out why on the trip to Oxford Services. Indirectly.

It seems that after I'd gone to bed, Desi had gone to Vicky's room, and neither of them wanted the rest of us to know what was going on unless there had been a real emergency. Before you jump to conclusions, they'd got together so that they could have an argument. About me.

I didn't get an apology from Desi in the morning, but she did say that she was going to pray for me. 'Vicky talked to me last night,' she said.

'Oh?'

'Yeah. She said that I had to open my heart to the idea that you and she had been called to do God's work, and that so long as you didn't lead her into evil, I had to give you the benefit of the doubt.'

'You should come back on Tuesday,' I said.

She looked uncomfortable. 'Not my decision.'

'But it's my house, my ancestor. You can act as chaperon.'

'You what? Who for? I don't have a problem with you and Mina, you know.'

I was so on my best behaviour that I didn't tell her that it was none of her business. Instead, I gestured towards London. 'It's Li Cheng. You can protect him from the Keeper.'

It took her a moment to work that one out. Instead of high dudgeon, she laughed. 'You're right. Dr Somerton would eat him alive. I'll ask Mum if there's anything on at Church.'

The rest of the journey passed in silence, because Desi took out her Bible and started reading. When I dropped her off, she thanked me for not smoking during the journey and said, 'Might see you Tuesday.' I'll settle for that.

Even in war, you get the occasional time-out, and this weekend was one of them. On Friday, I walked the parish boundary of Clerkswell with Myfanwy, so that she knew the limits of her prison. Half way round, she stopped and said, 'I've got an idea.'

'Good. What?'

'I'm going to tell people that I'm doing a detailed, three year survey of every plant in the parish for a PhD in biodiversity, and that I'm working for you to cover my board and lodging.'

That was actually a very good idea, given her specialism.

She continued, 'And I'll do it, too. On and off. Mind you, Conrad, I still don't know how I can explain to people why I can't leave the village.'

'You'll think of something.'

On Saturday, Mina and I went to Cheltenham, to get some quality time. There was a lot of holding hands and wandering around, and mostly people smiled at us. Over lunch, I brought up the question of her trying to get the maternity cover job at Merlyn's Tower.

There are only a handful of civilians in the King's Watch, one of whom is Maxine Lambert, the Clerk. She has a deputy, and said deputy is going on maternity leave in the summer. I had broached the idea of Mina doing the job, and Hannah was not exactly receptive.

'You saw the way she looked at me on the video call,' said Mina. 'She hates me.'

'She's done and said far worse things to me, yet she still made me Watch Captain at Large.'

'I don't want to go where I'm not wanted.'

'It's not Hannah's decision, not really. Maxine needs an assistant, and the assistant has to come from the world of magick. There's not many people willing to do the job. If there was a crowded field, you'd be at a disadvantage, but there won't be. If there's more than one application – yours – I'll be surprised.'

'I don't know.'

'I've got a plan.'

'Vishnu preserve us from your plans. What now?'

'You're going to do some research into why there's been a huge surge in the amount of Alchemical Gold in circulation.'

That stunned her for a second. Her response wasn't quite what I expected, though. 'But Conrad, I was an accountant, not an economist.'

'The market's too small for an economist to be of any use. This is a job for detail.'

'Where would I start?'

'It's going to be while before you meet Hledjolf the Dwarf in person. Thankfully, he's very much a twenty-first century Dwarf. I'm surprised he doesn't have a website. Maybe he does. All you have to do is talk him into handing over some anonymised data.'

'Oh yes, that will be so easy I'll get right on to it.'

'Good.'

'I was being sarcastic.'

'I wasn't. I'll send you his contact details.'

'You want me to call a Dwarf?'

'Email would be best. You're guaranteed a quick response. As far as I can tell, they don't sleep. Maybe they recharge at night.'

'I'll think about it. Now let's focus on lunch. There's shopping to do afterwards, and not just to buy you yet another new Barbour.'

'Let me guess: Myfanwy's given you a list.'

'Yes. It's a good job you have broad shoulders, Conrad. There'll be a lot to carry.'

'Talking of shopping, how did it go when you went to the village shop this morning?'

She brushed her hair away from her face and gave me a smile. 'Wait and see.'

Right. Thankfully, the waiter arrived at that moment.

And Vicky? She got very bored. She had to spend long periods flat on her back, with her legs up the wall. It's the only way to get swelling down. Consequently, she was bored and grumpy, but by Saturday night her foot was back to normal size. She spent a long time on her phone, I know that much.

On Saturday evening, Mina and Myfanwy shared the cooking because Vicky and I were expecting a video call from Hannah at sunset. Our boss is so hard to read, that I don't know whether she keeps Shabbos out of faith or so that she can turn her phone off and have a normal life for twenty-four hours. Either way, Hannah doesn't do Friday nights or Saturdays.

'About this Fae Countess,' she said. 'I've had word back from some people, and it seems that the Warden was right. It was a Squire.'

I said nothing.

Hannah squinted at me. 'What does he know about the Fae?' she said to Vicky, completely ignoring me.

See? If she can treat me like that and still trust me, there is hope for Mina.

Vicky sighed. 'I've been trying to avoid that topic. I'll tell him later. Have you any idea who the Squire's master might be?'

'No, nor am I likely to. That Squire hasn't been seen before, and he won't be seen again. Not for a long, long time. I've had the final report from Ruth, by the way.'

Ruth is Hannah's twin. They joined the Metropolitan Police on the same day, and Ruth is still there. Inspector Kaplan. She's our gateway to the mundane world of law enforcement.

Hannah picked up a printout. 'The car was hired with a false name and the CCTV of the transaction shows that a Glamour was used. There is no record of the bomber on any database – no fingerprints, no hits for facial recognition. The only genuine part was the credit card. Ruth is trying to figure that out as best she can.' Hannah put the paper down. 'You're definitely right, Conrad. This can't go on. Ruth can't get at the credit card details without logging it against an open case, and because there's no crime we're admitting to, there's no open case. She'll get there in the end. I've asked Iain and Annelise to start drafting a proposal for the Occult Council on data access. Anything else?'

'No, ma'am.'

'Good. Enjoy the holiday and call me the minute the summoning is finished.'

We stuck our heads in the kitchen to see what was happening, and there was rather too much excitement going on.

'Oh, good, you've finished,' said Myfanwy. 'We'll eat in five minutes and be ready for the start.'

'Start of what?'

Mina and Myfanwy looked at us as if we'd been on the moon. 'It's the launch show for Britain's Got Talent.'

I stared at them.

'What?' said Myfanwy.

'You are joking, aren't you?' I said.

'I don't think they are,' said Vicky.

I turned on my partner. 'Not you, too.'

She gave me a shrug so big that she lifted her crutch off the floor. 'I'm easy. I take it there will be wine involved?'

Mina gave me a grin as she put the plates out. It was time to put my foot down. I turned to Vicky and said, 'If it's wine you're after, we can adjourn to the library and you can give me that briefing on the Fae.'

'Aye. Fair enough. It's about time, now that they're definitely implicated.'

'Duw God,' said Myfanwy. 'Good luck with that, Vicky. Rather you than me.'

Over dinner, Mina said, 'We got chatting to Doctor Mirren in the shop this morning.' The "we" in that sentence was her and Myfanwy, of course.

Dr Mirren – Grace – is my GP. She's the GP to a quarter of the village, and most of the rest are with her male colleagues at their surgery in Bishop's Cleeve. Unlike the others, Grace is willing to take some patients privately.

'Good,' I said. 'And?'

Mina looked from me to Vicky. 'She signed up Myvvy, no problem, not that Mages need the doctor much.'

'True,' said Vicky. 'Unless your partner breaks your foot and gets you shot at.'

'She also agreed to take me as a private patient,' said Mina. She looked down at her half-eaten meal and pushed it away. 'She's given me a note saying that I shouldn't travel until Wednesday.'

Okay. That was unexpected. I'm not sorry that Mina will be here for another night, definitely not, nor am I bothered that she'd just (effectively) bribed a doctor to forge a note for the prison service. That was definitely a victimless crime. However, I could see what was coming next.

'And there's something else,' said Myfanwy. 'Mina and I want to attend the summoning.'

Vicky put her fork down and looked at me. This was my call.

'We had planned for Myfanwy to be the backstop,' I said. 'You could watch from the house and be ready to call the cavalry if something goes wrong. We need a Mage for that.'

Myfanwy put her hands on the table. 'It should be Rick. He's only two hours away, his childcare duties will be over and he can put up a proper defence if need be. I don't want Clerkswell to be at risk like … like the Brecon Beacons were going to be.'

I think she meant it. I think she really had come to see how close she'd been to helping initiate a Dragon-based apocalypse. 'Vicky?'

'Sounds good to me. I'll give him and Hannah a text.'

'Thanks. Don't mention Mina, though.'

She gave me a *Duuh* look.

After supper, we went our separate ways. Mina and Myvvy headed into the sitting room to spend the evening with Simon Cowell while Vicky and I made ourselves comfortable in the library.

Vicky shifted in her armchair so that she could keep her foot as elevated as possible. I topped up our glasses, and she began to tell me about the Fae.

'What do you think a female is?' she began.

'Female what?'

'Female anything. Human, raven, oak tree, mushroom…'

I'm good at geography and history; Vicky is good at biology, and especially good at genetics. Until tonight, for example, I thought everything more complex than a nematode worm had X and Y chromosomes, that the old joke about the birds and the bees implies a universal pattern for reproduction. Not so. I got lost around the time she mentioned *Haplodiploidy*. I thought she was drunk, but no, it actually is a thing: it's how the bees really get it off with each other. And wasps and ants … and, in a manner of speaking, the Fae.

I've met Gnomes, Dwarves, one god, one Dragon and one very aggressive Giant Mole. All of these creatures are special and different. All Dragons are female, for example, and Dwarves are silicon based rather than carbon based. If I tried to explain all the ways of Fae at once, your head would hurt as much as mine did, and that was before the hangover kicked in. I'll just give you the basic headlines.

The Fae have human features, but they are most definitely not human. Their lifecycle is complicated and shares features of both human and honey bee reproduction.

I know. I'm still scratching my head about that one. Anyway…

They've been around since well before the first dynasty of Ancient Egypt.

Periodically they disappear underground to change their form, and are all tied to the sídhe (underground realm) where their Queen lives. Fae family relations are complicated.

They have a very rigid hierarchy and love titles.

They are very powerful users of magick, but you'd probably guessed that already.

There is a Fae Duchess on the Occult Council. Everyone except the Warden thought that the guest in Newton's House was one of her *Hlæfdige* (which is the word from which 'Lady' derives. I've only used it because I went to the trouble of writing it down).

If only the Warden had said something when she/he first walked in, those two waitresses would still be alive. Shortly after that point, we went to bed. Mina was already asleep.

And if you're wondering, according to Vicky, the female of any species is the one who produces eggs. So now you know.

9 — *Batting Order*

Easter Sunday. The day for families to gather round and consume chocolate.

'I'm going to Slimming World on Wednesday, so it doesn't matter,' said Myfanwy handing round the eggs that we'd bought for her in Cheltenham. I'd had to make two trips to the car with that lot. Mina accepted hers gratefully and promptly passed it back.

'I don't want to ruin my appetite before my first trip to the Inkwell,' she said.

'Do I have to walk?' asked Vicky.

'No. I'll drive us. Someone will be able to give you a lift back here. Mind you, after last night, I'm not sure I want that much to drink.'

We were sitting round in the kitchen finishing off a hearty cooked breakfast (my cooking). Mina had brought down a bright red kameez, a vivid blue sari and a Western shift dress. For some reason, she seemed to think that I would have an opinion on the subject. And I thought she knew me so well.

'It's about who you want me to be,' she said. 'This is your local pub. I will be on display there, like a cricket trophy.'

Vicky coughed. She has been exposed to Mina's sense of the ridiculous a lot longer than Myfanwy, who was about to protest that Mina was not an object to be paraded around. I got in first.

'It's too cold for the sari,' I said, 'and that dress is too like something you'd wear to the office. Wear the kameez with the black leggings and Nike trainers.'

Mina does know me well. She knew exactly what I was saying. 'Indian, but not too Indian. Don't want to upset the natives, do we?'

'I wouldn't worry about that,' I said. 'Most of the village have eaten curry at some point, and some of them even like it.'

'Ha ha. Where are you going?'

'To look at a horse. And get rid of that body in the stables. Hannah told me to drop it off at an undertakers in Cheltenham. I'll be back before one o'clock.'

I'm not dense, you know. I am fully aware that a first trip to the village pub was going to be an ordeal for Mina and, to a lesser degree, Myfanwy. Most of the regulars have met Vicky and know that she's my work partner. I would have loved to take Mina there on my own this weekend, to have her to myself, but at least in a group she wouldn't stick out so much.

Who am I kidding? The only non-white customers in the Inkwell are members of visiting cricket teams. My family is one of the oldest in the village. Of course she was going to stand out.

We are lucky in Clerkswell. Our village pub nearly closed a few years ago, until it was bought out by Reynold and his then boyfriend, a chef. They spent a lot of money installing a micro-brewery in an outbuilding, and didn't have enough to renovate the kitchens, at which point the chef stormed off and Reynold nearly had to sell up. My father had paid for the pipe running from our well down to the pub, and this was a very long-term investment. I think he even lent Reynold some money to help him buy out his ex.

Reynold is now happily married to Mike, who keeps his feet firmly on the ground. The beer is excellent, the decor is classic rural chintz and the food is average.

There isn't much privacy in the Inkwell, but there is a table in a little annex that's been very popular over the years with adulterous couples from Cheltenham. They think they can canoodle in there without their spouses finding out, but Rosie the bar manager sees all. She wouldn't dream of actually posting pictures on Facebook, but a subtle hint at the right time means that she makes a lot of money in tips. Such is the reputation of that table that the cricket team even named it Nookie Corner.

It did at least mean that we had *some* privacy. Myfanwy sat in the middle, Vicky to her left and Mina to her right, next to me. I had to sit on a stool for extra leg room. I went to get the first round of drinks and run the gauntlet of Rosie and Neil from the village shop. Myfanwy had been to the shop at least four times already, including this morning.

'Has your friend heard from her agent yet?' said Neil.

I looked over to Nookie Corner. Mina and Myfanwy were grinning at me. Vicky was studying the menu.

'Which one?' I said.

'Your ... erm ... Asmina? Was that her name?'

'Mina.'

'Sorry. Yes. She told me that she was waiting to hear from her agent about an audition in LA.'

Right. What was I to say to that? Play along, I suppose. 'You must have misheard. She probably said *Bollywood* not *Hollywood*.'

'Oh no,' said Neil. 'That's what I said, but Mina was adamant: Universal Studios are making a TV version of *Excalibur*, and she was auditioning for Morgan le Fey.'

Okay. That was creative. 'Oh, *that* audition! She was in Mumbai first, *then* she went to LA. She's not very hopeful. She thinks that she was only there to give a bit of diversity.'

Rosie, of course, had been listening to every word. She put down two pints of Inkwell bitter and Vicky's large Burgundy, then said, 'That's not what Myfanwy said. She said that Mina was doing location scouting for *Midsomer Murders*.'

'That's next week. I'll have a double Jensen's with Fentiman's tonic, too. And a bottle of sparkling water.'

Very casually, with her back to me as she poured the gin, Rosie said, 'I didn't catch Mina's family name.'

Three could play at this game. 'That's because they've disowned her,' I said. 'They said she had betrayed them.'

Neil and Rosie were agog, and all three of us looked at Mina in her scarlet kameez as she brushed back her hair to point at something on the menu. Rosie and Neil clearly thought this betrayal was something to do with consorting with me. I left them hanging for a second, then said, 'It's because she trained to be an accountant.'

'An accountant!' said Reynold, who never misses a chance for gossip and had drifted over to join in.

'She doesn't practise any more, but show her your ledgers if you don't believe me. Put these on a tab, will you?'

I carried the drinks over and Myfanwy couldn't wait to sample the Inkwell bitter. She pronounced it good.

'Cheers, everyone,' said Mina. We raised our glasses, and she continued. 'I have an Easter treat for us. I've brought this.' She whipped out a DVD with the face of Rani Mukherjee on it. 'What do you say? Girls only, or is he invited?'

'What's that?' said Myfanwy.

'*Kuch Kuch Hota Hai*,' I replied. 'It comes with an oestrogen warning. I think I might go for a walk.'

Mina tried a sip of my beer and made a face. 'That may take some getting used to,' she said. 'Also the menu with so much beef. Roast beef, beefburgers, steak and ale pies. Rump steak. Urgh. As it's not our kitchen, the *no-beef* rule is suspended.'

We were chatting happily away and Mina was filling the other two in on the conventions of Bollywood when I realised that, since we'd all arrived on Thursday, the three women were constantly pairing off in different combinations.

I'm no expert on female friendships, but it did seem slightly odd that whenever they were all together, they were rarely a threesome. There was usually a pair and one odd one out, and that configuration could change by the second.

Mina and Myfanwy bonded because they were both in prison and would both have criminal records for the rest of their lives, whereas Vicky is an officer of the law.

Mina and Vicky bonded because they were both survivors of serious trauma, had both used violence to defend themselves, taking another life in the process, and because they'd been that bit closer to the Abyss than Myfanwy ever had.

Vicky and Myfanwy bonded because they were Mages, and because Myfanwy had brought Vicky back from the dead.

Most of the regulars had looked over to our corner, a few had said hello, but we'd not been disturbed until a group of three came towards us. In the lead were Ben Thewlis, captain of the cricket team and his sister, Carole. Behind them was a man whose face was in shadow, and who turned to leave when Ben said, 'Look, there's Conrad.'

I stood up, and Carole gave me a hug and a kiss. She turned round and frowned.

'Oh. I was going to introduce you to my fiancé. He must have gone to the car.'

I introduced Carole to the girls, and she lingered in particular over Mina. I had no doubt that a detailed report would be on its way to my sister before long; Carole and Rachael go way back. Mina made a point of saying how much she liked Carole's dress. I don't know why she said that – it looked like a perfectly normal dress to me, but Mina will have had a motive. She knows that, as well as being Rachael's friend, Carole is one of my exes.

Carole left to seek her man, and Ben nodded a hello. He's met Vicky a couple of times, but not the others. 'You know what, mate,' he said to me. 'I've just worked it out: fifteen per cent of the women under thirty in Clerkswell are now living in your house. Did you know that?'

'What percentage of the unattached ones?' said Mina.

'Forty,' said Ben, without hesitation. Did he look at Myfanwy when he said that?

'There are only five single women under thirty in Clerkswell?' said Mina. She's very good at maths.

Ben sighed. 'Don't I know it. Anyway, Conrad, I'm setting you a challenge.'

'Why do I not like the sound of that?'

'You need to show some leadership.'

It was Vicky who spoke first. 'Be very careful what you say next, Ben.'

He grinned. 'The challenge is this: that Mina, Myfanwy and Vicky either start a women's cricket team or they do the teas for the men.'

'Deal,' said Mina. 'Provided that the men do the tea for our first game.'

Ben leaned over and shook her hand. 'You're on, Mina.' He turned to me. 'You haven't forgotten tomorrow, have you?'

'Wouldn't dare, skipper. I'll be there.'

When Ben had gone, Mina turned to the others, expecting some banter, but Vicky and Myfanwy were giving each other a much more serious look. 'Did you notice?' said Vicky to Myfanwy.

'Yes. I could hardly miss it now, could I?'

'Notice what?' said Mina and I together.

Vicky leaned in draw us together. 'I reckon that right now, seventy-five percent of the Mages in Clerkswell are at this table, and the other one is Carole Thewlis's fiancé. I wonder why he didn't want to chat, and why he used a Glamour to slip out?'

We speculated, fruitlessly, then talk did turn to cricket. Vicky was very non-committal, but Myfanwy was keen, especially when I said that Ben was quite a good coach and would be glad to put them through their paces.

I left them to their DVD and got some exercise taking a long walk up the scarp behind the house, down and round back to the village.

I took a detour at the end so that I could check out Mr & Mrs Thewlis's house. Ben has his own place, a tiny old cottage behind the village green, but for Easter Sunday dinner, he would be with his parents, as would Carole. Strangely, there was no black Mercedes in the drive or nearby. Had the mysterious fiancé received an urgent call from London, or was he avoiding the Elvenham House Coven?

On Monday, while Mina and Vicky shopped in Bishop's Cleeve, and Myfanwy made up more beds, I turned out at Mrs Clarke's Folly, home of Clerkswell Cricket Club. Every Easter, the team has to show up and renovate the pavilion ready for the season ahead. And if you are on holiday, you have to send a substitute. We were all there, and I asked Ben about Carole's fiancé.

'Dunno,' said Ben. 'His name is Isaac Fisher, and I think he's too old for her.'

I gave him the eye. This was dangerous ground.

'Hey, I didn't mean it like that. It's a much bigger age gap than the one between you and Mina. Must be fifteen years at least.'

'Where did he get to yesterday?'

'Now that was weird. He drove to the station in Cheltenham for some reason and got a taxi back, then made me take him back to the station first thing this morning. Carole wasn't happy, I can tell you. They were supposed to visit wedding venues today, and he's buggered off to London. Carole's gone off with Mum.'

I sent Vicky a text, and she promised to ask around. By the time Ben released us, the pavilion was once more fit for purpose and my arms ached from painting the ceiling. Again. On the plus side, all the arrangements were now in place for the summoning tomorrow.

10 — Welcome to the Party

'That was delicious,' said Francesca Somerton as she put down her napkin. 'I haven't eaten so well for a long time.'

'And me,' said Rick James. 'Well done, both of you.'

There were two small islands of clean table, one round the Keeper and the other next to Mina. Everyone else had had great fun dropping rice, dripping yogurt and generally making a mess of the Gujarati feast conjured up by Mina and Myfanwy.

As everyone joined in the praise, the Keeper of the Queen's Esoteric Library turned her chair to the side and arched her eyebrows. 'I hope you're not going to be lumbered with the washing up while we go to the well.'

'I've got it covered,' said Rick. 'Conrad's shown me how to load the dishwasher.'

Mina wiped her hand and looked down the table. 'Myvvy and I were hoping to join you, Dr Somerton.'

Li Cheng, who had been the quietest diner, laid his fork down and cleared his throat. Li has a special role to play in the Watch, and gets his own title: Royal Occulter. It's his job to cover up manifestations of magick. He's also a pioneer of using technology to aid and direct Lux. He created Vicky's sPad, for one thing. Li is a very talented man, and very far from being a geek. He comes from old Chinese money (via Singapore, I believe), and his casual outfit cost more than all the women's put together.

'With all due respect to the excellence of your hospitality, Miss Desai, I don't see a place for the ungifted in this ritual, and I cannot run the risk of Miss Lewis's bindings having an impact on the summoning. Sorry.'

All of a sudden, it went very quiet. Mina looked down at her plate, Myfanwy bit her lip and Rick developed a fascination for the antique kitchen clock. This might be my house and my ancestor, but it was Li's operation. I could ask nicely, but I couldn't order him.

'Myfanwy isn't bound when she's on my property,' I suggested. 'The Cloister Court have allowed her to practise all magicks at my discretion. I don't see a problem.'

'The bindings are still there,' snapped Li.

'You're the expert,' I said. 'But you should know that no one pushes a Desai. If Mina wants to walk up to the well, I'm not going to stop her.'

Li gave a flash of a smile. It was over between ticks of the clock. 'Perhaps we should call the Peculier Constable for guidance,' he said, knowing that Hannah would go ballistic if she found out that Mina was involved in any way.

Francesca picked up her napkin so that she could throw it down again. 'Don't be such a prig, Cheng. I thought you were better than that.'

Vicky looked alarmed. She doesn't like confrontation at the best of times, and this was too close to home for her. 'I think you're being a bit harsh,' she said to Francesca, then turned to glance at Li Cheng. I was about to get annoyed with her, then she turned back to the Keeper. 'He won't like me saying this, but I don't think Cheng's being awkward. He's not a Summoner. He's just being careful. It's not personal, is it?'

That put Li in a difficult place. He either had to say that it *was* personal or admit that he was scared. Saying the first would make a lot of enemies, saying the second would mean losing face.

Francesca turned to Desi. 'It's a good job you're here, my dear. If we put you upstream of Conrad, could you act as a cutout for Mina and Myfanwy? I can show you how if you haven't done it before.'

Desi didn't want to answer that question. She had been very quiet since the London party arrived and was looking very uncomfortable. Whatever she said would upset someone.

I don't like Li Cheng. He's a dickhead in all sorts of ways, but I do respect his magick and his intelligence. He used the latter to step in. 'That would work, Keeper. An excellent suggestion.'

'Good,' said Francesca. 'Is someone going to make coffee? We haven't got long before sunset.'

'We'll sort it,' said Vicky, meaning her and Desi. 'Go through to the lounge.'

'And I'll start clearing up,' said Rick.

Mina joined me in the outhouse, to where I'd been driven by the near-total smoking ban indoors.

'Thank you,' she said, pulling me down for a kiss. 'Will he go telling tales to Hannah?'

'Mmm. Yes and no. We haven't told him about Pramiti, yet, and I wouldn't ask him to lie in his report, so yes, you'll be there. If he's got any sense, you'll just be a name in an appendix.'

'Good. I'm going to get changed.'

The foul weather we'd been having had blown over and the sun had left behind a cloudless sky when we set off from the house. Li, Vicky and Desi went ahead to suss out the scene, followed by Mina and Myfanwy, leaving me to offer my arm to Francesca as we brought up the rear.

'The house hasn't changed much since I was last here,' she said, looking round, 'though I'm sad to say that the gardens have deteriorated a bit. I'm sure you'll have them in hand.'

'That's Myfanwy's project.'

'Couldn't think of anyone better.'

'I'm afraid that I was unconscious for most of our last meeting,' I said, slowing down even more. 'I wish I'd got to know your brother properly. I'm so sorry.'

She patted my arm. 'Thank you, dear. It's not how he wanted to go, but it summed him up completely, sacrificing himself like that. He'll be furious that he couldn't save the young girls. Furious.'

That was ominous. The use of the present tense was either a sign that she was losing the plot, or…

'Keeper, are you saying …?'

'That he transitioned successfully? Yes I am, but I'm the only one who knows. He had to leave more behind than he wanted, and he's made a lot of enemies in the Spirit world over the years. He'll be keeping his head down until he knows whether he's viable.' She smiled. 'Hurry along, they'll be wondering what we're up to.'

'Whose idea were these?' said Francesca as she lowered herself into a camping chair. Vicky and I had been up to the well earlier to tidy things up a bit and make arrangements.

'Mine,' I said. 'I don't want Vicky standing on that foot any longer than she needs to, and you…'

'…and I'm an old bat. Not going to argue if I get a seat.'

Given that she was there on sufferance, you'd think that Myfanwy would keep her head down, like Mina was doing. Oh no. 'I'm so looking forward to this,' she said.

'Really?' said Francesca.

'Oh yes, Dr Somerton. I've seen some of what Vicky does, but not proper Quantum Magick.'

I could see her point. There are as many magickal traditions in the world as musical ones, and that's why even the allegedly science based approach of the Invisible College still refers to it as The Art. The Invisible College made even a poor Mage like me a Master of the Art of Alchemy, and graduates of Salomon's House are known as Chymists. Myfanwy, of course, is a Druid.

All music makes sound waves, and all magick makes a change in the nature of the universe. It's how you get there that counts, and the biggest difference in schools of magick is that QM does without most of the sideshow elements – incense, candles, long speeches in Latin. That sort of thing. They still go in for circles, though.

The dagger with which Rick had dispatched the Pyromancer is a Dwarven steel weapon with a twelve inch blade. Vicious. Li Cheng has a dagger, too, but not one designed for combat. Solid gold does not take an edge well.

The Royal Occulter checked that we were all ready, then began to prepare himself, drawing the short bladed gleaming Artefact and holding it in front of him. When the summoning began, Li was going to stand two metres from the well, and we were all in our support positions. Vicky would be at his right shoulder, resting her left hand on him, just as Francesca would do with her right. They were his supporters and would contribute some of their Lux to the ritual.

I was to Francesca's left, then Desirée, then Mina, then Myfanwy. All of us would be touching, making a chain, as soon as Li had finished the circle.

He started at the north point, on the other side of the well, and began saying a mantra to help him focus. He spoke in Cantonese – the words didn't matter, only that he used them to draw Lux as he processed counter-clockwise round the well, enclosing us all in a Work of Alchemy that would confine any summoned creature. At least, that's what he was supposed to be doing. For all I knew, he could be reciting a Chinese nursery rhyme, something that the Keeper spotted.

'You can't see a thing, can you?' she whispered.

'Nope.'

'Let's join up. That way, your girlfriend can see it, too.'

I placed my hand on Francesca's shoulder, then Desi and the others joined in. Francesca was still seated, and I was too tall for Desi to put her arm comfortably on my shoulder, so we were holding hands. She wasn't happy about that.

My arm tingled, as if it were going to sleep, and my head throbbed as if my heart had relocated there, beating behind my eyes and blurring my vision.

'Ow!' said Desi. 'Don't squeeze. Take deep breaths.'

'Sorry.'

I relaxed my fingers and closed my eyes. The pounding lessened to a dull thump of pain, and I risked opening my eyes. Wow.

I could see the pole star above us, which was wrong, because it wasn't dark yet, and it seemed as if Li's golden cord were being drawn down from the sky. It hovered at waist height as he drew it round the well, paying out behind him like a climber's rope, and like a rope, it was braided with colour. Two of the threads were pure gold, the other flashed from rust to silver to orange in pulsing lights.

From my left, I heard Mina whisper to Myfanwy. 'Is it always like this? I can't believe it.'

'Oh no,' said Myfanwy. 'He's good. He's very good.'

'Shh,' hissed Desi. 'I'll lose my grip if you don't focus.'

Li stopped to touch Vicky on the way past and draw some Lux, then moved quicker as he finished the circle. When he came back to his starting point, he didn't tie a knot of light, he used both hands to sweep the lines together into an unbroken ring, and the faint connection to the sky withered like an umbilical cord. With a flourish, Li let go of the light, and it drifted slowly to the ground, still bright and unbroken. He let out a huge sigh of relief and moved stiffly to the well, where he sat down and picked up a bottle of water.

'You can let go for a bit,' said Desi.

When I released my fingers, she couldn't help herself, drying her hand on her jeans to wipe away my sweat. As soon as I let go of Francesca, the ring of protection faded. I was tempted to put my arm back, just to reassure myself it was still there.

I looked around, trying to sense it. Nothing. Then I saw a black shape in the sky, getting bigger. If I wasn't mistaken… Yes.

'Incoming raven,' I said to the group. 'I think we've got company.'

'Good heavens,' said Francesca. 'You're right.'

'And that's not all,' said Myfanwy, pointing west, to where the sun had set behind us.

'Two ravens?' said Mina. 'Hugin *and* Munin?'

The bird from the north glided softly down on a current, dipping his wings at the last moment and raising his claws to clamp on to the limb of an oak tree. So large was the bird that the branch shook. My former patron, Odin, was here in some sense. It felt like the stakes had just been raised and we weren't playing for pennies any more. The bird cocked his head to look at us, then turned to the west and let out a mighty *caw caw* when he saw the other raven. He didn't sound happy.

'That's not Odin,' said Myfanwy pointing at the second bird. 'It's…'

'Lord Jesus preserve our souls,' said Desirée.

'Oh, shit,' said Li Cheng.

'This is going to be fun,' said Francesca, rising from her seat and turning to face outwards. Vicky was already on her feet.

The second raven had been coming from a long way away. Either that or it got a lot bigger as it grew nearer. Much bigger than a natural bird, so big that its wings became a cloak of black as it landed and shimmered into the form of a woman, growing even further to reach an impossible height that was definitely taller than me. Myfanwy dropped to her knees and said something in Welsh.

The newcomer was beautiful and deadly in equal measure, and hadn't stinted on the accessories. Her hair was the colour of raven's wings and it flowed down in a river, cascading off her shoulders and disappearing down her back. High cheekbones drew down to a sharp nose and sharp chin. The only soft thing in her face was the blood-red lips, matching her blood-red nails and toning in with the emerald necklace. Were those emeralds shaped into skulls? Yes. They were. Oh dear.

Her outfit was … different. On top was a low-cut, short, white tunic, held in to her waist with a black leather belt. Below the tunic she wore silver fish-scale leggings, black knee pads and no-nonsense black fell-walking boots. If you're wondering how come I noticed her nail polish, it's because her right hand was on the hilt of a huge sword that hung from her belt.

I was once in the presence of The Goddess. Briefly. Despite the protective circle, I knew that the woman outside was not at all the same being. A goddess, yes, but *the* Goddess, no.

Francesca and I bowed low at the same time. Mina joined us, as did Vicky and Li. Desirée took a step backwards and remained upright. Instinctively, Mina stepped left to be closer to me and stand sentry.

Desirée opened her mouth and began to sing. 'Yea, though I walk through the valley of the Shadow of Death, I will fear no evil.'

And as she sang, to a gospel inspired melody in a minor key, the magick built round her, and she lifted her arms. Mina dived into the shelter of my arm and stared. Myfanwy looked aghast, shocked and awed, and Vicky looked alarmed.

It was Francesca who made the first move. 'No, Desirée. Not here. Not now. We are all guests in this house. We are safe.' She moved to the young woman and reached a hand to rest it in the small of her back. 'Would I bring you to that valley? Here are only green pastures. Peace.'

Desi slowly lowered her arms, a flush of red rising under her dark brown skin.

Francesca took two steps towards the edge of the protective circle (which had flamed into life when Desi sang). 'Great Morrigan,' said Francesca. 'You honour us with your presence. We are not worthy.'

'Rise, child,' said the visitor to Myfanwy, in a deep, throaty Irish brogue. To the rest of us, she nodded.

'You are thrice welcome,' said Francesca. 'Would you accept our hospitality?'

'Won't that break the circle?' whispered Mina.

'That circle has just become the proverbial chocolate fireguard, my dear,' said Francesca. 'This is the Morrigan, battle goddess of the west and gatherer of the slain. Here, though, she comes as a guest.'

The Morrigan looked up at the tree, where Odin's raven was staring back. Her fingers gripped the sword a little more tightly, before relaxing and dropping away. 'I would drink of the well,' she said, 'for I am but a thirsty traveller.'

Francesca moved, until I put my hand on her shoulder. 'This is down to me,' I said. 'My house, my well and all that.'

'Are you sure?'

'Yes.'

In the holdall by the well was a pewter tankard, an eighteenth birthday present from my grandmother. I took it and reached into the well, skimming the top of the water. When I set off towards the Morrigan, I started to regret my decision the second I crossed the circle, which snapped and broke under my feet. With its scant protection gone, the smell of blood and earth washed over me.

The ten steps I took after that were the longest of my life. It felt like walking into the open door of a blast furnace. The magickal heat poured off her in a river of fire. I knew I wasn't going to burn, but that didn't help. Sweat ran down my neck, my titanium tibia heated up from the inside, and my eyes watered so badly that I was walking blind. I had to hold the tankard with both hands to stop it spilling everywhere. When the heat became a physical barrier, I had to stop.

'Thrice welcome, my lady,' I croaked. 'You honour my home.'

'The honour is mine.'

The flow of Lux diminished slightly, and I blinked the tears out of my eyes. Up close, she was so stark of face that she didn't look human. Maybe she was one part human to three parts fire. She looked over my shoulder to the tree and called out, 'Allfather! Would you drink with me?'

A loud screech came from the raven, and a beating of wings as he dropped from the branch and glided towards us. I stepped back to give him room to land, and the Morrigan stretched out an arm for a perch.

Next to the goddess, the raven was a shadow. Literally a shadow, a black space where her magick didn't flow. I moved to take advantage of the shade, and offered the tankard to the Morrigan.

'Let him drink first. Saves putting his whole head down.'

I put my left hand under the tankard for extra support and offered it to the raven. He looked at me with one eye and blinked, then stuck his head into the vessel, yanking it back and craning his neck to swallow. He did it again, then shuffled his wings.

'Stand back,' said the Morrigan, and I moved just in time to avoid a wing in the face as the raven returned to the tree.

She took the tankard from me and drained it in one, wiping her lips. The blood-red colour in them didn't smudge, it dripped slightly, running red down her chin until she wiped it again, leaving a rusty smear on her tunic.

She held the empty tankard in the air, and more Lux flowed from her. Around the side, the faded birthday message melted away and was replaced with gleaming silver writing in a script I'd never seen before. She leaned down (have I mentioned that she was seven foot tall? It certainly added to the effect) and whispered lava words in my ear. 'When you wed, Chief Clarke, fill this cup from your well and call my name.'

With a graceful twitch of her fingers, she rotated the tankard to offer me the handle. I gingerly took it, and the runes vanished.

'Thank you,' she said, aloud. 'Now hurry up, you lot. I've places to be.'

I limped back to the group, and Mina stepped forward to take my hand. 'Are you okay?'

'I think so.'

Li Cheng stood up and took out his dagger, then stopped and looked around. He hadn't a clue what to do next.

With a clash of swords in her words, the Morrigan spoke out. 'Hear all, this place is under my protection while here I stand.'

'I guess we'll skip the circle, then,' muttered Li. 'Places everyone!'

We reconvened and restored the magickal links. Francesca and Vicky remained standing for this part.

Li lifted his dagger and stared at the well. My head started pounding again, and I saw a shimmering ribbon of gold form between Li and the water. I had to force myself not to crush poor Desi's hand again as my fingers burned with transferred power. Li's mouth became a rictus of pain, and the dagger shook in his hand. He shouted something in Cantonese and the ribbon of light became a laser.

Vicky groaned and her hand gripped his shoulder so tightly that his jacket bunched up and Francesca had to tug back to stop Vicky pulling him over. Then, with a scream, he fell to his knees, and a flash of golden light blinded me, like turning to look at the sun when you're flying above the clouds.

'Hello, son,' came a voice in front of me. 'Which one's your girlfriend?'

I'm not sure, but I think Vicky said, 'As bad as each other.'

11 – Unto the Tenth Generation

The burning in my fingers eased, and Desi pulled her hand away from mine. I heard the rasp of fabric as she gave it a wipe, and I dropped my arm from Francesca. As my eyes cleared, the shape of my 11xGreat Grandfather came into focus.

Spectre Thomas doesn't resemble me that much, but he's a dead ringer for a younger version of my dad, an idea emphasised by the sharp three-piece suit in blue pinstripe and by the red tie.

I cleared my throat. 'Grandfather, this is …'

'…The Keeper of the Library. Well met, madam.'

Francesca shocked me by stepping forward and shaking his hand. Li Cheng must have put a *lot* of Lux into that summoning for Thomas to have full corporeality.

'Francesca Somerton,' she said. 'How d'you do.'

'Thomas Clarke,' said Grandfather in a strong Lincolnshire accent. He let go of Francesca's hand and turned to me. 'Give me a hug, Conrad. We'll only get one chance.'

So I did, and his suit was as real as Father's, even down to the weave of the cloth. His face was warm when we kissed, and he held me close and tight. When he released me, he finally looked round properly and caught sight of the Morrigan, now glowing in the darkness that had fallen.

He bowed low and said, 'My Lady. Here we are again. Where are the others? And who…' He pointed to the tree where Odin's raven was perched.

Again? What happened last time?

'Well met, Thomas,' said the Morrigan. 'Much has changed since then, and that is for Conrad's generation to worry about. I am here to give you safe passage to rest with Alice, so tell your tale and be gone.'

He bowed again. 'Thank you, great Lady,' he said, then turned back to us and spotted Vicky. 'Sweet Witch, thank you for your help.'

Vicky coloured slightly, but stepped forward to embrace him. 'No one's called me sweet for years,' she said, 'but you're welcome.'

Li had collapsed into one of the camping chairs and was wiping his face with a handkerchief. Thomas was looking at the other three women, but if I didn't introduce Li first, he'd get the hump.

'May I present the Royal Occulter, Dr Li Cheng, also today's Summoner.'

Li dragged himself to his feet and shook hands. Instead of releasing his grip, Li held on and frowned. 'It wasn't just you,' he said. 'So much Lux – where's it gone? Is there someone else?'

'Aah. About that,' said Thomas. 'She'll be along when I've gone.'

Li let go and turned to me. 'What's this?'

'You can shout at me later,' I said. 'Let's move on, shall we?'

I introduced Desirée, then Mina gave him the full namaste and said, 'It is an honour beyond words to meet such an ancestor.'

Thomas bowed back and gave me a sidelong wink. 'I wish I could stay to know you better,' he said.

When I introduced Myfanwy as our new housekeeper, he sighed and said, 'So many Mages together. I wish I could stay and learn, and Alice would be thrilled.' He leaned in and whispered something to Myfanwy, who then gave me a funny look.

Vicky and I had brought quite a few bits up to cover contingencies, and one of them was an old cloak we'd been keeping. I spread it on the wall around the well, and invited Thomas to sit. I also slipped him my hip flask, then moved away to stand with Mina and light a cigarette. Francesca took one of the camping chairs, and after checking that Li was okay, Vicky took the other.

Thomas took a swig of the Islay malt, raised his eyebrows and said, 'So that's what I've been missing. Thank'ee Conrad.' He took his time screwing the cap back on, and looked at his feet for a moment.

When he looked up, he stared at where the Morrigan was glowing patiently and said, 'How many generations does it take to wash clean a sin? It is written that a bastard may not come into the Lord's congregation until ten generations have passed.'

'What is he talking about? Is he illegitimate?' whispered Mina.

'No idea, love,' I said.

Then Thomas looked directly at me and said, 'This is the story of Brother William. First of the Clarkes.'

Thomas spread his arm to encompass my house, the land around it and the village beyond. 'In the time of Edward, King of the Sea, this was all church land. Every acre belonged to Winchcombe Abbey and had done for generations.' He paused to take another sip from the hip flask. 'That would be Edward III to you. Middle of the 1300s, and there was no village called Clerkswell. In fact, there were only two stone buildings at all: the chapel of St Michael and the farmhouse. Elvenham Grange. That was where William was born.

'He didn't have a family name, but they didn't call him William Witchborn for nothing. From birth, the monks in St Michael's Chapel kept an eye on him, taught him to read and took him to Winchcombe to join their chapter, for Winchcombe Abbey was a Sanctuary House.'

'It means they took in Mages,' I said to Mina. 'And locked them up, effectively.'

'William was barely a man,' continued Thomas, 'when the first travellers brought stories of God's judgement, of how the plague was spreading throughout the kingdom, sweeping all before it. And one day, a French Monk arrived at the Abbey, seeking shelter and bringing with him a book.'

Thomas turned to look at Francesca. 'I'm glad you're here, Keeper,' he said. 'It will save me a lot of time knowing that you can fill them in when I'm gone. You know, don't you.'

Francesca had recoiled from my ancestor and was chewing a finger, unable to speak. She waved at Thomas to carry on. This did not look good for my family's reputation.

'The monk was Father Stephen of Potigny, special Inquisitor, and the book he brought was the *Codex Defanatus Britanniae*. Not long after Father Stephen arrived, so did the plague. In the confusion, Brother William killed Father Stephen, stole the book and fled home. To Elvenham Grange.'

Thomas looked at me again. 'That was the sin, Conrad, and he compounded it.'

I didn't think it could get much worse. The rest of the group were stealing glances at me already, but my ancestor had more. Oh yes.

'William had always known that here in these woods was a weak spot, a place where sometimes the Fae could appear. When he returned from Winchcombe with blood on his hands and the book in his bag, he made a Calling, and brought forth a Fae Count. In the dead of night, he made a compact. A bargain. He did a deal with the unhumans.' Thomas smiled grimly. 'It was bad, but I can't throw the first stone. Not after what I did.

'William's compact was simple. He was to dig a well. This well. And then to use his magick to make a door into the sídhe of the Fae. The Fae Count was to keep the *Codex Defanatus*, and so long as an offering was made every seven years, the waters of the well would keep the village safe from the plague.'

'An offering?' said Mina.

'A boy child,' said Vicky, grimly. 'A boy child was to be handed over. I'll explain later.'

'During the first seven years, refugees from plague-struck settlements flocked to Elvenham, and the village grew. The chapel of St Michael became the Church of St Michael at the Clerk's Well, and William became known as William the Clerk. The Abbey granted him Elvenham Grange as a hereditary tenancy.'

Desirée was giving me daggers. It looked like I'd gone back to being top of her hit list.

'William resigned his office and married,' continued Thomas. 'And when the first seven years were up, he did the one decent thing in all this. He refused the offering and the plague did its worst, but by then the village was big enough to survive, and survive it has. The Fae Count kept the book, William died, and his son was no Mage. The compact was forgotten and things remained that way for generations. My grandfather married an heiress from Lincolnshire and removed himself to her lands. Elvenham Grange was rented out. When he died, he left the Grange to my father, also Thomas, who was his second son.'

Francesca coughed. 'And your father was the first Keeper.'

'He was, and I followed him. My father was a great scholar, but barely a Mage. Many of the volumes in the Esoteric Library were sealed with enchantment, and he never opened them. I did, and one of them was the Oxbridge Scroll.'

'No!' shouted Francesca. 'You can't have!'

Thomas looked at his hand-tooled brogues. 'I did.' Then he looked up. 'Blame the King. My Alice was a known Witch. If he'd let me marry her and retain my post as Keeper, none of this would have happened.' There was a grim set to his face, and no one said anything. 'I fled here, and brought the Oxbridge Scroll with me. When Alice and I settled in the Grange, we found the Fae door. It was hidden behind the Dragonstone, the one that now sits above the doorway, Conrad.'

'That explains a lot,' said Vicky.

'The Fae Count returned the book to me, as he had to, and that left me with a dilemma.'

Francesca was rigid with fury. 'There was no dilemma. You had both codices. You should have returned them.'

'No,' said Thomas. 'I was the Keeper. I kept them, and kept them safe. I even joined them together – one *Codex Defanatus* covering the whole of England. I know about the world because I've read the newspapers and watched the news, or I used to, but I know nothing of the world of magick save what I've gleaned from Keepers who've come looking over the years. Sixteen of them, and some of them two or three times.'

It was getting distinctly uncomfortable out there by the well. Desi had moved slowly to stand by Francesca, and Li was now next to Vicky. Myfanwy didn't know which way to turn.

'Tell me this, fellow Keeper,' said Thomas. 'How would your Invisible College have faired with access to the *Defanatus*?'

Francesca wanted to argue, to defend the integrity of her predecessors, but something stopped her.

'I thought so,' said Thomas. There was a shimmer from the garden, and we turned to look. The Morrigan was getting restless. Thomas gave an ironic smile. 'Making the single book was a mistake. That's when the Dæmons started appearing.'

'Like real demons? From Hell?' said Mina.

'Amongst others,' said Thomas. 'Many others. I had to act, and I had to keep the book safe.' He looked towards the impatient goddess beyond the well. 'I threatened to destroy the book. Once word got round, there was nearly a pitched battle, here at Elvenham Grange. Thank you, great goddess, for your aid. I was unworthy.'

'You were unworthy, and you still are.' The Morrigan's words boomed across the grass. They could probably hear her in the Inkwell.

'There was a … a gathering, you could call it,' said Thomas. 'It lasted all of one winter's long night. Sixteen long hours, and at the end, there was an agreement. A bargain made that avoided what everyone feared and gave us all the promise of a future.'

'All?' I said. 'Who was there?'

'Some of this I can remember,' said Thomas. 'The Morrigan stood guarantor, and the rest of us signed in blood. Count Ealdhun of the Fae, the Dwarf Niði, the Bull of Evesham, the Spirit d'Houllac and at least two great Dæmons. Their names have gone. And there was Helen of Troy.' He paused and took a sip of whisky. 'I'm not going to forget her. The terms of the agreement were that the Fae Count would be promoted and allowed a new land. He is long gone, and his doorway sealed. What the Dæmons wanted or received was expunged from my memory. The Bull was on my side – he wanted the book gone, and that was what I couldn't achieve. The *Codex Defanatus* survived, but it was sealed under the great seal of the Morrigan.'

I've spoken to Thomas before, of course, and I could guess what was coming next.

'It was up to the Morrigan to decide for how long, and the Morrigan being who she is, no date was set. She said that the book would be sealed *Until the Clarkes leave Elvenham or until Thomas is born again to his own mother.*'

Mina had slipped her hand under my coat to wrap around my waist. She looked up. 'Is this going to make sense? Ever?' I pulled her even closer and let Thomas continue.

'I did one more magickal thing before I committed my greatest sin, the sin of self-slaughter. Alice and I rebuilt the Grange farm house, and when we did, I put the Dragonstone over the lintel, and I enchanted it. Did you work it out, Sweet Witch? My apologies. Did you work it out, *Doctor Robson?*'

'I'm no more a doctor of Chymic than I am sweet,' said Vicky, 'but I did work it out. I didn't believe it, but I worked it out.' She turned to face me. 'Your ancestor bound himself to the stone in a special way. His sons, and his sons after him could only conceive children in that house.'

'What on earth for?' said Myfanwy.

Francesca answered, 'To ensure the Clarkes carried on living here, I imagine.'

'True,' said Thomas. 'I did that, and I spent over three hundred years nudging them to stay. The odd haunting, the occasional manifestation. Just a nudge. It worked.'

I spoke out, 'Until it came to pass that Alfred Clarke wooed a girl from Cambridge, a girl who'd grown up in the Fens. My mother.'

Thomas picked up the thread. 'And your mother was my sister's daughter's daughter's daughter up to the fifteenth generation. Alfred Clarke had my father's Y chromosome, and Mary Enderby had my mother's mitochondria. In you I was born again to my own parents.'

'No!' said Myfanwy. 'Really?'

'Close enough,' said Thomas. 'Give or take the odd X chromosome. When Conrad was born, the *Codex Defanatus* was unsealed. I must say it's taken a long time for it to come into circulation. Thirty-seven years. And I had so little energy, I couldn't stray beyond the house. Thank you, Doctor Li, for giving me the Lux to manifest. It is now time for me to join my Alice and wait for God's Judgement.'

'You'll have a long wait,' said the Morrigan with the sort of laugh that makes you very worried. 'My promise to you is discharged, Thomas Clarke. I have made sure your story was heard, and now I shall go.' Her hard, haunted eyes scanned the group. 'One of you, at least, I will see again in this life.'

Deities, I've discovered, don't do goodbye. She turned to where Odin's raven had been watching, and bowed her head. The raven cawed in return, and then she was gone, leaving nothing but an image of glory on the retina.

'You can't go now,' said Francesca, struggling out of her chair and pointing at Thomas. 'What was in the full *Codex*? And where is the *Codex*?'

He moved off his perch on the well, brushing lime and grit from his suit. 'I don't know what was in it, because I had to forget. I only remembered Helen of Troy when Conrad met her and told me she was free.' He shrugged. Badly. Out of practice, I suppose. 'As to the book's whereabouts, I last saw it disappear down a hole in the ground under the arm of Niði the Dwarf. You'll have to ask him. Now, Conrad, will you and your lady escort me to Alice?'

'But ...' said Francesca.

Thomas stepped forwards and took her hands. 'Hush, Keeper...'

She snatched them back, 'Don't you dare talk to me like that! I am not a serving girl to be hushed. You will stay and answer for what you did.'

Thomas bowed. 'Forgive me. I did not mean to insult your sex, Doctor Somerton. Be that as it may, King James could not keep my Alice and I apart, and neither can you. I must take me leave of you all. Conrad?'

'Aren't you forgetting something?' said a rich, Indian voice from behind us.

We all whirled round to see the curvy form of Pramiti, hands on hips, by the well. I've mentioned her figure because she was naked, and you sort of couldn't ignore it.

'Put the cloak on,' I said. 'I left it out for you.'

She flicked her hair and picked up the cloak, drawing it round her and making sure that there was plenty of Pramiti still visible. I also noticed that instead of a gaping wound in her side, she had a scar. So that's where all our Lux had gone.

'What is the meaning of this?' said Francesca, boiling over with fury and directing it at Thomas and me with equal venom.

Mina upstaged her by marching up to the Nāgin. Pramiti was on a slight rise, and a good six inches taller than Mina anyway, but that didn't stop Mina jabbing her in the chest with a finger and saying something in Gujarati.

Pramiti replied in a language that sounded different. Hindi?

Mina shook her head, jabbed her finger again and ranted at Pramiti for a good ten seconds. Then, without waiting for a reply, she turned round and came back to me. She turned to Vicky and said, 'Give her food and send her on her way. I want her gone by the time we get back, and Vicky?'

Vicky was not looking happy. No one was looking happy. Even Pramiti looked like a vegetarian who's won the meat raffle.

'Aye?' said Vicky.

Mina darted to Vicky's side and whispered in her ear. Before anyone else could react, Mina grabbed Thomas's arm, then mine, and dragged us away from the well.

12 — You can Choose your Friends

No one followed, and Mina slowed down as we passed Rachael's dilapidated tennis court. She let go of Thomas's hand, keeping hold of mine. 'That was scary,' she said. 'And it was a good job I've felt magick before. I would not have liked that to be my first time.'

'Conrad never told me where you were from,' said Thomas. 'I know enough to know that you were born in England.'

'My parents were both born in western India,' she said. 'Papa-ji was from the country in Gujarat and mother was from Mumbai. Bombay, as we still call it. I grew up in Ealing.' She gave him a grin. 'I bet it was all fields in your day.'

Thomas grinned back. 'I remember a very welcoming inn at Ealing. It was a good place to stop if you couldn't make London before the curfew.'

We were past the house and on to Elven Lane.

'Did you know Pramiti was there? Did you talk?' said Mina.

'No,' said Thomas. 'Not until the summoning. We were both asleep, what you people would call *suspended animation*.'

Mina laughed. 'I've had my share of racism, and I've been called *you people* often enough, but never because I came from the twenty-first century. A nice change, Dādā-ji.'

'Might I ask what you said to her? It sounded fierce.'

I was very interested in this, too.

'I told her that the wise tiger is wary of the shepherd.'

'Aah. Of course you did.'

Mina pulled her hair all the way off her face. 'It took a while to get the message over, because her Gujarati is not wonderful, and my Hindi is very rusty. So is my Gujarati, but don't tell anyone. *The Wise tiger is wary of the shepherd* is my family motto – Desai means shepherd. I also gave her the modern English version: *No one pushes a Desai*, then I told her that if Conrad is hurt trying to get her jewel back, I will hunt her down and stick her with a spear.'

'Ouch.'

'And what did you say to Vicky?' I asked.

'Not to tell anyone else about the price on our engagement. That detail would not help me get in Hannah Rothman's good books. If she has any.'

We reached the churchyard, and I opened the gate, casting around for visitors. Now that Easter was over, the church had gone back to its habitual slumber, and tonight was not choir practice.

'This way,' said Thomas. 'When I had the Lux, I would come here every day. I had terrible trouble making sure that our grave wasn't disturbed when they re-laid the churchyard.'

'Our grave?'

'Oh yes. Don't forget, my first body was buried there, too.' He gestured to his suit and the form underneath it. 'All this is just a temporary clothing.'

I got out a torch for Mina's benefit, and Thomas led us round to the almost empty south section of the grounds. When I was chasing the Pyromancer last week, I must have run over his grave. There was just one headstone here, hard by the wall and covered with moss and lichen.

'You had something to tell me, Grandfather?' I said. 'Isn't that why you dragged me away from the others?'

He looked bemused. 'No. I just wanted your company on my penultimate journey.' He laughed. 'Joking!'

Mina hit him. 'You've been watching too much television. Stick to the sexism, it sounds much more natural.'

Thomas took out the hip flask. He unscrewed the top and said, 'A toast. To family.' He drank, and offered the flask to Mina.

She joined in, and seemed to be acquiring a taste for Islay malt. 'To family.'

When it was my turn, after what I'd heard tonight, I wasn't sure that my family was worth drinking to. Then again, it was the only family I had. 'To family.'

'I'll just say this, Conrad, then I'll be gone. There have been Clarkes in Elvenham Grange and then Elvenham House for at least twenty four generations. Even so, with no magick, it's only bricks and mortar. Remember that.'

'Thanks. I think. Goodbye, Grandfather.'

He shook hands with me rather than give me a hug. That, he saved for Mina. I don't blame him. I'd rather hug Mina than hug me.

'Clean up after me, will you.'

And those were his final words before he sank into the ground. Or some of him did. There was a simultaneous melting and burst of fire. Mina and I jumped back as his suit and body turned into fizzing water, rushing air and a blaze of light.

When it died down, we both had wet feet and there was a thick white powder exactly outlining the shape of a grave.

'What was that all about? Is he gone?'

'He's gone to wherever Christians go when they die. I think the fireworks and shower were something to do with the human body being nearly all water, gas and calcium. That white stuff must be lime. Better get rid of it before it kills the grass.'

Too late. It had already singed the turf, so I used a branch and brushed it to the wall. I wonder what the vicar will say about the sudden burnt patch by the Clarke headstone when the churchwarden sees her.

We linked hands and walked the long way round the churchyard, and I pointed to where my paternal grandparents had been laid to rest. James

Clarke, builder of Elvenham House, is actually inside the church. Money will always get you a good seat.

'A graveyard in the dark. Not the most romantic date, Conrad.'

'I can't say I'm anxious to get home.'

'Me neither, but it is warm there. Come on.'

A shadow lingered under the lychgate. A shadow that had something of the raven about it. As we got closer, it stepped out and brushed back the hood of a dingy grey sweatshirt. The Allfather was going for grizzled combat veteran tonight, complete with scars and a bloody bandage instead of a regular eye patch.

His voice rasped, as raw as the cuts to his scalp. 'A good night's work, Dragonslayer. I had to wait here, for obvious reasons.'

'Odin Allfather, may I present Mina Desai.'

'Ohmygod. Sorry. Namaste, Allfather,' said Mina, almost toppling over as she bowed and joined her hands.

'Well met, Mina Desai,' said the second god of the day.

His one eye bored into mine. 'What are you going to do?'

'Follow orders, sir. If I were the Constable, I'd send me to find the Dwarf, but I'm not the Constable. Personally, I'd go after the Pyromancer's friends. They tried to kill me.'

He nodded, as if I'd passed a test. 'Don't forget, you still have an answer and a boon to claim from me.'

'Sir.'

He turned to Mina. 'Ganesh made a mistake, I think. You would have made a great warrior, Miss Desai.'

Mina shook her hair and held his gaze. 'There are many ways to be a warrior, great lord.'

He laughed, a much more human laugh than the Morrigan's. Still scary, though. 'As you say. Go well, both of you.'

We bowed, and when we looked up, there was no shadow. As I said, not big on goodbyes, these gods.

'Is your heart going at one forty beats?' said Mina. 'Because mine is. I need a drink. I still think we should have had one before the summoning. Is it like this every day when I'm not with you? Is he going to turn up at our wedd…'

I kissed her until she'd calmed down. I knew better than to tell Mina to *hush*.

We started off down the road, and had got ten paces before Monti's Czardas rang out from my pocket. I may not have a smartphone, but it does do ringtones. For 79p, I now know when Hannah is calling without having to check the screen.

'Yes, Boss?'

I was expecting wailing and gnashing of teeth. What I got was a throaty chuckle. 'I knew that the Lord was testing me, and now I know that the Lord has a sense of humour.'

I raised my eyebrows to Mina, who was trying to reach up and listen. 'Ma'am?'

'There I was, staring at a bottle of wine, unopened, thinking that it would be hours before I heard anything, and suddenly Rick calls me. "Hannah," he says, "The Morrigan is in Conrad's Garden. I can feel her." And now I hear that Odin was there as well, and somehow you walked away.'

'Limped away, ma'am. My titanium implant is playing me up for some reason. It seems to be hot all the time.'

'Shut up. I don't care. Well, I do, but not very much. Do you know what's so funny? Do you know why the Lord has a sense of humour.'

I'd bent down and put the phone on speaker so that Mina could hear. She mimed drinking a glass of wine and pointed to the phone. I shook my head.

'No, ma'am.'

'Because, on my watch, he has unleashed the worst magickal crisis in two hundred years. This he has done to test me, but he has also sent you, which is why he has a sense of humour.'

Mina couldn't restrain herself. She can be polite to gods and ancestors, but bosses she has a problem with. 'Conrad is not a joke, Constable Rothman.'

A loud sniff carried all the way from North London over the speaker. 'No, he's not, Miss Desai, even if he thinks he's funny. The Lord has sent him so that I can blame his family, and every time I have to rely on him – which I will – the Lord is reminding me that his family caused this mess. That's why the Lord has a sense of humour.'

I held my finger to my lips in case Mina decided to deepen the hole we were standing in.

'You're up to speed, then?' I said.

'Yes. Vicky and Li called as soon as they got to the house. I'm glad, in a way. It removes the vague sense of impending doom and replaces it with the certain knowledge of impending doom. That, I can cope with.'

She took a deep breath. 'You can tell the others this. No one outside the group tonight can know what we've discovered, and the group includes Cora Hardisty. Cora has already been in touch to discuss our approach, and she agrees with me. She left hospital today, by the way. For now, Francesca and I will try to find out what we can – with help from Desirée. You and Vicky will carry on with Project Talpa this week, and you will go on the firearms course in Gravesend. Then, and only then, will you go looking for the Dwarf. Clear?'

'Yes, ma'am.'

'And how was it for you, Miss Desai?' said Hannah, acid in her voice.

'I learnt something tonight, Constable Rothman. I learnt that Thomas Clarke loved his wife more than I thought was possible, and if Conrad loves me one quarter as much as Thomas loved Alice, I shall be the luckiest woman in the world.'

There was a silence, then Hannah coughed. 'Not quite what I had in mind, but thank you for sharing. Now, can you give me a moment with my Watch Captain at Large?'

'Of course. Goodbye.'

I took the phone off speaker and stepped away.

'I need you, Conrad,' said Hannah. 'I need you on our side, but I swear that I will cut my own throat if you pull another stunt like the snake woman and I don't fire you.'

It took me a moment to disentangle her syntax, but I think I got there. 'I understand, ma'am. Full disclosure from now on.'

'Good. And I don't believe for one minute the load of hogwash Vicky told me about why that woman was in your well. Should I be worried? Honestly?'

'Honestly? I don't know. She's not a threat to anyone but me, and only indirectly, I can tell you that much.'

'Good. Now go and get drunk. That's what I'm going to do.'

We'd been walking slowly as we talked to Hannah, and we were back at Elvenham House. I wasn't sure I was ready, but I took Mina's hand and we crunched over the gravel towards the kitchen.

There was already one empty bottle of wine on the table, and not much left in the second. Given that Rick was drinking coffee, the others were well on their way. Even Desirée had a large glass in front of her. There was no sign of Pramiti.

'Are you all right? Where've you been?' said Myfanwy, rising and getting two more glasses.

'Is he gone?' said Francesca.

I took her to mean Thomas rather than the Allfather. I was only going to share that encounter with Vicky. 'He's at rest. Finally.'

'Hmmph,' said Francesca.

'You clearly knew about these books, scrolls or whatever they were, Keeper, as does everyone else, I imagine.'

Myfanwy held up her hand. 'Not me.'

Francesca was the only one who hadn't taken off her outdoor coat. The lines in her face were drawn together even more tightly than normal, and she was gripping her wine glass like an anchor. She took a sip and said, 'You know about the system of Sanctuary Houses, yes?'

I'd mentioned them to Mina, but there was much more. I looked at her and said, 'It was how the church controlled magick. The Inquisition of St Michael scoured Europe for Mages and convinced them to join monastic orders. Men and women. They were allowed to practise magick, but only within their institutions. And of course they couldn't start a family. That all ended with the Reformation.'

'It ended before that,' said Francesca. 'It ended with the Black Death, where William's story started.' She sighed. 'All over Europe, there were little Sanctuary Houses, each with a few Mages, and not enough Inquisitors to keep track of what they were really up to. And then the plague came, and the Grand Inquisitor realised what was going on. Dæmons. Lots of them had gathered around the Sanctuaries like flies, and the first thing they promised was, "We can show you how to stop the plague." Terrible. The Grand Inquisitor sent out his best men to visit every Sanctuary and root out the Dæmons. They were also supposed to gather the more dangerous rituals and Artefacts and bring them back to Avignon.'

'Avignon?' said Myfanwy. 'Why there?'

'The Pope was based there during the Plague. Not important. What is important is that all the special Inquisitors returned safely except one. Stephen of Potigny disappeared. It was known that he was in the Midlands, but everyone thought he'd made it to Oxford. He'd started in Lindisfarne, gone round the coast and only had the two universities left. We know that from his letters. Because the Codex never turned up, most people thought he'd been victim of a mundane robbery and that the Codex had been lost.'

'What does *Defanatus* mean?' said Mina. A good question. My Latin is non-existent.

'Profane,' said Desirée. 'Something unclean in the sight of the Lord.'

Francesca pushed on, keen to get the story over with. 'The Grand Inquisitor sent John of Arles to investigate and finish the job. He couldn't find Stephen, obviously, but he did visit Oxford and Cambridge and he produced the Oxbridge Scroll, which he took back to Avignon. When all the books were together, the Grand Inquisitor sealed each one, and sent them out all over Europe. There was far too much power to have in one place otherwise. The Oxbridge scroll went to Spain, and again we thought it lost. That monster Don José must have brought it with him, which is why it ended up in the Esoteric Library. Briefly. Until your ancestor stole it.'

'Kept it,' I said. I was determined that Thomas's name would not be blackened any further than he deserved.

'You're not trying to defend him, are you?' said Desirée.

'He's my ancestor,' I said. 'I have to be his advocate. In this case, I can see why he did what he did. Would I have done differently? I don't know.'

'Sounds like you've inherited his values,' she replied, 'as well as his house. What he did was monstrous.'

Vicky had decided that Desi needed to get this off her chest, so she said nothing. Francesca looked too tired to intervene, and I was in agreement with Vicky. It would blow itself over.

Mina doesn't know her well enough, yet. There's a line with Desi between outrage and action, and this was still on the side of outrage. Mina either hadn't picked that up, or she was drawing the line in a different place.

She put her glass down carefully and gave Desirée a smile. 'I have heard this before, you know. To a Hindu, there is no problem because the father will pay for his own actions in the next life. To you Christians, you are always arguing about the Sins of the Father.'

'I didn't...' said Desi.

Mina wasn't finished. '...Have you heard about *my* father? He was a wholesale importer of heroin and he died on remand in prison. Are you going to judge me for his actions?'

There was a stunned silence, into which Mina rose and said to Francesca, 'Dr Somerton, I believe that Conrad needs to talk to the others, including Desirée. Shall I light the fire and make us more comfortable.'

Mina's timing was impeccable. Francesca drained her glass and said, 'That's very kind of you, my dear, but no, I shall take myself off to bed.'

'I'll show you the way,' said Mina.

I got up and said, 'Thank you, Dr Somerton. Tonight would not have been possible without you.'

'I wouldn't have missed that for anything, Conrad. Now, you lot,' she said, glaring at everyone, including Myfanwy, 'I expect all of you to pull together. I want to be the Keeper who brings that book home, and I need your help. Goodnight.'

When Mina and Francesca's voices had faded, Myfanwy said, 'Are you sure I should be hearing all this? I know this is my home, and I had a right to be there at the summoning, but the rest isn't really my business is it, not that I'm not fascinated and all that. Oh! And I forgot! I gave Pramiti that Volvo XC90 to get her off the premises. You don't mind, do you? Have you got her number? Does she have a phone?'

If you spend long in Myfanwy's company, you get used to this, or you go mad. I think I was getting used to it.

'Yes, she's got a phone, no I don't mind that she's taken the car, though Mina might, and yes, if you promise to keep quiet, you can hear what I've got to say.'

'Thank you. I'll get another bottle. Good job we stocked up. Is anyone hungry yet? I'll make toast.'

'Good. I've had our orders. Desirée, you're with Francesca on research, and that comes from the Dean, not from the Constable.'

Desi nodded.

'Rick, Li, you're back to business as usual until we know more. Vicky and I are on Project Talpa this week, then I'm off to Gravesend. After that, it's a Dwarf hunt.'

'Yeah,' said Rick. 'That's what we were talking about after Pramiti left. I told them that Niði has gone dark. All his work goes through the Gnomes in Birmingham.'

'And you know how much I love Gnomes,' said Vicky. It was the first time she'd spoken since I got back

'Thanks, Rick. How was Pramiti?'

'Arrogant and a pain in the arse,' said Vicky.

'Completely,' agreed Myfanwy. 'A right bitch if you ask me, and it might be a while before you get your car back, if I'm completely honest.'

'I'd say she was a creature of Satan,' added Desi, 'except that creatures of Satan are easy to get on with. Until they steal your soul.'

You will have noticed that the two men at the table had said nothing. Li is very good at hiding his emotions in company, and the poor bloke looked shattered. Rick had stood up and put his mug in the nearly empty dishwasher. Rick must be a nervous cleaner, because the kitchen looked spotless. He must have done all that while we were busy with Thomas.

'Thanks, Conrad. I'd best be off,' said Rick.

'No toast?' said Myfanwy.

'Better not. Thanks for the meal. See you all later, guys. Don't worry, I know my way out.'

'And I know my way to bed,' said Li. 'Goodnight.'

'Well I'm hungry,' said Myfanwy.

'If you don't mind,' said Desi.

'Me too,' said Vicky. 'I'll bet Conrad's going for a smoke.'

I was, with a glass of wine, and I was still out there when Mina appeared, nibbling a slice of toast.

'What did you want with Francesca?' I asked.

'Her help. I now have the number of someone called the Steward of the Great Work. He's going to help me with the inflation report. Did I tell you I'd heard from that Dwarf, Hledjolf?'

'No.'

'Well, I did, and he said he'd help if the College vouched for me. This Steward person will do the vouching.'

'Excellent.'

She brushed toast crumbs off her hands and tilted her head. 'Have we been using condoms unnecessarily before now? Am I really immune from pregnancy away from here?'

I shook my head. 'Vicky says the Work in the Dragonstone discharged when I was born.'

She smiled. 'Not that I've got the energy tonight. I've had an email from the prison, too. No leave this weekend because the prison service have finally got their act together. I'm being taken to Preston on Monday morning for a pre-release interview with a probation officer. Are you sure you're happy for me to put Elvenham House down as my residence?'

'I wouldn't want you anywhere else. Let's go back in.'

13 — To the Ends of the Earth

We had to leave before the others (apart from Myfanwy) were up next morning. If Mina wasn't back at HMP Cairndale by noon, there would be real problems that not even Dr Mirren could get round. We made good time through the interminable roadworks on the M6, good enough time for a visit to Ribblegate Farm. Before we arrived, Mina spent most of her time staring at her phone.

'This data on Alchemical Gold is fascinating,' she said at one point.

'Clearly, and clearly a lot more interesting than me.'

'Mmm. If anyone asks, I've called it Project Midas, and I need a proper computer. The spreadsheet on this phone won't do.'

'Do you want me to have a word with the prison governor?'

'No, I ... Very funny, Conrad.'

It was a big day in the Kirkham household: the kitchen fitters had arrived. We got a cup of tea, but didn't linger. I took Mina to meet Scout, and the little puppy crawled over the straw to say hello as soon as we appeared in the doorway. When he licked my hand, I could feel the heat of Lux flowing through my fingers, and that dog will be on television, one day, I swear. There must have been more than a transfer of Lux, because when he'd finished with me, he went straight to Mina and rolled on his back. He somehow knew, even before he could see her, that Mina was a crucial part of his future.

She was oblivious, and immediately fell in love with the little familiar.

Shortly after, there was a heartbreaking scene when Mina parted with her phone until her next outing from prison. At least that meant she had to talk to me for the rest of the journey, about half an hour. The main topic was what to do during the middle of my course.

'I'd love to go to London,' she said. 'But it just won't work, and it would be dangerous for you to drive up and back twice.'

'You're right, but I'll miss you.'

'And I'll miss you.'

'What will you do?'

She looked out of the window and back again. 'I asked Dr Somerton for something else last night, apart from the information about the Steward. I asked her for details of Hindu temples that have magickal practitioners. Like you, she is old, and happy to put them in a letter, and she thinks there is one in Bolton. Kelly Kirkham will help me sort things out.'

'Are you sure?'

'I am sure. It may not help me get any closer to Ganesh, I have learnt this, but it certainly won't do any harm.'

'You'll be careful, won't you?'

'As careful as you,' she said, with a grin.

TENFOLD

She knows me too well.

It was deathly quiet in Elvenham House when I got back that afternoon. The London party were gone, and so was Myfanwy. Off to Slimming World. Vicky was curled up in front of the fire with a pot of tea and half a cake from the village shop.

'This was Myfanwy's totally bonkers plan,' she said. 'Stuff herself before the first weigh-in. I did try telling her, but she didn't listen. I hope she changes her ways after tonight, 'cos I'm in need of some collateral dieting.'

'Collateral dieting?'

'Aye. When the cook goes on a diet, so does everyone else. Make us a fresh pot of tea, will you?'

'Don't get used to being waited on. You're back in the tender embrace of Doctor Nicola this weekend.'

'If she still remembers who I am, and hasn't let out my room.'

I returned with tea and grabbed what was left of the cake.

'Is it true? About Mina's dad?' she asked.

'That he died in prison? Yes, I'm afraid it is. You know her eldest brother was murdered.'

'I meant the heroin. That's ... I can't believe it. In bulk?'

'In bolts of cloth from Pakistan. He ran a fabric import and wholesale business.'

She looked at me over her mug of tea. 'I want you to be honest, Conrad. Did you have anything to do with that?'

I shook my head. 'No. And neither did Mina. I have smuggled alcohol on to British bases in Afghanistan, and done other stuff, but I have never assisted, directed or been in any way involved with drugs. Other than as a consumer. I give you my word.'

She put down her mug. 'I used to do that, you know: confess to something small to hide the really bad things. I'm willing to bet that "other stuff", as you put it, was a hell of a lot more serious than illicit hooch.'

I said nothing.

'Fine. I'll find out one day. I'm too shattered to do any work.'

'Me too. You never did tell me Desi's speciality. I didn't know the Invisible College had a course in being a Bard.'

'They don't. Strictly Druid magick, that. Desi started as a specialist in Glamour. That was her Proof when we took our Fellowship exams, but she always wanted to explore using song. Her tradition is Gospel, not Welsh, obviously. They allowed her. Last night was the first time I've seen it. You might not know, but she was close to losing control. Can I trust you on this?'

I put my mug down. 'You should know by now, Vicky. While I'm your commanding officer, your safety and your trust is my number one priority.

99

Even if I weren't your CO, you'd come high on the list, being my honorary niece and all that.'

'Aye, well. It's awkward. We were more at risk from Desi last night than we ever were from the Morrigan or the Allfather.'

'Thanks. That is good to know. What about …' I never got to ask, because there was a loud knocking at the back door. 'I'll get it.'

I was very disconcerted to find a teenage girl. She was dressed for running, and though her hair was pulled back, I thought I recognised her from somewhere.

'Sorry to bother you, Mr Clarke' she said. So, she knew who I was.

'No problem … ?'

'Emily. Emily Ventress.'

Aah. 'Sorry, Emily, I didn't recognise you. You're Jake's daughter, aren't you?'

Jake Ventress was in the class above me at primary school. And he had a daughter this old? I felt ancient.

'Yeah,' she said. 'I was, erm, looking for a Miss Lewis.' As she said this, she checked her phone.

'She's due back later. Do you want me to give her a message?'

'I saw her note in the shop. About the women's cricket team. I was going to run up to Langley and I thought I'd see if I was too young. I'll text her.'

'I think fourteen's the minimum age.'

'Oh. Good.'

'And I'll tell her you called.'

'Thanks.'

I waved her off on her run and went back to tell Vicky.

'She's the third today,' said Vic. 'We had two round here after the school run this morning. Mind you, I reckon that one of them just wanted a neb round your house. You should have seen the looks on their faces when they saw Desi, Cheng and the Keeper sitting round the table.'

'Isn't it the school holidays?'

'After the nursery run, then. I don't know. I was in me dressing gown and trying to pour coffee down Cheng's throat so he could drive them back to London.'

I grunted. 'You know what?'

'What?'

'What I'd like more than anything is to watch some rubbish on the telly.'

'That is the best idea you've had in ages.'

Between Wednesday afternoon and Saturday morning, I learnt an awful lot about Slimming World, and yes, there was a fair bit of collateral dieting. It came as quite a shock.

When Vicky and I set off for London, Myfanwy had already started to arrange visits from landscape gardeners, cleaning agencies, the roofer, the chimney sweep and the mobile hairdresser. She'd also done more gardening in one afternoon than I've done in the last eighteen months, and she'd arranged the first meeting of the Clerkswell Women's Cricket team. Item One on the agenda was going to be whether they should, indeed, be Women, or whether they should be Ladies.

'You've got yourself a whirlwind, there, Conrad,' said Vicky as we drove out of Clerkswell. 'Do you think she'll be all right on her own?'

'She'll settle down. She'll get some knocks, too. The village doesn't always embrace new people in the way they'd like to be embraced.'

Vicky laughed her Geordie laugh. 'Are you talking about a certain cricket captain?'

'I couldn't possibly comment.'

There was a riot going on behind the wall. I could tell that because someone shouted, 'Riot!' and they all rioted until the guy shouted, 'Stop!' and they stopped. Welcome to Kent.

The Met Police Specialist Training Centre is a concrete wasteland next to the Thames and opposite the huge container terminal of Tilbury. It's not somewhere you go to feel good about our green and pleasant land; it's somewhere you go to learn how to protect it. The voice over the wall shouted, 'You're not angry enough!' I don't know whether he was talking to the rioters or the police cadets who were supposed to be containing them. To be fair to the rioters, I find it hard to get too angry first thing on a Monday morning.

Once I'd got in the compound, I was directed to the firearms section, which is strictly segregated from the mock buildings, aeroplane fuselages and other bits of urban terrain where the riot practice was going on. It's not often you can look on a firearms centre as a haven of peace and quiet.

I got in to the reception area, and was kept waiting for twenty minutes. About par.

A stocky, middle-aged police sergeant finally appeared behind the desk and stared at me. I stared back. He was white, had even less hair than I do and had dry skin. I could go on, but the receptionist got agitated and pointed to me. He finally spoke.

'Conrad Clarke?'

I stood up.

'Go through that door.'

He disappeared into the back office, and I was buzzed through by the receptionist into a cold and dispiriting police interview room, complete with audio and video recording. I leaned against the wall and waited.

He didn't take long this time, and returned with a folder. I thought about offering a handshake, until I saw the frown on his face. Oh dear. Like that, is it? At least things can only get better.

'ID,' he said.

I laid my RAF ID, driving licence, police warrant card and passport in a line on the desk and stood back.

He moved the driving licence away with his finger, ignoring it, and gave my passport some serious scrutiny. He put that on top of the licence and picked up my RAF badge. He glanced at this, compared the number to something in his file, then put it down on top of the passport. That left the warrant card. This, he picked up and tapped against the folder.

'You know you're the only candidate this week, right?' His voice was London through and through.

'Yes, sergeant. Is there a problem?'

'Put it this way, Special Constable Clarke from Lancashire. The Chief Super doesn't have a problem with you. The HR department don't have a problem with you, and Janet on reception doesn't have a problem with you. All of which should mean that I don't have a problem. And then I get this.'

He held up a piece of paper, full of empty boxes with a few words at the top. He showed me the other side, too. That was just as blank.

'I am happy to believe that you *are* Conrad Clarke, and that you are thirty-seven years old. The rest of this set-up has my few remaining hairs prickling on the back of my head.' He made a show of reading the paper. '"Date joined police service: two weeks ago." And that's it. Every box about your career, your experience, your psych evaluation, qualifications and medical history are blank. In the section for *References*, it says, "Refer to Security Liaison." So, Special Constable Clarke, what the fuck are you doing here? If you're a spook, why don't you go to spook school?'

'Westmorland,' I said.

'Eh?'

'You said Lancashire. I'm mostly based in Westmorland, and it's like the Wild West up there, sergeant.'

I thought he was going to explode, which wouldn't have been a good start. Then he burst out laughing.

'Herds of armed sheep? Ninja ramblers? At least you've got a sense of humour.'

'Do you want the truth, sergeant?'

'No. Just tell me a story I can live with.'

'May I?' I asked, pointing to my adjutant's case. He waved for me to go ahead, and I took out a photocopy from the *Gloucestershire Echo* of the medal ceremony when I got my DFC, the year before last.

He studied it carefully, checked the date on the top, made a note of the other articles on the page and grunted before passing it back. I had no doubt that Janet would be checking this before we got to morning coffee.

'Special protection, sergeant. I will be providing special protection to … certain people in Westmorland, and I have to do it as a warranted police officer. Did they not put Commander Ross's name down?' He shook his head. 'Commander Ross, Cairndale Division. He won't tell you any more, but at least he's a real police officer.'

He picked up my credentials and handed them back. 'This way.'

We returned to reception, he had words with Janet, and I was finally issued with a security pass. He also told me his name. Police Sergeant Smith. It could be his real name, I suppose. We entered the inner sanctum and headed for a training room. 'You must have had personal weapons training in the RAF,' he said.

'Yes, sergeant. Mostly pistols. I've not handled anything like the MP5 for some time.'

'Here, you're a beginner. Understand?'

'Of course. My boss won't be happy with anything less than humility and application.'

He stopped and looked at me. 'Is that what he said? Humility and application? Who the fuck do you work for? Father Brown?'

That was good. I liked that. I shall have to give it to Hannah as a codename.

'She, not he. What she actually said was, "Don't get arsey down there and keep it zipped, or I'll make you watch Arsenal videos until you beg for mercy." She meant it, too.'

He weighed his keys in his hand. No swipe cards or pass-codes back here, just old-fashioned mild steel keys. He passed the training room and took me deep into the complex. A steel plated door led to the service hatch for the armoury, and PS Smith drew a Glock 17 pistol and rounds. Under his own name. He took us to a bare room with a high workbench in the centre. Next to the bench was a one metre high metal tank full of soft sand.

'This is the live round demonstration room. Normally, we don't get here until Monday evening.' He laid the Glock and the ammunition on the table. 'Show me.'

It took me thirty seconds to get suspicious. After one minute I asked him to turn the task lights on and double checked. 'The sights are at least one degree out, sergeant.'

'Good. Should mean an earlier finish.'

And it did. I knocked off mid-afternoon most days, and I forced myself to go to a yoga class. Somebody, somewhere will appreciate the contrast between the two. On Friday morning, a taciturn counter-terrorism specialist came to examine me. After half an hour's wait, PS Smith shook my hand and handed me a Part One certificate.

'There's no rushing Part Two,' he said. 'See you Monday morning.'

On the train back to the City, I fantasised about pulling a sickie and driving up the M6 to meet Mina at the prison gates. A weekend of Hindu rituals sounded infinitely preferable to what I will actually be doing on Saturday, but we'll come to that later. First up was a Project Talpa briefing.

I'd just left the train at London Bridge when Mina called. She was using the prison phone, so not only would the call be brief, it would be monitored. Probably.

'How's it going?' she asked.

'Good. I passed Part One today.'

'Of course you did. Any updates on the book?'

'I'll find out this afternoon. Have you heard anything?'

She breathed out, air catching in her nose and echoing. It sounded like she was exhaling a breath she'd been holding for over a year.

'Yes. I saw the probation officer, and he has graded me low-risk. I have to register in Gloucester, and after that it will be by telephone.'

'Really? They do that?'

She gave a hollow laugh. 'You don't know the half of it. I also have a date: Friday twenty-second of May.'

'I can't wait, love.'

'Me too. Oh, and I have other news. I saw the governor yesterday, and I asked him if he'd seen any good videos lately, meaning Bollywood, of course.'

She didn't mean Bollywood (although Mina has started a trend with them). She meant the video of Mina being racially assaulted by an inmate while a prison officer watched.

'And had he?'

'He had. He has moved me from numeracy workshops to supporting the IT teacher. I will be able to start on Project Midas next week.'

There was a bleep on the line – the ten second warning. You can say *I love you* a lot of times in ten seconds.

14 — Of Dwarves and Coneheads

'Good afternoon, Mr Clarke. Not a good day for your leg, is it?'
I hadn't even got to the top of Merlyn's Tower when Tennille
Haynes' voice carried down the stairs. She has very good hearing. It wasn't a
good day, actually. My titanium tibia has taken to getting *hot*, which it
shouldn't, being an inert metal object. I was beginning to worry about it
getting infected, though again, that shouldn't happen. I waited until I'd
emerged into her zone before I replied.

The King's Watch has been based at Merlyn's Tower since its creation in
1618. Our home is in the outer curtain wall of the Tower of London, squat
and strong, and invisible. Even to satellites. Last year a drone flew into the
roof because its operator thought our building was a terraced house.

The Peculier Constable has the top floor, with views over the Thames
from a substantial office (and a back staircase to the basement). Outside
Hannah's robust oak doors is an open space where Tennille sits facing the
staircase, protecting Hannah and striking fear into the young Watch Captains
who have to get their expenses signed.

I was not looking forward to this. Tennille is Desirée's mother and is fully
versed in the ways of magick, even if she has none herself. Her stare said it all:
she had received a full and frank account of the goings-on in Clerkswell from
her daughter. I held up the flowers as a peace offering.

'Did you get any for Maxine?'

Sadly, Tennille and Maxine don't get on, and it can't be just rivalry because
both of them are good people and good at their jobs.

'No.' Nor would I dare: Tennille will check later. What she won't see is the
half case of Three Choirs Cuvée, a sparkling wine from Gloucestershire that
Maxine and Cleo have already split and hidden away.

'The vase is over there,' she said. 'I won't make you go down and get the
water. Have you got something for me that's not a bribe?'

I carefully placed the flowers in the vase and turned round. 'I emailed my
expenses. You saw me when I was unconscious, so you can't argue about my
claim for a new uniform.'

She frowned. 'Every fibre of my being wants to ask how you are, and say
how sorry I felt for your poor mother on that day. Last night I prayed to Jesus
for charity in my heart, but I am a mother.'

She is. We know this. I kept my peace while she tapped a pen on her desk.

'I can't help it,' she continued. 'My little girl was nearly called before her
time because someone hates you, and because of you, she had to sup with the
devil at your house.' She leaned as far forward as she could get. Tennille and
Maxine have contrasting figures. 'But my Desirée is caught up in this, and so
is her friend. Victoria is a good girl, Mr Clarke. You know that better than

anyone. If my child is put in the line of fire, I want you there to protect her, and to do that you need to get your Firearms Certificate. Hand it over.'

There was a logic in there somewhere. Maternal logic, I suppose. I passed over the paperwork as we turned to listen to new footsteps. 'And here they are,' said Tennille.

Vicky and Desirée appeared from the stairs. Tennille really does have excellent hearing. Vicky gave me a grin; Desi didn't. It was a good job her mother was there.

'Guess what we've been doing,' said Vicky.

'Given the potential situation in Clerkswell, I hope you've booked some indoor net practice.'

'Not until I get the all-clear for me foot. We've been decorating. See?' She showed me some dark spots on her hand. They could be paint, I suppose.

'Decorating?'

'Aye. The Watch Office in Salomon's House.'

The Watch has two rooms in the complete warren that the Invisible College calls its home. One is the Constable's, and is quite grand. The other is a conference room that has the worst case of institutional decay I've seen for a long time. Even the picture of the Queen looks disappointed.

'Project Talpa is going to be based there from next week,' she continued. She also glanced at Tennille's back and said, 'We did have some help.'

Aah. That would be Maxine. Things have clearly got worse recently.

Tennille had got up to put the kettle on, and I went to help, but she waved me away.

'You and Victoria go straight in. My girl can give me a hand.'

Desirée might be Vicky's friend, but she's not in the Watch. Hannah has very clear boundaries about that sort of thing, as Mina has discovered. I knocked and went in.

Hannah has a four-seater coffee table by the window, but today she was at the conference table, papers spread in front of her and two empty mugs already pushed aside. 'Sit down,' she said, pointing to the right side of the table. 'I hear it went well, Conrad.'

'By that, you mean there haven't been any complaints, ma'am?'

She laughed. 'I already knew you could shoot. Now I know you can play nicely with others. Sometimes. Seriously, all okay?'

'I did enjoy using the MP5. Is there any chance…'

'No. I am not giving you a submachinegun.' She got up and moved to the window, stretching her arms massaging her back and staring at Tower Bridge. 'I'm expecting visitors from Salomon's House in a minute. The CobroM committee decided that Project Talpa would be extended to cover the operation to retrieve the Codex and investigate the bombing. They also insisted that it be a truly joint operation with the Invisible College.' She turned round and made a face. 'We'll have to live with it for now. Today is just a briefing for your benefit. As soon as you get your Part Two certificate, I want you round here to collect your ammunition, and then you two are off on the Dwarf hunt.'

'Yes, ma'am. I can't speak for Vicky, but you know my views on that.'

She sighed. 'I know that your priority is to find who was behind the bombing, and I'm not sure I wouldn't feel the same, but you got the Pyromancer. You saved Rick and Myfanwy. The enemy couldn't stop the summoning, and now the cat is out of the bag. We're on to them, and the best route is to follow the Codex.'

'Don't forget those poor lasses,' added Vicky. 'Those catering staff didn't sign up for this.'

'I haven't forgotten them. Trust me, you two. I might even have some news after the briefing.'

Vicky and I exchanged glances. It was good to know we were on the same page, and she gave me a tiny nod. We'd keep our powder dry for now. There was a loud knock, and Tennille opened both doors to usher in three visitors from the Invisible College.

Francesca led the way, accompanied by another senior member of their Inner Council. After dressing down for her visit to the country, Francesca was restored to her twin set and pearls. Now that I know her better, I'm sure that she wears them to upset some of the female Mages at Salomon's House, the ones who hero-worship the woman with her: Heidi Marston, the Custodian of the Great Work and the most senior Artificer in the Invisible College. Desirée is in Heidi's gang; Vicky is not.

Heidi's magickal speciality is creating Artefacts, enchanted items of all descriptions. This can be an intricate process akin to jewellery making, or it can be hammering hot metal in a forge. Heidi is of the hot hammer persuasion. She wears her hair tied back by a leather braid, something that emphasises her strong jaw and full lips. For clothes, she favours ethnic smocks with broad belts, black jeans and boots. Vicky once said to me, 'Somewhere there is a mother who looks at Heidi and thinks, "What happened to my little girl?"'

The first time we'd met, I hadn't registered her spectacular enamel earrings. Vicky tells me that she makes a new pair first thing every Monday morning, just to show that she can.

Burdened with trays of refreshment, Desirée and Tennille brought up the rear. They put down the trays, and Tennille left, closing the doors behind her and leaving her daughter to distribute the cups. I had stood up, and made a point of shaking Heidi's hand, just to show that there were no hard feelings. At that meeting of the Inner Council, she had voted against my registration as a Mage, nearly ending my career in the Watch before it had started.

Her hands were rough, calloused and scarred, but not dry, and her fingernails were painted a luminous pink. 'Nice to meet you again,' she said. 'I can't wait to hear about the Dragonslaying. According to rumour, there were some serious Artefacts in play.'

Her voice was what I'd imagine a soprano sounds like when not singing – high pitched but *big*, and with just a hint of flat vowels. Whatever the reason she'd had for voting against me, it clearly wasn't personal.

Hannah got us to sit down. 'This is only a briefing, not an operational meeting. Vicky, you've got the final word on the original Project Talpa files, I believe?'

'Yes, ma'am, I…'

'Ma'am!' said Heidi with a hoot of laughter. 'Since when did you get them calling you *ma'am*, Hannah? That's a new one.'

Hannah stared at me for a long second, then turned slowly to the Custodian (that's Heidi. Just reminding you of her title). 'It's him,' said Hannah. 'I had to write an order forbidding him from saluting me unless we're in uniform.'

'I'd forgotten that he turned up to Salomon's House in uniform,' said Heidi. 'He does scrub up nicely, and I do love a man in uniform.' She turned to Vicky, sitting almost in her shadow, and said, 'And a girl in uniform, too. Obviously. Sorry, I shouldn't have interrupted. You were about to say something?'

Vicky stared at a blank piece of paper. 'Aye, well, erm, yes. Now that we have Conrad's date of birth as the earliest time for the Codex going into circulation, we have a cut-off point.' She looked up and managed a smile. 'I suppose it fits, you being a Sagittarius. There's nothing since then that we can definitively tie down to Codex material, except Helen of Troy and the Dragon. Of course, there's a good few cases where we've no idea what the magick involved was.'

Hannah looked at Heidi and Francesca. 'We did try to establish some connection – any connection – between Keira Falkner and Adaryn ap Owain, and we got nothing.'

'I'm afraid that I haven't got much to add,' said Francesca. 'Ten days ago, we had no idea that either part of the Codex existed, so we're starting from a long way behind. All the direct records of what was in them have vanished, but there are plenty of references and stories about what the monks and scholars of England were up to in the fourteenth century; the challenge has been in sorting the wheat from the chaff. At least we have a few starting points now. It would be premature of me to say anything else, other than to thank Desirée for her help. The Dean has told her doctoral supervisor that Desirée will be working in the Library for the foreseeable future.'

'Thank you,' said Hannah. 'That brings us to the Dwarf, Niði.' She turned to me. 'Like you, Conrad, the only Dwarf I've met is Hledjolf.'

'And the same for me,' said Francesca. 'Despite my best efforts.'

'Which is why I've asked the Custodian to come. You actually worked with Niði, didn't you, Heidi?'

Heidi nodded. 'A long time ago. I even lived in his Halls for a few weeks. You should get on with him, Conrad.'

'Sorry? Why?'

'Didn't you know? Niði was the Dwarf who put Humpty Dumpty back together.'

I gave her a blank look.

'Niði was the one who re-forged the Allfather's Imprint. He found the shards buried underneath the battlefield. Somewhere in the Midlands.'

'I thought…'

She was ahead of me. 'Hledjolf made a huge fuss about it, but all he did was provide the Lux. Niði did the work, and that was at some point *after* he was seen leaving with the Codex under his arm.'

I recalled a box that Heidi had shared with me at my testing, a beautifully crafted piece of art with a diamond inside it. 'Niði made *The Heart of a Dwarf*, didn't he?'

Heidi nodded. 'He did. It was a gift when I left him. There's no such thing as a typical Dwarf. You won't know this, Conrad, but there are only four in England, and Hledjolf is nothing like the others. When I saw him, Niði was your typical broad-shouldered, bearded blacksmith. He even smoked.'

'Good heavens,' said Francesca. 'What does a silicon based life-form smoke?'

'Something that produces germanium sulphide. You would not believe the smell.'

'I've been to your workshop often enough not to be surprised by any odours, Heidi.'

'Fair point. I don't know that there's a lot to add. I was there over twenty years ago, and Niði hasn't dealt with anyone other than the Gnomes of Earlsbury for at least ten years. I don't think that even Hledjolf is in contact. He's gone very deep.'

'Do you mean that literally?' I asked.

'Both. The further down they dig, the more dangerous it is.'

I could see Vicky going paler and paler, and she doesn't have much colour to start with. Vicky does not like *underground*. She likes Gnomes even less, and I could see where this was heading.

'Thanks,' said Hannah. 'Conrad, Vicky, I'll set up a meeting with the local Watch Captain for Monday … no, that's a bank holiday. For Tuesday the fifth of May. Any questions?'

Vicky clearly wanted to ask *Do I have to?* But she didn't.

The intercom on Hannah's desk buzzed, and Tennille's voice came over the air. 'She's here.'

109

'Send her in,' shouted Hannah. 'I think we're done,' she said to us. 'And Heidi, I have a treat for you.'

Like most female Mages over forty, Heidi doesn't look her age in any way. She must be at least sixty, but only Vicky (who has a magickal gift for this) could tell you how old she really is.

Tennille opened the door and showed in Hannah's twin sister, Inspector Ruth Kaplan. In her police uniform. Hannah, that was very naughty of you. Funny, but very naughty.

'What?' said Ruth, going red as a variety of snorts, humphs and frowns greeted her appearance.

'We'd better be going,' said Francesca. As she stood up, she turned to me and said, 'How's young Mina getting on with Project Midas?' When she heard the sharp intake of breath from Hannah, and saw the cringe on my face, she said, 'Oh dear. Have I said the wrong thing?'

I got the distinct impression that she knew exactly what she was saying. There was going to be an uncomfortable conversation in the very near future.

Ruth stood aside as the Salomon's House group left, then closed the door behind them. 'What?' she said to her sister.

'Nothing,' said Hannah. 'Don't worry. Heidi knows you're a married woman.'

Ruth gave her twin a hard stare, then joined us and took out an opaque plastic wallet. Ruth and Hannah are not identical twins, Ruth being darker and slightly taller. It's hard to make further comparisons, given that Hannah has suffered so much trauma and that I've only met Ruth a couple of times. 'I have some news on the bomber,' said Ruth.

Hannah looked at me. 'See? The old police cliché about *several lines of enquiry* is true in this case. And while I remember, Iain has started to draft that paper for the Occult Council on increasing our access to national data sources.'

Ruth rested her hands on the folder. 'Given that we couldn't get a forensics team down to Clerkswell, you all did a great job with gathering evidence. It's paid off: we have a name for our bomber.' She popped the snaps on the wallet, but left it closed. 'There were no fingerprint matches in the UK, and I had to jump through all sorts of hoops to go international, but we got a hit. Here.' She opened the wallet and took out a passport in the familiar blue and gold of the United States. She slid it across the table to her sister and said, 'Meet Arcangelo Rossini.'

Hannah picked up the passport and opened it to the picture page, turning it so that Vicky and I could see. 'This him?'

'Aye,' said Vicky.

'Yes, ma'am.'

She flicked through the pages. 'Brand new. First time out of the US. How did you get this?'

'Once the fingerprints came through, it was a matter of old-fashioned police work, or picking up the phone as it's now known. He had rented a room at Heathrow, and they kept all his stuff when he didn't turn up to check out.' She took out further papers. 'The one thing we didn't find was a phone, but I have credit card statements, some CCTV sightings around the airport. Not a lot to go on, and the whole identity was created less than a month ago. Before that, no official record of Mr Rossini anywhere.'

Hannah looked the passport again. 'Coneheads or private enterprise?'

Ruth gave a very Jewish shrug, identical to Hannah's when she was relaxed. 'That's your department, though I can tell you that no one has reported Mr Rossini missing.'

Hannah turned to me. 'Before you ask, *Coneheads* is our affectionate nickname for my opposite numbers in the States.'

'Numbers? Plural?'

'I know you love history, Conrad, but now's not the time. I'll just say that the Constable of the Commonwealth of New England – CCONE – is one of many. Too many. And this is a complication I don't need. Ruth, keep at it. See if you can find any evidence of any associates or meetings, but keep it off the system for now.' Ruth nodded and put everything back in the wallet.

Hannah leaned back and stretched again. 'Are we all done? Good. I think it's home time. What are you two up to this weekend? Any trips up north planned?'

Vicky made a face. 'Physio on me foot, tonight, then if you want the Watch room finished for Monday, I'm wielding a paint brush tomorrow.'

I grinned. 'You know I'd help you if I could, but I have to have get fitted for my new uniform and have dinner with my sister.'

'Thanks, Vicky,' said Hannah. 'I won't forget this. I need a word with Conrad.'

Ruth stood up. 'Have a word tonight, Hannah. Conrad, if you're not busy, would you like to join us for Friday night dinner?'

Hannah sat bolt upright and stared at her sister. 'Seriously?'

'Why not? There's going to be a crowd anyway, with Moses' family there.' She turned to me. 'Meet us outside Finchley Reform Synagogue at half past seven when the service finishes. We'll walk back after that, and don't drive. You'll be well over the limit. Probably.'

'I'm honoured,' I said. Well, I wasn't going to say no, was I?

15 — *Family Time*

There was an ulterior motive for asking me. I knew there would be, it was just a question of what it was, whom it concerned and when it would be revealed. If it had anything to do with Hannah then any budding friendship with Ruth would be very, very short-lived.

Apart from one moment in the garden, it was a very enjoyable (if somewhat chaotic) Kaplan family evening, and had nothing to do with magick whatsoever. The ulterior motive was a teenage nephew of Moses Kaplan who was doing an A level history project which required him to garner my first hand experiences of Afghanistan. After twenty minutes, Ruth came along and took me away.

'You're scaring the boy,' she said. 'I could see him going white from across the room. What were you telling him?'

'What it's like in an Afghan family compound. He did ask, and I hadn't got to the bit where the Taliban come calling.'

'Let's give him a break, shall we? You can smoke in the garden.' She handed me another glass of wine and pointed to a bench under an awning.

Hannah joined me five minutes later and we took a moment to enjoy the breeze. When she'd emerged from the synagogue, she'd been wearing her explosive red wig. She'd taken it off when we arrived at Ruth and Moses' very tasteful house, and replaced it with a luxurious Liberty print headscarf, a million miles from the simple prints she wore to work.

She'd spent the whole evening shepherding Ruth's girls, by far the youngest of the whole crowd, and I hadn't seen her for some time.

'I've been playing with the girls upstairs,' she said, staring at where the stars would be if it weren't for the light pollution.

'They're very cute. I can see why you spend time with them.'

'You just wait. You'll see how cute they are. You know the real reason Ruth invited you, don't you?'

'To talk about Daniel's project,' I said.

She waved that away. 'A convenient excuse. Daniel's mother now owes Ruth a favour, but she could have dragged you out here any time for that.'

'Then what?'

'To make Moshe's brother jealous. Or scare him off. One or the other.'

I pondered my next move while she drained half a glass of wine. It was not her first, by any means.

'You haven't narrowed it down,' I said. 'At one point I thought *I* was one of his brothers, there are so many.'

She laughed. 'And they're not all here. His mother won't go to the Reform Synagogue, so the other two are at her place, and two of the guys tonight are brothers in law. I meant the one with the weird daughter who sat as far from you as possible.'

'She's not that weird.'

'Wait till you talk to her. He's divorced. Her dad. Ruth has been trying to match-make for over a year.'

This was very dangerous territory. Hannah finished her wine and bent to pick up my glass. With no apology, she tipped half of it into hers. I grabbed what was left and moved it to the other side.

'You're really happy with Mina, aren't you?' she said.

'So far.'

'I'm glad. What the hell is Project Midas, and why am I hearing about it from Francesca Somerton?'

'If I tell you, will you remember it in the morning?'

'Are you saying I'm drunk, squadron leader?'

'No, ma'am. I wouldn't dare.'

She gave a hollow laugh. 'Will it put her in danger?'

'No. Definitely not.'

'Then we'll forget about it. Does she have a release date?'

'Twenty-second of May. Four weeks today.'

'Good for you. I was going to get our standing orders amended to bar her from applying for the job, you know.'

'And are you still?'

She shook her head. 'Not any more. She can put in her CV for the maternity cover with all the rest. I have too many battles to fight.' She raised her hand to stop me speaking. 'Don't thank me. She'll still be bottom of the pile as far as I'm concerned. Come on, let's go in. I haven't suffered enough today, so there may well be dancing.'

There was dancing. Somewhere, there may even be mobile phone footage of me dancing with several brothers and nephews. Let's hope not. Ruth's daughters also showed their dark side, but I'm sure Ribena will come out at the dry cleaners. The hangover was epic.

I hate to say this, but dinner with my own family was a lot less pleasant than dinner with Hannah's.

My sister lives in a very expensive flat in Mayfair. It's worth more than Elvenham House. 'Where are we going?' I said when she let me in.

She frowned. 'Nowhere. Maybe later. Did you see him?'

'Who?'

'Delivery guy. I thought we'd have Chinese, given that you're no doubt spoilt for Indian now that you've got one of your own.'

That was vicious, below the belt and quite unlike Rachael.

She wandered into the living area. 'Drink?'

I leaned on the wall and folded my arms. 'Not if it's as bitter as the welcome.'

'What did you expect?'

'I expected a nice meal with my sister. I even bought a new shirt.'

She picked up a chunky crystal tumbler full of artisan gin and handmade tonic. If the bottle on the table was new tonight, she would be even drunker than Hannah. I thought young people (she's twenty-seven) didn't drink so much any more.

'And a very nice shirt it is, too. I'm sure your little jailbird will appreciate it,' she said, waving her glass in my general direction. She saw the look on my face, and that fact that I'd stood up and unfolded my arms. 'Joke, Conrad. Joke. I hear she's made quite a stir in the village already, to say nothing of the rest of your little harem.'

'You should be ashamed of yourself, Rachael. Not one man, not Ben Thewlis, not Old Tom, not even the creepy guy from Water Lane has made a single reference to harems. And you're supposed to be a feminist.'

'Says the man who's benefited from male primogeniture all his life, even to owning the family home and stuffing it with other women. For God's sake, Conrad, you've installed some Welsh floozy as your housekeeper. Is she to keep you amused when the other one's locked up?'

'Take that back.'

'What?'

'Myfanwy saved Vicky's life when I couldn't. Take that back.'

'What's going on, Conrad?'

I stood, waiting.

'Okay, okay. I take it back. You do not have a Welsh tart in our family home. I'm sure she's a nice person. Carole thinks so, and Carole thinks your Indian … and Carole thinks that *Mina* is lovely, and as for Vicky, if she didn't have nice parents of her own, Dad would adopt her tomorrow. Regular hero, apparently. What's going on?'

I had absolutely no idea what had brought this on. I was tempted to have a drink, just to numb the pain. The entryphone buzzed loudly into the awkward silence.

'Go and get that, will you? Don't forget to tip him.'

When I got back with two carrier bags full of the Luxury Banquet for Two, Rachael had put some plates and chopsticks on the little table in the corner. Her flat may have two bedrooms, but there's only one other room. She has the smallest kitchen I've ever seen, only slightly larger than the Aga in Elvenham House. The only part that's full-size is the fridge, out of which she took a bottle of craft beer and held it out to me.

'It's not Inkwell Bitter. Would you prefer wine?'

'Beer's fine.'

I spread the containers round the table and found myself a fork. Never could get away with chopsticks.

'How's work?' I asked, to give the wounds a chance to stop bleeding.

'Fine. Good. Very good. That's why I asked you round.'

Rachael is ten years younger than me. She is apparently a legend in the wealth management industry, if you can call looking after very rich people's money an industry. She didn't, however, sound very fine.

'What's the problem?'

'You are.'

'Me?'

'You and your associates. You remember that journalist, Juliet Porterhouse, who was sniffing around. She knows people.'

'I would hope so. Wouldn't be much of a journalist if she didn't.'

'Stop it. I'm trying to be serious. My firm want to second me to the Financial Conduct Authority for six months to help them with a project on … well, you wouldn't understand. Mina would. That's the problem. If I go to the FCA, they have to vet me, my name will crop up in the news feed at the *Sunday Examiner*, and Juliet Porterhouse will be all over it like a rash. She might not be able to print anything about you, but I'm fair game.'

I helped myself to another beer. 'Vicky saw you in that gossip rag, you know. On the arm of the Earl of Morecambe Bay, no less. You weren't so publicity shy then, were you?'

It was a good job Rachael was drunk. It slowed her brain down to something like my speed. I am in awe of her, you know. She may be a brat, but she's an awesome brat. 'What was she doing reading *OK* magazine? I thought you were all above that sort of thing.'

'My vice is smoking; Vicky's is royal gossip. Are you going to eat the rest of those dim sum?'

'Help yourself. You don't get it, do you? If this Porterhouse woman can't write about your black ops, she'll write about me, and about Mina. I can see it now: "FCA adviser's brother lives with money launderer." I can't have that, and the firm desperately want me to do the job, so you can see that I'm between a rock and a hard place. I can't imagine Mina would be very happy either, not if she wants a quiet life.'

Rachael had been rude, aggressive, vicious and just about racist. I still love her though, and yes, I had to sympathise. I leaned back from the table, stuffed. They do a mean takeaway in Mayfair. This might need some thought.

'I can tell you one thing,' I said, making sure to keep a straight face. 'Mina doesn't want to be the black sheep of the family. Brown sheep, yes, but…'

Her eyes flicked round the room as if she were checking for an unseen audience. 'Did you just…?'

I stood up. 'Can I still smoke out of the window?'

'There's a key by the door with a red fob. Go upstairs, as far as you can. That key lets you on to the roof.'

Rachael's flat may be worth more than the family home, but it doesn't have a view. Even the roof looked on to taller roofs around it. I gave her dilemma some thought. I was inching towards a solution when she joined me with two glasses of Burgundy and asked for a cigarette.

'How about this?' I said. 'You've never been big on the family motto, have you?'

'We don't have one.'

'Yes we do. *A Clarke's Word is Binding*. I've never made a promise I haven't kept.'

'That's because you're a lying, shifty sod, Conrad. You just make people believe you've made a promise when you really haven't.'

'Not all the time, and not to people I care about. Remember the May Ball?'

'I remember. I still see him occasionally. In the distance. He avoids me.'

'Good. Let me know if he doesn't. I can't promise anything, Rachael, but I have got a plan. I'm not promising anything because it's not up to me to make the final decision, but I will do my best, and I need a couple of favours from you.'

She glanced at her phone before responding. 'What's your plan and what are the favours? I'm not saying I don't trust you, but I don't.'

'I'll have a word with Security Liaison. They should let me give Ms Porterhouse an off-the-record interview, and then the plan is that I get Mina a job in our place, so that Juliet can't write about her. I do have a Plan B as well, but you don't want to know about that.'

'A job? You want to get an ex-con a job in the security services? Your Plan B had better be good, that's all I can say. What are the favours?'

'You should come down for the bank holiday next weekend. You can meet them all.'

She looked upset. Really upset, as in about to cry. 'Not yet. Too soon. One of them will be in my room, won't they?'

I pointed first to the stairhead and then to just west of due south. 'Your room's down there in your flat, or over there, in Spain. You're scared you'll like them, aren't you?'

She smiled. 'Maybe. It's still too soon, though. Perhaps for Whitsun. What's the other favour?'

'I need you to give someone an interview. For a job.'

She looked genuinely regretful. 'Sorry. We don't advertise, we only headhunt. Except for the admin staff, and they all come from a recruitment agency. We're not a huge company, in terms of staff, you know.'

'It's for a postgrad student. Just six months, minimum wage. It's only eight grand. You could afford to pay him yourself. Say you need an assistant to cover some tasks while you do your secondment.'

'It would cost more than that, but money isn't the problem. What's he like? And why?'

'Can't tell you why. He's sharp, I know that much. Comes from Bordeaux. He's working at Praed's Bank at the moment. He's very keen to work for you.'

She looked at her phone again, unlocking it and staring for a second. She grunted and returned it to her back pocket. 'Tell me the truth. Is this *anything* to do with your job? If I brought a spy into the firm, my career would be ruined. We have a lot of foreign citizens as clients, and we're always tap dancing around the Foreign Office, MI6, HMRC. If I brought a mole into the firm...'

'No. To my knowledge, he is not connected to any British security service. I promise you that.'

'Is he hot?'

'I couldn't possibly comment.'

She pulled her lip, a gesture she has 100% inherited from our mother. 'No guarantees? Just an interview?'

'Just an interview.'

'If you tell me something, it's a deal.'

'What?'

'What happened at the medal ceremony before Easter? It's freaked Mother out. I've never seen her so distracted as when they came that night, but she made me promise I wouldn't ask. Dad was oblivious to everything. Usually it's the other way round.'

'You promised, but you're asking anyway.'

'As you pointed out, I've never been bound by the family motto.'

I moved round to light a cigarette. There was something different about Rachael's eyes... 'Before you came up here, I thought you were clearing up. You've done your makeup.'

'Very observant. I'm going out. You can come if you want. Now, tell me what happened at that place.'

I looked away, trying to make out which buildings I could see in the distance. 'There was an incident,' I said. 'A serious one. Mum saw it, and Dad didn't. She also saw that my new job is more hands-on than she realised.'

'Thanks, Conrad. You know she won't admit it, but she does worry about you. She has, ever since I was old enough to know what *worrying* was.'

'She worries about you, too.'

I don't know whether Rachael heard me, because her phone buzzed, and when she saw the message, she said, 'Come on, I need to get changed.'

Back in her flat, I was sorting through my jacket when someone called the entryphone. 'Let them in, will you?'

I released the street door and took her flat door off the latch. I stood outside her bedroom and said, 'I'll be off. I'll tell Alain to ring your PA, shall I?'

'Alain? Oh, the French guy. Yeah. Whatever. Hang on.'

She came out with a pair of GHDs on a very long lead in one hand. 'Kiss. You'll sort that journalist, won't you?'

I was giving her a peck on the cheek (and trying not to get burnt) when the door opened and two young women came in, both dressed in outfits that cost more than my entire wardrobe.

'Wow, he's *taaaall*,' said the blond one, lifting her sunglasses. 'Where did you get him, Rachael, and why haven't we seen him before. So delish.'

'So old,' said the one with black hair.

'And so related,' said Rachael. 'This is my big brother.'

'Who is just leaving,' I said. 'Thanks, Raitch. Nice to meet you, ladies.'

The one with black hair pointed to her companion. 'She's the Lady, I'm only an Honourable, and Rachael's no lady at all. Ha ha.' The laugh at the end was more like *Fnaa Fnaa* than Ha Ha. As I limped down the stairs, I felt almost sorry for Rachael.

By Sunday afternoon, the only truly happy person in all this was Alain Dupont. He was over the moon.

16 — One of our Own

Part Two of the firearms course was more interesting than Part One, though a lot less fun, and I got to meet instructors other than PS Smith. On Wednesday afternoon, a Commander came down to discuss the finer points of solo work. You have to remember that this is the basic course, designed to make sure that police officers were safe to carry weapons, not an advanced course for decision makers.

We went through Threat Evaluation, where you ask how much of a threat the target poses, and Risk Assessment, where you ask whether someone else might get hurt.

'What about Mission Objectives?' I asked. Entirely innocently, I might add. I thought it was a sensible question.

For some reason, the Commander sucked in his cheeks and PS Smith coughed. 'What "Mission Objectives"?' asked the Commander.

'When you ask yourself, "If I don't shoot, will the bastard get away?" sir.'

The Commander blinked. PS Smith grinned. 'Get many of those missions, do you Clarke? Do tell. I'd love to know.'

Oops. I'd forgotten where I was. 'Sorry, sir. I could have phrased that better.'

After the Commander left, PS Smith said, 'I thought Licence to Kill was just fiction.' He was being serious, and he'd been straight with me. I owed him an answer.

'I've never shot anyone who wasn't trying to kill me, Sergeant, nor will I.'

He grunted. 'Fair answer. Just don't say anything like that in your oral exam on Friday, or you'll be dead in the water.'

'Point taken.'

'Come on, let's get the daily reflection written up, then you can get off to do your downward dogs and tree postures. Is there a pose where the dog pees up the tree?'

'Yes, but that's for the advanced class.'

I'd had to demonstrate touching my toes before PS Smith actually believed I went to yoga classes and not the pub. The daily reflection was a learning journal, completed together and a crucial part of my qualification. We were heading to the break room for coffee when Janet stuck her head into the corridor.

'Visitor for you, Conrad.'

PS Smith visibly bristled, and my antennae were twitching, too, but I let him go first.

'Who is it?' he demanded.

'A visitor for Conrad,' repeated Janet with a very delicate shrug, as if Smithy's question were redundant.

'How did he get in?'

'I let him. He asked what time you were due to finish and left a note. I'll go and get it now I know you're not busy.'

This smacked of magick. Of Glamour at the very least. Before PS Smith could jump in with both feet, I spoke up. 'Janet, could you also bring my case out here? Please?'

'Yes. No problem,' she said, and disappeared.

Smithy turned to me. 'What's this?'

'I don't know. I have my suspicions, but believe me, this is nothing of my doing, or my boss's, or my partner's for that matter.'

Janet came back with my case, which she'd looked after every day since I first arrived. It's a wonderful Dwarven gun case, complete with a protective Work that makes strangers want to look after it for me. Very useful. She also had the message, which I glanced at and shared with Smithy: *Meet me at Shornemead Fort. Four o'clock. 1600 if you like. Mack McKeever.*

'Do you know this clown?' asked Smithy.

'Yes and no. I know who he is, but I've never met him. I was supposed to meet him next week. In Birmingham. He's one of my gang.'

'Is he, now?'

'Yes. I've seen the signs to Shornemead Fort. What is it? Where is it?'

'It's one of the old naval gun posts, in the middle of a bird sanctuary, about a mile and a half along the footpath. Nice day for a walk. And a trap, but I think you've guessed that.'

'Mmm. I'll have to go, though. Shall we get this reflection sorted, Sergeant?'

Smithy grunted and said no more about it.

If this was to be my last day on Earth, there are worse places to finish. The walk from the firearms centre to the fort was bathed in April sunshine, making the emerging spring green look like a leprechaun's playground. A gentle westerly breeze blew away the sounds of shipping on the Thames and let the mating lapwings have the airwaves to themselves. The short path from the road joined up with the Saxon Shore Way, and I got to see why so many people found the Kent estuaries either bleak or beautiful. Or both.

You couldn't miss Shornemead Fort, which was sort of the point. It commanded the Thames in both directions and would have given any invader a torrid time. It was also difficult to miss the man standing on top of the old casemates – the big stone wall with holes for guns. He was the first person I'd seen since leaving the road, and he'd seen me, too.

For a moment, he disappeared from view, and I activated my Ancile. I also looked at the surrounding marshes for flight options. He reappeared at the bottom and gave me a wave.

It meant getting my feet wet, but I cut across a boggy pasture so that I could approach the fort from the open side, near the metalled track that led to the main road. The man waited until I was about 100m away, and opened his coat. From his hip, he drew a substantial dagger, standard issue for Watch Captains. There was a flash of light as the sun caught the blade, and the shadow of a woman holding a sword appeared behind him. Nimue, nymph and patron of the King's Watch, holding Caledfwlch, aka Excalibur. I touched the same mark on the Hammer, and felt the tingle of magick. If this wasn't "Mack" McKeever, Watch Captain of the West Midlands, it was such a powerful Mage that I was doomed, and he wouldn't bother with all this subterfuge: he'd have walked into the firearms centre and blown me to bits. Or done the same when I caught the train.

I lifted my hand in acknowledgement and lengthened my stride. When I got closer, I recognised his face from the noticeboard in Merlyn's Tower. Watch Captains don't usually plan long careers in the service and have moved on by their late twenties. Mack was one of the longest serving, and had the biggest area to cover outside Rick's vast territories in Wessex and Cornwall, so what the hell was he doing stalking me down here?

He spoke first. 'So this is what a Dragonslayer looks like. I can't say that I was expecting someone taller, because that would be blatantly untrue. Thanks for coming.'

His voice gave nothing away, polished and public school. He had sandy hair that was blowing a lot in the breeze, and needed a good cut, as any RAF Sergeant would tell him. He was stocky, wrapped in several layers and had the pale skin that goes with pale hair. Pasty, my mother would call it. He was also a much stronger Mage than I was.

'No problem,' I said, 'though you could have just sent me a text. I'll have some explaining to do tomorrow.'

'Thought I'd pop down and see what the brave new world of the King's Watch is all about. Why have you got two guns, by the way?'

'Well, Captain McKeever, as you no doubt know, one of them is empty. Until I get my enhanced ammunition, the mundane weapon has a place.' I'd done my threat evaluation, and my risk assessment. It was time for a cigarette. When I'd lit one, I said, 'Go on then.'

'Have you ever read *Great Expectations*? The opening was set down here, in the Kent marshes. I've seen all this from the Eurostar, but I never thought I'd actually come here. I wouldn't like to come back in winter, that's for certain.'

'Enough,' I said. 'I've loved the walk and enjoyed listening to the lapwings, so we'll forget about all the rules you've broken so far. Now, before I go and get my train, is there anything you want to say that warrants dragging a senior officer out of his way, because a discussion of Charles Dickens won't do.'

'You're not a senior officer, but I won't argue the point. I hear you're interested in the Dwarf Niði.'

'I am, and the proper time to have this conversation is when my partner is with me. Saves me having to repeat myself and besides, she's much cleverer than me.'

'So I hear. You know that you need to start with the Gnomes?'

'Yes.'

'You'll find Clan Flint between Earlsbury and Dudley on an industrial park. Their cover name is Sparkshave Engineering and Metalwork. They even have a website, so finding them shouldn't be a problem. You have dealt with Gnomes before, I take it?'

I'd had enough of this, and I went in hard, with the tone I used to use on newbie pilot officers who hadn't checked the weather forecast from two different sources. 'What are you doing here, captain? I could have found this out from asking Maxine.'

He flinched, and when he did, he gave himself away with a glance down to the grass.

The spot he looked at was just to my left and on the margin of the path. With any other enemy, I'd have backed away. With Mages, it pays me to get up close and personal. Safer that way. I took two steps closer and barked, 'McKeever! What's going on?'

'I quit!' he shouted, not aiming at me but at that point on the grass. He took a step to his right, away from me but circling the mystery location. There was something there, hidden by magick, but I didn't have the time or talent to investigate. I manoeuvred him off the path and into the bog.

'I resign my commission!' he said. 'Please. Let me draw my Badge and hand it over.'

If I'd had any ammunition, I would have arrested him. More for his safety than anything, because the bloke was clearly scared of something, and that something wasn't me. 'Fingertips of your left hand. Slowly.'

He pulled back his coat and gingerly extracted the dagger. Runic inscriptions flowed along the blade, and the Mark of Caledfwlch glowed on the hilt. I've got one of those. It only glows when I really think about it. He must have a *lot* of Lux.

He held the dagger carefully away from his body as he sank to his knees. What's this all about? I took another step towards him.

His knees splashed in the bog, and he moved with lightning speed to grab the dagger with both hands. I started to dash towards him, drawing a knife of my own. It's the only thing that works inside the circle of an Ancile, but my knife came from a survival shop; his came from the Dwarves.

Before I could close on him, he plunged the dagger blade first into the small pool in front of him. 'From water you came, to water return. So mote it be.' He garbled out the words before I could get to him, and something made me drop down, turning away. Good job I did.

TENFOLD

There was no bang, but there was a great explosion of light and Lux in equal measure and someone left the area. A tiny portion of Nimue had been in that mark, as there must be in mine, and she was gone, returned to the water.

All my nerve endings were tingling and my left leg was burning as I rolled on to my back to see what was going on. McKeever had already moved away from the dagger, and was groping towards that spot of grass. The blast of magick had stripped away the Glamour, and I could see a mobile phone sitting there. We must have had an audience for our conversation.

McKeever hadn't got to his feet yet, which gave me just enough of an edge. I dug in and set off like a sprinter out of the blocks, hoping my bad leg wouldn't give way. It didn't, and I dived to reach the phone before Mack got there. That left me with the phone, and him close enough to grab my leg and give me a huge electric shock.

Aaaaaaargh … Aaaaargh …

Everything was locked. Every muscle had seized in a spasm. Every tingling nerve was now screaming in protest, but my left leg was screaming loudest of all, and I used every ounce of willpower to move my right arm to grab it. When I moved one muscle, the others unlocked with a jump and started shaking. I grabbed my shin and some of the pain seemed to leach up into my arm, enough to balance things and give me a sliver of attention to devote to something other than pain.

The water rushing through my ears drained away and I heard a car engine scream from down the access road as it sped away. I forced myself to come up on all fours, but I couldn't balance because my left hand was a fist, and inside the fist was McKeever's mobile phone, now bent into an alarming shape. There were a few angry cuts on my fingers, as if McKeever had tried to peel them back while I was out of it, and dug his nails in during the failed attempt. Serves him right. He shouldn't have given me such a big shock.

I looked up towards the path and saw a pair of black combat boots.

'How is Inspector Rothman?' said Smithy.

'It's Dame Colonel Rothman, now, and she's in rude health. Emphasis on the rude. Are you going to help me up?'

'Not yet. Try sitting for a while, until the shaking stops. I'll get some water.'

That was excellent advice, and I crawled to a dry patch, where I sat with my head between my knees until I heard Smithy's footsteps crunching down the path. I took a deep breath and sat up. He sat next to me and passed me a bottle of water.

'I never had you down for the King's Watch,' said Smithy.

'What did you have me down for? And is your name really PS Smith?'

123

He sounded indignant. 'Leave it out. 'Course it is. I'd say *call me Smithy*, but you already have. I saw you write it in one of your notes to Janet. I never thought of the King's Watch. I had you down as a cleaner for MI5. Lots of plausible deniability.'

I tipped the water bottle to him. 'Cheers. How did you come across the Watch?'

He stared at the top of the casemates, remembering. 'I worked in the same nick as Hannah when she was an Inspector. She was good. Could have gone all the way to the top if she'd played her cards right. Then she ups and leaves. Wouldn't say where she was going, so we all knew she must be joining the cloak and dagger brigade. Even her husband got transferred to another station and promoted to DI.'

'You knew him?'

'Yeah. Sergeant Mikhail Rothman. We used to call him Mothman. Handy in a fight, and sharp as a tack. Transferred to CID when Hannah got Inspector. He even told us why – no one would compare their careers. Detective Sergeant is a good rank to stick at.'

He went quiet, and I gave him some space. I checked my pulse, and it had come down to less than one hundred, so I lit a cigarette.

'Next time I saw Hannah, I was first on the scene. I went with her in the ambulance. I even took some bits of her skull with me, to see if they could put them back together. Is she really still at work? The last time I saw her, she was only just conscious. I insisted on breaking the news about Mothman. I can't believe she's back at work after that.'

'Very much so. She's … you can see the damage. Some of it. Best CO I've ever served under.'

'Good for her.'

'You don't have to answer this, Smithy, but what happened? She won't talk about it.'

He gave me a sardonic smile. They teach that on sergeant courses. 'Something unbelievable, I know that much. Something that no one ever explained to me, because I didn't want to know. Do you want to know what little I saw?'

'Please.'

'When Mothman left Southwark, he moved to the Fraud Squad at West End Central. I moved to Counter Terrorism. One night we got a shout for something serious at an address in Mayfair.'

'Mayfair?'

'Upper Brook Street. Do you know it?'

'No. My sister lives a bit further north. Sorry. Carry on.'

'We were on our way back to HQ, and the control room said there was an officer in danger. We got there in less than a minute. There were already flames coming out the top of the building and the first floor windows had been blown out. Glass everywhere.'

'You went in, of course.'

'Of course. You would, too.' I nodded. 'It was weird. Big front door standing ajar, so I shouted a warning and kicked it fully open. Instead of a huge hallway, there was just a little box with a black curtain, half torn down. Behind it was another door. I shouts another warning and kicks that one down, too.' He paused to take in some water. 'Other side of that door was Hell. With a capital "H".'

'The building had been hollowed out, and the inside was all one space, and it was on fire. Bodies everywhere. Inspector Rothman was … on the floor. I won't describe it. She deserves some dignity. I thought she was dead at first, and I scanned round for any threat or any survivors. I saw her husband in the corner. Well, I saw his head. On a spike. Then this woman, stark naked, comes out of the fire. Carrying a sword.'

Smithy was on the edge. This story was taking him to a place he hadn't been for a long time.

'Do you know why I'm telling you this?' he asked. 'Because I'd forgotten all about the inside of that house until I saw her again, the sword-woman, that is. Here. When you marched up to that guy, I saw her, standing over him. Just for a second. Then I saw her again, when he did the thing with the knife in the ground. I may never forgive you for making me remember that.'

I had stopped shaking from the human taser, and was now shaking from the cold. The breeze was definitely picking up. I stood up, to see how I felt. Just about okay. 'Sorry,' I said. 'I know someone who might be able to take it away again, but I think if Nimue wanted you to remember, she must have a reason.'

'Nah,' he replied, still seated. 'I'll live with it. Nimue, you say? Well, she takes this sword and lays it next to Inspector Rothman. I can't remember the next bit, but she says, "Help her." And then I realised I was on my own. I dropped my MP5, picked up the Inspector and took her outside. My whole team, and the paramedics, were getting back in their vans, and there's these three blokes standing there, two of them holding daggers like that one in the ground. One IC1, old, one IC3, young, and one IC5 juvenile. "Who are you lot?" I says, and they say they're the King's Watch.'

IC1, IC3, IC5. If you don't speak police, that's one white male, one black and one Chinese. I'm guessing Rick and Li Cheng for two of them, and Hannah's predecessor as Constable for the old white guy.

Smithy continued. 'I screamed at the paramedics, put the Inspector down and ran back in. The fire had well got hold by now, no one else was moving, and all I could do was pick up my weapon. And what was left of the Inspector's skull.'

I held out my hand and helped him to his feet. 'And this is the first time you've remembered what happened inside?'

'Swear to god, Conrad. When I gave evidence at the inquest, I had to make it up because I couldn't remember. And the only person who'd been found inside was Mikhail Rothman. No trace of the other bodies, and cause of fire, unknown. Death by misadventure. They found some references to the address in his notes on a fraud case, but that's it. Are you gonna leave that knife in the grass?'

'What dagger?' I said. It seems that Nimue had taken more than just the badge of office, and McKeever's Artefact had disappeared completely.

Smithy stared at the shallow pool and grunted, then started walking down the road. It was getting later, and dog walkers were starting to appear. I fell in step and we arrived at a car park. The four other cars had all given the marked police vehicle a wide berth. Smithy looked around and opened the boot of the patrol car.

'There's another reason I'm telling you this,' he said, and showed me a sniper's rifle in the boot. 'I came out of curiosity, Conrad, and because I was worried about you. I had you under obs, all the time, but when that bloke legged it back here, I wasn't going to tackle him on my own. You going to meet him unarmed was either brave or reckless.'

My two guns are protected by Dwarven magick. When they're in their holsters, only strong Mages can see them. 'Who says I was unarmed?' I said. 'Outgunned, clearly, but not unarmed.'

'Figures. That's why I let him go past me. I've got him on film, though, and the index of his car. Give me your private email address and I'll wing it over.'

I passed him a card, and he shut the boot. 'You're not catching the train. I'm going to take you to Tesco, and then the Premier Inn, and I'm going to put a constable with you tonight, not because they'll stop any of this nonsense, but because you might go into shock or cardiac arrest. All right?'

'Thank you, sergeant.'

'Good. But first we're going back to base. There's a doctor on the way to check your heart, and I imagine you'll want to call someone.'

When we got back to base, I passed him a Merlyn's Tower Irregulars badge. 'What's this?'

'You've got my mobile. If anything happens, and you can't get hold of me, call the number on the back of that badge. Merlyn's Tower is a real place, as it happens. It's where Nimue lives.'

He put the badge carefully in a pocket. 'Thanks, but tell her not to invite me for tea, will you?'

TENFOLD

17 — 'War by other Means'

Of course I wanted to call someone. I called Hannah on her personal mobile from the privacy of the firearms centre medical room as soon as the doctor and his portable ECG machine had given me the all-clear.

In all the jokes I'd made about the firearms course to Hannah, I hadn't mentioned Smithy by name, and I didn't do so now. One day, we'll talk about the Revenant of Upper Brook Street, but not today. There was no swearing in Yiddish when I told her about McKeever.

'Why?' she said when I'd finished.

'Blackmail. Threats to his family, if he has one.'

'He's engaged to a Mage from America. They met when he went to some function at Salomon's House last year. Why do you say that? Why don't you think he's part of this group?'

'He didn't want to kill me.'

'Are you sure?'

'He wanted someone on the other end of that phone to hear him serving up that rubbish about the Gnomes, then he was going to resign, duty done. He knows more. A lot more, but he'll be at Heathrow, I reckon. Unless you want to put a stop on his flight and get down there yourself, we'll have to let him go. For now.'

She managed a laugh. 'I am not sending you to the States to follow him. We don't have the budget for that, but we do have Li Cheng. I'll send him down to the Premier Inn to pick up that phone. Does it still work?'

'Don't know, ma'am. Thought it best to isolate it.'

'Good. And you're sure this police officer saw nothing?'

'He saw me get into a fight. I told him that McKeever had tasered me.'

'Then I'll let you get some rest. Are you going to be able to finish the course?'

'Yes. I am not going to be without ammunition again. What are you going to say about McKeever?'

'This is Project Talpa restricted. What happened to him was because of the Codex, and we'll keep it to ourselves. I'll just put out a statement that he brought forward his resignation suddenly for personal reasons.' She laughed. 'And I'll tell Tennille to hold all outstanding money until he comes in for an exit interview.'

'No cloud without a silver lining, ma'am.'

'Take care, Conrad. See you Friday.'

Because of staying at the Premier Inn, I didn't get to read Mina's letter until Thursday afternoon. I'll give you an extract:

127

Bolton is a very strange place. I thought places like that only existed on television. It's very Northern, isn't it? Have you been? You seem to have been everywhere. Maybe you have. It took a while to work out why they were staring at me. The men were looking at my head, and I thought it was my jaw. Then I heard comments. In Urdu. I think they were saying something about my not dressing modestly. Whatever. The reason they were staring was that I couldn't find the temple. Francesca didn't give me an address, just directions. To an empty street. It's a good job that Kelly waited in the car, because I'd have been stuck there.

Kelly took me to her mother's house, you know. That was very strange, too. We Googled the regular temples, and Kelly took me to one after lunch. I made Puja and then I spoke to the priest, and showed him the directions from Francesca. He took my number and said that someone would get back to me. To say thank you to Kelly, I insisted on babysitting on Saturday night so that she and Joe could go out. I have not slept on a camp bed since my cousin's wedding in India. When I was nine years old.

They did get back to me in the end. I shall tell you all about it at the weekend. My train gets into Cheltenham at four o'clock, and I shall get a taxi. I can't wait…

At one o'clock on Friday afternoon, I handed my Part Two certificate to Tennille and was shown into Hannah's office, where Vicky was already ensconced at the coffee table. She'd finally been cleared to drive, and in a first for our partnership, she was driving her own car down to Clerkswell this afternoon with me as a passenger.

'Congratulations,' said Hannah. 'I believe that these are yours.' She held out a box with thirty-two 9mm enhanced magickal rounds.

I took them, opened my gun case and began to stow them away. 'I don't think I'll need them on the way home. Thank you, ma'am.'

'You do realise that you've just started an arms race, don't you? As soon as word gets around, Mages will be trying to improve their Anciles.'

'That thought had crossed my mind, ma'am. A teacher once told me that there would always be someone taller, stronger, faster and smarter than me just round the corner. It stops me getting above myself.'

'Could've fooled me,' said Vicky.

'I'm still alive, aren't I?'

'Sit down,' said Hannah. 'I'll let Vicky fill you in on the details of the Project Talpa Steering Committee later. That was before your encounter with Mack, of course.'

'There was nowt,' said Vicky. 'Now you know.'

Hannah gave her a stare. 'I was going to say that the structural issues were more important than the content.'

'I don't believe you, ma'am. Structure has never been interesting.'

'What if I told you that Salomon's House will be represented by five Mages? The Keeper and Desirée, yes, but also the Chaplain, the Provost and the Custodian.'

I made a face.

Vicky saw me and said, 'That's what I thought, too. Not exactly friends of the Watch, are they?'

'What about Cora?'

'Poor woman,' said Hannah. 'She overdid it and pulled out two of the internal stitches. Had to have emergency surgery.'

'Ouch. I know how she feels. When I was convalescing with my leg, I overdid it and got sepsis. It was touch and go for a while. Mina believes that Ganesh saved me.'

'I won't try to top that,' said Hannah. 'Let's just all count ourselves lucky to be alive, shall we? And give thanks at dinner tonight, wherever that may be and whoever may be with you.'

She straightened her headscarf, and I couldn't help thinking about what Smithy had said. *His head. On a spike.* Had Hannah seen that before she was attacked? What was the real extent of her injuries, and how much of a role had Nimue played in her survival?

She caught me staring at her. 'What? Isn't it straight?'

'Erm. Sorry. I was admiring your earrings.'

'If you say so. Now. About McKeever.' She picked up a piece of paper. 'That was a burner phone you brought in. Cheng got it working, so it's gone to Ruth for her to pursue it through police channels. Nothing's come up yet. What I can tell you is that Mack, and his fiancée, flew out of Heathrow on Wednesday evening. Not only that, but there was no activity on her phone for 72 hours beforehand. Completely dark until three hours before the flight. That supports your theory that Mack was coerced, Conrad.'

'Mmm. Sorry to be ignorant, ma'am, but how do Watch Captains with territories work? Do they have a base? Will there be records up in the Midlands?'

'They're supposed to file everything with Maxine, and only keep rough notes at home. I've checked the file on Clan Flint – bland to the point of innocuous. He was a bit preoccupied recently, but Mack was a good officer before that. All of this leaves us back at base camp with a big mountain in front of us. Or a big hole, as we're dealing with Dwarves.'

'I'll stick with mountains, thanks,' said Vicky. 'Until I have to think about holes, I'd rather not, if it's all the same, ma'am.'

Hannah turned round her empty coffee cup. 'Don't take this the wrong way, Conrad, but I've been talking to Iain, as he's part of the Talpa team, and he's got a lot of experience.'

'Good,' I said. Iain Drummond does have a lot of experience. His field experience might be decades ago (I checked), but he has his finger on the pulse.

'When we go to Clan Flint, I'm going to lead,' said Hannah. 'There's too much at stake. And I'm going to try something risky – a writ of Habeas

Corpus. Gnomes don't like lawyers, or the courts, and it will make them show their hand. They may be innocent, complicit or guilty. Who knows. Iain and I will go to the Cloister Court on Tuesday morning, and I'll travel up with the writ after that. Can you pick me up from Birmingham?'

'Of course.'

'Well, have a nice weekend, both of you.'

We stood up. 'Give my love to Ruth,' I said, 'and give her this.' I passed over a dry-cleaning receipt.

'You can't give her that!' said Hannah. 'It was an accident.'

I turned to Vicky. 'No it wasn't. It was a deliberate act of criminal damage. By a four-year old, yes, but definitely deliberate.'

'Even so,' said Hannah.

I blinked at her. 'You know why I'm sending it. You were there.'

'Yes. Ruth made you promise to give me the bill to pass on.' She checked it. 'You've paid it, haven't you? Good. Well, I didn't promise anything, so consider your promise fulfilled.'

She screwed the paper into a ball and dropped it in the bin as we left.

Vicky waited all of five minutes to get down to the important stuff: what was Ruth's house like, and did Hannah really get drunk. I lied. A bit. I did give her the gist of our chat in the garden though, and of my campaign to get Mina rehabilitated, which led to Rachael and my problems with my sister's reputation. Vicky was sympathetic, of course, but she didn't have much to say until I told her about the two Chelsea girls who'd turned up.

'How do you know how much their outfits cost?' was her considered, incisive question. 'They might have been from Primark for all you know about fashion. Don't forget, you're the man who wears cords to go to the pub.'

'As I was leaving, I heard Rachael say, "My God, JJ, is that the new Versace?" so I think I'm covered on the cost front.'

'Aye. Fair enough. You reckon Rachael can afford that lifestyle, so what's the problem?'

'She wasn't born to it.'

It was a good job we were stuck in traffic, because Vicky forgot she was driving and turned right round. 'Hey! What do you mean *born to it*? I suppose I was born to work in Tesco's because me dad was a lorry driver, was I? And should I tug me forelock to you as well as saluting? Never heard such rubbish from you before, and that's saying something.'

I held my hands up. 'Sorry. How about this: all wealth tends to corrupt, and enormous wealth…'

'Now you sound like a vicar, and I don't see you selling all you have to give to the poor.'

'It was her sunglasses. JJ was wearing shades well after dark, and I saw why when she went to give Rachael a kiss. She'd had a *lot* of coke before she came out. The Dispatchers in Helmand sometimes took it when they had to work a twenty-four hour turn.'

The driver behind us blared his horn to tell Vicky that we were finally going to get on to the Hammersmith Flyover. 'Wind your neck in,' she muttered, then nearly crashed into the vehicle in front by sending a massive power surge through the transmission. 'I'm still getting used to this car, as you may have noticed.'

It was a bright red Audi Quattro TT convertible, seized from one of the Dragon brigade. I said nothing, and let her get the measure of the Friday afternoon traffic. When we'd reached a cruising speed of twenty miles an hour, she said, 'What about you? Did you ever need stimulation? You said you'd been a consumer…'

'Just cannabis. The Afghans used to grow it in their compounds to sell on the base.'

'And it's very commendable of you, Conrad, to resist temptation. You can be very strong-willed, so why can't your sister? Who's to say she'll join in?'

'Point taken. Let's focus on the weekend.'

'You do realise that I haven't played cricket since I was eight, and that was on the beach. I'm not sure I'm going to be much use to Clerkswell Ladies. Is it Ladies or Women?'

'According to Myvvy, they decided that *Ladies* was more euphonious. *Clerkswell Ladies* rolls off the tongue better than *Clerkswell Women*. You're going to be there to support Mina, who's going to be there to support Myfanwy, but that's on Sunday. You'll see a proper game tomorrow.'

'I can't believe that Myfanwy – and Mina – have agreed to help with the teas. That's so … patriarchal. Sorry. I know you love the game, but getting the women to do the tea. Come on.'

'It's so last century, is what you really mean. It varies, but clubs rarely do the actual prep themselves. There's a healthy competition in the local outside caterers to supply them, and all the non-players do is put out the tables and fill the teapots.'

'So who pays for all that?'

'The players, with our match fees. And general fundraising.'

'Fair enough. You said that Rachael mentioned Carole Thewlis. Did she mention Isaac Fisher? I'm not happy that a Mage would avoid the Watch like that. Even those who aren't in our fan club usually say hello.'

'Sorry. Rachael has never met him. Honestly. And there wasn't an opening last Saturday to bring him up. Maybe next time.'

We got a shock when we arrived at Elvenham. Well, I did. Vicky and I got out of her car and both saluted the dragon, then something very strange happened: the front doors opened. That usually only happens for weddings and funerals. I thought one of them was rusted shut.

Mina, in full sari, stepped out and made namaste. 'Welcome home,' she said.

I heard Vicky mutter something, and I was stumped. What's this all about? I bowed in return, and Mina lifted her skirts to walk down the three steps. I went up to her and she broke into a big grin, holding out her arms.

'What was that all about?' I whispered into her hair as we embraced.

'I wanted to practise being lady of the manor,' she giggled, 'welcoming home her lord, or other VIPs. Myvvy got the builder to re-hang the doors for me. And fix the bell.'

The doors are very big, taking up most of the tower front, and Vicky had given us a wide berth to go inside. I gave Mina an extra squeeze and a big kiss. 'How did it feel, *Ōha mahāna rājakumārī?*'

'You've been at Google again, haven't you?'

'Yes, Oh Great Princess.'

I took her hand, and we walked inside. Wow. How much was Myfanwy paying these new cleaners, and could I afford it?

'It looks lovely, Myfanwy,' I said. 'Thank you.'

Vicky and Myvvy were standing at the side of the hall. 'Apparently the sad singletons are going to the Inkwell,' said Vicky, 'so that youse two can have a date-night. Don't overdo it, mind, you've got a match to play tomorrow.'

'Aah. About that,' said Myfanwy as we drifted through to the kitchen. 'Ben gave me a message.'

'Oh, aye,' said Vicky. 'And when was that? Been on a date yet?'

Myfanwy waved her hands in embarrassment, and I took a good look at her. The tunic dress she'd bought in the Undercroft was already loose on her. Either there was magick involved, or Slimming World should be prescribed on the National Health, a point I made to Mina later. She told me it *is* available on the NHS, and that several of her larger fellow prisoners were looking forward to starting on it. Oh well.

'It's complicated,' said Myfanwy. 'Ben's asked me twice to go to Cheltenham with him. I reckon that he thinks it's too public in the Inkwell and it would be too creepy to ask me round to his place on a first date. I don't know what to do.'

'Bring him here next week,' said Mina.

'Maybe,' said Myfanwy. 'Anyway, the message. He says you'll understand, but he's got two leg spinners and only room for one in the team. The other guy has been to every practice, and you haven't. He says he wants you both in the nets at eleven o'clock tomorrow.'

Vicky was going to make a joke about that cramping my style. I'm sure she was, until she saw Mina's face.

'Who is it?'

'Stephen Bloxham. His wife is coming to the first meeting of Clerkswell Ladies on Sunday.'

Vicky didn't notice my lack of response, and said, 'I thought you'd had the first meeting, hence the name.'

'I set up a Facebook Group to start with, and we voted. First IRL meeting on Sunday. Here.'

'Myfanwy,' I said, cutting across them. 'Who suggested meeting here? Juliet Bloxham, maybe? You do know that their house is the biggest house in Clerkswell.'

'Bigger than this?' said Mina.

'By far,' said Myvvy. 'The old manor house on the Winchombe Road. Yes, it was Jules who suggested meeting here. "More central," she said.'

'Can you do me a favour? If you show them round – and this is your home, so that's up to you – Jules Bloxham might ask about the safe. Tell her the key has been lost for years, and no one knows for certain what's in it.'

'But I know what's in the safe. You showed me. And where the key is.'

James Clarke, builder of Elvenham House, was a lawyer. He had a big safe built in so that he could work from home occasionally.

'Just trust me on this one, and I'll move the key. Then you won't know where it is. Makes lying easier.'

'Are you … Never mind. You know these people.'

'And you'll get to know them. I'll explain soon. Promise.'

'Right you are. More tea?'

Mina got changed and came down in something more comfortable. While the sad singletons got ready to go out, we curled up on the sofa, and I filled her in on McKeever and the Gnomes, then she told me about the temple in Bolton.

'It was the same priest,' she said. 'Mundane? Is that the word?' I nodded. 'The same priest officiates at the mundane and magickal temples, and he has no magick himself. He said so when he gave me a lift. His wife is the Mage, and she put up Wards around the building, not that I could tell. I'd stood outside it, feeling a fool on Saturday. On Sunday, we went round the back. Very rich inside. A lot of gold, and a lot of very angry people.'

'Are you okay? What happened?'

'The third degree is what happened. I had a cover story ready, like Francesca suggested. I told them that I had seen magick in a road traffic accident, that I had saved the life of a Witch by doing first aid and calling 999. I said that I had been invited to the lakeside ceremony. That lasted less than five minutes. One of the men must be like Vicky. A Sorcerer. "She has been touched by Ganesh," he announced. "A Nāgin has a lien on her fate." It's a good job I know what a lien is or I'd have panicked.'

I've got a lien, too, on the cricket ground. It means having an interest on property until a debt or obligation is discharged.

'Then things got really bad,' said Mina, squeezing my hand. 'The Sorcerer pipes up, "I smell Nimue. You are an agent of the King's Watch!" and he points his finger at me.'

'Ouch, love.'

'Very much so. I saw hands reaching for daggers, until the priest stepped in. "Tell us the truth, child, before Ganesh." And I had to kneel before the altar and tell them about you. It was very dusty, and tucked in a corner. I had to tell them about us. Not much, just who you are and that we are … an item. I didn't use that word, though, Conrad. Nor did I say "partner". I said that our souls were bound together. I hope you don't mind.'

I kissed the top of her head. 'You told the truth. Why should I mind?'

'Good. After that, the priest shouted at them. In Bengali. He took me to his private room and said, "Ganesh sees all, Mina. You should make puja in the mundane temple until he calls you to his secret gatherings. For today, you are welcome, though." Then his wife and I made puja to Ganesh while they got ready a sacrifice to Shiva. The altar to Ganesh was only there because it would be rude not to have altars to Shiva's wife and children. Shiva is their god. When we had finished, the priest's wife dropped me at Lostock station, and I caught a replacement bus to Preston. I tell you, Conrad, the trains up there are terrible.'

'So was the welcome at the temple. Do you want me to look into this?'

'No. You have enough problems. Perhaps one day.'

Myfanwy knocked on the sitting room door and stuck her head in. 'We're off. Have fun.'

We did. I don't know what time they got back, because we were asleep by then.

'I don't want to do this, Stephen, but you can see the problem,' said Ben. It very much looked as if Stephen Bloxham *couldn't* see the problem. In his head, he'd been to practice, he was the current chairman of the club and he deserved to play.

Now that I've had Spectre Thomas's testimony, I know that the Clarkes really are the oldest family in the village, but we've never been the richest. For a long time, that honour fell to the family of the knight who got all the land when Winchcombe Abbey was dissolved. His descendants built the Big House, Clerkswell Manor, and quietly got on with the job of being rich and oppressing the peasants for generations. Until World War One. That did for three of them, and the widow sold up. Four families have lived there since, and the Bloxhams for nearly thirty years. Stephen's father was a builder, though Stephen prefers to call himself a *property developer*. I know, I know. Stop being such a snob, Conrad. I could almost hear Vicky getting on her high horse when I thought it.

'Does that sound fair enough?' said Ben, desperate to get Stephen's buy-in for the eliminator.

'When did you last play?' asked Bloxham.

'In Afghanistan, before my injury.'

Bloxham looked at Ben, as if to say *Give him a game some other time. Like when I'm at my villa in Greece.* Credit to Ben: he stood his ground.

'Look, Stephen, I can't bat against you because everyone knows that Conrad is my mate.' This was code for *We're proper locals.* The implication was not lost on Bloxham. Ben continued, 'You choose one of the team to face two overs from each of you. If it's too close to call, you play today. Fair enough?'

Bloxham held up his hands. 'Fine. Let's get it over with.'

Half the team was here for morning nets. The other half was at Tesco's, delivering children to parties or at work. Bloxham looked around, and suddenly we were on our own. The others had seen what was going on and made themselves scarce, leaving only one: Ross Miller, teenage fast bowling prodigy. He was watching from a distance, already padded up. Bloxham frowned, looked around, and turned to Ben. 'It'll have to be Ross,' he said.

Ben called Ross over and said, 'Give it your best shot, to both of them. You could do with the practice against spin bowling anyway.'

'Yes, skip,' he said and went to collect his bat and helmet. I took a few moments to stretch my back and legs while Ben got some wicket keeping gloves.

'Heads Conrad goes first, tails it's Stephen,' said Ben, tossing a coin. It came up heads. I took the ball off him and measured out my run up.

For the first over, Ross played a very straight bat. I appealed for LBW on one ball and Ben said, 'You'd have been given out for that, Ross.' On the last ball, Ross cut my delivery sharply to leg. 'Runs there,' said Ben.

Ross played much the same during Bloxham's first over, trying to get his eye in. Bloxham didn't get a wicket.

The home of Clerkswell CC is known as Mrs Clarke's Folly, and it was very good to be back here, in the spring sunshine. You really could forget that somewhere underground in the Black Country was a Dwarf who had had dealings with my 11xGreat Grandfather, and who was part of a magickal situation that had already cost … how many lives? More than a dozen, if you included the Dragon, and a lot more that we don't know about yet.

It was my turn again. Ross opened up his bat and tried to score some runs. Exactly what a batsman would do at the end of a game when time was running out. I clean bowled him once, had one go to slip and probably a couple of fours conceded. Not bad, but Ross is not a specialist batsman. Then it was Bloxham's turn.

Not only did he fail to get through Ross's defence, he was hit all over the net. Ross was vicious. Bloxham didn't wait for Ben's verdict, he just headed for the changing rooms.

'What was that all about?' I asked, when Ross had gone.

'You won't know, will you?'

'Know what?'

'The reason Ross's dad left was that he caught his wife with Stephen Bloxham. To be fair to Stephen, that was before he married Juliet. I try to keep Ross and Stephen apart at practice, and Jules tries to keep Stephen on a short leash. Well done, Conrad. See you at the game.'

18 — *Gnome is where the Hearth is*

We won the match. Just. I played my part, but I wasn't man of the match by any means. That would be Ross Miller. On Sunday, Myfanwy, Mina and Vicky hosted the Clerkswell Ladies, and I did the shopping.

While I was gone, the Ladies elected Juliet Bloxham as their Chair, and she did indeed ask Myfanwy about the safe. When Myvvy asked me why, I changed the subject.

The rest of the long weekend shot by in a flurry of plans for the garden, eating, drinking and an away cricket match on Monday. We lost that one. 'Stephen can bat much better than you,' said Ben ruefully.

'I'll be at work next weekend,' I said, diplomatically.

After the away match, Myfanwy invited Ben round to Elvenham for a drink during the week. I know this because she said to us, 'I give up. I can't go out of the village, he won't go to the Inkwell and he said he'd feel funny coming here, what with it being Conrad's house and all that.'

'Get him to give you a one-to-one coaching session,' said Mina, stirring something aromatic. 'That way you can get hands-on in the nets. Does this need more wine?'

I didn't mean it to happen. Honestly. I had it all worked out: Mina would catch the 12:15 to Cairndale, and we'd park up for an hour until Hannah's train arrived at 13:00. Vicky drove the Volvo so that I could help Mina with her case and kiss her goodbye. If there wasn't a free drop off place, Vicky could dump us and circulate.

There was a space, and Mina and I were saying goodbye when she pushed me away and stepped to the side. 'Namaste, Constable.'

Oh dear.

'Ms Desai,' said Hannah. 'Sorry to interrupt, but I got the early train. I was going to call, then I recognised your car. I didn't realise that you had company, Conrad. I'll get in with Vicky. Have a safe journey, Ms Desai.'

'That is without doubt the most awkward moment of this year,' said Mina. 'Why doesn't her sister tell her that she looks like a clown with that wig, and even I think it's too hot for boots. She has strong eyes, though. I will miss you, Conrad. Just twenty days.'

'We should go away. Anywhere you like.'

'You mean anywhere that I'm allowed to travel by the probation service. No, that would be good, and try not to get killed before then.'

Hannah was discussing routes to Earlsbury when I got into the car. According to Vicky, her only comment about Mina had been, 'She's a lot smaller than I thought.'

I'd never been to Earlsbury before. None of us had. I went to Birmingham fairly often before I joined the RAF, but my knowledge of the Black Country is very limited. It even feels strange to call it that, but the locals are insistent. If you can understand them.

The RAF is drawn from all over the UK, and you have to get used to hearing twenty different accents before breakfast. Without doubt, the two most impenetrable are rural Northern Ireland and the Black Country. Earlsbury isn't as big as its northern neighbour, Dudley, but it does have its own centre, as we saw when we drove up the high street and past a quaint little Saxon church that wouldn't have been out of place in the Cotswolds. It looked rather forlorn on top of the hill.

Sparkshave Engineering and Metalwork has the biggest premises on the King's Common business park, and unless there was more magick in Earlsbury than London, most of the space must be devoted to mundane operations.

'Do they know we're coming?' I asked.

'No. I've got a list of the directors, and Mack's notes did say that the clan chief is Wesley Flint. He's the Exec Chairman of Sparkshave Holdings.'

We were parked down the road from the squat grey buildings, and a heavy lorry rumbled past full of scrap metal. It headed on to the site and disappeared round the back.

'Not here,' I said. 'Gnomes like to keep their businesses at arm's length. Are any other companies listed?'

Hannah flicked through some papers. 'Sparkshave Developments. Sparkshave Services. They're both registered at an address back in Earlsbury town. Flint House.'

'I'd start there. I'm sure there's any number of the clan out here, but not the chief.'

'Good point,' said Vicky.

'Fine. Take us to it.'

There was no market on today, and plenty of spaces in the high street. When I saw the old coaching inn, I remembered that Earlsbury had featured heavily in one part of the Operation Jigsaw story. I might have to get in touch with Detective Chief Inspector Morton if we were here much longer, though I doubted that even Tom would have come off best against a clan of Gnomes.

'Down here,' said Vicky.

Hannah looked like she always does, but Vicky had dressed down, sporting a pair of walking trousers, trainers and a baggy top. Gnomes are *almost* human, but not quite. And they're nearly all male. Very male. On our first encounter, she'd dressed differently. Taking one for team, she'd called it. If a woman had eyed me up the way she'd been surveyed by Henry Octavius, I'd be in therapy. They're not all like that. Well, they are, but the younger ones hide it better.

It started out looking like a normal narrow street between Poundland and a charity shop, both occupying converted original buildings. By the time we'd got past their delivery doors, the road had narrowed to about an inch wider than the average van. One side was a featureless wall; the other was an elaborate monstrosity in smoke-begrimed red brick and limestone that had been subject to years of acid rain. There may have been carvings, once. If you'd asked me to define it, I'd say the building was the bastard child of a Lancashire cotton mill and the Old Curiosity Shop. Dickens would have loved it.

The alley curved slightly to allow the building to have railings and a drop down to the basement area. Up the stairs, the door was imposing, black, and had a bronze boss in the centre, featuring a grimacing gargoyle. I was getting the impression that the Flints were a very traditional clan. To the right of the door was the only polished object in sight: a brass plate with just two words: Flint House. Underneath was a wooden board with the names of the registered companies, so faded that they might as well be anonymous.

Vicky pointed to the wooden board. 'Haven't seen that in a while.'

'You're right,' said Hannah.

'And you've lost me,' I added.

'See that company?' said Vicky. 'Sparkshave 1926? While you were getting bowled out for a duck yesterday, I was keeping my eye on the ball and doing my homework. That company was only incorporated a year ago. They've used a Work to deliberately age the board, make sure the place looks abandoned.'

'I was unsighted. A plastic bag blew in front of the sight screen.'

'Well done,' said Hannah. 'And there's no doorbell or knocker, either.'

'Not even a keyhole,' said Vicky.

'We don't have one,' I said. 'The front doors at Elvenham don't have a lock. Why have a lock when the servants can unbolt it from the inside?'

'Is he like this at home?' said Hannah.

'Only when he doesn't get his own way. Most of the time he's quite normal. You should have heard the row when Myfanwy wanted Radio 1 on.'

'And are we going to stand here all morning?' I said.

Hannah looked at Vicky. 'Is my hair straight?' Vicky nodded, and Hannah said to me, 'Use your Badge of Office. Strike the door boss three times. Lightly.'

Vicky's Badge is stamped on to a golden pickaxe round her neck. It's purely ornamental. Hannah's Badge is Caledfwlch itself, and only comes out of the Tower on special occasions. It's not easy to carry on the train, either.

I took the Hammer out of its holster, ejected the clip and cleared the chamber. You don't use a loaded gun as a doorknocker, no matter how gentle you are. I tapped three times. Slowly.

'In the name of the King, open!' said Hannah in her best beat bobby voice.

I reloaded while we waited.

Hannah didn't jump. Vicky didn't jump. I did.

'Who's there?' said a voice from under our feet. I peered over the railings and saw a Gnome staring up at me from a hidden doorway.

'The Peculier Constable,' said Hannah, gathering her skirt to stop him looking up. I'm not saying he would, but…

His black eyebrows shot up and he emerged from the doorway to stand back at a more respectful angle. 'Constable! Welcome. Do you want to come down? It's a lot quicker.'

'We go through the front door,' said Hannah. 'As it is commanded. Sorry and all that.'

'Won't be a tick,' said the Gnome, his Black Country accent coming out. He disappeared and we went back to waiting. It took a lot longer than a tick. It took nearly two minutes, and it was getting cold out there. I doubt they get sunshine even in July.

There was a crack as paint ripped, a groan as timbers shifted and a whoosh as the great door was pulled back. The Gnome from downstairs had been joined by an older relative to help him get a grip, and we waited until it was fully open before following the Constable over the threshold.

'Welcome, Constable,' said the older Gnome. 'I am second in Clan Flint. To what do we owe the honour?'

'Thank you for your welcome,' said Hannah, leaving a slight pause before she continued. 'I require an interview with your chief.'

The subtleties of this were beyond me, but I know a power play when I see one. Of course the chief of Clan Flint would see the Constable, but she was *requiring* it. She must know what she's doing.

'As you say,' said the older Gnome. 'Please, follow me.'

The hallway behind the never-used door was a beautiful example of high Victorian decoration: chessboard black and white tiles, Lincrusta panels under the dado rail and a gloomy flowered wallpaper above it. There was even a green baize door at the back, standing ajar. Half way down each wall were oversized doors that looked as little used as the one we'd just come through. The only furniture was a pair of scroll backed chairs close to the front door. Thirty years ago, my father would have given his eye teeth for those. Was the whole above-ground portion of the building just a shell?

We got our answer when the clan second led us through the servants' door and into a brightly lit, modern corridor, running parallel to the alley. He hurried us past an office with windows on to the corridor, an office with modern desks, computers and a mixture of staff. I say mixture, because you can spot a Gnome from a long way away. They are all short. The human men and women were all taller.

Past the office, the corridor opened out into the hallway I'd expected: airy, open plan and relaxed. It also had the biggest thing missing from the false hall: a staircase. I didn't want to be rude, so I didn't try examining for magick, but I couldn't work this place out. Had it been built as a shell originally, or converted into one? I didn't get time to inspect the plasterwork, because we were off up the stairs.

The first floor accommodation was much more Gnomely. The large landing had a Barbie clone at a reception desk, guarding three highly decorated pairs of doors behind her.

'Louis XVI,' I whispered, pointing to the doors while the clan second spoke to Barbie.

'You what?' said Vicky.

'Downstairs was all Victorian, and this is all pre-Revolutionary France. Weird.'

'Knowing the difference is weird.'

'Shh,' said Hannah.

'One moment,' said the Gnome. I reckoned that Hannah would give him twenty seconds.

He disappeared through the central doors and I started counting. I'd got to fifteen when he reappeared, opening both doors to let us into an antechamber. That's the only way to describe it. Louis XVI himself would have been proud of it.

There was a generous skylight, but no windows to break the white panels round the room. Barbie's older sister was sitting in a corner, behind a tiny desk that had only a telephone and a stack of papers on it. If she got bored, she could always look at herself in the mirrors or recline on one of the chaises longues. Behind her was a badly concealed hidden door, and if I know Gnomes, her real workplace would be through there, as would be the kitchen.

The matching doors opposite us were already open, so Hannah strode straight through into the clan chief's lair, and we were back in the land of Dickens.

If the building were as old as it pretended, then this room was original, right down to the small fire burning in a large hearth to our left. Was that …? Yes. They were using sulphur coal, illegal in a smokeless zone. A pair of two-seater couches sat perpendicular to the fire, and were an island of calm and good taste. From there on out, chaos slowly took over, reaching its zenith at a metalworker's bench against the right hand wall.

Nuggets of gold were interspersed with crucibles, half-finished spring-driven contraptions and several black glass bottles. I could feel the heat from the coal fire on one side and the deeper warmth of magick radiating from the bench. Everything looked yellow, and that was either a side-effect of the magick or the consequence of lighting your room with gas lamps. Yes, really. Hissing gas lamps. You can take authenticity too far.

An array of straight-backed chairs clustered around a coffee table in front of the monumental desk opposite the doors, and here was the clan chief, standing in front of his paper-strewn desk and smoothing down his suit jacket. No, it wasn't a suit, because the pinstriped trousers didn't match the long, almost frock coat in plain black. A black waistcoat was stretched over his paunch, and a gold watch chain led to a fob pocket. And then I noticed the most unexpected thing of all. A woman.

An Asian, perhaps Iranian, woman in loose black trousers and a plain white shirt stood up from a chair at the desk's side and took up a position to the Gnome's left. She was the oldest female I've seen in the company of Gnomes, with lines on her forehead and grey in her hair. And gold bracelets covered with runes. Aah. A Mage.

The clan second had been standing by the doors. When we were inside, he announced, 'The Peculier Constable, Watch Captain Clarke and Watch Officer Robson, sir.' And before you ask, no, we hadn't given him our names. He left and closed the doors behind him.

Wesley Flint bowed. 'I am the chief of Clan Flint and you are welcome in our hall. Would you accept our hospitality? It would be an honour.'

I did wonder. As a rule, you should *always* accept hospitality in the world of magick. Even from the Fae. Especially from them. It means you're less likely to be eaten yourself, though it does change your status from *visitor* to *guest*, which means that you can't attack your host either.

Hannah gave the slightest of bows in return. 'And I am honoured by the offer, but we have matters to discuss.'

Wesley pointed to the chairs. 'Will you at least sit down? It must have been a long journey from North London.'

Vicky didn't get it, I don't think, but in my opinion, the clan chief had just made an anti-Semitic jibe at our Jewish leader.

'In a moment, perhaps,' said Hannah. She turned to the woman and had a dig of her own. 'Do you work here, or are you family?'

'This is Irina,' said the Gnome. 'Counsel to Clan Flint.'

The two women acknowledged each other, and Hannah turned back to the chief. On the way up the stairs, she'd been rummaging in her battered leather tote bag and had found some paperwork. She held it up for everyone to see and said, 'I got this in the Cloister Court this morning. It's a writ for you to appear before the London Stone.'

'On what matter?' said Irina, with enough challenge in her voice to let everyone know that she was there with a job to do.

'I'd rather not serve it,' said Hannah. 'Budget cuts, and all that. Just tell us what's happened to the Dwarf, Niði and how much you were paying my Watch Captain to turn a blind eye.'

'Are you accusing the Clan of bribery?' said Irina.

'You tell me,' said Hannah, still addressing the chief.

Gnomes may all be short, but they do have broad shoulders. Literally and metaphorically. Wesley Flint's were particularly impressive, and they needed his paunch to balance his shape – without it, he'd look like an inverted pyramid. Above the shoulders, his neck barely rose above his collar before it merged into his head. His black hair was all brushed back, and was gathered into a loose bunch. I hesitate to use the word *ponytail*; think *Viking braid* instead. There were deep lines all over his face, and a red patch along his jaw that looked like a burn trying to heal.

'Sit down, Constable,' said the Gnome, 'and I shall tell you of the Dwarf. Please.' He echoed his words with an outstretched arm.

Hannah took a chair with arms and made herself comfortable, crossing her legs and straightening her skirt. I waited until the chief and his counsel were sitting opposite Hannah, and took a chair with its back to the window for myself. Vicky sat next to the boss.

Hannah put the writ in front of her on the coffee table and said, 'Go on.'

Wesley glanced at Irina, who nodded. He began his story, and I finally figured out what was going on with his accent. Yes, there was a hint of the Black Country to it, but if we weren't sitting in Earlsbury, I'd have said that he was the child of a German father and a Welsh mother. Perhaps he was.

'I have known the Dwarf all my life,' he said. 'I first went to his halls before I could walk, carried on my father's shoulders. What has happened to him is none of our doing, and I would swear that on the London Stone.'

In other words, everything he said from now on would fail the *truth, whole truth and nothing but* test.

'Niði has his Hall to the north of here. The old entrance was through Dudley Castle, but that's history. For generations, the way to Niði's Hall was by boat.'

'Boat?' said Hannah. I had an idea where this was going.

'Along the Dudley Canal, where it goes underground. One of the canal's branches leads towards the Wren's Nest, and we provided the boats. Amongst other things. That's how he got round, too. After all, there are more miles of canal in Birmingham than Venice.'

Hannah was getting impatient.

Wesley held up his hand. 'The canal is important, Constable. Bear with me. It was closed for a while, and Niði lived elsewhere. It was not long – not long in our terms – after the canal re-opened that he dug a new Hall. A deeper Hall. And then, one day, my father's boat disappeared. If nothing else, his death should be in your records.'

Hannah took out her phone, and was surprised when she looked at the screen. I wasn't. Why have gas lamps in your lair? And an oil lamp on your desk? Because there is no electricity. Her phone was dead. She gave the Gnome a hard stare. 'What's this?'

'Don't worry,' said Irina. 'It will power up when you get outside. If the device was vulnerable, we would have warned you.'

Hannah stuffed her phone back in her bag and took out a crushed, folded and stained set of printouts. Tennille would be appalled to see what had happened to her work. Hannah flicked through the pages. Then back. Then forwards. Her eyebrows rose and fell. 'Thirty years ago,' she said, then read out, '"Wesley Flint is acclaimed chief of Clan Flint on the death of his father. Circumstances unknown."' She refolded the papers and replaced them in her bag. 'Sorry for your loss, Chief Wesley.'

'Thank you. My brother and I took arms and went to see what had happened as soon as our father's boat was missed. You'll see yourself what I mean, because I know you'll go down there.' He glanced across the three of us. 'Perhaps not the Constable, but one of you.' Vicky's nose was flaring. She was trying to control her breathing. Wesley continued, 'There is a branch off the canal, just inside the Wren's Nest Tunnel. Heavily concealed and dislocated, with a gate, too. The gate was open when we arrived. We drew our boat down the tunnel, as slowly as we could, fearing a rock fall, until we smelled the smoke.'

Vicky couldn't help herself. 'Fire? Underground?'

'Mmm,' said Wesley. 'The Dudley Tunnel complex has quite a few sections that are open to the sky. Niði's dock is one – the sides of the opening are too high and too steep to get down, unless you abseil. Because of the opening, most of the smoke went straight up. My father's boat was half under water, still tied to the dock. The doors to Niði's Hall were standing open, and the two humans who'd been with the chief were lying dead on the landing stage, smashed against the wall and half-burnt.'

'You went down,' said Hannah.

'We did. We got as far as the upper Hall, where there had been a battle. Our father was there.' He had placed his hands on his knees when he started to speak. The only part of Wesley that moved, besides his mouth, was his knuckles as he made his hands into fists. 'I'm telling you this because you need to know. He had been slashed open. There was more fire, more destruction. And the sounds. We feel them, you know.'

'I know,' said Hannah. She turned to me. 'Gnomes can touch the rock and hear for a long distance. What did you hear, Chief Wesley?'

'We heard two heartbeats. The Dwarf's and another. Something I've never heard before. The Dwarf's was fainter, deeper in the rock. We left before the other thing came looking for us. Every year I go back, and every year I hear them still: two heartbeats, one above the other.'

The chief fell silent, his hands still clenched into fists, his eyes now on the past. By his side, Irina watched his face closely. It wasn't quite *concern* in her expression, more *observation*.

Hannah gave him a moment to gather himself, and began her questions. As PS Smith noted, she is a very good copper. 'And you have no idea what this entity in the tunnels might be?'

'No. The Dwarf's presence is so strong down there that we couldn't use any magick to work it out. Your guess is as good as ours.'

'Forgive me, Chief Wesley, why have you not reported this? Would that have anything to do with the fact that you've been taking commissions on behalf of Niði for three decades?'

'Read the small print,' said Irina. 'It says, *The commission will be completed to Dwarven standards by Niði or other Artificers.* Chief Wesley has fulfilled most of them himself. The most difficult ones were completed by Haugstari and other Dwarves.'

I couldn't resist it. 'And how does Clan Skelwith feel about you doing business on their patch?'

'What's it to you?' said Irina. 'Are you going to tell them about it? Over a glass of Nimue's water perhaps?'

I made a doodle in my notepad, as if I were writing things down. It was full of doodles. 'It might come up in conversation,' I said with a smile.

Irina rocked back, just a fraction. So, they don't know everything about us. Reassuring. By the way, I am not in a hurry to go back to the Lakeland Particular. Unless that's where Mina wants to go for our first holiday.

The chief raised a hand to still Irina. 'That's over now. May I ask why the King's Watch is interested in Niði?'

Hannah ignored him. 'This arrangement has benefited the Clan greatly. You could argue that it's all worked out very well for you.'

Wesley blinked at Hannah. 'The same could be said for the death of your husband. It's worked out nicely for you, Constable. I lost my father; the Clan lost its chief.'

That must have hurt Hannah. She licked her finger and wiped something off her skirt, and when she looked up, her face was just a fraction less animated. 'Watch Captain McKeever. His reports into Clan Flint are borderline fraud, and he ran away rather than answer questions. Why would that be?'

'I wouldn't know,' said the chief. 'Perhaps you were working him too hard, and he'd had enough.'

'His area was huge,' added Irina. 'I'm sure he did his best in the circumstances.' She turned her left hand over in a sort of Persian Shrug. 'He may have guessed that we were selling on behalf of a Dwarf who couldn't fulfil the bargains, and he may have turned a blind eye.'

Unless she served the writ, Hannah wasn't going to get any more out of them, and she knew it. 'Very good. Are there other entrances to Niði's Hall?'

'The Castle entrance is sealed. There is an entrance from the Wren's Nest, but that is blocked. We will provide a boat and escort to the dock, should you wish. If Niði made an entrance to his lower Hall, we know nothing of it. Perhaps now you could tell me why the Constable has come all this way to investigate a Dwarf?'

We'd planned this. There was only one way to conceal the truth: hide it behind an enormous lie. Hannah looked at me.

I showed my troth ring, a gift from the Allfather. 'Odin has brought it to our attention. I'm sure you know about his link to the Dwarf.'

Irina's head jerked to look at Wesley. 'Him? He is behind this?'

Hannah took up the reins. 'Once we knew of a potential issue threatening the King's Peace, of course we were interested.'

Wesley looked dubious. Irina flat out didn't believe a word. I wonder why? Whatever the reason, they weren't going to argue about it.

Hannah looked at Vicky and me. 'Anything else?'

Vicky shook her head, but I coughed and said, 'One thing, ma'am.' I turned to the Gnome. 'How bad is inflation round here? I'm talking the value of Alchemical Gold: have your prices had to go up?'

The Gnome sat up straight, and Irina stepped in. 'Why do you want to know that?'

I kept my eyes on Wesley Flint. 'Have they?'

'You know they have. You wouldn't be asking otherwise,' said the Gnome. 'We have had real problems, as have others. Is the Watch interested in this?'

'There may be a crime here,' I said, 'and we are looking into it. If Clans Skelwith, Octavius and Farchnadd all agree, would you supply anonymised data? Salomon's House and Hledjolf are already on board with this.'

Irina pursed her lips. 'I don't think…'

'Yes,' said the chief. 'Ask my nephew, Lloyd. He's the clan second, and he's the one who will sort out access to Niði's Hall. Unless the Constable *requires* another interview, of course.'

Hannah was on her feet. She picked up the writ from the coffee table and handed it to me. 'Burn that, Conrad, would you? Chief Wesley, thank you for your co-operation. We will be in touch.'

She and Vicky shook hands with our hosts while I crossed to the open fire. Could I feel Irina's gaze on my back? I placed the writ carefully in the flames and got a powerful whiff of magick. They weren't just burning sulphur coal for nostalgia – it was doing something, and that something was up the chimney, somewhere, because the magick wasn't flowing into the room until I disturbed the coals.

Chief Wesley rang a big bell on his desk, and the doors opened as I shook his hand, 'Good luck,' he said.

'I hate it when people say that, sir. Makes me think they know something I don't, and they usually do.'

Wesley laughed, for the first time, and said, 'Then I withdraw it. Go well, Conrad.'

Irina's fingers barely touched mine, and her bracelets were glowing as if they'd cut off the supply of blood and Lux to her hands. They subsided when I stepped back.

146

19 — Train-ing

Back in the antechamber, the clan second was passing out and receiving business cards. 'Would you like to leave by the car park entrance? If you come back, it's easier to get in that way.'

Hannah nodded, and when we'd returned to the ground floor, he showed us through to the general reception area, at the back of the building. After more handshakes, we found ourselves in a small car park behind Earlsbury's high street. As one, we turned round to see what was going on.

The back of Flint House was really the front. A modern concrete building had been somehow welded to the Victorian Gothic nightmare we'd gone through. Hannah looked at Vicky. 'Why did you take us round the other side?'

'No idea, ma'am. This side didn't seem to be Flint House at all.'

'Look. Up there,' I said, pointing to the roof. 'See that smoke? I think there's something very weird going on with the fire in the clan chief's room. Don't ask me why.'

'Bloody Gnomes. Hate them,' said Hannah. 'Let's get off their land.'

Hannah and Vicky walked across the car park, but I couldn't resist turning back for a last look at the grimy slate roof of the old building and the yellow tinged smoke drifting out of the chimney. I left Flint House with two lasting impressions – that they were hiding something important in plain sight, and that we weren't finished here.

Once off the premises, Hannah saw another alley, away at an angle, and quick-marched down it until we were out of sight of the Gnomes.

'Conrad, turn round and watch the road. I need to get this thing off my head before I kill one of you for no reason and regret it later.' I did as she bid, and there was a much happier looking Constable when I turned back. Today's headscarf was a bold imperial purple.

'Lunch,' said Hannah. 'I'm starving. Let's try the George. Seems okay.'

We wandered in and found a corner. I got in the drinks and menus. 'What are you having?' said Hannah.

Vicky and I looked at each other. 'Beef!' we chorused.

'That bad?' said Hannah.

'Forbidden beef is always juicier,' I replied. 'Excuse me first, I'm going for a smoke.'

You wouldn't describe the George as a gastropub, but those burgers were just what Vicky and I needed. You can guess what Hannah ordered, I'm sure, and she finished well before us.

'This is going to take a while to sort out,' she said. 'I'm not sending you down a canal tunnel, even with your ammunition, until I've done a lot more thinking and talking and planning.'

That was a relief. Vicky looked undecided: if she had to go there, she might rather do it today and get it over with, even if that meant certain death. She really doesn't like underground things. I mumbled my support with a mouth full of beef.

Hannah checked her notes. 'There's the obvious questions, such as whether anyone else has heard anything and what might be down the tunnels. I also want to know about that woman. Those bracelets hid her magick like wearing a full face veil. I couldn't get any sort of a clue as to what manner of Mage she was. Did you get anything, Vicky?'

'Sorry, Boss. I reckon I could decode her imprint, but I'd need Conrad to hold her down first.'

'Thank you for that image. So, this business with magickal price inflation. That wouldn't be Project Midas, would it?'

I wiped my hands. 'Yes, ma'am. If the Gnomes cough up some data, my outside consultant should have something to report in a couple of weeks.'

She looked ticked off. 'You can use her name, you know. Will she really have something to say, or is it all just a gesture?'

'I honestly don't know. She's doing it for nothing, so it won't be coming off your budget.'

'Hmmph.' She looked at Vicky, who was wiping a chip round her plate as if we weren't there. 'You're keeping out of this, aren't you?'

'Out of what, ma'am?' said Vicky, as if she had a full pat of unmelted butter in her mouth.

'Fair enough. While we gather intelligence on Nið-i's Halls, there's a lot else on my plate, including the whole of the West Midlands now that Mack's no longer with us, and I've been thinking.' She saw the look on my face and pointed her soup spoon at me. 'Don't say a word.' She put the spoon down. 'I want you two to cover as Watch Captain for the region, until we can make more progress. It's the only option that doesn't risk a real crisis. I hate to say this, but neither of you could do it on your own. Yet. Together, you'll do a great job. I can't force you, Vicky, but he'll be living at home, and would you mind lodging in his guest wing for a bit?'

'It's not that big,' I shot back. 'But yes, there is room for Vicky, on one condition: you pay her an overnight allowance and a contribution to the running costs.'

Vicky is very short of money. A lot of what she earns goes to pay her grandmother's nursing home bills. She looked both embarrassed and grateful.

'Of course,' said Hannah. 'Seems fair. Why are you standing up for Vicky's welfare, Conrad? You're up to something, I just want to know what.'

'That's easy,' I said. 'The Clerkswell Ladies need her, and she needs intensive work in the nets.'

'He's got you playing cricket? How? Why?'

'To be fair,' said Vicky, 'it's Myfanwy who's got me roped in. I did suggest a women's football team, but that went down like the proverbial.'

Hannah looked at her watch and her phone. 'Let's check out the Dudley Canal. You can drop me at somewhere called Coseley. There's trains from there to Birmingham every half an hour.'

The Dudley Canal is now a tourist attraction, attached to the Black Country Living Museum, through which we walked to get there, just like a weird family on a day out. I don't know what Hannah did at the ticket office, but she came back with passes and I saw no money change hands.

We did look round a bit, and Vicky said that it was clearly modelled on Beamish in County Durham, where she spent a lot of time when she was a kid. 'Beamish is better, of course,' she added. 'At least you can understand the guides. What did he say back there?'

Vicky averted her gaze when we walked past the guided tour of the coal mine, as did Hannah when we came across a man selling pork scratchings from a tray.

The big thing with trips through the Dudley canal tunnel is that there is no towpath and no ventilation, so diesel engines are banned. If you want to get through, it's electric or lying on your back and "legging" it along the tunnels with your boots on the side walls.

'Not me,' said Vicky. 'Too weak.'

'Me neither,' said Hannah. 'Dodgy knee.

'Titanium tibia,' I added. 'We'll have to get some Gnomes.'

The one piece of useful information we got was that the Wren's Nest tunnel had been closed for decades.

'Take me to Coseley,' said Hannah. 'That's not a sentence I ever thought I'd utter. I'll get Maxine to forward you all of Mack's current caseload and give you access to his files.'

It's funny, you know. Since joining the King's Watch, I've tackled Spirits, a Dragon, a mad Lakeland revenger, and I've been nearly blown up. None of those things is part of a Watch Captain's normal duties, as I found out over the next two weeks. It was challenging, yes, and the visit to the Foresters of Arden was a real eye-opener: for one thing, I got to know my friend Chris Kelly's mother. I learnt a lot, too, but those stories are best told by Vicky. After all, she did most of the magickal heavy lifting.

A lot else happened during those two weeks, if you add it all together. Myfanwy worked in the garden, and spent at least two nights at Ben's cottage. She looked a lot happier. At one point, I had to make a difficult phone call to Rachael, informing her that her childhood pride and joy, the tennis court, was going to disappear in Myfanwy's plans for the landscaping. She took it better than I thought she would, and said that she'd been impressed when she met

Alain Dupont for lunch, impressed enough to arrange for a formal interview by the HR team at her firm.

I even got Vicky out of the house occasionally to go for a walk and get some exercise. I know. Wonders will never cease.

Mina returned for the first weekend. The Clerkswell Ladies had gone from strength to strength, at least in terms of numbers. A couple of students away from home had promised to join in at the end of term, and on the Saturday, they had a dozen volunteers ready for their first coaching session, led by Ben and ably assisted by Yours Truly.

'I thought you were at work,' said Ben as we surveyed the assortment of spare junior equipment we'd cobbled together.

'So did I. We've been reassigned for a bit. Stephen deserves a game. He is the Chairman.'

'Thanks, Conrad. And thanks for bringing Myfanwy here.' He concentrated on examining the helmets and didn't look up. 'She's from your world, isn't she? Cloak and dagger brigade?' I said nothing. 'I know I'm a bloke, but I'm not stupid. Do you know something: Old Mrs Evans and Mr Jones have been out of the village more often than she has. Two of her best friends are the DPD courier and the Tesco home delivery guy.'

'I can't speak for her, Ben. I can vouch for her, but I can't speak for her.'

He put down the helmet as we heard voices outside the pavilion. 'Fair enough,' he said. 'But the big question is, can she bat?'

'Let's find out.'

I have coached women before. In the RAF. The proper coach was much better than me, and she was a woman. Then she got posted, and I stepped in for a month. Do you want my considered opinion on the difference between male and female sportspeople? No? Well, you're getting it anyway. Take two groups of inexperienced players, one male and one female, a bit like the group waiting for us outside. In my experience, the women will form a team bond much, much more quickly than the men.

I knew most of the women by name or by sight, and it was nice to see that Myfanwy had made friends who weren't delivery drivers. Ben took the net for batting, and I handled the bowlers. Fast bowlers can be angry people, and Emily Ventress lived up to the legend.

She was good. Unfortunately, she was the only one who'd actually been taught how to bowl properly, and she had a real tendency to no-ball. Also, she was shy and reluctant to try coaching the older women on her own. In Ben's net, things were going much better, and yes, Myfanwy could bat.

I was having a smoke and wondering how to move on from absolute zero when Mina came over.

'Your knees will be killing you, keeping wicket all the time,' she said to me. 'Let me have a go.'

Ben had been rotating his group behind the stumps as they finished batting, but I'd done it all myself for convenience and to get a good look at the bowlers' line and length. Mina had already found a pair of gloves small enough, and I wasn't going to say no. It was only when I'd been relieved of my duties that I started to notice things other than how bad the bowlers were. There were fingers being pointed at the back of my net. At Mina.

One of Myfanwy's new friends is Rosie, bar manager at the Inkwell and local legend for joining in everything that happens in the village. She's also the Slimming World consultant, which is how she'd got talking to Myvvy. I took a second to ask Ben how Rosie was doing with the bat.

'Too slow,' said Ben. 'Shame, 'cos she's keen enough.'

'Can I borrow her to try out for bowling?'

He gave me a strange look. 'Of course, mate. All yours.'

I'm afraid she was no good at bowling, either, but I did get her on her own. 'What are they saying about Mina?'

Rosie is the nosiest person in Clerkswell, and that's saying something. 'It's just gossip,' she said. Oh dear.

'Spill, Rosie. Don't make me put you in to bat against Emily Ventress.'

'I'm sure it's not true.'

'I mean it. She's just getting warmed up now.'

'Mina was in the shop last weekend, and she dropped her credit card. Someone picked it up and looked at her surname. They reckon she murdered someone, and that's she's in prison and that's why she keeps disappearing.'

'That someone wouldn't be Juliet Bloxham, would it?'

Rosie shook her head and handed me the ball. 'I'd better go. My shift starts in half an hour and I need to get changed.'

'Thanks, Rosie.'

'What for? I didn't say nothing. See you later.'

I tossed the ball in the air and went to see Ben. 'Can we swap for five minutes. I think Mina's got the makings of a good keeper, but I'm biased. I want you to check her out and I'll put some spin down for your batters.'

'Good idea.'

After a couple of overs, it was Juliet Bloxham's turn. As she came past me, I stopped her, pointed to the ball and stepped into her personal space, as if demonstrating something. 'It's all true, you know, except that it was self-defence, not murder. Big difference.'

Juliet took a step back. 'An unarmed man against a gun? I wouldn't call that self-defence.'

I took a step closer. 'Well, I'd start doing so, if I were you, and I'd start doing it now, before it's too late.' I stepped back and let her make her way to the crease.

'What was that all about?' said Myfanwy, who'd been watching closely.

'The truth is out there. About Mina.'

151

'No! What can we do?'

'Stick by her. Talk to Rosie and put her straight. She's come through worse.'

'She has. Did you just go easy on Jules when you bowled at her?'

'Yes. I'm giving her a chance to put things right.'

I needn't have bothered. At the game that afternoon, Stephen Bloxham came up to me while he was waiting to bat.

'Do that a lot, do you? Intimidate women? Jules was *that* close to reporting you to the committee after this morning.'

'Yes,' I said. That threw him.

'Yes, what?'

'Intimidate women. If I need to. Especially when they want to kill me. You should remember something, Stephen: Clerkswell Manor may be made of stone, but it's very much a glass house.'

'What do you mean?'

'That you should both think twice before making accusations. Leave Mina to make her own way.'

'Maybe we'll start a youth team,' said Bloxham. 'Then everyone will have to do a criminal records check. I wonder who'd fail?'

'Go and calm down or you won't concentrate when you're batting.'

'As if you care.'

'I do. I'm a team player. If you get fifty, I'll be at the front of the queue to buy you a drink.'

Clerkswell – or Clerkswell Men, as I'll no doubt have to call them in future – did scrape a win, because Ben hung on like a solo yachtsman in a gale. The Ladies' practice this morning must have sharpened his edge, and my money was safe in my pocket because Stephen Bloxham was out for a duck, lashing at a full toss and missing completely. Ben hit the winning runs in the next over and allowed Myfanwy to give him a kiss when he carried his bat off the pitch.

I was under no illusions about the Bloxhams. They were not going to warm to Mina, and Juliet would definitely continue her campaign, if she thought it would hurt me. On the other hand, they were both practical people. Nasty, but practical. If the village embraced Mina Desai, the Bloxhams would join in enthusiastically.

Later, in the Inkwell, Ben took me to one side. 'About the Ladies,' he said. 'I've got two groups, I think. One needs polishing, because they've got the basics, and the other group will need a lot of work before they're ready for a game. Unfortunately, we haven't got eleven in the first group. Is there any chance you could help the bowlers?'

'If I can. How did the Elvenham contingent get on?'

'Myfanwy's well on the way and Mina has the makings of a good keeper. Her batting's a bit rusty, though.' He looked over to the corner, where Vicky was talking to Nell from the village shop. 'I'm afraid that cricket doesn't come naturally to Geordies. If she practises a *lot*... maybe?'

'Cheers, Ben.'

On Monday morning, Vicky said, 'I know when I'm beat, Conrad. Now that the team's up and running, I'll walk away. Until the autumn, and if I'm still forced to live in your house, which is most unnatural by the way, I'll start a *women's* football team or die trying.'

'My house is not unnatural.'

'Your house has been visited by two gods, a Spectre, an Indian snake-woman and has a sídhe door in it, and that's just since I've been here. The food's good, though.'

20 — Let's go on a Dwarf Hunt

There is no weekend out for prisoners ahead of their release on licence, at least not at HMP Cairndale. Mina says that this is because so many of her sisters in jail have a tendency to mess up, especially before release, and this rule saves them from themselves. You have to be very, very bad to get called back once your licence has been issued.

Vicky and I left Clerkswell on the Friday afternoon following the first Ladies' coaching session. I think Vicky was getting lonely, or bored, or just missed the city. At Paddington, she headed for the taxi rank with a smile on her face, and I headed to the City for a drink with Alain, after a meeting with Hannah that she'd made me keep quiet about.

Everyone else was packing up for the weekend, and Tennille had already gone. We were good, though, because Shabbos didn't begin until ten to nine tonight. Hannah, to my amazement, was wearing a loose pair of linen trousers and a much baggier shirt. Perhaps she'd joined the Heidi Marston fan club. No. Not going to happen, and that reminded me of something, but before I could ask, Hannah offered me a dram of the finest whisky that's ever been distilled: Dawn's Blessing. No one knows for sure, but I reckon that they use an enchanted still. And the barley must be harvested at midnight by elves riding unicorns. It's that good.

She even gave me an embrace when I arrived.

'Thanks, ma'am,' I said, raising the glass. 'What's the occasion?'

'Oh, nothing,' she said, waving her hand. I would have described it as *waving her hand breezily*, but she didn't quite pull it off. Hannah goes from *calm* to *tempest* without passing through *breeze*. 'Just to say thank you for coming all the way over to Merlyn's Tower. And for not telling Vicky about this meeting. Was that hard?'

'You gave me an order, ma'am.'

'Hannah, not ma'am. Just for once, please. I know I gave you an order, but that doesn't make it easy to obey.'

'You've got your reasons, Hannah, and you'll tell me in a minute, when you've finished buttering me up. If I said it was really, really hard, would I get another drink?'

'Oy vey, have I missed this? Yes. My life has been too easy without you.' She tossed back her Dawn's Blessing and rolled it round her tongue. 'First, I wanted to say thank you. I was reading the final paperwork on your trip to Gravesend and I spotted a familiar name. Smithy. I rang him, and he told me that he'd talked to you. Thank you for not bringing it up. That means a lot.'

There was nothing to say to that. Anything I did say would make it worse.

'I never thought I'd say this, but that was the easy part of the conversation. The rest is about Vicky. Is she fit to join you on the Dwarf hunt?'

So far, I'd only smelled the whisky. I took a tiny sip and savoured it.

'I'm not a psychologist, Hannah. With a Xanax, probably, but they do take the edge off things. Long term? I'd say that she needs therapy and, maybe, something like joining a martial arts class.'

'She needs toughening up, you mean? Are you going to tell her that?'

'She's tough enough. I think she needs practice going through the pain barrier. She's done it, but only when the chips are down, and she's paid a high price for that. You know what I'd do in your shoes?'

'Limp, probably. Your feet are huge. No, go on.'

'Promote her to Watch Captain, conditional on undergoing a psych evaluation, then you can get someone else to tell her. If you make it a challenge, she'll get through. And you can recruit a new Watch Officer then.'

'Good. I like that. If everything goes well next week, that's exactly what I'll do.'

'Next week?'

'Tuesday. I've fixed it with Lloyd Flint for Tuesday morning, but that's not all.'

We were now getting to the really difficult bit. I could tell that because she gave me a tiny top-up.

'Niði's Halls are too risky for the two of you to handle on your own. I don't want to broaden the circle beyond those who already know about the Codex Defanatus, and that doesn't leave many.'

'Hannah, I don't have a problem with Rick. He had my back in the ambush, remember? He can lead the operation for all I care.'

She was already shaking her head. 'Not Rick, though I'm glad that you two are good. I've asked Desirée, and that's why we're on our own. Tennille stormed off to shout at her daughter and tell her not to go.'

This needed an immediate drink. 'Will she succeed in talking her out of it.'

'You've seen Desi in action. You've had her in your house. What do you think?'

'I think she'd walk over hot coals to look after Vicky, and I'll be glad to have her. If you give her a temporary commission.'

'Good one. I like that.' She laughed until she saw my face. 'You're serious, aren't you?'

'I don't joke about staying alive. I'm not going to argue about it, but if I'm the ops commander, then everyone is either under orders or a passenger, and this isn't an op for passengers.'

Hannah gave it some thought. 'That might be the only thing that puts her off, you know.'

'Tell her she doesn't have to call me *sir* unless Vicky does, and Vicky only does it when she's pissed off with me.'

'That might work. Leave it with me. I've got an incentive for you, anyway.'

'Oh?'

'Wait there.' She stood up and got some paperwork from her desk. 'Here you are. Not two, but *three* tickets for the rearranged medal ceremony. Friday 22nd May at two o'clock. I've spoken to HMP Cairndale and they've said they'll make sure that Ms Desai gets out before breakfast. They'll put her on the eight o'clock from Lancaster, arriving at eleven. I know you wanted to meet her at the gates, but I need you here for a meeting. I hope this will be compensation.' She gave me a smile. 'And your parents can make it, too. And Vicky's. I'm footing the bill for all of them, given the events last time.'

I leaned over and took the tickets. Hannah was going the extra mile for me. 'That means a lot. Thank you.'

'Good. One last thing.' She held up a printout. 'You took a Volvo XC90 from the Druids, didn't you, and you haven't changed the registration to your name, yet.'

Oh dear. I didn't like the sound of that. 'No, ma'am. Sorry.'

'The lawyers dealing with Surwen's estate have had a blizzard of parking tickets, speeding fines and congestion charge penalty notices. It took a while to land on my desk. Ruth can make this go away, but I need a sensible explanation, and if it's Vicky's flatmate or your disreputable uncle who's responsible, they'll have to take it on the chin.'

'It's Pramiti. I loaned her the car to get away from Clerkswell, and it looks as if she's taken things a bit far.'

Hannah gave me a dark look. 'Do you think she's up to no good?'

'Undoubtedly, but … she's got diplomatic protection. Well, divine protection. Up to a point.'

'I'll put a warning on the system. Next time she parks illegally, it'll get towed away. I'll tip off Eddie and Oscar as well. Right. There's no point having a planning meeting, because there's nothing to plan. I've no more idea what's in those tunnels now than I did when we left Flint House, and there's no trace of Irina, either. I've told Desirée to get in touch with you to arrange things.'

This time, when she stood up, it was time to go.

Alain was half way through a bottle of Bordeaux when I got to the Churchill Arms. He was hanging out with a couple of his colleagues from Praed's Bank, and seemed to be in a good mood. He was twenty-three, had money in his pocket and it was Friday night. Why shouldn't he be in a good mood? His friends drifted away when they saw me.

I grabbed a glass. He filled it and raised his own. 'Salut. To the Clarke family. I would say that I am in love with your sister, but I 'ave seen you shoot three men.'

'Cheers. My father is still alive, so it's him you have to answer to, not me.'

''Ow many people 'as 'e shot?'

'None. None that I know of.'

'Then I will answer to you, mon ami. She is so clever, so chic, so graceful that I cannot possibly get a job with 'er. That would be paradise.'

'Are you sure you want a job with her? I only have to spend Christmas with her. You'd be stuck with her all day, every day.'

'Non. I think she would give me all the shitty jobs to do, which is what I want.'

He'd gone serious in the space of a sentence, like a downpour at Wimbledon. I looked over my shoulder to check that Cliff Richard wasn't about to sing. 'If that's what you want, Alain, is there anything I can do to help?'

He shook his head. 'The less I know about 'er background, the better it is. If she thinks you 'ave been telling secrets, she won't want to 'ave me around. You 'ave done enough. Merci, Conrad.'

I sat back and enjoyed the Bordeaux. It was from the vineyard of a distant uncle, I think. Alain's uncle, obviously. 'I'll tell you what,' I said. 'If she mentions my name at all, just say that I've taught you how to keep a secret. That should be a tick on the form.'

'Again, thank you. Now, how is Victoria? She is well?'

I once, mistakenly, tried to set them up on a date. Vicky was not impressed, and Alain said that she looked like "a 'orse", which she does. A bit. On the other hand, Alain likes to play percentages. If young people still used little black books, his would run to several volumes.

'She's good. She's very good. Are you not going out tonight?'

He gave me a vintage Gallic shrug and checked his phone for a few seconds. When he looked up, he grinned. 'It looks like I am going out, after all. But we still 'ave time to finish the bottle. It is too good to waste.'

I lifted my glass and drank to that.

'Anybody fancy some pork scratchings before we head underground?' I asked, as we made our way through the Black Country Museum complex on Tuesday morning.

'Gross,' said Vicky. 'I can still taste me cooked breakfast, and what's that smell? It was in the car? Is it you, Conrad?'

It was me, but not me. If you see what I mean. It was something I was carrying. 'Curried worms,' I said. 'That was the best piece of advice the Allfather gave me. Always carry curried worms underground.'

'Does he always talk in riddles?' said Desi to Vicky. They were doing that a lot – talking about me as if I weren't there. Good job I don't have problems with self-esteem.

'Sadly, yes,' said Vicky. 'That's him over there. Lloyd Flint.'

'Go and say hello, Vicky. I need a moment with Desirée.'

'What for?' said Desi, surprised that her friend would just walk away and leave her. And that was why I needed a word. Vicky knows when I'm giving her an order, Desi doesn't. I took a moment to buy a bag of scratchings, telling myself they were full of salt and protein. Could be useful underground.

I coughed to get Desirée's attention, then took out a small box and my car keys.

'What?' said Desi, looking at Vicky and the Gnome, not me.

'Here,' I said. 'Your rank badge.' I opened the box and showed her the pair of bronze pips that a second lieutenant is issued with. I'd bought them from a militaria shop yesterday, because Hannah had bottled out of a confrontation and delegated the power of field commission to me, saying that it was my idea and that I should sort it. I hate it when she does that.

'What the fuck?'

I had decided that I had one shot to get this right, and one way of doing it. I held the keys in one hand and the pips in the other. 'You take a field commission or you go back to the car, Desirée. If you take the oath, I promise not to tell Vicky. That will be your decision.'

'Why? So you can order me around?'

'Yes.'

She looked stunned. 'You … you don't order Vic around, so why me?'

'I do, it's just that I don't make a fuss about it. Neither does she. Last chance…'

I started to close the box with the brass pips inside with one hand and simultaneously held out the car keys with the other.

'I'll do it,' she said. 'Quickly.'

'Repeat after me. "I Desirée Haynes, do swear by Almighty God…"'

'What was that all about?' said Vicky. 'And why did you end up saluting him?'

I hung back to see what Desi would say.

'He pressganged me,' said Desirée. 'Made me take the oath and salute once. "For the Queen," he said. Then he gave me these.' She quickly showed Vicky the box, but Vicky took it off her and opened it fully.

'Just the one pair?' said Vicky.

'Yeah.'

Vicky burst out laughing. 'Now you have to salute me as well. I'm a captain and you're only a second lieutenant.'

Desirée snatched back the box and stuffed it in her pocket as Lloyd Flint came over. I'd pretty much ignored him at Flint House, but now it was time for a closer look. His suit was gone, and he fitted right in with our selection of outdoor wear and running gear. Gnomes don't age like humans: they tend to stick at one point, then jump straight to the next. Sort of quantum ageing. If you see what I mean. Lloyd was at the point a human male would be just before he gets grey hair and needs glasses. In other words, he was in his prime.

We greeted each other and he asked if we were ready. Vicky took some water to wash down her Xanax, and we were good to go. Lloyd took us to a small boat, proportioned like a very short barge with the middle cut out. It had the yellow handles for legging down the tunnels as well as a bulky housing at the stern. 'Don't worry,' he said. 'This one's electric and fully charged. As soon as the tour boat comes out, we'll nip in. Make yourselves comfortable.'

I'm going to call Vicky and Desi *the girls*, if that's okay with you. It's what they called themselves. The girls took the seat furthest forward while I had a last smoke before we disappeared underground. I was looking for a waste bin when a much bigger barge glided out of the black mouth of the tunnel. It was full of small children in red school sweatshirts, all shouting. With that lot in full flow, the noise in that confined space must have been excruciating. I untied our boat and got in behind the girls. As soon as we left the quay, Vicky pointed to the brick wall above the tunnel entrance.

'Wow,' said Desi.

'What?' I said.

'Look. Concentrate.'

I reached out with my Sight, and I got it just before the black hole swallowed us up. On the retaining wall, above the footbridge, was the glowing red crest of Niði. I made out an anvil, of course, and the crossed short hammers of a Dwarf, but it was the bit above that really stood out: the Valknut, sign of Odin. Well, if anyone was entitled, it was Niði. Before I could comment, we were through the arch and into darkness. For about five seconds.

'I can see a light,' said Vicky. 'That's good.'

The first part of the tunnel system is Lord Ward's Tunnel. At 196 feet, you barely get going before you reach the open air again at Shirt's Mill Basin. It would take longer if you had to leg it. A lot longer in my case.

At the basin, trees were coming into leaf right the way down to the water, descending the steep limestone walls like the half-finished painting of a fairy grotto. It looked other-worldly until you saw the beach of mud outside an old mine entrance. In seconds we were into another, shorter tunnel, and Lloyd slowed the engine so that we could drift into the Castle Mill Basin, another oasis of green.

This was even bigger, big enough for the tour boats to make a 90 degree turn into the much longer tunnels to the left. We headed right and pulled up at a low dam. 'They put this here to seal off the Wren's Nest Tunnel,' said Lloyd. 'The system is open to any boat, and some idiots would go down there if they could.'

'Not that we're idiots, or anything,' said Vicky.

Lloyd used a strong arm to hold the barge steady while we climbed on to the dam. Desi stared into the tunnel. 'We're not going to swim, are we? No way.'

159

'Can't swim in there. Too shallow. You can wade if you want, or get in the boat. Hang on while I tie this up.'

He stared into the Wren's Nest Tunnel. This one really was black, with nothing to see beyond the first few metres. He curled his arms like a weight lifter, and a small boat, just big enough for four, floated gently towards the dam. Impressive.

'Where's the oars?' said Desirée.

'Or the engine,' said Vicky. 'Either would be good, but an engine would be better.'

Desi and I braced the boat against the wall so that Lloyd could get in. 'Rope line,' he said.

He pushed us away from the wall and fished under his seat. The boat rocked alarmingly as he found a metal hook with a short wooden handle and reached up. The hook glowed with Lux, and as it did, a knotted rope of energy, hanging from the ceiling, became visible. He put the hook down and opened his arms.

Slowly at first, the boat moved out of the light and into the tunnel. Lloyd's breathing got more ragged until he stopped and relaxed. The boat had picked up speed, and carried on moving without his intervention. As we passed a brick support, a lightstick flared into life. 'We call it drawing the boat,' he said. 'There's not many who can do it any more. Another minute and we'll be there.'

We were all trying not to move. No one wants to rock the boat, do they? After the third lightstick, he opened his arms again and took an Artefact from under his fleece, a flat iron disk. He held it up, and a pattern on the disk glowed with golden light – Niði's crest. Ahead and to the left, a section of rock shimmered and changed into a portcullis gate that was already rising out of the water.

'Duck,' said Lloyd. The boat turned towards the gate before the portcullis had fully risen. We scrambled to get down, and I had to lie on top of Desi to stop the boat overbalancing. She was not amused. 'I never get that right,' said Lloyd. 'I'm always going too fast. Never mind, nearly there.'

There was natural light ahead, and then we were in a tiny basin, a fraction the size of Castle Mill. Wesley Flint was right – the cliff walls were so sheer that only trained climbers could come down here, and I've no doubt that the top was magickally hidden.

Niði's dock was longer than a full-sized barge and ten feet deep. The roof sloped down to an elaborately carved door. Even after thirty years, you could see soot marks on the rock from the fire, but thankfully no bloodstains. We got out of the boat and stared at the door. This time I didn't need to use my Sight. It positively glowed with Lux.

'I'll get the stuff we arranged,' said Lloyd. 'I brought it down this morning. Didn't want to overload the boat.' He walked off to a small heap under a plastic tarpaulin at the far end of the dock, and we turned our attention back to the doors.

Dwarves like stone. After all, they're made of it. In a way. Stone and rock do not like to move. They like to sit still. They make good walls, but they do not make good doors, because doors are twin-natured. Doors have to admit and bar; a door that does one but not the other isn't a door. The doors to Dwarven Halls are made of stone. Show-offs.

The anvil and crossed-hammers was etched into each half of the door, and the Valknut shone out from the keystone above. Desi approached the doors and held her fingers towards the engraving, a look of wonder on her face.

'Don't worry, I've got the key,' said Lloyd. 'Here we go.' He laid out an array of kit on the floor. Half a dozen pre-charged lightsticks, bottles of water, a couple of robust Thermos flasks and a piece of electronic kit that looked familiar. Aah, yes. A mobile repeater. I've used one underground before, but surely the Halls would be far too far from the surface? Lloyd picked it up and went to the wall, where a tiny piece of trunking ended in a connector.

'There's no signal down here,' he said, 'so we put an aerial on the top and use a booster. It's how you can call to get someone to pick you up.' He looked at Desi. 'That way, you won't have to wade out to the basin. I'll just test it.' He plugged in the box, switched it on and made a call. 'Chief, it's Lloyd. They've gone under. I'll head off to the Smethwick foundry and wait for them to call me … No, no problems … Yeah. Talk to you later.'

Vicky and I exchanged glances. There was something going on here. Lloyd had gone back to the tarpaulin, from where he retrieved a metal box, a soft zip-up plastic case and an axe. A great big double-headed battle-axe. My hand went to the butt of my gun.

There was a leather harness attached to the head of the axe, and Lloyd made a point of carrying it by that, to show he wasn't going to swing it at us. When he got closer, he put the items down, and I recognised the metal box. I let Lloyd explain himself first.

'What did chief Wesley say about my father?'

'That he and your father came down here looking for their father.'

'Thought so,' said Lloyd. 'That's true, actually. What he didn't tell you was that my father was the older brother, and that he died down here. It never made it into the records, and we're supposed to forget all about it. The dead chief – my grandfather – was laid to rest in the First Mine at midnight, with just a few of us to make the cairn. There is no cairn for my father.'

'Does that make you the rightful clan chief?' I asked.

Desirée gave me a pitying look. 'It doesn't work like that. Gnomes don't do strict primogeniture. They choose from the late chief's surviving brothers and heirs. You were too young, weren't you, Lloyd?'

'I was. I'm not now, and I'm coming with you.'

'Or what?' I said. Always useful to know what the stick is before you get to discuss the carrot.

'Or you can open those doors yourself. After I've gone down on my own.'

'Sounds good,' I said. 'You can weaken the enemy, then we'll follow you down and finish it off.'

Desi span round to face me. 'You wouldn't! That would be evil.'

'He would,' said Vicky, not taking her eyes off Lloyd. 'Squadron Leader Clarke doesn't do good and evil, Desi. Not like you do. You'll get used to it.'

Desirée was appalled. 'What about you, Vic? Have you lost sight of good and evil, too?' When her friend didn't answer, she turned to me. 'Pressgang him, like you did me. He can take the oath.'

'That won't work,' said Vicky. 'Gnomes are not loyal subjects.'

'We're not,' said Lloyd. It was his patience that won me over. We'd gone head to head, and he hadn't blinked once.

I spoke up. 'The King's Watch does not take Gnomes as officers, but it does take them as guides. Vic, have you got a tenner handy?'

Vicky took a ten pound note out of her pocket and held it out.

'Guide and escort, bound by contract,' I said. 'How does that sound?'

'Better than going down on my own.' He was about to take the money when I held up my hand.

'And I'll take custody of the detonators, thanks.'

'What?' said Desi.

I pointed to the metal box. 'That's pelletised TNT. High explosive. The detonators will be in the case.'

Lloyd picked up the case and tossed it to me, then accepted the ten pound note with a bow. 'Let's get ready.' He got his phone out again. 'If you go to any other Dwarf but Hledjolf, their Hall messes your tech right up. I really would power off anything you can.' He took his own advice and showed us the shutting down screen.

We stowed the gear and turned off our phones in silence. All I knew about what we'd face was that there would be a lot of Lux about: the doors told me that.

Dwarves are creatures of Lux. They have a sort of biology based on silicon, but without Lux they would just be lumps of stone, which is what happens to them when exposed to daylight. A Dwarf's Hall isn't just a home, it's more of a living infrastructure that provides ambient Lux. Don't ask me how. Don't ask anyone how, because I don't think anyone, even Hledjolf, truly understands. The presence of Lux would stop me getting a migraine if I left my Ancile powered on, which is good. Less good was that it also provided energy for whatever was down there.

'Set?' said Lloyd. I checked the others and nodded. He took out the disk again and said something in a harsh Germanic language. With grace and elegance, the doors swung slowly out. I took one last look at the sky, searching for a raven or any other sign. Desi started saying the Lord's Prayer and Vicky kept her eyes firmly on the ground and clung to her lightstick like a drowning woman with a lifebelt.

Lloyd switched the grip on his axe to hold the haft, and runes lit up on the blades, red on one half and black light on the other. There was nothing more to say, so he led us through the doors and into who knows what. There was no raven, by the way. We'd be on our own down there.

21 — *All ye who enter Here*

We didn't need the lightsticks at first. Not all of Niði's smokeless, heatless torches were still working, but enough of them flickered into life for us to see our way down the passage.

Dwarvish art lined the walls in a series of friezes, all intricately carved or shaped. There is a dissertation to be made of those carvings, and maybe someone has, but we couldn't linger. I took a moment to examine one panel, where a bearded Dwarf raised a tankard to a hopelessly out of scale Dragon.

Gnomes are all shorter than humans, and Dwarfs are even shorter. Mina would tower over Hledjolf if she ever met him, but in Dwarven art, the Dwarf is always the largest figure. Even larger than the Dragon. I lengthened my stride and caught up with the others.

The tunnel sloped down sharply, so sharply that a human engineer would have put steps in. Dwarves don't do steps, because they push things around on trolleys or in mining carts. With their strength, no slope is too steep. The tunnel curved to the right, and Lloyd held up his hand. 'The old Hall is round the corner. I've been a few times, and there's never been anything there. Let me listen.'

He rested the axe on the ground and leaned towards the wall, touching it with his splayed fingers. 'Still below. Slowly, now.' He picked up the axe and edged round the corner. I had my hand on the Hammer. 'Clear,' he said, and swung the axe up to rest it on his shoulder.

Niði's old Hall reminded me of a trip to the Mezquita at Cordoba in southern Spain. Instead of one great overarching high cavern, there were rows and rows of columns and arches. The stone blocks that made up the columns must have been cut and brought from somewhere else, because they weren't limestone, and this hill is all limestone, which was why humans had built the canals. Niði had hollowed out a space, forming the roof and the arches out of the native rock, and then built up the pillars from imported stone to meet the capitols. It was beautiful and quite disturbing at the same time, because in a few places the pillars had been knocked away, and the rock above had collapsed. I could hear Vicky's breathing getting shallower as the weight of the hill pressed down on her mind.

The Dwarf had clearly abandoned the Hall before he was attacked, because it was empty and disused. A few forges stood idle, covered in dust but clean and neatly arranged. There were stone tables, a couple of what looked like coffins (stone chests), and in several places there were red stains. Oh.

Lloyd pointed to one of them. 'This is where my father and Wesley found their father.' He pointed north west. 'The door to the Wren's nest is behind that rock fall. And the way down is over there. Due north.'

'Excuse me,' I said. 'That can't all be your grandfather's blood, can it, if you don't mind me asking?'

'Well it's not Dwarf blood, is it?' Dwarves don't have haemoglobin, true, so the red stain wasn't Dwarf … fluid, let's say.

'Vicky, could you tell, after all this time?'

'Sorry? What?'

Desi put her hand on Vic's shoulder, and I repeated myself. 'Could you tell whose blood that is? Or even if it's all Gnomish?'

'Might do. There's enough Lux to preserve some of the Imprint.'

She got out her sPad and squatted by the stains. She stared into the screen, then ran her fingers over the rock. She took a good look at Lloyd, then turned back to the rock. 'This here, where Lloyd was pointing. That's the blood of his grandfather. Or his father. Gnomes are hard to tell apart in the direct family line.' She moved a little. 'This here, that's not Gnomish. Not enough iron. I'm getting a weird mixture. It's very degraded, but I'm getting human, equine, and something else.'

'Equine?' said Desi. 'Like a horse? Down here?'

Vicky stuck out a hand, and I helped her up. 'Aye. I studied horses a lot on our last case, and I'm definitely getting the feel of something horsey. I can't even tell if it was one creature or two. Either way, it didn't die here.'

We hadn't noticed, but Lloyd had raised his axe a few inches. When Vicky finished, he lowered it back again. 'Thank the gods. For one second, I thought you were going to tell me that my father had died here. That would not have been good for the chief.'

'What do you know about what happened?'

'Wesley only told us once. He said that when they got down to the old Hall, the piles of coal were burning, and the chief's body was still warm. My father ran down to the lower Hall while Wesley was still checking for a pulse, or so Wesley says. When Wesley went to the ramp down, he felt my father's heart give out, and he retreated. If that's true, I don't blame him.'

Having something to do had helped calm Vicky down, and I seized the moment. 'Let's go.'

Lloyd led us down an arcade of columns, many of which were damaged with slashes and gouges. Not the random damage of an explosion, but something like a weapon. Two somethings, I reckoned. One was thin and sharper than diamonds, and had been wielded with huge strength. 'Look,' I said. 'These marks. They're too high for a Dwarf, but those, the gouges. They're the right height.'

'You're right,' said Lloyd. 'I never thought. I've been on at the chief to get the Watch involved for years. Or another Clan. You've told me more in five minutes than I'd figured out in hours spent down here.'

'Why didn't he?' said Vicky. 'Why didn't the chief get us down here? Was it just greed?'

Lloyd shook his head. 'Fear, I reckon. Greed was the excuse, especially after Irina joined us, but deep down I reckon that Wesley simply doesn't want to face up to whatever's in the lower Hall.'

Now would have been a good time to ask about Irina. The only reason I didn't was that Vicky was on a timer, and useful though the information might be, it would be of no use if she collapsed and we all got killed. I didn't have time to change my mind, because Lloyd was already half way to the ramp.

The ramp to the lower Hall, or whatever it was down there, took a sharp turn to the left not long after we started down it. Lloyd stopped and fingered the wall. 'We're getting closer.' Instead of moving on, he put down the axe, placed both hands on the wall and sniffed the rock. 'Well I'll be blowed,' he said, in the thickest Black Country accent. He smiled and stepped back. 'That's the 30ft seam.'

'Seam?' said Desi.

Vicky and I had done our homework, and I let her speak. 'A seam of coal. It's not actually thirty feet wide, but you get the picture. It's why the Black Country is black. They had it easy down here. My ancestors had to dig a lot deeper.'

'This is deep enough,' said Lloyd. 'It runs down and under the limestone, and below that is haematite. Everything you need to make the best iron. God's little gift.'

Desi was going to say something about God until she caught Lloyd's eye. She made do with shaking her head, and Lloyd picked up his axe.

'It's dark ahead,' he said 'Lighting up time.' Vicky had to show me how to activate my lightstick. Desi looked on, slightly appalled. She doesn't think I'm Mage enough to be doing this sort of thing.

'Spread out,' I said. 'You two behind me.'

The ramp got steeper, as if it were impatient to get to its destination, and then it ended in a landing.

Lloyd edged up to the arch and glanced in before stepping through. I had expected a straight tunnel, but beyond the arch it was like getting out of a hotel lift, with two tunnels, left and right, and Niði's crest glowing in the middle of the opposite wall. Lloyd took out the disk and compared it to the wall.

'There's something different on this crest. No Valknut.' He hefted the key. 'And this isn't in tune with the lower level. Niði must have done that for a reason.'

'Which way?' I asked.

Lloyd touched the wall, then the floor, then the wall again. 'Something's wrong. Whatever is down here is on this level, and the Dwarf is deeper still. But I can't get a fix on it. It's like the heartbeat is everywhere.'

166

We stood in the entrance to the new section, looking both ways. Neither tunnel was lit. 'Desi? Which way? Pick one,' I said.

She pointed right from the entrance, going north again. Lloyd headed off and we followed. This time I took the rear.

With no general light, we moved more slowly, and Lloyd took a couple of sonar readings that told him nothing, nor did the plain stone walls and flagged floor. We soon came to a side passage to the left, as featureless and clueless as the one we were on. Lloyd could just make out a turn to the right ahead. 'Shall we try down here?' he said. I shrugged, and we turned.

I tried to expand my Sight in the vain hope of finding something. I did find something. Something very wrong. 'Stop!'

'What?'

'We're still heading north.'

'Still?' said Desi. Vicky, who knows me better, was looking worried.

'We've just made a ninety degree turn from a northerly passage, and we're still heading north.'

'We're sitting on top of a vein of iron ore,' said Lloyd. 'Niði could have used it to confuse things.'

'He could, but why? He hasn't scrambled the compass, he's made it dance to his tune. That must take a lot of energy.'

'Keep a look out.' Lloyd started stroking the walls and floor of the tunnel while we anxiously stared into the darkness. 'I need to touch the roof.'

'Seriously?' said Desi. 'You got a trampoline in that backpack?'

'Not the middle. The edge will do. The walls and floor are faced with limestone. The roof is sandstone, and that has to be for a reason.'

The wall was about three metres high. Ten feet, if you prefer. I'm just under two metres tall, so I could see what was coming next. 'Get on my shoulders.'

Lloyd didn't waste time. I braced my back against the wall and linked my fingers to make a stirrup.

'Do you have to have the axe on your back? That thing must weigh a ton.'

'It does, but I need it, and it's tied to my blood. No one else can pick it up, and if it's not on my back, it might swing round and slice into you.'

'Go on, then. Desi, Vicky, you keep watch.'

He put his foot in my hands, and I did my best to boost him up. It's a good job he's strong. He seemed to use the wall like Spiderman, dragging himself with his fingers when he was half way there, and then his feet were on my shoulders. Oww, that hurt. Really hurt.

'Hold still, Conrad. I need to get the axe out.'

'I'm as still as I can be. You need to diet more and work out less.'

He carefully took the axe off his back, leaned out an arm and swung it up to nick the roof with the black-runed head. When it touched the rock, a flash of light lit up the corridor, and Lloyd was thrown backwards. I tried to grab him to break his fall, but the flash had dazzled me, and he hit the ground with a thump.

'Something's coming,' said Desirée, who'd been watching ahead.

'Vicky, help Lloyd. Desi, get down,' I said, drawing the Hammer and going to one knee to Desi's right. She looked bewildered for a second, and then she hit the deck. Behind me, I could hear Lloyd groaning and Vicky frantically asking him if he were okay. From the blackness ahead of me, I could see nothing, but I heard something. I heard metal-shod feet. Four of them, trotting towards us. That would be the equine contingent, then.

'Desi, get to your knees and look behind. What's happening?'

'Lloyd's sitting up. His arm's hurt, I think. Nothing coming that way.'

'Good.'

But there was something coming towards us.

'Desi, power up one of the lightsticks, and on my word chuck it as far down the tunnel as you can. We're sitting ducks here.'

'Right.'

She took a lightstick, but instead of illuminating it, she just held it for a second. Then she stood up, took two steps back, ran forward and hurled it like a javelin, way faster and truer than a stick should fly. In mid-air, it burst into light. That was good. That was very good, unlike the horror it revealed.

'Lord Jesus preserve us!'

'Oh fuck.'

'Mmmmm.'

'Someone tell me what that thing is!'

I can tell you what it looked like. It looked like a nightmare horse, black with red eyes and a red hot, glowing spike of iron in the middle of its head. On its back was a humanoid figure that looked to be made of coal and burning itself from the inside out, smoke wisping from volcanic fractures in its skin. And it carried a black sword.

The horse pulled up in front of the lightstick.

'En Svartálf,' said Lloyd with horror in his voice, which was not a good sign.

'And a Black Unicorn,' said Vicky.

'Hell-horse,' said Desi. 'Black does not always mean evil.'

I agree with her, as it happens. It's a good job the horse and rider were stationary, though. This was not the time or place.

'Get up, get up,' said Vicky to Lloyd.

I still hadn't looked behind me, nor could I afford to. I really hoped that the axe-wielding Gnome would get up soon, because I was feeling very exposed.

The Svartálf raised its sword and shouted something in the Germanic language that Lloyd had used to open the doors to Niði's Hall. It said it twice, I think.

'Nej! Nej!' shouted Lloyd. *No No*. I got that much at the start; the rest of what he said was loud, impassioned and incomprehensible.

The Svartálf spoke again, and again Lloyd said, 'Nej!' this time with a finality that I couldn't miss.

Then the Svartálf dug in its heels and the horse broke into a gallop, lowering its sword so that it could cut us down like wheat before a scythe. I aimed at the horse and fired.

The bullet broke through the creatures' Anciles with a flash of energy and it struck the Hell-horse in the chest. That should have been that. It should have broken every synapse in its brain, disrupted every nerve in its body and killed it like submersion in a bath of neat neurotoxins. Nothing. Shit. I stood up and fired at the Svartálf. Ditto. Time to panic.

'To the right!'

If we could avoid the Svartálf's sword, we might stand a chance. I swapped the Hammer into my left hand and drew my machete, probably pointless, but you never know. I scampered to the wall and risked a look behind. It was not good.

Lloyd had hurt more than his arm. He was trying to stand on a clearly broken ankle and reach his axe, which had skittered well away from him along the tunnel. Vicky was desperately trying to help him to his feet, and instead of hugging the wall next to me, Desirée was standing in front of them, singing.

The Hell-horse was nearly on me. The rider was focused on the group ahead and didn't swap his sword arm, so all I had to face was a galloping horse with a red hot spike in its head. I went en-garde with the machete and tried with all the life in my body to put some magick, any magick into the blade. The most powerful magick I've encountered is that of Nimue, water nymph. Not much use underground, but it was all I had. I thought of spring flowers, sweet breezes … and the horse veered its spike away from me at the last moment, and I chopped at its shoulder.

I didn't make contact. Something turned the blade away at the last moment, and I missed. The hind quarters caught me a glancing blow and slammed me into the wall. I bounced back, falling down as my bad leg gave way, and I looked left with my heart in my mouth.

Desirée stood firm in front of Lloyd, who'd collapsed back on to the floor, with Vicky on top of him. The Svartálf raised its sword and delivered a cavalry slash at Desi. Oh no.

She made a circle with her right hand, never missing a beat of the psalm she was singing, and a disk of blue light appeared. The blade slashed through the circle, and I heard the crash of metal on metal as it was deflected away from her head. The blue light flashed off, the horse jumped over the prone couple and Desirée collapsed in a heap.

I got up and ran to them. There was blood welling out of Desirée's jacket. She'd been slashed in a line across and down from her right breast. It was bad, but she was alive. For now. I glanced ahead. The Hell-horse and rider had disappeared, and it struck me that they were too big to turn round easily in this tunnel. We had a few seconds to do something. Anything.

'Get me up,' said Lloyd. 'I need that axe.'

'Desi!' said Vicky.

'Vic, first aid. Now,' I said, pushing her to her friend.

I moved to Lloyd, braced my back and lifted him to stand on one foot. Slinging his left arm over my shoulder and bending forwards, we hopped to get the axe. He stooped, picked it up and leaned against the wall. I leaned next to him.

'It hurts, Vic,' said Desirée. 'God help me, it's bad.'

'What the hell?' I said to Lloyd.

He wiped his mouth. 'It's my grandfather,' he said. 'The old chief.'

'What???'

He gestured down the tunnel. 'That Svartálf is my grandfather. The body we buried must have been my father. No time to explain now. I need a wall, something for them to run at. In the open, like this, they'll cut us down one by one. What was going on with your gun?'

'I need to have words with Hledjolf. It seems that his ammunition only works on humans.'

Lloyd gave me a look that said it all.

His arm wasn't badly hurt, not really, but his ankle was completely useless. He touched the wall and said, 'They're coming round again. From the same direction. We need to get back to that junction. I need them running at me, and your only hope is to get some of my blood on one of those bullets.'

'Do you need a knife?'

You'd think I'd asked his mother out on a date. 'It has to be spilt in combat. Just get me down there and have a bullet ready.'

'How long?'

'About a minute.'

I limped over to the girls. That Hell-horse had done nothing for my left hip. 'How bad is it?' I asked.

Vicky's hands were shaking. She'd opened Desi's clothes and examined the wound. The Svartálf's blade hadn't hit an artery, but her friend was bleeding badly. Vicky was trying to get some tape out of the first aid kit, which was the right thing, but we didn't have time for the right thing.

'Help Lloyd. We need to get to that junction. I'll take Desi.'

'Wha…?'

'Now.'

Vic struggled to her feet and went over to Lloyd. I looked in the rucksack for something soft. Aah. It looked like Tennille might save her daughter's life from a distance. Tucked in the bottom of the rucksack was a woolly scarf.

Perfect. I grabbed it, balled it and shoved it on to the wound. 'Hold that,' I said to Desi, moving her hand into place.

Her eyes came into focus. 'Vic?'

'Hold tight. We're moving. Help me if you can.' I rolled her, lifted her and got her to her feet. 'Come on, Desi. You can do it.'

I didn't so much help her as drag her down the tunnel. Lloyd was already in place, propped against the wall facing me. I had absolutely no idea what he was doing except making himself a brilliant target, but he was the only one with any clue about what was going on. Vicky came to help, and we got Desi out of the firing line. Unless the Hell-horse came round the other way, in which case she was doomed.

'Incoming,' said Lloyd. 'Ready, Conrad.'

I ejected the clip from the Hammer and took out one round. Behind me, I heard the sound of surgical tape being torn. From the left I heard the sound of hooves. I dodged to the corner and peered round. The Hell-horse had come to a stop about thirty metres away, giving it enough distance to build up a head of steam. Now that Lloyd had the axe, the Svartálf knew that it couldn't just charge. Lloyd might not be mobile, but one blow from that axe would finish off anything on two legs or four.

The volcanic rider, allegedly the Gnomish chief, spoke again. Lloyd growled and lifted the axe. That was weird. He was holding it with his left hand, and it was obviously a two-handed weapon. With ease, he waved it in front of him, the red runes leaving an after-image of Lux in the air. The Hell-horse took a step back. I wouldn't want to charge that axe, either.

The Svartálf leaned forwards and whispered to his mount, patting him on the neck. Again, it would take more than a pat on the neck to get me charging a mad magickal axe-wielding Gnome. Oh. They weren't words of encouragement and a pat. They were a Work of magick.

The red-hot spike on the Hell-horse's head grew until it was about seven feet long. Gnomes have long arms, but even with the axe, Lloyd's reach was not that long. The Hell-horse's neck bowed with the extra weight of iron, until its rider dug in and spurred it on.

I took a step back to provide what little cover I could for the girls, and watched the Hell-horse charge, its iron horn aimed at Lloyd's heart. He raised the axe. Even with his strength, he wouldn't be able to move fast enough to parry that spike, and he didn't even try. He just leaned to the right and let the Hell-horse drive its horn through his left arm.

Vicky screamed. The iron tore through flesh, but when it hit his blood, something happened. The rock behind him boiled, and instead of snapping or slipping, the red hot horn drove through the rock then stuck. Stuck fast.

The rider pitched forward and lost his grip, tumbling off and rolling into the wall. The Hell-horse whinnied and shook itself, but its head was fixed.

What happened next will haunt me forever. Lloyd grinned. He reached under the horn and took the axe in his right hand. He moved his grip close to the head of the axe and, in one quick movement, chopped off his left arm, just above the spike. Behind me, I heard Vicky retching. I couldn't take my eyes off the arm pinned to the wall. Black blood was running down the stone. Blood. Gnome blood. Shit. That was my cue.

Lloyd stepped to his right and dropped his grip to the end of the handle. He swung the axe at the Hell-horse and buried it in the creature's head in a flare of Lux. With a cry, he fell to his knees and collapsed.

I was running to the wall, but the Svartálf was getting to his feet.

'Conrad! Get his Ancile down,' said Vicky.

The creature could have finished off Lloyd easily, but the Svartálf dodged round the horse and came for me. His skin was a shifting, cracking crust of coal, and he was on fire inside. This close, I could smell the sulphur and see flames in his eye sockets. I also realised that Lloyd could well be right. The creature was hellish, yes, but it had the height and proportions of a Gnome, not a human.

I couldn't turn my back on him to get the blood. I had one round in the chamber, and I fired at his heart. As soon as I'd raised the gun, Vicky had started to send scythes of air at the Svartálf, all of which bounced off his Ancile. When the bullet pierced it, his Ancile collapsed long enough for the blast of air to stagger him back.

In a close match, victory comes in the margins. I turned round, and the hours of practice I'd had in Gravesend with Smithy paid off. I didn't drop the next round when I wiped it in the blood. I didn't fumble when I pressed it into the clip and turned round.

The Svartálf's Ancile was back in place, and he was coming for me. He was close. It was death or glory, so I aimed for his eye and squeezed the trigger.

22 — *Where there's Life*

The Svartálf's head snapped back and he dropped his sword, clutching his head. I thumbed out another round, ready to anoint it with more of Lloyd's blood, then I stopped. The fire under the Svartálf's skin dimmed and crusted over. He sank to knees and raised his head, still clutching one eye with his hand. His coal face changed subtly, from pure carbon to charred flesh, and the fire in his left eye flickered and became a pupil with a brown cornea. He parted his lips, and I saw the pink of healthy flesh inside his mouth.

A noise of gargling fire, came from his throat and he collapsed to the floor. The hand fell away from his eye and he lay still. The sword had stopped glowing, too, and was now bare metal.

'Is he gone?' said Vicky. My ears were ringing from the shots, and I hadn't heard her come over. In this tunnel, without ear defenders, I'd have been deaf if I hadn't also practised a mini-Silence recently. I may not have much magick, but you do what you can. As I said, it's all in the margins.

'I hope so. You check Lloyd, and I'll watch the Svartálf.'

'Lloyd's alive, and his arm's been cauterised. I'll put him in the recovery position.'

Lloyd groaned and said, 'Don't bother. I could murder a drink, though. Give me a minute.'

'What about the Svartálf?' I asked.

'Gone,' said Lloyd. 'You don't need to stand guard.'

I holstered the Hammer and went to check on Desi. Vicky had done a good job with the tape and a dressing, but it was already going red in places. The bleeding had been slowed, but not stopped. Before the fifth horseman of the Apocalypse had ridden for his last charge, Vicky had propped Desi's head up on a rucksack. She'd seen the whole thing.

'Do I get a medal?' she said.

'If I have anything to do with it, yes.'

'That makes it all worthwhile, then.'

'Where's there's sarcasm, there's hope. Well done, Lieutenant.'

'It hurts. Really bad. Raked all my nerves.'

'Hang on.' I rummaged in the first aid kit and found the good stuff, the OxyContin tablets I'd saved from when my leg was in bits. I gave her two and a drink of water.

'Give us a hand,' said Lloyd to Vicky. She stared at his stump and looked slightly sick. 'That wasn't a joke, love, I've still got a broken ankle.'

'Sorry. Here.'

The Hell-horse had ended up as a sort of sculpture. The iron spike was still embedded in the wall (and still stuck in Lloyd's arm, but we'll draw a veil over that). The rest of its body had collapsed in a heap underneath it. Vicky gave

Lloyd a hand, and he pulled himself up, using the spike to steady himself. With a grunt, he pulled the axe from the Hell-horse's body and tossed it to the ground. Vicky put her arm round his waist and helped him over to us. When he got near, he hopped to the wall and slid down into a heap. 'About that drink?'

'Islay Malt?'

'Seriously?'

'Present from my girlfriend,' I said, taking out the replenished hip flask.

He examined the engraving and grinned. 'To teamwork,' he said, and took a healthy pull.

Vicky and I drank too, echoing his toast. When I'd finished, Desi said, 'I'm good, thanks. Those pills are amazing.'

The pills would help her cope, but they wouldn't do anything for the wound. I leaned over to Vicky and whispered, 'Is there nothing you can do to heal her? There's plenty of Lux about.'

She shook her head, choking back a tear. 'I did a quick heal on Lloyd's hand, but there's too much damage. When I healed that lion bite on your arm in Wales, I had access to an open Ley line and only had to patch some muscle. This is different. I'd kill one of us if I tried it.'

'I hate to rain on our own parade,' said Lloyd, 'but you do realise we're still trapped down here?'

'Any other life?'

He checked the floor. 'No. Just the Dwarf, down below.'

'Good. Anyone mind if I smoke?'

'Yeah, we all do,' said Vicky. 'But we'll let you off if you sit over there and pass the Thermos. Whisky's good and all that, but I need a coffee and a flapjack more.'

We needed a moment. Just the one. I took a good look at Lloyd. If anyone was going to go into shock, it should be the one who's just performed an auto-amputation. He seemed fine. Perhaps Gnomes feel these things differently. I decided to avoid the obvious questions.

'Lloyd, that all seemed to kick off when you struck the ceiling,' I said.

He gave me that look again. The one that says *And what did you bring to the party? Rubber bullets?*

He swallowed some more water and looked up. 'It all goes back to Crete, and I'm not talking where I went on my holidays.' He looked at me. 'When you said we were still going north, I thought you were using a compass. Then I saw the look on Vicky's face, and I knew you were a Navigator.'

'A what?'

'All Gnomes have a bit of it, but only a few can do it properly. Dead reckoning by the Earth's magnetic field and other things. I suddenly remembered the legend, and the only way to find out was to check the roof.

That's where the Work is built in. And I was right. Niði has built himself a Labyrinth.'

'Of course. Knossos. The Minotaur. Are you saying that was a real thing?'

He looked at Vicky. 'What do you think?'

'Never been big on legends, me. That's one of the downsides of the Invisible College; we tend to look for evidence, not stories.'

'Big mistake,' said Lloyd. 'There are two legends: the human and the Gnomish. The human legend has Theseus, the Minotaur, Ariadne and all that. The Gnomish story is different. I reckon the human version is about Zoogeny, creating unnatural creatures. To us, it's all about metal.'

'It would be,' said Desi, trying to keep up despite the opiates working through her system.

'Our version has a Dwarf, a Dwarf who gave the secret of iron to humans.' He held up his hand to forestall interruption from the girls. 'I know, I know. Humans want to believe they found it for themselves. Can we agree to differ? Good. King Minos invited the Dwarf to Knossos, but he wouldn't pay the price for the Dwarf's secret and tried to kill him. The Dwarf couldn't get off the island, so to protect himself, he built the Labyrinth and hid underneath it.'

'Are you saying the Dwarf was the Minotaur?' asked Vicky.

Lloyd shook his head. 'No. We say that the Minotaur is from a different story and got merged into this one. In our version, Minos filled the Labyrinth with spiders.'

Vicky flinched back. Spiders are second in her phobia hierarchy. After tunnels. She tries not to think of the two together.

Lloyd didn't notice and carried on. 'Theseus killed the spiders and liberated the Dwarf. Our legend also has details about how the Labyrinth works, and when I used my axe to knock the ceiling, I realised that it was true. I also disrupted the part of the Work that was keeping us and the Svartálf apart from each other. That was unfortunate, but we'd have had to deal with them sooner or later.'

Vicky gave him a dark look, then pointed at me. 'I am not letting this get out. It's bad enough that people call him the Dragonslayer. I am not having him known as "Conrad Dragonslayer, the new Theseus." That would be unbearable.'

'Hear hear,' said Desi.

'No danger of that,' I said. 'I would never have abandoned Ariadne. After all…'

'… A Clarke's Word is Binding,' said Vicky. 'Yeah, yeah, we know.'

I wanted to deal with something else before we got back to the Labyrinth. 'So, Lloyd. About your Grandfather? What was going on there?'

He looked grim, and for the first time, he rubbed the stump of his arm. 'Can you get my fleece?'

I wasn't ready to stand up yet, so I crawled to the rucksacks and got out his thick fleece. Perhaps he was going into shock, and getting cold. I helped him get it on, and he said, 'Tie up the left sleeve, will you?'

When I'd done what he asked, he leaned back and looked at the opposite wall. 'You know we're mostly human, right? Well, the bit of us that's not human is part rock and part Dæmon. When we're underground, we get access to Lux and other powers that humans can't even begin to understand. We're also vulnerable to possession. It's our blessing and our curse, and that's what happened to the old chief.'

Vicky and I looked at each other. This was clearly news to her as well.

'A Dæmon must have attacked Niði. I think it must have happened when my grandfather opened the doors. That's why the barge was blown up, and why the humans died up there. The chief must have gone down to help the Dwarf, and during the battle, he must have overreached himself, and the Dæmon possessed him. Turned him into a Svartálf. When my father and Wesley came to investigate, my father must have been killed trying to drive the Dæmon down to the lower level.'

'Sorry,' said Vicky. 'I should have checked more closely. I knew that the bloodstains and death site were from either your father or your grandfather. I should have narrowed it down.'

'Wouldn't have made a difference. It does now, but we'd have found out anyway.' He gave her a smile. 'You were spot on about the horse. You're good.'

'Aye, well what about the Fae?'

'The Fae?' That was my question.

Vicky answered the question. 'Only the Fae can tame a Hell-horse, or Black Unicorn as we used to call them. There must have been one of them involved at some point. There's no trace of Fae magick up there or down here. And you should tell him, Lloyd. He won't figure it out for himself.'

I do like Vicky, and one of the reasons is that she never skates delicately around my ignorance.

'Tell him what?'

'What the old chief said.'

Lloyd tried to look innocent. Gnomes don't do that very well. 'I didn't know you spoke Old High North Germanic, Vicky.'

'Don't need to. He told you to get out. Told you it wasn't your fight, didn't he?'

I had figured that out on my own. I was waiting to use it later. Never mind.

'Yeah. A Svartálf can't – won't – attack one of its own brood. When I made with the axe, it used the Hell-horse to attack me, and that was the only way I could get it to spill blood. So now you know.'

'And you didn't do that for ten pounds, did you?' I said. 'Or a medal. Or because you love us. And don't try the Shylock routine.'

'You what?' said Vicky.

'*If you prick me, do I not bleed?*' said Lloyd. 'Shakespeare. We get taught that early. You're right, though. I did it because it needed to be done, and because I could only guarantee to get one of them, and because I'm going to ask you for a boon in return.'

I paused. 'You can ask. Later. First, tell us about the Labyrinth. We need to get out of here.'

'It's like a living maze. It's part of the Hall in some way beyond my understanding. There are only a eight tunnels in a Labyrinth, like a noughts and crosses board with a border. Trouble is, any tunnel can be closed or opened dynamically, and they can move while you're inside them. The legend says that Ariadne went down the tunnels with Theseus. She was a red hot Geomancer, and she followed the trail of Lux back to the start, and that's where the Dwarf was.'

'Sorted,' said Vicky, hauling herself to her feet.

Lloyd frowned. 'You're not a Geomancer.'

'No, I'm not, but I know someone who is. It's time for Maddy to go into bat, isn't it, Conrad. We need to get a move on, before one of us conks out.' She held out her hand to me. 'Here. Your leg will be stiff.'

It was. I used her help and went to get the Egyptian Tube from my rucksack.

23 — As One Door Closes…

The first person who had any time for me as a Mage wasn't Vicky, it was a Witch from Lancashire called Julia, who is Mother to a coven at a remote location near the Trough of Bowland. Thanks to them, I was given a powerful dowsing rod to help make use of my Talent for Geomancy – detecting and following the flow of Lux, usually through Ley lines. The only trouble is that the dowsing rod is possessed by the spirit of a woman called Madeleine.

All I know about Maddy is that she died in 1902 and that she has unfinished business somewhere in the Lakeland Particular. She makes a damned good dowsing rod, though.

'What if we get sucked in by the Labyrinth?' I said.

Vicky shrugged. 'Makes no odds. Just means we'll die in two groups instead of one. You need me to hold the lightstick while you frolic with Madeleine.'

Desi briefly zoned in and said, 'You've definitely been spending too long with him if that's your attitude.'

'Sorry, Desi, I mean…'

'I know what you meant. Hurry up, yeah?'

Vicky looked at me as I shook the Egyptian Tube like a maraca. 'What you waiting for, Conrad?'

'I'm trying to remember which way electrons flow relative to the magnetic field.'

'Eh? Won't there just be a Ley line in the floor, or in the roof?'

'If only. That Dwarf has generated a pseudo magnetic field, and that only happens when there's electricity – or Lux – flowing *round* the field.'

Vicky's eyes glazed over. Physics has that effect on her. I feel the same about genetics. I rubbed my chin, turned to face what my senses were telling me was the South pole and moved my arms in a circle, to mimic the flow and get it fixed in my head. Right. That way. I hope. I opened the tube and took out the dowsing rod.

There was so much Lux in these tunnels that I didn't need to go deep into the wand to activate its powers. Around me, the vague sense of warmth turned into a rotating heater, like being in the centre of a giant tumble dryer. Better yet, a heated corkscrew, because it was slowly moving, and coming from that way, the way we'd come.

I moved down the tunnel, almost to where we'd entered, and instead of Niði's crest on the right hand side and an opening on the left there were two blank walls and a right turn. Fine. I turned right and soon came to a T-junction. Vicky came next to me and waited. How the hell did this work? I looked at the roof, and I could see a line where the two tunnels joined. As best I could, I planted one foot in the tunnel we'd come from, and one in the new passage. I moved the rod from side to side, across the line and closed my eyes. Deep in the stick, Maddy woke up.

She always appears to me in a vision associated with water, perhaps because she drowned, or because she was a water witch. One or the other. Usually, we're on the bridge of a ship, sailing on an ocean. Today we were in a canoe, with me in the back, paddling upstream through a rocky gorge, and struggling to hold our own against the current. Maddy was wearing her usual Edwardian costume and paddling gracefully. She didn't turn round. We were coming to a widening of the rocks, a pool with two ways out. I tried to figure which way the water was flowing *in* to the pool, but I couldn't get a grip on the currents.

Madeleine has only ever spoken once (she said *Oh!*), so I wasn't expecting a reply when I muttered, 'Come on, Maddy, give us a clue. Which way is it coming in?'

She took one hand off the paddle and pointed left. Wow. I withdrew from the vision carefully and blinked my eyes open. 'That way,' I said to Vicky.

We came to two more junctions, and both times the vision became more real. I got sounds, I got spray in my face, and I got the clean, cold zing of mountain water in spring. The third time, when I tried to go into the dowsing rod, it trembled, and Madeleine pushed herself out. With a shimmer, she glowed into form in front of us.

'I'll go to the foot of our stairs,' said Vicky. I couldn't agree more.

'Where am I?' said Maddy, looking around with fear creeping into her eyes. As a fully materialised Spirit, she was completely different. For one thing, she'd borrowed most of Vicky's wardrobe. The white blouse and long black skirt had been replaced by a long purple top and skinny jeans. She'd forgotten her head, though.

'Hat?' said Vicky. 'You might want to lose the hat. And we're in the Halls of a Dwarf.'

'What hat?' said Madeleine, pronouncing it *Wot het?* With a very plummy voice. She turned to the wall and sketched a rectangle with her fingers that immediately turned into a mirror. 'My Lord! How silly.' She brushed her hands over her head and the straw boater disappeared. Long black hair cascaded over her shoulders as the pins vanished, too. Vicky had said that Maddy was thirty-nine when she died. She looked a lot younger than that now. Her inner image of herself, probably. I look nowhere near thirty-seven in my head, so I don't blame her.

I glanced at the floor. Maddy wasn't casting a shadow, so she hadn't materialised in the flesh. She looked around again, nervous eyes flicking down the tunnels. She pointed to the right. 'Down there. A hundred yards on the left, that's where it's all coming from. So much power.'

She grew an inch taller. No, she didn't, she floated an inch off the floor. She wasn't going to last long like this.

'How can we help you?' I asked.

'I need to find my daughter. They took her from me. She … she was so young, so small, and I haven't got long. Until the Spring Equinox next year, then I have to go.'

'Just wait until I get my hands on Sister Theresa,' I muttered.

'What? Never mind. Look, squadron leader, I know my actual daughter won't be with us any more, but her daughter's daughter will. I need to find her. I need to tell her.'

'Tell her what, Maddy?' said Vicky. 'If you give us the message, we'll get there in the end.'

Madeleine shook her head. Freed from the pins, her hair flew around. 'I can't tell you. Only her. Please…'

She faded from the extremities, blurring and erasing herself. When she was gone, I looked at Vicky. 'I'll kill her. She did that deliberately.'

'Who? Sister Theresa?'

'Yes. I'll murder the old witch, and before you say anything, she is undeniably old and a Witch. She gives Madeleine a year to find peace for her soul, then bars me from going to Lunar Hall to ask what happened. And I doubt she expected Maddy to materialise so early.'

'You don't know that. You could be barred for other reasons, such as being a man. I'm not barred. I'll go and find out.'

'Thanks. Now let's find that Dwarf.'

It was easy to trace the Lux to its source. Getting beyond that would be another matter. To the mundane eye, it was just a wall, and even Vicky couldn't tell that this bit of tunnel was where all the Lux came from. With my dowsing rod, it was plain as a pikestaff. I took out the Hammer and got ready to eject the clip.

'Shall I knock thrice?' I said.

'You can if you want, but you're not the Constable, so I doubt he'll answer.' She was looking at the gun, and switched her attention to the hand holding it, focusing on my Troth Ring, a gift from the Allfather. 'Try your ring. If anyone's gonna answer the door to a friend of Odin's, it's Niði.'

'I am not the Allfather's friend.'

'You gave him tea and biscuits. Hurry up.'

I focused on the Valknut symbols in my ring and knocked as hard as I could on the wall with the back of my hand, making sure that gold touched stone.

'And if that doesn't work?' I said while we waited.

Vicky was scanning the wall, scratching her head in lieu of using her powered-down sPad. 'We could … never mind. He's coming.'

We both stepped back, and a segment of wall slid down into the floor as quietly and efficiently as every other piece of Dwarven work. Behind the door was a well-lit tunnel, and in the tunnel was a Dwarf.

'You!' he exclaimed. 'You! You're the key! What are you doing here? And where is Odin?'

'We come in peace to your Halls,' I said quickly, before the Dwarf could panic and shut us out again. 'We have been hurt and we seek sanctuary.'

The Dwarf stroked his beard, of which there was a lot. You may remember that Hledjolf is a sort of dark-side R2D2, more mechanical than magickal, and creepy as hell. I'm glad to report that Niði was as thoroughly traditional as village cricket. Yes, his face was a bit grimy, as if the stone were leaking out from inside, but his skin looked like skin, his black beard looked like hair and his eyes were proper eyes, not a pair of diamonds.

'You seek sanctuary? You come in peace?' he said.

Dwarves do like to repeat what you say. Perhaps it needed a little reinforcement.

'As Odin is my witness.'

'Then welcome.'

'Our colleagues...'

'...I know. Wait.'

He took a small geologist's hammer from his belt and moved to the wall. He used the pick end to scratch something into the rock, then turned to face the entrance, gazing behind us at the blank wall. I heard a rumble of stone on stone and turned round to look. Another section of rock dropped down and we were one tunnel's width from Desirée and Lloyd, who were lying just the other side of the impaled Hell-horse. Vicky didn't wait. She dashed over to see how Desi was faring.

'Was this your doing?' said Niði, pointing to the bodies.

'Lloyd of Clan Flint took out the Hell-horse. I eliminated the Svartálf.'

Niði walked through to survey the scene, touching various things on the way, rubbing his hand over the Hell-horse, the sword, the axe and making his way to Lloyd. 'You must come down. I will carry the Gnome.'

He went to pick up Lloyd, who looked a little panicked. 'Easy, master. And the humans cannot carry the other one. She is too badly injured.'

Niði glanced at Desirée, then whistled. As easily as picking up a pillow, he rolled Lloyd onto his shoulders and moved towards the entrance to the lower level, collecting the axe on the way. So it wasn't just Gnomes who could use it. I was about to say something when a trolley came up the ramp and shot over the threshold. Vicky and I had to dodge out of the way as it careered into the dead Hell-horse.

'Follow,' said Niði as he disappeared down the slope.

We examined the trolley dubiously. It wasn't a hospital trolley, and I'm sure there were chemical stains on the top. Nor was it padded, but it was that or leave her here. At least it was a smooth runner. With great care, we lifted Desi onto the top. She only screamed once.

The ramp down to the lower level was mercifully short. We were well under the limestone now, and the walls had a reddish hue, as far as I could tell in the dim, Dwarf level lighting. For his new, lower Hall, Niði had opted for a Gothic look. It looked rushed, unfinished, and several of the slender arches were only half knocked through. The spaces beyond were barely lit at all. In one of them, a shadow flitted across the light, something long and low, even lower than a dwarf.

It was hot down here, and three forges were glowing at various points, long iron handles sticking out of the coals. Niði had placed Lloyd on a stone bench and was examining his leg. They conducted a conversation in their Germanic language, and Lloyd pointed to us, or to the trolley where Desi was lying. Lloyd got quite animated and sat up to make his point. The Dwarf rubbed his beard and came over.

'The Gnome would have you take the female to safety urgently, before our business is done, and one of you must go with her. I have a new door, but I have not used it yet, and I am not ready to share it with others. Would you agree to travel with dark minds?'

'He means asleep,' clarified Vicky for my benefit. 'Yes, we would.'

'Then take the trolley through there and wait.'

We followed his directions, through an arch and into a cavern about the size of an underground station. Instead of train tracks, a canal flowed next to the platform, and on the water were three barges. One was a heavy-duty rock carrier (half full of sandstone), the second was a beautiful rendition of the traditional residential narrow boat. I would have loved to linger and admire the way that Niði had used iron instead of wood to create a curved top and gemstones instead of bargework painting, but we were headed for the third boat, a plastic mini-barge with a flat bottom and buoyancy tanks fore and aft. Plastic? Had he had it for thirty years, or had he branched out from metalwork and jewellery and into synthetics? By the time we were there, Desi had drifted into sleep.

'I'll have to go,' said Vicky, 'and before you say anything, it's not because I don't like Dwarves. I like them fine when they're not underground. I can't cope much longer down here, and this is how bad it is: I'd rather speak to Tennille than spend another minute down here.'

'Call Hannah first. She can pass on the news.'

'Oh, I will call Hannah first, but if I don't call Desi's Mam meself, I'll be in the deepest shit ever. Even deeper than you're gonna be. How do we get her in there?'

Niði appeared on the dock, carrying what looked like a dead animal. Oh. It was a dead animal, sort of. He had an armful of furs and pelts. 'Who's going?' he asked.

'Me,' said Vic.

He threw a selection of furs in the boat and told Vicky to get in and arrange them. When Vicky had realised that they didn't smell as bad as they looked, we worked quickly, using the Dwarf's enormous strength like a crane to swing Desirée over the dock and into the barge.

He took two small rubies out of his apron and said, 'When I put these on your foreheads, your minds will go dark until daylight hits the gems. If you could leave the boat adrift afterwards, it will find its way back to me. Lie down and close your eyes.'

Vicky made herself as comfortable as she could. The Dwarf licked the ruby and placed it quickly on her forehead, where it started to glow, ever so gently. He repeated the process with Desi and cast off the boat. With a thump from his hammer on the stern, it started to move, soon disappearing into a dark tunnel.

'I didn't know Dwarfs could make water run uphill,' I observed.

'We can, but not on this scale. Half a league along, there's a boat lift.'

I was suddenly very grateful for the ruby on Vicky's head. If she were awake during the transit of an underground boat lift on her own, she'd have a breakdown. The Dwarf turned and headed back to the main Hall.

24 — Another one Slams in your Face

In the time it had taken Niði to fetch the furs, he'd also stoked up one of the forges. He went straight over to it, and I checked in with Lloyd.

'He's going to give me the glass fix,' said the Gnome.

'Sorry?'

'For certain fractures, we can take a glass replacement or repair. Only Dwarves can do it, though, and he's making it a freebie.'

'That sounds … painful. Can he do anything for your severed arm? Do you want me to retrieve it?'

'Thanks, but no thanks. It's tainted, I'm afraid. I'll get a prosthetic of some sort eventually.'

The Dwarf lined up some surgical instruments and said, 'It has been so many years since we had visitors. There is ale to drink, but not yet. The sooner I do this, the better.'

Without waiting to see if I watched or turned away, he went to fetch a small crucible, glowing red hot. He carried it at arm's length in a pair of tongs towards us and placed it on the floor. He placed his left hand on Lloyd's shin and picked up a scalpel. He made an incision into the top of Lloyd's foot, and the Gnome bucked with the pain. Or most of him did. The leg under Niði's hand didn't move a millimetre.

I hated myself for watching, but having had several major operations on my own leg, I was fascinated. My titanium tibia itched in sympathy with Lloyd.

The Dwarf dipped a spatula in the crucible and lifted a blob of glowing glass. Surely, he wasn't going to …

He was. With a deft flick, he pasted some of the sluggish liquid into Lloyd's ankle and smoothed it with a piece of leather. He dropped the leather and placed his other hand on the wound. He grunted with effort, and the temperature in the cavern rose several degrees as the Dwarf gave off a huge amount of Lux. Some of his beard actually fell out in front of my eyes, and my ears were battered when Lloyd screamed. At that point, I looked away.

''Tis done,' said Niði. 'I'll fetch some ale.'

I went over to Lloyd, not sure if I could do anything other than be shouted at. Don't underestimate the importance of being a lightning rod when someone is in pain. It can make a huge difference.

'Was that as bad as it looked?' I said.

'Probably worse, but it's over. Help me up and we'll see how good he is.'

'Are you sure?'

He held up his hand, and I hauled him upright. With way more confidence than I'd have felt, he put his foot on the floor, pressed down, and sat back. 'My boot's over there. Would you? This floor's hot.'

TENFOLD

I shook my head and handed him his boot.

One of the chambers off the main Hall was full of more pelts, skins, animal rugs and furs. Niði told us to help ourselves and pointed to a stone table with stone benches. Lloyd and I grabbed a couple of sheepskins and made ourselves comfortable.

The Dwarf fussed about, putting three tankards on the bench and wheeling over an empty barrel. A wooden barrel. I wonder where he got the wood. While he went looking for something else, I admired the tankard. It was pewter on the outside, but lined with a thin layer of glass. Lead poisoning is never a good idea. The pewter was engraved with a swirling, organic pattern that turned silver in certain lights, and then I realised that the silver was *moving* around the design, like mercury in a children's maze puzzle (in the days before mercury poisoning had been discovered).

It was beautiful and captivating. When I looked up, Niði was filling the barrel from a new plastic hosepipe. He'd definitely branched out. When the barrel was half full, he wandered off.

'Desirée was telling me about your well,' said Lloyd, 'while we waited for the cavalry. She said she likes the Inkwell Bitter, but won't admit it. This should be a treat for you.'

'It looks a bit weak.'

'It's water. Dwarven Ale is made to order. When it's your turn, say, "May your fires never dim." Here he comes.'

Niði carried not a red-hot poker, but a white hot poker. Instead of plunging the end into the barrel, he dropped the whole thing into the water. Steam roiled and blew into the chamber, and I caught a whiff. Eurgh.

The Dwarf collected the tankards and dipped them into the barrel. Liquid was running down the sides when he thumped them on the table. 'Drink,' he commanded, raising his tankard.

We picked up ours and slammed them all together. 'Hearth and Home,' said Niði. We repeated the toast and all drank deeply.

That was good ale. That was very good ale. I could drink a lot of that – it cut through the taste of blood and pain from the encounter with the creatures above and had a kick to follow. I'd still rather be drinking Inkwell Bitter, though.

Lloyd raised his tankard. 'To the earth, our mother.' Now I got it. We drank.

'May your fires never dim,' I said.

When we'd taken a third drink, I forced myself to put the tankard down. Breakfast was a dim and forgotten affair, and I might have to drive soon. I opened my rucksack and slid out the smelly package that had upset Vicky in the car. Have you ever tried to buy germanium sulphide? I had to use my police warrant card in the end. It's easier to buy guns in this country.

'A gift,' I said, sliding over the package.

The Dwarf's eyes lit up. 'It's been many years. Many, many years. Thank you. I shall savour this later.'

You've no idea what a relief that was.

Niði turned his attention to me. 'You are the key. What are you doing here? You had no fire in your veins when you were born.'

'He means you had no magickal Gift,' said Lloyd.

'The Allfather had his eye on me,' I said. 'Whether he knew about the Codex or not is a question he's not answering, but here I am, and I think you know why. Thomas Clarke told me that he last saw the Codex Defanatus under your arm, four hundred years ago.'

The Dwarf finished his drink and pushed the tankard aside. 'And it should still be here.' He rubbed the patch on his face where the beard had fallen out. There was already a healthy stubble there. 'It would still be here if I had not been robbed and tricked. Robbed and tricked.' He fixed me with his nearly black eyes. 'You want it, don't you? And not for yourself.'

I laid the Hammer on the table, with my Badge of Office showing. 'That book has left a trail of blood. It will soon become a river.'

Niði said something in North Germanic that sounded like a question. Lloyd rubbed his chin and replied, 'That would be 1689 CE in the human calendar.'

'More ale?' said Niði. I shook my head. He took a small jewellery box out of his apron. It was made of some sort of lacquer, and I was starting to recognise Niði's style. He'd made that box. He put it, still closed, on the table.

'I was owed a debt,' he said after more beard rubbing. 'The Count of Fae whose sídhe had a door on your land. He owed me a great debt, and I took the book in payment. I didn't think it would take so long for that woman's curse to be lifted.'

'The Morrigan?' I asked. Niði agreed. Dwarfs live a long time. He could afford to wait for the Codex to be unlocked.

'In 1689, I was approached by a human Mage. I could tell that he was using a cloak to hide his true shape. Of course I could.'

'He means a Glamour,' said Lloyd.

'Please don't tell me that I have to learn a whole new set of jargon. I still can't cope with Quantum Magick vs Circle Magick.'

'I'll translate.'

Niði gave us the eye. 'I kick myself for a fool now, but I should have torn his cloak aside when I had the chance. And then I saw what he brought. Is there ever a bigger fool than a Dwarf who sees a bigger seam in the next gallery?'

I had a stab at that one. 'Let me guess: the grass isn't always greener on the other side of the fence.'

Lloyd raised his tankard. 'In one.'

Niði was having trouble telling this story. We were all trying to avoid the word *greedy*. It rhymes with Dwarf in the same way that *human* rhymes with *mortal*. It's just what they are.

He put his hand on the box. His fingers were so big that I couldn't see it any more. 'You have to understand that it came in a flask. A glass flask filled with our Mother's tears.' Before Lloyd could jump in, Niði said, 'Only we Dwarves have the secret of Alchemical Gold, but some of the other races can make the Earth, our Mother, weep tears of Lux. They do not last long, but they can carry much.'

'Sorry,' I said. 'This was a bottle of liquid Lux. Pure magick? Can humans do that?'

'Not a bottle. A gallon flask.'

Lloyd drew breath. 'A gallon?'

'Yes. And in the centre was a Rockseed. Don't ask now. The Gnome will tell you.'

'It's a delicate subject,' said Lloyd.

'I was robbed,' said Niði. 'The Rockseed was a fake. The flask had been enchanted, but in my haste, I didn't think. I didn't think that the container might be a cloak in itself. I traded the Codex for the flask, and the Mage was gone. Before you ask, the Mage could have been male or female, Fae or Dæmon. Only the Mother's tears were real. I hoarded them until I could use them, and I used them to re-forge the Allfather. I have nothing more to say than that this was what the trickster left behind.'

He opened his hand and opened the box. Inside was a huge diamond, as big as the Great Star of Africa in the British crown jewels, but shaped like a lozenge not a teardrop. It glinted as the dim light refracted through its myriad facets. He slid the box over to me. 'Take it, as a gift to you in thanks for killing the Svartálf. You will find the trickster's mark on it somewhere, I'm sure. That is who has your book.'

He snapped the lid closed and sat back. Lloyd made a sign for me to take it off the table, and I quickly stuffed it in a pocket. My poor brain couldn't process this. There was too much to think about, and I had a lot of questions to ask. Niði, however, had folded his arms. I wasn't going to get any joy there. Not only that, I was shattered. 'Time to go, Lloyd. I just need a quick word with our host. In private.'

He nodded and drained his tankard. 'Thank you, master. I cannot speak for the Watch Captain, but Clan Flint will keep your secrets, and we will not broadcast it around that you are free again. Until you wish it.'

The Dwarf and Gnome shook hands. Lloyd nodded to me and walked out of the chamber towards the main Hall and the exit.

When he was gone, I took out one of my enhanced 9mm rounds and put it in front of Niði. He picked it up, sniffed it and examined it with a jeweller's loupe. 'Hledjolf,' he said, putting the round down. 'I might have known that he would be the first to make such a thing.'

'What will it work on?'

'Don't presume on my generosity, mortal. I would normally charge a fee to answer such a question.'

Without the Gnome at the table, Niði was suddenly less … human, I suppose. The whites in his eyes had disappeared completely, for one thing.

'But this isn't normal, is it, master?'

'Your weapon will work on any human. On a Gnome, it will work if you get it within an inch of the spinal cord or brainstem. On Spirits, a direct hit on the Imprint will work. On anything else, it might or it might not. It certainly won't work on a Dwarf.'

I put the round back in front of him. 'No magick, just an engraving. Can you engrave one word on it. In whatever script you use for North Germanic.'

He took out a stylus. How much stuff did he have in that apron? 'What word?'

I told him, and it took him less than two seconds. I put the round in my rather bulging pockets and stood up.

'Were you truly trapped down here, master, or were you just keeping your head down, as we say?'

'Let me show you something on the way out. It won't take long, and you'll be the first mortal to see this since I first came to Albion.'

He led me away from the main Hall, deeper into the rock. We took a side tunnel, and it was almost pitch black. The tunnel twisted, and the Dwarf had to touch a rod on the wall to bring more light. At the end of the tunnel was a bare rock face. In the rock was a relief sculpture. A sculpture of Niði. Only it wasn't a sculpture. It was another Niði, emerging alive from the rock. I couldn't see that, but I could feel it.

There are lots of Hledjolfs in Hledjolf's Hall. I did wonder why there was only one Niði. Soon, there would be two.

'Did you like my Labyrinth, Theseus?' he said.

'I'll pass on that name.'

'As you wish. This one was better than the one in Knossos, though I do say so myself.'

'You…?'

'Yes. I was the Dwarf on Crete. I was imprisoned by Minos and rescued by Theseus. When we returned to the mainland, Odin Allfather was waiting for me, with an offer. I took it and left the sunlands behind for winter's night.' He looked up at me. 'In your language, I left the Mediterranean and headed to Scandinavia, and that's why I re-forged Odin when he fell. One debt for another. Those creatures in the Labyrinth that you killed, they drained so much Lux from the Hall to keep themselves alive that I could barely lift a hammer or swing a pick, so yes, I was trapped. Now that they are gone, I will grow again.'

He flicked off the light and we returned to the main Hall. Lloyd had already hoisted his axe onto his back.

'If you would not have the name *Theseus*, what should I call you?' said Niði.

I was about to say, *Try Conrad*, when Lloyd spoke.

'He is a Dragonslayer.'

Niði's busy eyebrows clenched. 'Then farewell, Dragonslayer. You have shared my table and you are always welcome in my Halls.'

I shook hands. I once shook the hand of Britain's Strongest Man (he'd just won the title), and the Dwarf was ten times stronger. At least ten times.

25 — Diamonds are not Forever

We didn't speak until we'd left the lower level and returned to the scene of battle. The hind quarters of the Hell-horse were starting to sink into the floor and the body of the late chief had already disappeared. If only the floors in Elvenham House absorbed rubbish quite so neatly, that would save me a fortune on cleaners. Then again, if I got to keep that diamond…

I stopped walking. This seemed a good place to have a difficult conversation.

'That boon you wanted, Lloyd.'

'Yes. I was…'

I tossed him the round I'd shown to the Dwarf. He caught it easily in his one hand. 'This is no use to me without your gun,' he said.

'Have a close look.'

He peered at the casing until he caught sight of the engraving. 'What does this mean?'

'You've heard the saying that there's no dodging a bullet with your name on it. That's the bullet with your name on it. Literally. And you've just dodged it. That's your gift from me.'

He was furious. 'That is no boon. I saved your life. All of you.'

'And for that, I have spared yours. You knew exactly what the Labyrinth was. You led us in there so that we'd be trapped. If you'd told us what it was, you knew I'd retreat and get help to deal with the Svartálf and the Hell-horse, and that you'd be cut out. You used us. You put us in peril for your own ends. You risked my team, and for that I should kill you.'

He stared at the round of ammunition. 'You are more Odin's son than you admit.'

'I am Alfred and Mary Clarke's son, and I need no more than that. Nor am I one to bear a grudge. You did a good job down there with the Codex. Either you had no idea what I was talking about or you managed to worm it out of Desirée.'

He grinned. 'Poor kid. She was half out of it on opiates. I told her we had to keep talking to stop her falling asleep. Then I waved my stump around and told her that she could at least tell me what I'd lost an arm for. She didn't tell me everything. I've no idea what your personal connection to the damned thing is, but I know what it is and some of the grief it's caused. And you don't have to tell me to keep my mouth shut about it. What happens in the Halls stays in the Halls.'

'Good. Let's go and you can tell me what a Rockseed is.'

'Don't you want your prize? The chief's sword is yours.'

'From my experience, taking the chief's anything is likely to lead to reprisals. Surely that sword belongs to the clan.'

'I may be young for a Gnome, but I am the Clan Second. Weapons are in my gift. If you took it, you would be a Swordbearer, the highest honour for a human. You'd have some clan rights, so it's not to be sneezed at.'

'And would I have any clan obligations, to go with those rights?'

By way of an answer, Lloyd bent down and picked up the sword by the hilt. He ran his eye over it for a second, then shoved the hilt under the stump of his left arm. He fingered the blade. 'Do you know anything about swords?'

'That's either an early eighteenth century double-edged cavalry sword or a very good copy. The point of balance is a closer to the tip, to make it easy to use on horseback. Does it have magick?'

'Oh yes. Most of it wouldn't work for you, not being a Gnome, but the edge is ever true.' He held it by the blade so that he could offer me the hilt. 'Every clan has a First Mine. It's where we keep our treasure and bury our dead. After I've had some answers from my uncle, I shall be going to the First Mine to re-dedicate the burial cairn now that I know my father is lying there, not the chief. If you became a Swordbearer, we could call on you to defend the First Mine.'

'What if I had a warrant to search it, and you weren't keen?'

'Swordbearers have the right of access, so there wouldn't be a conflict of interest.'

I was so tempted. Very tempted. Lloyd had deceived me before and put my team at risk. On the other hand, he'd done it for reasons I could understand. Gnomes drive a hard bargain, and you have to know what you're letting yourself in for, but they're not Dæmons. They don't kill you with small print. I reached out and took the hilt. That grip could have been made for my hand.

Lloyd let go. A wash of magick flowed up my arm, then flowed back down when it didn't find a Gnomish Imprint to bond with. Was there a residual tingle, or was that my imagination? It was heavy, of course, far heavier than a fencing sword, and it would take a lot of getting used to. 'I am honoured to be a Swordbearer of Clan Flint.'

'Good. Can we go now?'

'Assuming we're not trapped in the Labyrinth again.'

He took a small plastic disk from his pocket, about the size and weight of a high end casino chip. He held it up to show me Niði's crest. 'The master gave me a new key. We're good.'

We left the scene of battle and took one turn. We were back at the entrance to the Labyrinth, the tunnel up to the old Hall ahead of us. Lloyd showed the chip to the crest on the wall and we moved on. As we climbed the ramp, the back of my neck tingled with magick. The trap was now re-set.

'Rockseeds,' said Lloyd. 'I thought you handled the master well, given that Hledjolf is the only Dwarf you've met before.'

'I think I can see the resemblance. Greed, pride, lack of empathy. They're all in Niði, just not so bad. And Niði is an artist. That's the biggest difference.'

'It is. Our master is the oldest Dwarf in Britain or Ireland, but hasn't been here the longest. That honour goes to the guy in Cornwall. Did the master show you the spawning rock?'

'The one with a new Niði emerging? Yes. Very creepy.'

'Tell me about it. You know that a Dwarf and his Hall are linked?'

'I do.'

'They're more than linked. They are different aspects of the same creature, though most humans don't believe that. When Theseus took Niði from Crete, there were two of them.'

It is quite mind-bending. I could accept that the mostly digital Hledjolf has a shared consciousness, like a distributed computer. It was harder to believe with something like Niði. I guess that's magick for you.

'What happened to their Hall on Crete?' I asked.

'It was collapsed into one of the Niðis. When they got to what we could call Denmark, and they couldn't have got that far without Odin's help, they dug down. One of them cut himself and bled out into the rock. He became the new Hall.'

After what I'd learnt about the breeding habits of the Fae, this wasn't so shocking. 'I think I've got that.'

We were back in the old Hall. Lloyd took a moment to touch the spot where his father had fallen, thirty years ago. He took his axe and chipped a bit off the wall. 'For the cairn,' he said.

We headed for the dock and daylight. 'You haven't mentioned Rockseeds,' I said.

'Just coming to that. To the Dwarves, a Rockseed is like the Philosopher's Stone, the Holy Grail and the Ark of the Covenant all rolled up in one. A Rockseed allows one Dwarf to plant a second Hall and share them.'

'So Niði could plant a Hall in Nottingham and be present in both Halls at the same time?' Lloyd nodded. 'And I thought that General Relativity was hard to understand.'

We had reached the doors on to Niði's dock. Lloyd took out the new key and held it up. 'If you had the Codex, would you swap it for the Philosopher's Stone?'

'Of course not. It's way too good to be true. No deal could be that good.'

'Which is why you'd make a terrible Dwarf. Not nearly greedy enough. Let's see that diamond again before we leave.'

I took out the box with the diamond in it. When I was applying to join the Watch, I went to see the Crown Jewels. The Great Star of Africa is worth about $400,000,000. That's right. Four hundred million dollars. The stone in this box was bigger.

'If the Dwarf is so greedy, why am I walking out with this monstrosity?'

'Do you want my honest answer?'

'What use would any other kind be?'

'Gnomes can be just as greedy as Dwarves. Niði got rid of your sidekick before he told his story, didn't he? And it wasn't me who said that Desi needed urgent medical attention. You're the only one not of the rock who knows of his stupidity. He expects me to kill you up here, round about now, and take the diamond.'

'And why aren't you?' I said. Was I scared? Of course I was bloody scared. You'd be scared if you had to look at that axe.

'Because I'm not a Dwarf, either. Killing you would be too easy, compared to the reward.' He pointed at the diamond, using his axe as a pointer. 'That thing is either cursed, or it's not what it seems. There's far too much Dwarven magick in the Hall for me to tell, but I can guarantee that you are not about to walk out with a half-billion diamond in your hand.'

'Let's find out, shall we?'

He opened the doors and we walked out together. Boy did that Black Country air smell good. We must be due a storm, because there was very little light coming down. It must have clouded over. Funny. That wasn't in the forecast.

As soon as the doors closed behind us, the gem started to turn black, its atoms rearranging themselves from diamond into graphite. *Allotropes.* Not a word you use very often, but that's what we had here.

'So obvious,' said Lloyd, frowning. 'I'm losing my touch. So bloody obvious. The one who tricked the master used Lux to make a temporary diamond, then immersed it in a flask of Mother's tears. Try rubbing it, but don't use your fingers. That pure graphite is a bugger to get off.'

I had a small towel in my pack. I tipped the black blob on to it and rubbed. The graphite smudged and broke up. At the heart of the blackness was a much smaller diamond. I showed it to Lloyd.

'May I?' he said, hovering his fingers over the stone.

'Of course.'

He rolled it round his fingers, held it up and frowned. 'Three point seven carats. Not a bad reward in the end. You must get it analysed, because there's magick in there. The master wasn't lying about this being the fake Rockseed. Whoever tricked him has left a trace of themselves behind.' He gave me a very Gnomish grin. 'And when you've analysed it, bring it back here and I'll get my cousin to set it in a ring for you. I'm sure that Mina would love an enchanted engagement ring. If you haven't already proposed, that is.'

That wasn't a bad idea, in its way. She'd either love it or throw it down the well. Women are funny like that.

He blew away the last of the graphite and returned it to the box. 'I'll get some of that tarpaulin to wrap your sword in. It might cause a bit of a stir if you carried that through the museum.'

I'd been carrying the sword, because I didn't have anywhere else to stow it. I put it down next to the wall for Lloyd to deal with and focused on priorities. I put my pack down and got out my phone and my cigarettes. I also got out the bag of detonators so that I could return them. I pressed the button to power on my phone and lit a fag. Lloyd wrapped up the sword, and did some other housekeeping. When he saw what I was doing, he said, 'I'd forgotten about my phone. Good idea.'

I stared up the narrow cleft in the hill, trying to see sky. I'd thought it was dark because of cloud, but I could see a couple of stars and therefore it was night time up there. I checked my watch and it was only three o'clock? What? My stomach agreed, saying that it had missed lunch, but not tea and supper, too.

I was about to check the clock on my phone when I heard a noise from the left and glanced at the light in the tunnel. There should not be a light in the tunnel. It should not be coming this way. I stepped aside so that I could watch the expression on Lloyd's face. 'Who's that?' I said.

'What the fuck?'

Gnomes have a good poker face, but they're not actors. Whatever was coming down the tunnel was as much of a surprise to him as it was to me.

26 — A Warm Welcome

The noise I'd heard was splashing from the nose of an inflatable boat as it slapped the water. They must be using an electric motor, or magick, because I couldn't hear an engine. I lit the last of the lightsticks and placed it further down the dock. The boat appeared from the tunnel a few seconds later.

I could see a male figure in the back, holding the arm of an electric outboard, and a very familiar female figure in the front.

'What's your boss doing down here?' said Lloyd.

'Your guess is as good as mine.'

'Thank God you're alive,' said Hannah. 'Where've you been?'

'Didn't you get Vicky's message, ma'am? And how did you get here so quickly?'

The boat had drawn up to the dock, to the left of the little raft we'd come in on. The man in the back had black hair, wore black and was quite short. Very likely a Gnome. He tossed up a rope, which Lloyd caught and fastened.

Hannah waved her hand. 'I was always here. This mission was too important not to have backup. Not that I don't trust you, of course.'

I held out a hand for her to get out. 'And Vicky's message?' I was worried that Hannah didn't know what had happened to Desirée, and the sooner she knew that, the sooner we could get the shouting over with.

'I won't get out. This skirt's too tight, and I'll be getting back in soon. There's no mobile signal down here, not in the other basin anyway. How did it go, and where is Vicky, anyway? She must be all right or you and the Clan Second wouldn't have been having a little bromance on the dock.'

'Long story, ma'am. Do you mind if I make myself comfortable?'

'Put that cigarette out if you're going to sit anywhere near me.'

I stubbed out my fag and took off my coat, taking a packet out of the pocket first. Lloyd was waiting politely to the side. I tried to catch his eye, but he was messing with his phone. Typical. The next few seconds could be very, very important.

I opened the little bag and popped a pork scratching in my mouth. 'You must be starving ma'am. Have these. It's all I've got.'

I handed the packet of scratchings to Hannah, who glanced at the grinning pig on the packet and put them down. 'In a minute, when you've told me how you got on with the Dwarf.'

I was still leaning down by the boat, having passed over the tasty pork product. Hannah had come closer to me, too, so she was in easy reach. I shouted. 'Lloyd!' as loudly as I could, and made a grab for Hannah's throat, diving into the boat as I did so.

As soon as I touched her, she burst into a bubble of violet smoke. I was pushed hard back and bounced on the inflatable side of the boat then up into the dock wall. The smoke filled the boat. I couldn't see anything, but I did hear a splash from my left. A dagger appeared out of the smoke and stabbed at me. The other person clearly couldn't see anything, either, and I was able to roll away. The knife stabbed into the rubber, embedding itself with a hiss.

Lloyd blasted air across the boat to clear the smoke, and I found myself face to face with Irina.

She was scrabbling in the bottom of the boat. Over her shoulder, I could see the other person wading towards the tunnel, and Lloyd, standing on the dock, torn between pursuit and helping me. I had a split second. Did I go hand-to-hand or reach for my gun? I went for the gun as she picked up a plastic spray bottle.

I had the Hammer out of the holster, but I was half on my side and I couldn't bring it round before she had the chance to spray me with that bottle. I rolled away from her and brought my left arm over my face. Liquid hit me and started to burn straight away.

'Help!' I shouted, and drew in my right hand to avoid more spray. I also worked my legs round to try and kick her, then something slammed into my right hand, and I was disarmed. Half a second later, there was a splash. I couldn't risk taking a look, in case she still had the bottle of acid. I bucked and thrashed, trying to connect with legs, arms, anything. Until she punched me in the groin.

If that wasn't bad enough, more liquid landed on my head. There is no pain quite like an acid burn. It's like putting a cast iron pan on the hob and trying to pick it up an hour later, but you can't drop it, you have to keep holding on to that pan no matter how much it burns because you can't let go. What the hell was Lloyd up to? If he'd gone down that tunnel, I was in serious trouble, because the pain from my groin washed up to meet the pain from my head and there wasn't a lot of me left in between.

The boat rocked. I heard the rasp of the knife being pulled out of the rubber tubing. That was my one chance. I dug my feet in to the side of the boat next to the dock, still keeping my arm over my face, and launched myself out, out of the boat and into the canal. When the cold water hit my head, the pain doubled and trebled, but at least I'd let go of that hot pan.

It was deeper here than in the tunnel. Deep enough to take a stroke and get myself out of acid range. I surfaced, shielding my eyes with my hand in case she'd followed me into the water. When my head broke water, I saw why Lloyd hadn't jumped to save me: we had company, and they hadn't come to rescue us.

Another boat had come out of the tunnel, longer and carrying three men and three women, all wearing black helmets, black balaclavas and black combat fatigues under hefty stab vests. Their boat was at the far end of the dock from me, and three had already jumped out. The boat containing Irina was in the middle, and Lloyd had retreated to the near end, because that's where he'd put his axe down.

Irina saw me and raised her hands, feeling the air for magick. The canal was about five foot deep. Sodden and wearing boots, I couldn't swim, so I started to circle left, towards the dock, because I knew what she was checking for. As soon as she'd robbed me of the Hammer, my Ancile had collapsed. I was about as close as you could get to being an actual sitting duck in the water.

Five of the six wannabe ninjas were now out of the boat. The three men and one of the women took a defensive position on the dock, protecting another woman at the back. That would be the boss. The front four had knives out already, until the sixth member of the team tossed them a selection of weapons from the boat. Taking turns to cover each other, they started to pick up shields, machetes and in one case, a spear.

I could only spare them a glance, because Irina had figured out my vulnerability and I was still four strides from the dock. She drew back her arm, ready to launch a blast that would cut me in half. The bed of the canal was sloping up, just a bit. I reached for the dock, still ten feet away, and I saw Irina adjust herself. When she brought her hand down, I used the sloping bed to launch myself backwards.

I've been next to an exploding grenade before. It's what blew my leg to pieces. This had more energy, but the water saved my life. Her blast struck two metres in front of me, and the wave pushed me back like an involuntary surfer. A sonic boom reverberated around the dock basin as my back smashed into the opposite wall. The good news was that I was alive. The bad news was that I was now even further from the dock.

'What happened to your Ancile?' screamed Lloyd.

I coughed water. 'On the gun,' was all I could manage. Irina was winding up for a second go.

'Shit,' said Lloyd, then he did the only thing that might save me – he charged at Irina.

If I'd been the boss of the black-clad muppets, I'd have moved forward to protect Irina, but no, they'd stayed at the opposite end. That meant she was stuck in the middle when Lloyd ran at her, swinging his axe.

The posse realised the danger to Irina and started forwards, but they were never going to get there in time. Irina pivoted round and used the blast meant for me to cut the rope tying her boat to the dock, pushing her out at the same time, so much so that she overbalanced and landed in a heap in the boat.

Lloyd stopped in his tracks and backpedalled, which is exactly what I wanted, because I was across that canal and rolling onto the dock when he got back to cover me with his Ancile. When Lloyd had retreated, the posse had stopped their charge and waited for orders.

I took a second to scan the opposition. None of them were short enough to be Gnomes, a good thing. The three men were armed with thoroughly illegal machetes and small riot shields, and the woman with them in the vanguard was holding the spear. I couldn't see much under their balaclavas, just enough to know that one of the men was black, and everyone else was white. There was just enough room on the dock for the front four to spread out.

'What do you want?' I shouted. 'I wasn't lying about Vicky. We got through to the Dwarf, and Vicky left by the new exit. She's long gone. Killing us won't change anything, and most of you will die trying.'

Irina glanced at the posse, then turned to us. 'Stand back, Lloyd. This isn't your fight. You can walk away, and I'm sorry about your arm. You've given a lot on Watch business, and what has the clan gained? Let the King's Watch fend for themselves. You don't have to give your life to them as well as your arm.'

'Too late,' said Lloyd. 'When you attacked the Watch Captain, you attacked a Swordbearer. I stand as clan second.'

I'd been holding my breath during Irina's little speech. Holding my breath and glancing around. When Lloyd backed me up, I breathed out and bent down into the shadows. Gnomes are very tidy, and Lloyd was no exception. I flipped the catches on the black box and unzipped the soft case.

Irina blinked. Just once. 'He is no Swordbearer. Only the chief can confer that honour. Stand aside before you go down with him.'

'I am clan second. I chose the Swordbearer. Bring Chief Wesley down here and see what he says.'

The woman in black, the boss, said, 'Here,' to Irina, pointing to the dock. Irina didn't look happy about that. She would have preferred to sit in her boat, away from the dock. She reluctantly obeyed, twisting the grip on the electric motor and guiding the inflatable as best she could given that one of the air chambers was ruptured.

'Hold still,' I said to Lloyd. 'Just a few more seconds. What can you tell me about them?'

Irina didn't try to dock. She brought her boat to the bigger one and the sixth ninja helped her out.

'There's only one Mage. The one at the back,' said Lloyd. 'Plus that bitch Irina, of course. They've all got Anciles, though.'

'Was that a Gnome on Irina's boat.'

He spat on the dock. 'Fuck, no. When you punctured the Construction, I saw him for what he was. A Fae Squire. He'll be half way to Birmingham by now.'

A Construction is more than just a Glamour. It's a total magickal makeover, which is why I'd believed that the woman in the boat was Hannah.

'I'm done,' I said, standing up with a groan after I'd shoved the black box against the wall. *'Geh langsam vorwärts.'* My mother made me choose German over French at school. One of the men in black understood me and looked round for guidance. Lloyd also understood, and we moved forward, very slowly.

Irina had made it out of the other boat and was about to confer with the Mage in black. Before they could plot anything, I spoke up. 'This is what's going to happen.'

They stopped talking and looked at me.

'See that box? It's pelletised TNT. You can see the blasting caps.' I held up my hand. 'And here's the remote control. We're going to advance to the doors. Lloyd is going to open them, and we're going inside the Hall. When the doors are closing, I'm going to set off the TNT. If the blast doesn't kill you, you'll all die under thousands of tons of rock when the roof collapses.'

Unfortunately, the doors to Niði's hall were closer to them than us. 'Block the doors,' said the woman in black. They advanced slowly, as did we.

I took the chance to whisper to Lloyd. 'Keep going until I can get near that tarpaulin.'

'Bit bloody close,' said Lloyd, but he kept going. Yes. We were there.

When we stopped, and when the opposition had blocked us from the doors, Irina said, 'Fine. I get it. If you're going to die, you'll bring everything down on top of you. I can believe that. No one has to die. Give us the diamond and we'll walk away.'

Lloyd flicked a glance at me. I shook my head, ever so slightly. He nodded.

'Why don't you lot leave?' I said. 'That way, no one dies.'

Irina turned her attention to the clan second. 'Lloyd, this really isn't your fight, and now you don't have to protect him. All he has to do is hand over the diamond and you can both live. I know you'd die for a Swordbearer, but are you going to die for a bit of rock?'

Lloyd was done talking. He lifted his axe and rested it on his shoulder, ready to swing at anyone who came any nearer.

I stared at the four who stood in our way, making eye contact with each of them. 'You've seen how shallow the water is. You don't need a boat. You can jump off the dock and wade out of this basin. If you don't, who's going to die first? Is it you? Is it you?'

Why did the men go over the top at the Battle of the Somme? There was a module on that in officer training. All sorts of reasons, but fundamentally, because each one believed that someone else would die, not them. When there's only four of you, that gets a bit harder. And it got harder still when I bent down, lifted the tarpaulin and picked up the sword. My gun has a name – the Hammer. I reckoned that the sword deserved one, too.

'This is the Anvil,' I said. 'Who wants to test their mettle on it?'

199

'Just so you know,' said Lloyd. 'That was a terrible joke, and that spear has a poisoned tip. One scratch from that and you'll be dead in minutes. I might last a bit longer.'

Adrenaline had kept me going since the fight on the boat. I was soaked, and that dock wasn't warm. If they decided to wait it out, I'd have hypothermia before anyone came looking. I was going to give it a few more minutes before suggesting that we attack, then the woman in black made up my mind for me.

'Get Clarke. You know the drill.'

One of the men, the black one, said, 'C'mon! Let's go!'

'Lloyd. Outside channel,' I said and braced myself for the attack. He stepped right, towards the water, and swung his axe off his shoulder.

The three men made a sort of tortoise around the woman with the spear and prepared to shuffle forwards. They'd clearly practised this.

'Get down, Conrad,' said Lloyd. 'Use them.'

I backed off a step and crouched lower. Their Anciles were now my Anciles, leaving Lloyd free to go for Irina and the woman in black.

Their boss didn't fancy that, and shouted, 'Number Four! Stop the Gnome.' The white guy nearest the canal broke off and went to intercept Lloyd, leaving one less for me. Now I was only facing three. Wonderful.

They'd done their homework. The remaining white guy was a leftie, machete in his left hand, and that meant they could protect the spear wielder, keeping her safe behind two riot shields while their blades stopped me flanking her.

It also meant that most of the spear was useless. I couldn't reach her, but they'd have to get quite close to reach me. It would be hard for her to kill me like that, but she didn't have to kill me, she only had to get a knick. They started to move forwards.

Lloyd wasn't going all out against Number Four because his left side was too exposed, and was his one-handed swing a little less vigorous? Yes. He was slowing down, and that axe was a hell of a weight. It was time to take a risk.

I stood up, exposing my head for a second. Both women Mages tried to get an angle to blast me. I turned side on in the classic fencing stance and weighed up the guy on the left of their tortoise. His machete was almost as long as my sword, and much lighter. What it didn't have was a tip.

I took a half step to the right, and he started to bring his shield round. Before he could protect himself, and before the spear could get set, I lunged, dancing forward and sliding the tip of the Anvil into his forearm, just above his wrist. In, out, withdraw, then a blast from the woman in black blazed at me.

Most of it was deflected by her own team's Anciles, but enough got round to blow me back onto my arse, right in the open. I cringed for a second blast.

The guy I'd stuck with my sword had dropped his machete and gripped his wrist, screaming in agony. He also staggered in front of me, blocking the Mages. 'Get him now,' said the black guy, pushing the spear woman at me. She lowered the spear and charged the two steps. Big mistake. She had a poisoned spear. All she had to do was prod my leg. Maybe she didn't believe in the poison. Maybe she was a psycho. Either way, she aimed the spear at my chest.

I lifted my sword arm and waited until she was committed. A spear is deadly, this one doubly so. I'd still rather face that spear than a Ross Miller bouncer. His bouncers are a hell of a lot faster.

I didn't roll out of the way, I waited until the last moment, then swept the tip aside with my sword. It struck the ground just by my shoulder and skidded away. The woman had braced herself for a crunch, and her momentum sent her pitching down. She lost control of the spear, dropping it then rolling away as I got up.

'Shit,' said the black guy. He didn't fancy it, but he came at me to protect his unarmed colleague. I swept my sword in front of me, enough to stop him, and enough for me to find the spear with my boot and kick it back. It made a lovely splash as it hit the water. I looked my opponent in the eye, and he knew they were in trouble.

I went en garde again, moving him to get him between me and the magick and feinting at various exposed parts of his body. The woman had got up and scampered down the dock, where she joined the two Mages and the guy I'd stuck in the arm. My opponent fell back half a step every time I feinted, fearful of the lunge. I made several stabs towards his face until he raised his shield too far, then I dropped my blade and slashed down his thigh. He collapsed in a heap, dropping his weapon and screaming.

Lloyd's opponent started backing towards their boat. The woman in black screamed, 'Get back, get at them,' trying to push the wounded man and the spear woman towards us. They were having none of it, and got in the boat. Lloyd and I advanced on the two Mages and the one remaining combatant.

Irina broke first, getting in the boat, too, and starting to untie the rope. The woman in black took something from her pocket and chucked it over our heads. I watched it sail past us and land on her fallen comrade. Instead of a bang, there was a flash of magick. Lloyd and I stopped to let the woman in black and the last man get on the boat.

The sixth ninja, who'd never left their boat, started the motor and swung away from the dock. Their boat was just small enough to make a turn in the basin, and I expected them to race off, but they stopped in the middle on a command from the woman in black. She moved her hands, making a Work of magick, then bent down and picked up a black metal shape. I flinched instinctively; I always do when faced with a submachine gun.

She didn't aim at us. She aimed at the guy on the dock. The guy who'd been facing Lloyd realised what she was going to do, and tried to deflect her aim, but it was too late. She let her fallen comrade have most of the magazine then turned the weapon on the rest of her team, shouting something I couldn't hear because I'd raised a Silence.

She must have been threatening them, because they sat down and put their hands on their heads. Of course. She'd removed their Anciles. The woman at the back cranked up the motor, and they disappeared down the tunnel.

I checked the guy on the dock. Dead.

Lloyd collapsed down, sweating heavily. I laid down my sword and stripped off my wet shirt and base layer. I picked up my dry coat and shrugged it on. The diamond had been sitting on the dock, in my coat pocket, the whole time we'd been fighting, but I didn't tell Lloyd that. I got out my cigarettes and the hip flask, passing it to Lloyd and sitting down next to him.

'It's a good job you were no oil painting before,' he said. 'With those burns on your head, you're certainly not one now.'

27 — Sitting on the Dock of the Basin

'There's no signal,' I said, checking my phone.

Lloyd got up and went to the repeater box. 'Bugger them all. They've disconnected it. And there's this. Hang on.' He came back and showed me a small camera. 'No wonder they knew when to come after us.' He dropped the device and ground it with his boot, then he sat down again. 'I know that your boss is Jewish. I get that, but I take it you wouldn't normally offer her pork scratchings.'

'No more than I'd offer Mina a beefburger.'

'So what tipped you off about the Construction?'

'The Jewish bit. No one as observant as Hannah would say, "Thank God." She'd have said, "Baruch Hashem." Plus, the real Hannah would have wanted to know about the team first and foremost. She'd have been screaming about Vicky and Desi from the moment she saw us. Irina didn't even know that Desi had gone down there.'

Both our phones started pinging with messages when the network repeater came online. And mine did something else: its clock jumped forward by six hours. I showed it to Lloyd, whose phone had done the same.

'Bloody hell,' he said. 'I never believed that bit. You were joking about General Relativity before, yeah? The elders said that time in the Labyrinth flowed differently. It must have. Well, I'll be blowed.' He shook his head, put his phone down and turned to look at me. 'Did you really set those explosives?'

'No. Not enough time. I just needed them to see it in your eyes. You believed it so they believed it. They were half beaten before they took to the field, and with a leader like that, I'm not surprised. Thanks for standing by me, Lloyd. Now I really do owe you.'

He nodded his head. 'So what now, Boss? You need medical attention, I'm afraid.'

'I think you're right. I need to retrieve the Hammer, and we need some forensic samples. Can you deal with the body afterwards?'

'Yeah. Have you any idea what this was all about?'

'It was the third attempt on my life. The first two were to stop me summoning my ancestor's Spectre and finding out about the Codex. When that failed, they tried to stop me getting to see the Dwarf, when that failed, they tried to get the diamond. Who could have conned the master in 1689 and still be alive today?'

He shook his head. 'One of the Fae. Well, good luck with that one. There's two good things come out of this, Conrad. First, I can bury my father properly, and second, we've got rid of Irina. I'd say that was fair exchange for my left arm. Now, let's get you to hospital.'

I checked the first few messages. 'Can you get me to Queen Elizabeth's in Birmingham? That's where the girls have gone. I wonder if the staff there will remember me from when they put my leg back together.'

28 — The First Day

Desirée didn't get a medal, but she did get a Mention in Dispatches. For that, you're allowed to wear a small bronze oak leaf on your uniform. She was going to be presented with it this afternoon, when Vicky and I got our medals in the rearranged ceremony. Desi was out of hospital, but still in a wheelchair most of the time. The Svartálf's sword had sliced through her abdominal wall, and she wasn't supposed to put any strain on it.

She had actually been discharged before me, much to my embarrassment. They'd admitted me for observation, and during the night I'd fallen victim to something nasty that I'd swallowed in the canal. I won't go into detail. Vicky had been an absolute angel, running down to Clerkswell to get some stuff for me. She'd even contacted Mina.

On Friday morning, still feeling rather delicate, I'd walked out of hospital to meet Lloyd and be driven to the early train. He gave me a large box to pass on to Hannah, and I even got to meet his wife. That was most unusual, and wouldn't have happened if he wasn't waiting to get his car adapted for one armed driving.

When I got to Merlyn's Tower, it was strange to see a young white girl sitting outside Hannah's office. Tennille had told the boss that she was taking compassionate leave to look after her daughter, and Hannah hadn't argued.

'It's Amy, isn't it?' I said. 'You're from Iain's office.'

Amy is the daughter of a Witch from Surrey. Amy hadn't inherited any Gift at all, but she was part of the magickal world, and she was bright enough to get an internship with the Deputy Constable before going to read law at Cambridge. That meant she was eighteen. Life at school had not prepared her for this.

'You must be Conrad.'

'Well spotted. Perhaps I should grow a beard, then no one would recognise me.'

That went straight over her head. Oh well. Stick to business.

'Is the Boss ready?'

'Erm...' She searched through twenty Post-it notes of different shapes and colours. 'It was on a pink heart. Or a lemon.' She started to blush. 'Sorry. It must be here somewhere ... Ah. Conrad Clarke ... Oh.' She blushed more.

'What?'

'Erm. It says, "Under no circumstances sign Conrad Clarke's expenses until I've seen them. Why's that?'

Before I could answer, the doors opened and Vicky grinned at me. From further inside the office, Hannah shouted, 'Is he here yet?'

'Yes, Hannah,' said Amy.

'Then send him in before he enlists you in his private army and invades France.'

'Why would he …?'

'Never mind,' I said. 'You'll get the hang of it.'

'I hope not,' said Amy. 'I want to go back to the Annex building before I end up like you lot.'

'She means *old*,' said Vicky. 'She couldn't believe that I was only five years older than her.'

Amy went red. Something she probably did a lot. 'I didn't mean that. I meant that you're all sweary-bonkers, like my dad when he loses at golf, but you do it all the time.'

Hannah shouted again. 'Get your lanky arse in here, Conrad. Now.'

'See?' said Amy.

The others were already there, gathered around the conference table – Hannah, Vicky, Rick, Francesca and a very fragile looking Cora Hardisty. There were two sticks, one propped against Francesca's chair and one lying on top of a very expensive looking handbag. That would be Cora's.

As Vicky closed the doors, Hannah came over, carrying something in brown paper. She pulled at my jacket, forcing me to bend down so that she could kiss me on the cheek, then she wrapped her arms round me and squeezed for a second. When she stood back, I was blushing and everyone round the table was staring.

She offered me the brown paper packet. 'I got you this. Open it.'

I peeled back the paper and found a square of silk. It had been specially printed with the shield of 7 Squadron, my old unit in the RAF. My current unit, technically. I'm still on their books.

'You should know how to tie it,' she grinned. 'You've seen me tie mine often enough, and you can't wear your hat on those burns without something soft to protect them.'

This was the most bizarre, and most personal, gift I'd ever received. 'Thank you ma'am. I don't know what to say.'

Vicky had resumed her seat at the table. They were quite far away, and Hannah leaned up to whisper, 'Don't say anything. Just keep coming back, okay?' She patted my arm and went back to the head of the table. 'You can pour, Conrad,' she said. 'As you're standing up already.'

I made a point of asking after Cora's health as I served the coffees (with Vicky's help). The Dean of the Invisible College was still not fully healed, and she admitted that there had been magickal assistance during the first operation. I wished her well and joined the group.

'This is what we've got,' said Hannah. 'Thanks to Conrad and Clan Flint, the forensics from that attack on Niði's dock led very quickly to a martial arts group in West Bromwich. I'm afraid that four members of that group are missing, five if you include the one they shot. They all left home the night before the attack and haven't been heard from since. No phone trace, no bank activity, nothing. Even their cars were left behind. They're either dead or being held against their will somewhere.'

'That was a terrible, terrible thing to do,' said Francesca. She had aged a lot in the last week. 'To kill one of your own like that.'

Hannah turned to me. 'Clan Flint have also written to us on the subject of Irina, and we got her fingerprints from the boat. Nothing on the prints, but the Clan say that her family was definitely from Iran. She called it Persia, and they don't know whether she was born there or not. She'd been with the Clan for over fifteen years in one capacity or another, and been officially a Counsel for ten of them. She'd made a lot of enemies, but no more than you'd expect for a human woman in that situation. Even Lloyd said that most of her ideas were good ones, though being an outsider and a woman, he was never going to take to her. And that's it as far as leads are concerned.'

I'd expected as much. 'What about that submachine gun?' I asked. 'That was new and government grade. They won't have picked that up on the streets of West Bromwich.'

Hannah shrugged. 'We checked the bullets you recovered. None of them were on any firearms database, and that brings us to the big picture.'

'The Fae,' said Rick. 'It took me a while, but I tracked down that Fae Count who was living at the bottom of your garden.'

'It doesn't do to make fairy jokes,' said Francesca. A comment like that might sound prim and proper. It was nothing of the sort. Her tone made it clear she thought Rick was on dangerous ground. 'The Fae are never a joke to us, even though we might be a joke to them.'

Rick looked at me. At least one of the Fae was my enemy. It's always fine to make jokes about the enemy in my book, and I let Rick know that with a smile before saying, 'The Count got a promotion and new lands, according to Thomas.'

'He did,' said Rick. 'And an alibi. The former count is now Queen of New York. If ever there was a prime suspect for sending over that Pyromancer, it's the Queen of NYC.'

I made the obvious point. 'Did he – or she – come back in 1689?'

Rick shook his head. 'Whoever pulled a fast one on the Dwarf, it wasn't him, and he didn't become a her until 1870. Not only that, all the Works from the Codex that have shown up have been found here, not America. Thanks to the Keeper and some contacts in Glastonbury, I've been able to put together a list of all the Fae that we know for certain were around before 1689. Here.'

He handed out sheets of paper to everyone. I glanced at the list – it didn't mean that much to me, because the Fae have two identities, one magick and one mundane. The list said things like *Duke Alaric, resident in Manchester*. That was the name they used in the magickal world. To the world at large, they were …. Well, I can't say. If I told you that the front man for a well-known rock band was a centuries old non-human creature, I'd either be laughed at or get a call from his lawyers.

'And that brings us to our most difficult decision,' said Hannah. She stared at her papers, then looked up at me. 'I read your report, Conrad, and I agree. Someone close to the Codex Defanatus is leaking information, or worse than that, they're part of the team who've been splitting it up and selling it. It's the only explanation for their knowledge of your movements.' She took out the box from Niði and showed everyone the diamond that had nearly got me – and Lloyd – killed. 'This is our best lead. This will tie one of the Fae to the Codex, but I don't think that we can pass that knowledge outside this group.'

'I agree,' said Rick; Vicky nodded, too.

Francesca took a different view. 'If we move quickly, and use people that we trust, we can bring this dreadful business to an end before there are any more casualties.'

She had the right to say that. She'd had to see the savaged body of her brother, a brother who had saved my life.

'There is one problem,' I said. 'Irina and the other Mage who attacked us know that we have it. Even if you let it be known that you were keeping it at the bottom of Nimue's well, they might be tempted to grab it. They put a lot of effort into that ambush, and it came very close to succeeding. I certainly don't want people thinking that *I've* still got it.'

'You're all right, in a way,' said Hannah. 'This is what I propose. I'm going to Scotland next week on official business. I shall take the box with me and make sure it's seen when I hand it over to Napier College. By then, it will already be out of the UK. I'll say no more than that.'

'You're putting yourself at great risk, ma'am,' I said.

'Which is why both Rick and Vicky will be with me 24/7 until then.'

Rick did not look happy. 'But Boss, it's half term next week. Couldn't Conrad do it? He's used to working with Vicky, and now he's got his ammunition…'

Hannah stared at him. 'Conrad is taking a week's leave.'

Rick either had to say that I didn't deserve it or back down. He backed down.

Hannah checked her watch. The others were taking a taxi to Salomon's House and the official oversight committee for Project Talpa. I had told Hannah that nothing would stop me meeting Mina off the train at Euston. That and picking up my new uniform.

'The line I'm taking is this,' said Hannah. 'We'll say that Niði *sold* the Codex to an anonymous Fae in 1689. We'll put together a series of polite questions to ask the Fae on that list, and I'll seek authority for further discreet enquiries. For now, we're done. Anyone else?'

We all shook our heads.

'Good.' She picked up the diamond. 'Right now, this is going down to Nimue's well. I'll see you this afternoon, Conrad.'

It's only when I see her from a distance, in a crowd of people, that I realise how Mina must seem to others. She was the first out of the carriage when the doors opened, and a man in a suit passed her case down to her. Then waves of travellers washed over her, and for a second she disappeared. When other people see her, what do they notice first? Her (lack of) height? Her unusually long shiny hair? Her light brown skin? Her slightly pointy nose? The lines round her eyes that shouldn't be there? The glint in those eyes that says they see right through you? They'd have to look for a long time to see her smile, that's for certain, because she's very slow to smile amongst strangers, unless she's putting on a show.

I don't see any of those things. I see a Mina shaped package round the essential Mina who fits the hole inside me. I knew that's what she was the first time we met, when she pushed my wheelchair and tried not to let me see the damage to her face. If Joe Croxton hadn't murdered her husband, would we be together? I try not to think about that, because Miles Finch was a good man. If I get eaten by a Dragon or skewered by a Hell-horse, I hope she finds a better man than me.

'Are you going to stand there like Nelson's Column for ever?' she asked. 'And don't tell me he was a sailor, because that's not the point.'

We kissed for a long time, until well after the housekeeping carts had boarded the train. Finally, I picked up her case.

'This is light. Have you left another on the train?'

'No. I gave away all my prison clothes last night. All that's in there are things I've only ever worn outside the gates. Oh, and I left some things with Kelly Kirkham last weekend. We can pick them up when we collect your puppy. Where are we going now?'

'The Waldorf. I've paid extra to check in this morning so that we can get changed. Are you going to wear Indian for the ceremony?'

'No! I don't want to meet your parents like that. Tell the taxi driver to go to Oxford Street.'

We headed down to the taxi rank. 'Have you decided where we're going for our break?' she asked.

'We're staying at the Waldorf until Monday. After that, I have no idea. It can wait.'

We began in Selfridges (don't worry, I'm not going to give you a blow-by-blow account of the shopping trip). Mina held up her hand. 'Cherise did my nails last night, so whatever we buy has to match this colour.' She started gathering dresses from the petite collection and said, 'Who do I need to impress most? Your mother or your father?'

'Dad thinks you're gorgeous, and that's just from photographs. When he's seen for himself how clever you are, it's game over for him. Mother's more of a challenge.'

'Why?'

'Because she's a bit different. Just remember, no matter how odd she seems, I'm her only son.'

'Hmm. You are no use. Wait there. Do you think I've put on weight?'

'Not since Christmas.'

'So you do think I've put on weight?'

'Don't forget Rachael. She's joining us for lunch.'

She whirled round. 'Since when? Why didn't you tell me?'

'I said we were having a family lunch. She's family.'

'That changes everything. I need to rethink this. When are we eating? Which does she look more like, Kate or Meghan, and why have you never shown me a picture of her? And have you found out which member of the royal family this Duke of Albion is?'

'I'm giving you half an hour,' I said. 'Then I have to collect my uniform.'

29 — Of the rest of our Lives

Lunch was a great success, and not just because Rachael cried off (she sent Mum a selfie from the first class lounge in Heathrow to prove that she really had been ordered to the USA). If you're wondering, Mina chose a royal blue dress in the end. I won't tell you how much the matching bag cost.

Mother asked a few pointed questions about HMP Cairndale until she realised that Mina was neither proud nor guilty of what she had done, then after that the talk very quickly turned to Clerkswell, Elvenham House and, "What is that Myfanwy woman *really* like?"

At a quarter to two, we approached the back door to Newton's House and Dad said, 'Is there really no other place to have this? Won't it be a bit morbid?'

'No, Dad, is the short answer. I'm not going to give you the long one.'

The Counter-Terrorism squad were out on the pavement, and we were all given a thorough check. We were still being searched when Vicky arrived with her parents. There was an awkward moment in the Duke of Albion's Room when John Robson dragged me to one side and said, 'Are you sure you got the bastard who killed them lasses and the Warden?'

'Yes, and we're on the trail of his paymaster. Don't worry, John, I'll never forget them.'

He clapped me on the back. 'Good lad. That lass of yours is canny and no mistake. I think you're batting out of your league there, Conrad.'

'Good job I'm a bowler.'

He found that hilarious for some reason.

Shortly after, Maxine gave me the nod. I'd told her to tip me off when Tennille and Desirée were on their way down the corridor. I left Mina getting a crick in her neck talking to Chris Kelly ("If we get married, he cannot be your best man. I would look like a dwarf." "You look nothing like a Dwarf. Too tall and no beard"), and headed out to face the music.

Tennille was pushing the wheelchair, of course, and slowed down when she saw me.

'Good afternoon, Mr Clarke,' she said. Her voice had blown straight down from the Arctic. No wonder Desi had always done her homework if that was the alternative. 'I hope your parents are well and had a good flight.'

'Mum! You promised,' said Desirée. She braced herself on the arms of the chair and rocked up. Then she saluted. 'Sir.'

I gave my crispest salute. 'Lieutenant. How are you?'

Desirée sat down again before replying. 'Getting better, thanks. What have you got on your head? Under your hat, I mean?'

I carefully lifted my cap to show her the scarf. Mina had tied it for me; it's harder than you'd think.

'Please tell me you didn't buy that. It's hideous.'

'But functional, and it was a gift from the Constable.'

Tennille wasn't going to have this. She cleared her throat and said, 'Just tell me why. Why did you drag my girl into your world of pain and death? Why?'

'Leave it, Mum. It wasn't Conrad, it was Hannah. Your boss, remember?'

Tennille wasn't going to blame Hannah if she could find another candidate. She looked at me. 'You didn't have to say yes. You could have spared my girl. Why did you do it?'

I looked at Desi. 'Shall I tell her?'

She nodded. 'I still think you're an over-privileged white guy, but you got us out of that mess. You and the Gnome. Tell her, 'cos she wouldn't believe me if I told her, and besides, I have no idea what you're on about.'

I looked from daughter to mother. 'I said yes because of what she did last time we were here. She recovered first, and her instinct was to chase the bad guys because no one else could. That's why I said yes.'

Desi looked down. We'll find out soon whether she still has that instinct, because Hannah processed Desirée into the Army Reserve. She'll get paid that way, and we can call on her again if we need to.

Tennille sniffed. 'Move out of the way, Mr Clarke. We're late as it is.'

I had great fun watching Desi get out of the chair a few seconds later to salute Vicky.

Mina was making friends with Maxine, the parents were swapping stories and I checked to see if anyone else had turned up. They'd roped off a different corner today, and I saw Francesca staring bleakly at the spot where Roland had fallen.

I went over and said, 'I'd forgotten something. Something he said just before it happened.'

She gave me the tiredest smile. 'Really?'

'Yes. Do you know of Sister Theresa of Lunar Hall?'

She frowned, a stabbing frown. 'She's a monumental shit, I know that, and you'll know I wouldn't describe another woman like that without reason. How on earth did her name come up?'

'Theresa told me she'd known your brother. When I mentioned it to Roland, he seemed to think that he'd been sent a coded message. He was quite agitated, for Roland, and said he'd have to go and see her.'

'Are you sure?'

'All my short term memories came back in good order.'

'Then I shall have to go. For his sake, not hers. Ursula Forton. That was her name. Is she old and in pain?'

'No more than you, Keeper.'

'That's more than she deserves.'

'Would you allow me to escort you, if you go?'

'You're up to something, aren't you?'

'Yes.'

'Then I'd be honoured.'

Ian Drummond had replaced Tennille behind the scenes. He came out and asked us to take our places, then returned behind the closed door.

Vicky wheeled Desirée, and the three of us took our places in front of the lectern.

A door banged, away in the gloom, and Hannah's voice said, 'Attention!'

We stood, and the royal party made their way forwards. Hannah, as the host, was in the lead, looking as uncomfortable in her uniform as ever. The bright red RMP cap sat on top of a matching scarlet headscarf, and she had just the one medal: the Queen's Gallantry Cross. That one put all of mine into the shade.

On her right was the Duke of Albion, Rector of the Invisible College and royal patron of all things magickal. To the mundane world, she is the Princess Royal, and was wearing her uniform as colonel-in-chief of the King's Royal Hussars. Behind them came Iain Drummond and Michael Oldcastle, the Deputy Warden/Chaplain of Salomon's House. I don't like him.

Bringing up the rear was Annelise van Kampen, and leaning on her arm was a very old Mage – the Senior Doctor of Chymic. His morning suit was decorated with the medals he'd earned during a distinguished career in the Watch.

Hannah stood in front of the lectern and I gave my best salute. Vicky and Desi (from a seated position) joined in belatedly, and Hannah glared over my shoulder until Eddie and Oscar realised we were waiting for them. Finally, she returned their salute and asked us to be seated.

She glanced at a piece of paper and placed it on the lectern. 'Welcome to Newton's House and a very special ceremony. Those who were here last time don't need to be reminded of what happened, and we should never forget those who died. If you are able to rise, please rise and join me in a minute's silence.'

We bowed our heads and Hannah read the three names.

At the end of sixty seconds, she cleared her throat and spoke up. 'Thank you. Please sit.' She checked the piece of paper again and continued. 'I nominated Conrad and Vicky for these medals – gallantry medals – not for the Watch, but on behalf of those whose lives were saved by their actions. We can't know how many would have died if they hadn't done what they did. I am certain that it would have been a lot, and they both put their duty ahead of their personal safety. Both were injured, and Vicky nearly didn't come back. Nominating them was not only my duty, it was a personal privilege and a pleasure. Again, on behalf of the innocent, thank you.

'Since then, there have been more sacrifices, and once again Conrad and Vicky stood up for the Watch. This time they were joined by Desirée Haynes, and I was again proud to mention her in my report. She will also be honoured today.'

She bowed her head for a moment, then looked up and gave me a wry grin. 'There are some small changes to the advertised programme. These awards were signed off at cabinet level, I assure you, but the Distinguished Flying Cross has to come from the Air Ministry. Believe it or believe it not, they wouldn't let us have one unless I signed an affidavit saying that Conrad was flying a plane during the incident. I couldn't do that, because he wasn't, so today the Duke of Albion will be presenting not one but two Military Crosses and an oak leaf. Thank you, Your Royal Highness.'

Hannah stepped back, and the Princess Royal stepped forward. Hannah said my name and rank.

The rest you can guess. It's strictly against the rules to repeat what royalty say on these occasions, and who am I to get in trouble? How did I feel? Proud. Happy. Did I well up when Vicky got her medal and the well-deserved ovation that went with it? Yes. 100%.

When Desirée had her oak leaf, Hannah returned to the lectern and pulled out the box I'd been given by Lloyd Flint at Birmingham Station. 'The final change to the programme is another presentation. It gives me great pleasure to report that Conrad has been appointed to an honorary position with the ancient and noble company of Clan Flint in Worcestershire. By special dispensation, he is now allowed to bear this with his uniform.'

She pulled out the sword I'd recovered from the late chief. Lloyd had taken it from me, and one of the Clan had made a suitable scabbard, with both a belt and a shoulder harness. Hannah had insisted that this position go on the record, hence the presentation. The Duke didn't make a fuss; she just handed it over and gave me a strange look, the sort of look that said she'd met her share of Gnomes in the past.

Ian Drummond escorted the Royal Person away, and the whole thing had taken less time than it must have taken her to get into her rather splendid cavalry uniform.

When we fell out, I took my sword and medal straight to show my parents and Mina.

'Congratulations, son,' said Dad. Mum gave me a hug.

Mina gave me her secret smile. 'This is very good,' she said, 'but I can't deny being a little disappointed. Princess Anne is nice, but I was so hoping for Meghan.' She grinned and put her hand through my arm. 'We're being summoned. Over there. Look.' She pointed to Hannah. 'And the Constable wants both of us, not just you.'

'Can I have a proper look at that sword?' asked Dad. Mother was off to discuss something with Francesca, so I handed it over.

I kept Mina's arm in mine as we went to see Hannah.

'Good afternoon, Ms Desai,' said Hannah.

Mina gave a short bow. 'Constable. I thought you spoke very well. Your care for your officers is clear to see, especially when Conrad takes his hat off.'

The RAF cap was firmly in place on my head, and would be until I changed out of my uniform.

Hannah looked down. 'It doesn't look quite as good on him as I thought it would. I'll stick to malt whisky in future.' She raised her eyes and gave Mina a long look. Mina looked back. 'I have something for you, too. It's useful having a sister in the police.'

Mina said nothing. Hannah had retrieved her handbag. It didn't go with the uniform at all, but it made her look much more like herself. When she swung it round to get something out, Mina said, 'I'd love a Chanel tote like that. I hope you're listening, Conrad.'

'What's a tote?' I said.

Hannah looked at me. 'This. It was a thirtieth birthday present from Mikhail.' She turned to Mina. 'And that Marc Jacobs goes beautifully with your dress. As I was saying, I have something. Here.'

She handed over an envelope with the flap open. Mina peeked inside, and I saw the burgundy cover of a passport. She'd had to surrender it when she was arrested and was expecting to have to jump through all sorts of hoops to get it back.

Mina flicked to the main page, then looked at me. I shrugged. 'You've put it in my family name, Constable. That was very thoughtful of you.'

'I have an ulterior motive, but we'll come to that in a second. This is also for you.'

She handed over a USB drive, which Mina accepted with a quizzical look.

'Conrad got that from the Gnomes in Earlsbury. I've used my contacts to get more. It's the data you wanted for Project Midas, and I wanted it to come from me. If you're going to work on it, I want it official, and I want you to get reimbursed. If that's acceptable.'

'Of course. I have more free time now.' She said it as a challenge, when Hannah didn't bite, Mina put the USB drive in her new bag and said, 'And you should call me Mina. Please.'

'Mina it is, and I'm Hannah. I've got an appointment with the Vicar of London Stone this afternoon.'

'About Vicky?' I asked.

'Yes. I'm going to follow through on our idea and propose that she's promoted to Watch Captain.'

'Good. She's earned it.'

'She has, and now it's your turn, Conrad.'

She handed me an envelope. A padded envelope. A well sealed padded envelope.

'There's a voucher for business class tickets to the European capital city of your choice in there, departing tomorrow, and a government licence for the other item. Just text me your destination from the departure lounge, then drop it off at the Israeli embassy when you get there. Your time's your own after that. Don't worry, Mina, Conrad will explain everything. Have a good time and I'll see you a week on Monday.'

'Ma'am.' I shook hands, as did Mina, and we went to rejoin my parents.

'I fancy Madrid,' said Mina. 'Followed by a visit to the Costa Whatever. I could use the sun after winter in Cairndale.'

'Seriously? You want to stay with Mum and Dad?'

'The sooner we get to know each other the better. And you've told me often enough that they have room there.'

When I asked Mum, she actually smiled. A smile that got even bigger when Mina said, 'Mary, it would be lovely if you could teach me how to play bridge.'

'Then it's settled,' said Mother.

Dad held up the sword. 'I've never seen anything like this, son.' He drew out the blade a little. 'That workmanship in the hilt is beautiful. Subtle and at least two hundred years old.'

'How can you tell, Alfred?' said Mina. Did she give Mother a wink when she asked him? I think she did, you know.

'Because that scrollwork is a copy of a motif you only find in Ancien Regime decoration. It went right out of fashion after the French Revolution. It's the blade, though. This is a weapon, not an ornament, and that blade is razor sharp. Look closely. What do you see?'

He held it down for Mina to stare at. 'Nothing?' she said.

'Precisely,' he said. 'There's combat damage on the hilt, but not a trace of sharpening on the blade. Not so much as a nick. Where did you get it from, son?'

Mother stepped in. 'Alfred! You should know better than to ask questions like that. Anyway, we should be going if we're going to catch the flight. You've got work to do when we get home. That pool won't clean itself, you know.'

We embraced and they made their way round the others. 'Go on,' I said. 'What's your ulterior motive?'

'While she is telling me all about how to bid No Trumps, I will be getting all the dirt on Juliet Bloxham. I had a long phone conversation with Myvvy while I was on the train. This is war, Conrad.'

I almost felt sorry for Jules. Almost.

There were happy goodbyes all round, and the last to leave was Chris Kelly. 'So you met my mother,' he said.

I had. In the Forest of Arden, on the case of the Phantom Stag.

Chris gave me a rueful grin. He could guess what she'd said. 'Would you like to come for supper when you're back in town? You can make your own judgements about my home life then.'

'That would be lovely,' said Mina. 'Just remember, no beef.'

216

'Got it. And I need to talk to you, Conrad. Vicky was telling me about what you got up to in Niði's Halls. I think you need a lesson on Quantum Topology.' He saw the look on Mina's face. 'Not over dessert, obviously.'

He made a hasty retreat, and we were free to walk out of Newton's House and into the future. We held hands in the afternoon sunshine, and headed for the river rather than going straight to the hotel.

'Where's your sword?' said Mina in alarm.

'On my back. Feel it.'

'Oh, my. That's … that's magick, I suppose. Let's stop here. I'm out of practice in wearing heels, and I don't want to scuff these.'

We sat on a bench in Whitehall gardens. Neither of us could quite believe that this day had come, that there was no cell door waiting to slam behind Mina as she was locked up. I gathered her into my arms and stroked her hair.

'Am I worth the wait?' she said.

I kissed her and savoured the moment. 'Yes, but try not to get locked up again.'

She pushed me away and stood up. 'We're going to Madrid tomorrow, Conrad. We need to get changed and get back out there. My summer wardrobe won't buy itself, you know.'

Conrad, Mina and the rest of the King's Watch are back with *Nine of Wands*.

The first of the King's Watch Casebooks is available in eBook - *The Case of the Phantom Stag*.

The King's Watch Casebooks are short stories and novellas set during the action of the main books. The first four have been collected into a single paperback – *Tales from the Watch*.

217

Nine of Wands
The Fifth Book of the King's Watch

By Mark Hayden

Gold.
Beautiful and Deadly.

And when you mix it with magick, doubly deadly.

Conrad and the team are on the trail of a new source of Alchemical Gold that already has Dwarves, Gnomes and human Mages at each other's throats.

When the prize is gold, life is cheap, and nothing blinds like greed. Can Conrad keep his eyes open and see through the killing glare of gold?

When the Tarot says Nine of Wands, you know you're in for a bumpy ride.

Available in Ebook and paperback from:

www.pawpress.co.uk

Author's Note

Thank you for reading Conrad's latest adventure. I hope that you enjoyed it. And now, it only remains to be said that all the characters in this book are fictional, as are some of the places, but Merlyn's Tower, Elvenham and Earlsbury are, of course, all real places, it's just that you can only see them if you have the Gift...

This book would not have been written without love, support, encouragement and sacrifices from my wife, Anne. It just goes to show how much she loves me that she let me write the first Conrad book even though she hates fantasy novels. She says she now likes them.

And credit must go to the Awesome Rachel Lawston for creating the covers that have given the King's Watch such a distinctive look.

As ever, Chris Tyler's friendship is a big part of my continued desire to write.

Thanks,

Mark Hayden..

Printed in Great Britain
by Amazon

42526484R00128